A WAG ABROAD

Alison Kervin is an award-winning writer, biographer and journalist. Alison was formerly the Chief Sports Feature Writer of *The Times* where she wrote a weekly interview – The Kervin Interview – featuring stars ranging from Nick Faldo and Michael Owen to Prince Edward and Sean Connery. Before working as a newspaper and magazine interviewer, Alison was *The Times*' rugby editor, and prior to that she was editor of *Rugby World*. Alison also worked for the Rugby Football Union as the public relations manager of the England team, was the first woman presenter on *Rugby Special* and the first woman to referee at Twickenham. She holds coaching qualifications in ten sports and sits on numerous judging panels. Her début novel, *The Wag's Diary*, was a bestseller.

A WAG Abroad is her second novel. For further information about Alison please go to www.wagsdiary.com and visit www.AuthorTracker.co.uk for exclusive updates.

By the same author:

The Wag's Diary

ALISON KERVIN

A WAG Abroad

AVON

AVON

A division of HarperCollins*Publishers*
77–85 Fulham Palace Road,
London W6 8JB

www.harpercollins.co.uk

A Paperback Original 2008

1

Copyright © Alison Kervin 2008

Alison Kervin asserts the moral right to
be identified as the author of this work

A catalogue record for this book is
available from the British Library

ISBN-13: 978-1-84756-055-1

Typeset in Minion by Palimpsest Book Production Limited,
Grangemouth, Stirlingshire

Printed and bound in Great Britain by
Clays Ltd, St Ives Plc

Mixed Sources
Product group from well-managed
forests and other controlled sources
www.fsc.org Cert no. SW-COC-1806
© 1996 Forest Stewardship Council

FSC is a non-profit international organisation established to promote the responsible management of the world's forests. Products carrying the FSC label are independently certified to assure consumers that they come from forests that are managed to meet the social, economic and ecological needs of present and future generations.

Find out more about HarperCollins and the environment at
www.harpercollins.co.uk/green

First of all a big thank you to the fabulous Maxine Hitchcock, editor par excellence, for her advice, suggestions and patience as we took Tracie on an action-packed adventure to LA. Also to Keshini Naidoo and Sammia Rafique at Avon for being such stars and so supportive. Indeed many thanks to everyone at Avon for their unfailing help, you've been a joy to work with on two books now – that's more than any writer can hope for! An enormous thank you to Sheila Crowley, super agent and super friend, for all her support and encouragement. Thanks to Mum and Dad, as ever, though dad doesn't have time to read my books now, since he became a star of the letters page of *The Times*. Finally a special mention for Charlie Bronks and everyone on the Linda Uttley Committee who put on a magnificent display of what real friendship is all about when faced with illness to one of their number. You should be desperately proud of yourselves for all you did for Linda. I'm honoured to call you friends . . .

For Gorgeous George – the little boy who finds
it sooo embarrassing when I dedicate books to him.

Also for my brother, Gareth, whose knowledge of hair
extensions and spray tanning were a real help to me in
the writing, and to my sister Susan for her indepth
knowledge of football.

Featured in today's *Daily Mail* – the LAST column
by Tracie Martin, Luton Town Super Wag, and
our most popular columnist, as she prepares
for her new life as a Wag Abroad . . .

HOW SHOULD A WAG PACK FOR A LONG JOURNEY TO LA?

It's a question to trouble even the most confident and committed of Wags. How much stuff should you take on a trip to LA? The right answer is . . . take it ALL!! Pack the bloody lot – from your light-bulb-covered dressing-table mirror to the glittery, tassely, shimmering, skimpy dresses that would make you look overdressed at the Oscars, let alone on the terraces. Take the shiny long pink PVC lace-up boots and the barely-there, marabou-fringed knickers. Obviously take the home spray tan kit complete with portable tanning studio. (This should be in your hand luggage just in case your tan starts fading to yellow during the flight. Always remember – a Wag should be far more chicken tikka masala than chicken korma.)

Take the machine that glues in hair extensions that you bought but can't use because every time you try to glue the extensions back in yourself you manage to get

1

glue in your hair, on your clothes and all over the furniture, you burn your thumbs and stick your fingers together.

Take the collection of twenty-nine skin-tight white lycra dresses that show every cellulite-free inch of your orange thighs. Take the leather dresses, the ridiculous jackets, the huge handbags that cost more than most people's cars, and the tiny handbags that cost more than most people's houses.

What about the huge leopardskin-patterned fake fur coat and the impractical cream-coloured Ugg boots? Yes, yes and thrice yes! But what about the fact that you're going to a boiling hot country and there's no way on God's Earth that you could possibly wear them? Take them anyway. Just in case it cools down – who knows? What with global warming and all that stuff, perhaps the warm countries will experience global cooling. Maybe the smoking ban in Europe will hasten the melting of the ice caps which will cause polar bears to develop webbed feet and gills and swim to LA to live. All I'm saying is – it's possible. So take everything with you.

Take the earrings that are so heavy you can barely lift your head and the gold necklaces that are so chunky they give you whiplash every time you turn round. Take it all, then buy loads more at the airport while you're waiting for the flight that you will inevitably miss because you're too caught up in a shopping frenzy to even think about silly things like gate numbers or departure times.

There. I hope that advice is clear and concise enough. That's certainly what I intend to do. This is Tracie Martin bidding au revoir to Luton Town as I head off to my new life in LA. Welcome to my world . . .

Sunday 25 May
3 p.m. – I think. Los Angeles

Good heavens, doesn't it take a long time to get from Luton to Los Angeles? I mean, a really long time. I left on Thursday, for God's sake. Thursday! Can you believe that?

One of the cleverer footballers at the club told me that it would be a twelve-hour journey, but he was clearly lying through his pearly white, dentally reconstructed, gold-capped teeth. The flight may have been twelve hours, but the journey sure as hell wasn't, it took days!

Now I'm finally here – lying on a plump white leather sofa in my gorgeous new, bright and airy Hollywood home, surrounded by my family and a large collection of brightly coloured airport shopping bags.

Right now it's midnight in Luton and I know that all my mates will be enjoying the last few drops of their Bacardi Breezers in Spangles wine bar, singing footie songs and snogging the face off the nearest bloke. Hovering over them will be a tired barman and an angry landlord ready to wrestle them out of the door and onto the cold, hard, vomit-coated pavement of Luton High Street. Ahhhh . . . what fun. It's strange to be so far away from it all, lying here without a care in the world, with the blistering LA sun streaming through the windows and warming me from head to toe. What a journey I've just been through. Honestly – it's been such a traumatic few days. As I lie back, relaxed for the first time in ages, I feel myself drifting slowly off to sleep ... What a journey, what a journey, what a journey ...

The day before
Heathrow Terminal Four

I confess that I'm not much of a traveller. You'd look at me with my fabulous clothes and my sophisticated air and think, 'Gosh, she's cosmopolitan!' but the truth is that I start to get the shakes whenever I leave the Luton postcode area. As far as I'm concerned, travel is all about getting on the train to Liverpool, going into Cricket and buying a vast amount of tight pink clothing, glittery accessories and must-have handbags, then getting back on a Luton-bound train as quickly as possible.

So I'm not all that used to airports, and I certainly had no idea how many things there are to do there, like rushing into Boots and buying more miniature toiletry items than you can reasonably get through in a decade, as well as stocking up on medical supplies for the flight in such quantities that you could open a small on-board hospital.

Then there's queueing. Oh, yes, you wait in queues for all sorts of things at airports – for people to check your ticket, your passport, your bags, coats, pockets and even your shoes.

Yes ... your *shoes*!

I kid you not. And they don't just check to see whether

4

the shoes are genuine Louboutin or this year's Gucci. No, get this – these people are looking for an altogether more crazy concept in shoe wear . . . they are checking to see whether anyone's shoes have bombs in them.

'Can you get shoes with bombs in?' I ask, all excited. I mean, if anyone knows shoes, I do. I've seen shoes with buckles, bows, glitter and sequins . . . but never bombs. Imagine that! I've always fancied myself as a blonde bombshell and now I could do the look head to toe.

'Have you ever found any shoe-bombs?' I ask, but the uniformed lady just shakes her head mournfully, and I'm overcome with a feeling of total admiration for the way she fearlessly continues to search for the perfect pair of shoes – making everyone in the airport remove theirs and causing utter turmoil in the process.

'Good luck!' I say, blowing a kiss as she pushes my shoes through the machine. 'Really hope you find some.'

Her brave battle reminds me of my own search for Marc Jacobs pink-and-white diamond-encrusted wedges a few years ago. I found them eventually, after hiring a team of crack shoppers and personal stylists. I turn to tell the shoe-bomb lady about this, in the hope that it will encourage her, but as I do she emits a loud scream, four people dive to the floor and someone falls to his knees and starts reciting the Lord's Prayer.

'Seize that woman,' says a small burly man in an ill-fitting jumper, rushing to the lady's side and pointing right at me. He hits a big red button on the machine and screams for assistance.

'Help! Help!' he cries, in a not altogether masculine fashion. It reminds me of my husband Dean when I last took him to the dentist.

Shoe-bomb woman howls as a major alarm wails through the airport, and people in uniform come tearing across from all directions, many of them armed.

'Oooo . . . how exciting,' I say, looking up at Dean and giving my daughter Paskia-Rose an entirely unwelcome hug. Three policemen with vicious-looking dogs are sprinting towards me. I feel like I'm on a movie set or something. Dean's not quite as impressed.

'What the fuck have you got in your bag?' he asks, as the alarms grow louder and the panic in the airport rises to fever pitch.

But I can't answer above the sound of screaming and shrieking. Those who are still standing hurl themselves onto the floor. Suddenly I'm being thrown down next to them in the most undignified and unladylike fashion.

'I'm wearing next season's Chloe,' I scream, trying to pull my teeny-weeny, pink mini-skirt across my lady place as I fly backwards through the dirt and dust.

There's not a flicker of compassion or concern on the man's face. Does he have no idea how hard it is to get hold of Chloe four months before it hits the catwalk?

'Get up!' he growls. 'Follow me!' He speaks in a real Arnold Swarzenegger-type voice that, despite everything, makes me want to giggle.

I turn to Dean and say, 'I'll be back,' in a similarly stern fashion, but realize immediately that this is a big mistake.

'Ah, funny girl,' he says, leading me towards a severe-looking woman with tightly cropped brown hair who is snapping on latex gloves. 'Let's see just how funny you're feeling after this.'

An hour later

Not funny at all, actually. Not in the least. My sense of humour deserted me entirely as I was forced to endure the horror of a strip search conducted by a woman with no highlights and bad taste in knitwear.

'What is the problem?' I asked, as she ordered me to remove my clothing.

'I think you know what the problem is,' she said before searching everywhere you can imagine. Finally, when she was happy that I wasn't concealing anything that might constitute a threat to national security she told me to get dressed, and sat down in the chair opposite me.

'You look tired,' I said because she did, poor love. 'Have you been working too hard?'

'Something like that,' she said, as I slipped on my skirt. Then she sat upright. 'Can I ask you something personal?'

'Yes,' I replied.

'Would you mind telling me where you get your bikini line done? I think the stars and stripes flag looks great.'

Oh, so she's human after all. I gave her the name of the beautician whose handiwork with sequins, glitter and jewels she was admiring, and continued to dress.

'Does it hurt?' she asked.

'It doesn't hurt a bit,' I reassured her. 'It itches though, and you find jewels in the strangest of places, but it's worth it. Is it for a special occasion?'

The woman smiled and took off the gloves, flicking the glitter off them as she did so and removing an electric blue star from one of the fingers. 'A date. Tomorrow night,' she confided as she led me through the door.

'Wow. Have fun,' I said. 'Make sure you ask for Mallory when you call that number. She's the best.'

'Thanks,' she replied warmly, then she switched on her more formal self. 'I'll leave you with Mr Matthews.'

'Tracie Martin?' asked a tall, cross-looking man who wouldn't know a fashionable bikini line if it jumped up and bit him.

'Yes.'

'Take a seat, please.'

On the table in front of us were a small replica gun, dagger and hand grenade.

'Do these belong to you?' he asked.

'Yes,' I told him. 'I'm going to Los Angeles. It's quite a dangerous place. Have you not seen all the films? Everyone carries a gun out there.'

'Not everyone,' he said. 'And certainly not anyone who doesn't have a licence for one. Even if you have a licence, you can't take them on a flight.'

'But they're only pretend ones. They're only to scare people away if they try to attack me. What if a baddie is on the flight and tries to take control of the plane and crash it into Disneyland or something? If none of us has any weapons, what are we supposed to do? Let him fly us to certain death? I don't know about you but I don't want to die in a head-on collision with Minnie Mouse or some other fanciful Disney character.'

I was rubbing the tips of my fingers together as I spoke. I do that when I'm nervous. It helps to calm me down. I thought Mr Matthews could do with trying it, the poor bloke looked as if he was going to explode.

'I can't let you take these on the flight,' he said.

'Just the one?' I suggested.

'No.'

'OK, I'll leave them here then,' I said, but I have to say I was mightily disappointed. The gun was a beautiful accessory. It had an exquisitely carved wooden handle.

'You're free to go, Mrs Martin. Enjoy your flight.'

'Thank you,' I said, and I walked back out to Dean feeling wholly deflated by the experience. What a bloody fuss! If I was going to start bringing down aeroplanes, would I have put the weapons in my hand luggage? No, I'd have put them somewhere altogether more discreet.

'You awright love?' said Dean, rushing over to hug me.

'I'm fine,' I replied. 'They just fussed a bit about my weapons, but it's OK now.' I looked over at Paskia-Rose who had gone all pale. 'I thought they were going to throw you into jail,' she whimpered. 'We've been really worried.'

'There's nothing to be concerned about,' I said. 'I'm back, and we're all off to LA.'

'If we haven't missed the flight,' said Dean. 'Come on, we're gonna have to run like the clappers to get there in time.'

Dean and Pask went tearing through to the departure gate in their comfy flat shoes and matching Luton tracksuits. I did more sliding than dashing as I teeter, teeter, clatter, clattered across the shiny slippy floor in my 10-inch high heels.

I was tripping along like a baby giraffe when I caught sight of the others ahead, standing still next to a TV.

'We've missed the flight,' said Dean, pointing to the display screen. 'Look, it's gone.'

'Oh, no,' I sighed, dropping my head. I really wanted to get going. I didn't want to have to hang around the airport

9

for bloody hours waiting for the next one. I looked up at the screen again to see whether there was a later flight listed, but as I was scrutinizing the board, my eye was caught by something altogether more entrancing – twinkling next to me, pulling me towards it in a sweet, magnetic way . . . a shop! Glittering. I looked up. There were more! There were loads of them, everywhere! I was not sure whether I took a wrong turn somewhere and ended up in heaven, but this place was toooo wonderful for words. Have you seen what it's like in the departure lounge? Every type of shop you can imagine is there. It's my personal paradise.

I knew right there and then that I had to shop.

We missed the next flight.

I had to shop some more.

We missed the one after that, too.

I had to do more shopping.

We missed another, and another, and another . . . I couldn't help it! I couldn't – seriously. I spent a fortune. I don't remember when I was last that happy.

Eventually Dean decided that enough was enough, so, with me hanging onto the Chanel lipstick display in desperation, as if clinging to a dying lover, two passing airport security guards, a drunk looking for loose change and one businessman shopping for perfume for his wife and inadvertently caught up in the drama dragged me away. 'Tracie, come on – let go. There'll be other makeup counters,' said Dean as I sobbed pitifully.

Through tears I watched the jewel-coloured eye shadows, gorgeous nail varnishes, perfumes and sparkly powders fade into the distance as a security guy gave me

10

a fireman's lift to the plane, plonking me down in my seat.

'Right – there won't be any more trouble now, will there?' he asked.

'No,' I said. 'No more trouble.'

And I honestly don't believe there would have been. I think the journey would have passed entirely without further drama . . . if it hadn't been for the ladies wheeling their alcohol-laden trolleys up and down the aisles and offering booze to everyone.

'More champagne, madam?'

'OK then.'

'Shall I give you two bottles this time, madam? Just to save me coming back every three and a half minutes?'

'Good idea,' I said with a happy little smile.

'Have a few,' she insisted, passing a handful over to me.

By the time we left mainland Europe my seat looked like a bottle bank. Now I know where the term 'off your trolley' comes from.

The only bad thing about the flight was trying to get to the bathroom to redo my makeup while hideously drunk and with the plane bobbing through the air. Have you ever tried that? The combination of alcohol and a moving floor provides an experience not dissimilar to that of walking across a bouncy castle.

Still, it's by getting out of your seat and staggering around that you get to meet people, and that's how I came to meet the pilot, after falling into the cockpit clutching my make-up bag and a change of clothing. He let me lie on the floor there for a while, and he even joined in some of the football songs I was singing though he didn't know the Luton words. Then there was Flavio, an Italian architect who's moving to LA. I met him when we both found ourselves waiting in line for the bathroom. He invited me to join his club.

'I'd love to!' I said, and rushed back to tell Dean, bouncing off every seat and every passenger en route.

'What club?' asked my husband, wondering whether this guy was going to the LA City Raiders too.

'No, his club's called the Mile High,' I explained. 'He wanted to know whether I fancied joining it with him.'

Sunday 25 May
10.30 a.m. (LA time)

'Ladies and gentlemen, we will shortly be arriving in Los Angeles.'

It's really weird waking up on a plane with the sun shining brightly through the windows. I haven't woken anywhere but the bedroom in Luton for so long that I look up expecting to see my lovely murals painted onto the ceiling, like they are at home. Those paintings show Dean striding across a brightly painted football pitch, shooting for goals with a finesse and degree of accuracy that is wholly reserved for the world of art. Dean was a fabulous footballer in his day – he had the hair, the baggy trousers, the heavy jewellery and the attitude – but he was always a hopeless player. While his swagger into a nightclub screamed 'Drop your knickers, there's a footballer in the room,' his staggers across the pitch screamed 'Drop your hopes of victory, I'm about to score an own goal.' Yes, the truth is that whenever he got near a ball you'd hear a collective intake of breath ricochet round the stadium followed by complete silence, not because anyone truly believed that something magnificent was about to happen, but because they knew it was all over for Luton.

Happily, over the last year we discovered Dean was a far better coach than he ever was a footballer. No one was more surprised than I to see the astonishing result produced by his fledgling attempts at coaching. He trained my daughter Paskia-Rose's side (I know, girls playing football – what's that all about?) until they were so brilliant that they thumped a visiting Los Angeles team, and Dean was offered a job as head coach of the Los Angeles Raiders, with Pask invited to attend St Benedict's, the school associated with the team, and join the ladies' side as its premier striker.

To watch Dean coaching those girls was to watch the work of a genius. He had them fitness training every day with the sort of devotion that I reserve for tending to my cuticles. Honestly, their fitness training sessions were like those undertaken by the Royal Marines, and the way he had them marching around during the training drills put me in mind of the SS. My greatest fear was not that the team would lose, but that my husband would be arrested for child cruelty.

I was the only one excluded from the crazy LA offer, and I think Dean was a bit worried about whether I'd want to come because I became something of a minor superstar in England last year. I started writing this blog online which became a newspaper column, giving lifestyle advice to wannabe Wags. It got so popular that I ended up going onto all sorts of TV programmes, and was recognized in the streets and everything.

'Are you really sure you want to give all that up to come to LA?' Dean had asked me. 'You won't miss being famous?'

'No, of course not,' I had said, and I'm sure I won't,

because I plan to be busy partying and drinking till dawn with the crazy LA Wags. I am going to find a shop like Cricket on Rodeo Drive, meet glamorous film stars, get an open-top car and chew gum all the time. I'll definitely start to talk in a way that is, like, soooo American, and I'll be getting stuck into some serious cosmetic surgery. 'I'll be fine,' I told him. 'Abso-bloody-lutely fine!' and I will be, no question. I'm Tracie Martin and I'm in LA. Bring it on!

Arrivals Hall, LAX Airport, 11 a.m.

I'm still feeling sleepy after the flight as I walk into the terminal after the longest journey in the history of modern aviation. I come staggering out, struggling to put one white patent-leather foot in front of the other, and then I see him – the world's most beautiful man. Just standing there, brooding, dark and handsome. The male equivalent of Barbie. Perfection.

Everything and everyone else in the building seems to melt away as I watch him. He's like a movie star. He's spectacular. He's . . . holy fuck, he's walking towards me, he's walking right towards me. Oh my God. I swear I'm going to faint.

'Are you OK, Mum?' asks Paskia.

'Yes,' I say, as I look up into big brown eyes. 'I'm fine.'

'Hi. I'm Jamie. I'm your driver. Welcome to LA,' he says, relieving me of all my bags and taking a handful off one of the porters next to me.

I love this country already.

'I hear you're a bit of a celebrity in England.' He winks at me as he speaks, and I feel myself flush hot from the black roots of my blonde hair to their extended, plastic ends.

'No, not really, I'm just, um, me,' I reply modestly, smiling up at him, while inside I'm going 'Phooooaarr!'

Dean is walking ahead, pulling several of the cases behind him and moaning about how much stuff there is, and, how heavy the bags are. 'I'm a football manager, not a bloody air hostess,' he moans. 'Men shouldn't pull cases on wheels – it's gay.'

Jamie laughs. 'I'll take them if you like, mate,' he says. 'I'm Jamie – the driver.'

'No, you're fine,' replies Dean, seeing how much Jamie is already carrying. There are also three guys from the airport staff pushing two trolleys each.

'Are you feeling tired?' Jamie asks, and I find myself unable to do anything but bat my heavily mascaraed, false eyelashes in reply.

'Here's the car,' he says, opening the door. 'For you, beautiful lady.'

'That's fine. I can get that.' Dean appears by my side. 'You just look after the bags. I'll look after Tracie and Paskia-Rose, thank you,' he says primly. He seems almost jealous, which is strange. It's not like I'm going to run off with Jamie, is it? Dean's the only serious boyfriend I've ever had, and the only man I ever want. Me and Dean were made to be together. I'd never leave him, not even for David Beckham . . . well, not for Wayne Rooney, anyway.

'How long have you been a cab driver?' I ask Jamie. He doesn't look like any sort of cab driver that I've ever seen before. The man ought to be in the movies.

'I'm a photographer really,' he says. 'I'm driving while

I get my portfolio together. My dream is to work for a British newspaper – something like the *Daily Mail*. Do you know it?'

'Do I? That's the paper I used to write my columns for!' I say.

'Really? I'd love to pick your brains about how it all works there.'

'Don't pick too hard,' says Dean with a loud guffaw. 'There's not much there!'

Jamie looks horrified. 'Sir,' he says to Dean, 'your wife is a world-famous writer. You should be very proud.'

'Hmmph,' says Dean, jumping in the back of the car next to me and Paskia. 'I'm not sure she's *world* famous. Does this car have air conditioning?'

'Yes,' says Jamie, tipping his cap to me in the mirror. 'Of course it has. You're in LA now. Most people's handbags have air conditioning.'

'Ooooo . . . ' I'm wide-eyed with excitement. I'm on the other side of the world in a country where they have air-conditioned handbags. But then Dean lays his hand on my leg and says that Jamie's joking. Probably a good thing. I'm going to be spending enough time looking for shoes with bombs over the coming weeks, without having to search for handbags with air conditioning as well.

'LA is home to more bars, cars and movie stars than anywhere else in the world,' says Jamie proudly, as he eases the big black Chevrolet onto the road . . . on the wrong side.

'Would you like me to point out some landmarks as we go?'

'That would be lovely,' I say, 'but maybe I should point out that you're *on the wrong side of the road*!'

Paskia smirks as if I'm batty, and Dean shakes his head. It turns out that they drive on this side of the road in LA. Er . . . hello. How was I suppose to know that? How do people know these things? It's an English-speaking country. If they want our language they should have to put up with our road systems too.

I look into the mirror and Jamie smiles. Not a smirk, but a proper 'Don't worry, everything's fine' sort of smile. I watch as his eyes drop down to take in my outfit and I smile back. I'm wearing tight white hotpants that I changed into before the plane landed. Well, as the plane was landing, to be accurate. I ended up having to get changed in the aisle, which upset the other passengers, of course, and led to a formal warning from the hostess lady, but what choice did I have? Once Dean had told me all about the Mile High Club I was scared to go to the loo on my own.

The lovely thing about the hotpants, except for the fact that they're white and tight, which is in itself the very epitome of lovely, is that they have 'Wag' written in large, bright pink rhinestones across the bum. I've got bare legs, naturally (well, not naturally at all, because they're coated in fake tan, but you know what I mean) and cowboy boots in pink. On top I've got a tight-fitting jacket made out of about five million cerise ostrich feathers. I'm boiling to death in it, but *nothing* is going to make me take it off.

'Look, I've got a present for you, Candyfloss,' says Dean, and he hands me a slim gold wallet. I feel myself blush as he calls me by my pet name. When we were first married he called me Candyfloss and I called him Sugar Lump all the time.

'Oh, what is it? What is it?' I squeal, mentally running through all the things I can think of that would fit in there. A diamond necklace might, if the diamonds were small – but what would be the point in that?

On the outside of it there's my name and address. 'Ah,' I say, cooing. 'Our new address.'

I put the tips of my fingers into the wallet and pull out . . . oh, a map. There must be some mistake here.

'All it's got in it is a map,' I say.

'Yes. So you don't get lost.'

'Oh.'

'I thought you'd like it,' he says. 'You know how you used to get lost every time you stepped out of the house in Luton. Remember that time you drove to the post-box on the corner of the road and ended up going through Watford to get back?'

Paskia and Dean howl with laughter at the memory of my 200-mile round trip, while all I can think is, When did giving a map to a Wag become appropriate?

'Sweetheart, it's just so you know where you're going,' explains Dean gently. 'There are some little gold stars in there. I thought you could mark our house on, and where your favourite shops are, where the Beckhams live, and things like that.'

'Yeah,' I say, tucking it into the top of my hotpants. 'Lovely, thanks.'

What Dean doesn't realize is that our house is right next to the Beckhams'. Once I knew we were going to be moving to LA I set about finding us a house near theirs in the Hollywood Hills. I called House Hunters, this terribly American, enthusiastic and upbeat firm who promise to find you the house of your dreams.

'We have a great house in Malibu,' they said.

'Nope. Has to be the Hollywood Hills.'

'Bel Air?'

'Nope. Has to be the Hills.'

The reason for this? Well, as you'll soon realize, I'm completely obsessed with Victoria. I love her with all my heart and want to be just like her.

'Mum, why don't you follow the route home on the map as we're driving?' says Paskia-Rose. 'You can look out for all the landmarks on it, as Jamie says them.'

'I think I'll look at it later,' I say. What does she think I am – a bloody five-year-old doing a project on a school trip?

'Here on the left is Venice Beach,' says Jamie. 'Ever heard of it?'

Neither Dean nor I have. In fact, the only landmarks I'm interested in are the ones that sell clothes or champagne.

'I've heard of Venice Beach,' says Pask. 'Don't they do sports and stuff on there?'

'That's right,' says Jamie. 'They play volleyball and basketball, also softball. It's well worth heading down to the boardwalk if you get the chance. It's great. There are fire eaters, jugglers, roller-skating performers and loads of carnivals, fairs and markets. It's a fun place just to hang out. There are loads of artists, if you're into that sort of thing. A friend of mine sells her pictures there.'

'Oh, let's go there,' says Pask. 'Can we?'

'Of course we can, love,' I say, looking up into the mirror where Jamie looks back at me. He has beautiful, thick, glossy hair, so dark it's almost black. He has a square jaw that reminds me of Action Man every time I glance it in the mirror. His body . . . well, his body is simply perfect. He's like a gladiator. I find myself feeling irrationally jealous of his artist friend. I don't want him to have female friends – just me.

'When can we go?' asks Pask.

'Really soon,' I promise.

'This area here is Santa Monica,' Jamie says. 'And that's Santa Monica pier, which is fun. It has old-fashioned funfairs, and an aquarium. There's a carnival there most days. It starts at the pier and goes all the way along the front to Venice Beach. It's well worth having a look. People all get dressed up and just clown around.'

Everything about LA looks so clean and bright, with its beautiful, sun-tanned people in their brightly coloured clothes. I haven't seen any Wags yet, or any women with Wag tendencies, but it's early days; plenty of time.

The sea is the most gorgeous sapphire blue, sparkling and dazzling as we drive along the front. The white sand looks so warm, soft and inviting, like the lovely big Stella McCartney fur coat Dean bought for me last Christmas. There are people everywhere, enjoying the sun and relaxing in the cafés, smiling as we pass. 'Are they on happy drugs or something?' I ask.

Jamie just laughs. 'OK, we're moving away from the seafront now,' he says, and all three of us say 'Oh', without realizing.

'Sorry, guys, but I can't get up into the hills without going inland. We'll take the Santa Monica Freeway. Along here are a few of the biggest museums in the area – see that, over there? That's the Museum of Contemporary Art. The area's known as Downtown, and you've got your Performing Arts Center and loads of theatres there. It's the arty part of town.'

'Oh, is it?' I say. 'Is that where your friend the artist lives then?'

'No, she doesn't live here but she hangs out here a bit. Now then, we're heading up into Hollywood.'

'Ooooh,' I say, hoping we'll see Tom and Kate or Angelina and Brad. Perhaps Julia Roberts and Catherine Zeta-Jones will be out shopping.

'On the left is the Egyptian Theatre. That's a great old place. The very first Hollywood première took place there.'

'*Legally Blonde*?' I ask.

'No, it was a bit before that. It was back in 1922.'

'Really? I didn't know they had films then.'

'If you're interested, you should go down there. They show documentaries every day about the history of Hollywood, and how it became a movie town.'

'Mum, look over there,' squeals Paskia. 'Look!'

'Wooooooah!!' I shriek back. 'It's the Hollywood sign. Look, Sugar Lump. Look. Oh my God. I can't believe we're here. Dean, we're in Hollywood.'

And the truth is, I really *can't* believe we're finally here after the year we've just had. You see, there's one thing I haven't told you about me yet and that's that my mum, Angie, is horrible. I mean *really* horrible. I had a miserable childhood with her because she hated me. 'Nothing personal, I just don't like kids,' she used to say, as she got dressed up in chiffon and diamonds for another glamorous night on the tiles, leaving me in the house, alone and scared. But it all got worse last year when I became famous. Mum tried to sabotage me – selling articles about me to the newspapers about how horrible I was, and trying to frame Dean and make it look like he was being unfaithful. I thought that was bad enough, but I was even more heart-broken when I discovered that my father, who Mum said hated me and wanted nothing to do with me from the day I was born, was actually sending regular letters and money which Mum never handed over to me. It turns out that my dad lives in LA, so if I'm ever feeling strong enough I'll get in touch with him. Right now, though, it's the last thing I can face doing.

'Now this is the most important landmark in LA,' says Jamie, interrupting my thoughts.

'What is?'

'This,' he says, pointing to a very grand house in front of us. It's a buttery-coloured mansion with large turrets and a wrought-iron gate. It looks like a fairytale palace. 'Your staff are here waiting for you,' he says.

'Our home!' I squeal. 'Oh, we're here!'

'Wow!' says Paskia-Rose. 'It's like something out of a movie set.'

She's right, it is, and it *has* been in the movies. The house has been used as a location in several films. It used to belong to some bloke called Liberace who played the piano and had fantastic, though slightly understated, tastes in clothing and décor. All I had to do to the outside of the house was add a few flamboyant Tracie touches, like gold leaf to the fountain and statues next to the marble pillars, and it was sorted. Work needed to be done inside to Lutonize the place, but not that much – this Liberace chap may well have had a bit of Luton in him, because the pictures and mirrors on the ceiling are just my style.

While Jamie goes to the boot to get the bags and organize all the other cars following behind, the three of us rush inside, crashing into three men, neatly lined up just inside the doorway.

'Welcome. I'm Gareth,' says the first man. He's the youngest of the three, with receding sandy blond hair and pale green eyes that have a ruthlessness to them. If he weren't smiling I could easily mistake him for a serial killer, such is the intensity of that stare. He wears a small diamond earring in his left earlobe, and in his hands he carries a huge bouquet of flowers.

'Thank you so much,' I say, taking the floral arrangement from him. This is the guy who's going to be our driver.

'I'm Mark,' says a man with ginger hair and glasses. He's the DIY expert. He's supposed to be the best carpenter in LA, and has been busy for the past couple of weeks creating my dream home, here in the Hollywood Hills.

'I'm Peter,' says the final man. He's smaller than the other two and slightly older with dark hair and a considerable twitch that sends his head flicking from one side to the other every couple of minutes. I remember that he's the one who's absolutely brilliant at gardening. I got them all from a staffing agency called Buff Butlers & Weed Whackers and they couldn't have recommended this guy more highly.

Inside the house is a great, huge white palace of a place with six bedrooms and a truly awesome kitchen that leads to a major sitting room with white floors and three enormous white leather sofas.

'It's exactly the same as the house in Luton!' squeals Paskia-Rose, who's trailing along behind us. 'I don't believe it.'

I'm determined to create my own little piece of Luton wherever I go.

'I'll show you round, shall I?' says Mark, and we wander

through the house ooohing and ahhhing over how lovely it is. It is just beautiful – utterly spectacular. A house fit for a Wag in every respect, from the leopardskin-covered dressing table (made by Mark himself) to the large, multi-roomed dressing area. Oh, yes, let me repeat that I have a collection of dressing rooms, all linked together to form a dressing area.

The house has magnificent patio doors that open right up so you're in this great LA garden, designed and maintained by Peter. The lovely thing about the garden is that there's nothing wild or unkempt about it – it's staggeringly well manicured, making it look like another room in the house. I've kept the concrete piano left by Liberace at the bottom of the garden and had it painted pink and brought up to the top.

It's all even more perfect than I remember from the pictures and design templates. Employing Lisaa, my favourite interior designer from Luton and flying her over to LA, has worked a treat, and these guys have transformed all my dreams and her plans into reality.

'Thank you, thank you,' I say. 'There's nothing I don't like about it. It's absolutely perfect.'

The three men smile proudly. I think I'm going to like them very much.

'There we are,' says Jamie, as he indicates that all my luggage has been brought in. 'Is there anything else I can get you?'

'No thanks,' I say, lying down on one of the beautiful white sofas and feeling the sun on my face. I'm so glad to finally be here. It's been a hell of a journey. What a journey, what a journey, what a journey . . .

3 p.m.

'Tracie, love, wake up, wake up,' says Dean. I look at his watch. It's 3 p.m.

'What do I have to wake up for?' I ask.

'You haven't had a drink in ages. Don't you want one? You'll be dehydrated!'

'Ooooh, yes,' I cry, leaping up. 'I'm *dying* for a drink!'

There are stains the colour of marmalade on the sofa where the fake tan's rubbed off a little, and a clump of hair extensions where my head once lay.

Jamie is still with us. He laughs at my eagerness for a drink, shaking his head and saying that everything he's heard about English women is true.

'Pass my handbag, would you?' I say. It's full of alcohol. I watch as Jamie bends over to pick it up for me. He has buns of steel.

'I've never known a girl have alcohol in her handbag before,' he says.

'Well, I guess you've never met a girl from Luton before then.'

Now he's beginning to understand why I was so excited about the idea of air conditioning in handbags. Chilled Bacardi Breezers. Wicked!

With that, I pull out a couple of bottles of Cristal and we're off.

'You staying for a drink?'

'I really shouldn't,' Jamie says, turning serious all of a sudden. 'I should be out looking for a job.'

'As a photographer?'

'Now that *would* be nice. Sadly, no. I need to find myself work as a driver while building my portfolio.'

'I thought you worked for the club.'

'I used to,' he explains, 'then they terminated my contract. This is my last job for them – picking you guys up from the airport. The club has a policy of using lots of different drivers. They never re-employ the same ones once their twelve-month contract is up, so – I'm off.'

'That's ridiculous,' I cry. 'We must get Dean to have a word with them. He's going to be *very* important at the club. He'll make them change their mind. Won't you, dear?'

There's no sound from Dean because he has his head down and is rummaging through my bags in search of lager. When he emerges with a big grin and a four-pack of Stella I ask him again.

'I'll try, Candyfloss,' he says, distracted by his new find, 'but I can't make any promises.'

'There you go. Dean's definitely going to get you a job, so you don't have to worry,' I say. 'Have a little drink with us.'

'I'll just have a softie,' he says. 'I haven't drunk for years. I'm just not keen on alcohol and what it does to the body.'

'What? You don't drink at *all*?'

'No,' he says. 'Never touch it. Lots of people in LA don't.'

I knock back my champagne in shock and watch Dean as he plonks himself down on the other sofa, facing the 60-inch wall-mounted plasma TV. He pours half of his can down his neck before switching on the telly and giving his balls a right good scratch. Ahhh . . . *now* it feels like home.

'You all right, love?' I ask, and he looks round with a contented smile on his face.

'Just like Luton but with more TV stations,' he says, and I can hear the emotion in his voice.

'Come and sit here,' I say to Jamie, patting the sofa next to me. He sits down unnecessarily close and looks straight into my eyes. I feel strange inside, as if every major organ in my body is involved in a trampoline display. I can't breathe. I'm sure I'm going to have a coronary at any moment. My heart's thumping so hard, it's like it's going to smash its way through my chest and dance across the floor.

What's wrong with me? I never feel like this around men. I need to get away.

'I'm just going to check on my dressing area, then I'll be back for a chat,' I say in a peculiar high-pitched voice, staggering up the stairs.

My dressing area is still there, with its cerise-coloured walls and leopardskin carpet, and the hangers and drawers lined in velvet. There's loads of space in there and little velvet, leopardskin pouches for shoes, and stands for boots and handbags. I'm still trying to catch my breath after sitting so close to Jamie, so I sit down heavily on the bed and pull out the little gold map case from my hotpants.

I open it up and try to work out where our house is. There! I put a gold star right on top of us, then I pull out my piece of paper with Victoria and David's address on. OK . . . Beverly Hills, Beverly Hills. Whaaaaattt? Hollywood Hills and Beverly Hills are two completely different places. They're separate hills entirely. Holy fuck. We're living on the wrong hill. I drop the map and jump up.

'Dean,' I say, shrieking through the house as I hobble

down the stairs, taking them three at a time and moving with reckless speed. 'Dean!'

'What is it?' he says, coming out to meet me.

'This house is all wrong,' I say.

'No it's not. It's lovely.'

'Dean, it's all *wrong*. We can't live here, we have to move. Immediately. We have to, Sugar Lump.'

'I don't understand, love. It's all done out just like the Luton house was. What's the problem? If you don't like something, can't you just call Lisaa and get it changed, like you did when the chandeliers in the hallway weren't sparkly enough? Do you remember that, love? You sent the poor woman back to India to get more jewels. Then there was the time you wanted pink marble benches and Lisaa managed to find them in China.'

'No, Dean, the problem isn't the house. It's the place. I got my hills muddled up. I thought Victoria and David lived in Hollywood Hills but they live in Beverly Hills. Oh, Dean, it was my dream to live next to them and to see them every day. I can't believe it. It's too awful for words.'

'How far away is Beverly Hills?' asks Dean. 'I bet it's just round the corner.'

'It's four and a half acrylic nails away. I measured it, Dean. How many miles to a nail, do you think?'

'I don't really know,' he says. 'Jamie might.'

Jamie! Of course, he's bound to know.

'Jamie, Jamie,' I start howling, as I run into the sitting room. 'How far's Beverly Hills from here?'

'About half an hour's drive,' he says. 'Why? Do you want to go there?'

'Yes, urgently,' I say. 'I need to go now. Quickly. As

soon as possible. I need to see where the Beckhams live. It's of the utmost importance. If they don't live where they should live, we're going to have to move. Unless they will move instead . . . No, I think it's going to have to be us. They were here first. I'm not an unreasonable woman.'

'OK,' he says, a little confused, but getting to his feet nonetheless.

'See you later,' I say to Dean. 'Keep your fingers crossed that it's not too far because if it is we're moving the whole damn house, and I have a feeling that this big house is going to be hellishly difficult to shift.'

I'm in the car, next to Jamie, and even though he's gorgeous and I could hardly take my eyes off him before, I'm concentrating on nothing but Victoria now. How could this have happened? It's unbelievable.

'I know the Beckhams well, you know,' says Jamie.

'What did you just say? Pull over!'

He looks at me. 'I know them well. I didn't say anything earlier in case you thought I was being showy or something, but, yeah. You know – me and Victoria, we're pals.'

'Pals? My God. I think she's the most wonderful person on earth. I'd die if I could meet her. I think she's perfect.'

I'm struggling to breathe all over again. This is so exciting.

'I used to be her driver.'

'No!'

'Yep,' he replies. 'Their personal chauffeur. I'll introduce you some day, if you like. Not today – it would be rude to go barging in there – but someday soon.'

'Oh my God, yes!' I cry, leaping up and almost

breaking my ribs on the seat belt. 'Yes, yes, yes. Oh God, yes.'

I take a huge swig from the Cristal bottle wedged between my orange thighs and smile happily. Meeting Victoria is the one remaining goal in my life. For years I've dreamt of meeting her. I mean, I've seen her before . . . there was that time when I almost got arrested after following her from Beckingham Palace. I don't think I'll tell Muscley Jamie about that, though, in case he thinks I'm mad.

'Right. This is Beverly Hills. What did you say the name of the road was? I've forgotten.'

I read out the address to him as we drive past magnificent double-fronted detached houses. They're all imposing, square buildings, very new-looking with squeaky-clean windows and perfect gardens. There's something pleasant about that, but something a bit odd, too, because it makes the place feel sterile and unreal. It's as if all the houses are too perfect to be real and that they'll blow away in the first gust of wind. Where Dean and I live in a posh part of Luton there are loads of different types of houses on the same street. Some look like large cottages, others like mansions. They're all massive, impressive and eye-wateringly expensive, but each house has its own little history. They're all unique. Not like here where they all look the same. Aaaaahhhhhh . . . except for that one.

'This is it!' I scream, making poor Jamie jump out of his skin. 'Oh, look. It's just like all the pictures I've seen – only bigger, obviously, or it would be a tiny house that I could fit in my handbag.'

I leap out of the car with considerable athleticism for

a woman in bone-crunchingly high heels and walk towards the Beckhams' large white mansion. You can't see it properly from the outside because there's a huge wooden fence protecting it from prying eyes. I have to get nearer.

'Where are you going?' asks Jamie, alarmed.

'I want to get as close as possible,' I say, breathing deeply. 'You can sense her presence, can't you?'

Jamie parks and runs after me. By the time he reaches me I'm standing by the gate with my body pushed up against it, sniffing deeply. I can see that the other side of the gate there's a driveway up to a more substantial metal gate, controlled by a security guard.

'Can I help you guys?' asks a uniformed officer.

They have two security guards? Wow, that's impressive.

'We're just going,' says Jamie. 'Sorry, we were lost. We're just off now.'

'What's she doing?' asks the guard, pointing at me as I stand completely flat against the gate, inhaling deeply and trying not to squeal with excitement.

'I'm a gate inspector,' I say.

'Gate inspector? I've never met one before. What do you do?'

'I inspect gates,' I tell him. 'On behalf of the government. I just need to stand here a moment longer.'

'Do you have a pass or anything?' asks the man.

'I do,' I tell him, 'but I've left it in my Marc Jacobs bag. I wasn't thinking when I came out, and I brought the Prada by mistake.'

The security guard glances at Jamie with a look which says 'take her away now or I'll have her sectioned'.

'We're going,' says Jamie, leading me back to the car.

'Sir, I'm glad to tell you that your gate has passed the test. Everything is fine. Thank you for your time,' I shout.

The security officer looks alarmed, as well he might, but not quite as shocked as Jamie, who is now driving away as fast as he can.

'I touched the gate,' I tell him. 'And look at this . . .'

While I was standing there I dragged my fingernails down the gate and filled them with splinters of wood. I pick it all out and hold it in my hand. A look of astonishment has crept across Jamie's handsome features.

'What will you do with that?' he asks.

'Keep it forever,' I say. 'Forever and ever and ever.'

He looks at me as if I'm stark staring mad. 'I just think she's brilliant,' I say, almost shyly. 'Brilliant.'

'I'm going to help you meet her,' he says. 'I promise you. Stick with me and I'll get you an introduction to the Beckhams. Just don't pull any more stunts like that or we'll get arrested. OK?'

'OK.'

LA is brilliant. The City of Angels, it's called, according to Jamie. Well, I've definitely found one in him.

Monday 26 May
9 a.m.

I feel like I've been in a major car crash, and when I glance in the floor-to-ceiling mirrors situated just outside my dressing area I can see that my feelings are entirely matched by my physical appearance. Seriously. My hair is standing up on end and three days of makeup have layered on top of each other, papier-mâché style, to form a thick mask.

I wipe away most of the black from round my panda bear eyes, add a little lipstick, then a little more, a shed load of foundation and streaks of blusher. Happily, I'm still dressed, so that's handy, though my jacket has sick all down the front, which isn't ideal – it's ruined half the feathers, and my hotpants don't have much in common with the colour white any more. They are slightly greying at the front from where I was crawling over the floor looking for alcohol when we got back from the Beckhams' last night.

I turn away from the dressing area (did I mention I had a dressing area? Honestly, it's perfect. You must get one. Wardrobes are sooo yesterday!) and wander downstairs and into the garden where Dean's sitting at our long garden table, teaching Gareth, Peter and Mark to sing football songs.

'Luton, Luton.
Sing along for Luton.
The greatest damn club in the land.
You should always sing for Luton.
Luton, Luton, Luton.
Give the boys a helping hand.'

Honestly, it's poetry. I can't believe the guys have learnt all the words so quickly.

'Where's Jamie?' I ask. I don't remember much about last night. We got back from our Beckham trip, I drank bottles of champagne and I woke up in bed still wearing my clothes.

'Gone,' says Dean. 'He left after I put you to bed. I think he had to get up early to return the car to the club.'

Dean reaches forward and takes a bread roll from the table. Bread? Where the hell did bread come from? I stand, rooted to the spot, scared to move any closer to the table in case the carbs jump up and attack me. You have to watch carbs very closely indeed. I know a great deal about this subject, having kept my weight below that of the average six-year-old for my entire adult life.

I was on the Bacardi and bay leaf diet at one stage but that didn't seem to be a healthy way to live, so I tried the raw potato and whisky diet, which was hopeless. In the end I realized that the only way to look good is to eat sensibly and healthily, so these days I'm determined to eat properly and set a good example to my daughter. The only rule I follow is to avoid all fats, carbohydrate, protein and vitamins. Besides that I eat absolutely everything. As long as it's alcoholic.

'He left you this note,' says Pask kindly, handing me a folded piece of paper.

'Thanks, angel,' I say, blowing her a kiss, but she misses my spontaneous gesture because she has turned her attentions to Dean.

'Daaad,' she says in her 'I want something and I want it *now*' voice that she knows is so effective on her father. 'Pleeeeaaaasee can we go to the club today?' Her cheeks are stained red from the exertion of whacking a football against a wall relentlessly in the sun. She looks all bright-eyed and freckly and not for the first time I'm drawn to thinking that with a little makeup and a little weight loss she could be a really attractive girl. I want to cuddle her and hold her tightly and show her how to apply eyeliner and what foods to avoid, but she shows no interest in such things. 'Can we? Can we, Dad? You know – go to the club. Can we?'

Pask's a real tomboy. It breaks my heart to say that, but it's true. I know she might well grow out of it but right now she's more male than female in her clothing and actions. She's dressed in the Luton Town kit, and she's pushed the football between her great white thighs while she leans in to Dean.

'Of course, love,' he says, and they do a high five thing. Dean's big gold signet rings glint in the early morning sunshine as his hand smacks against Paskia's, and the two of them smile warmly at one another. I glance down at the note. It's got Jamie's number on it. Hoorah! He says he's going to spend the day at the club, trying to change their minds about the job. 'Pop in and see me if you're there, and we'll arrange a time to go and see Victoria,' it says.

'I'm coming to the club too, I'm coming too,' I squeal.

Dean spins round, alarm springing from every pore. 'Don't you want to spend the day doing your nails or shopping or something?' he says, spraying bits of bread around as he speaks. I duck, dodge and dive to avoid them. If that carbohydrate so much as touches my skin, I'll be three stone heavier tomorrow.

'I can do all that later,' I tell Dean. 'Right now I'd rather be with you and Pask.'

I know that if I go I'll get to see Jamie again, and further develop our relationship, and I'll also be able to make a better case for the club employing him which will keep him on my radar. Dean's rubbish at doing things like that. He's too understated about things. This needs an approach that is unsullied by subtlety. In short, it needs the Tracie touch.

2 p.m.

We're here. This is it – LA City Raiders. It's an impressive-looking, ultra-modern, shiny grey building, with a big sign outside and a long track leading up to the offices at the front. The pitch looks perfect, according to Dean and Pask.

'Come on, love,' I say. 'Let's go and find a bar for a quick one before we meet up with the geezer in charge.'

'Yeah,' says Deany, rubbing his hands together at the thought. His earrings shine brightly in the sun. Bless 'im. We're like peas in a pod, we two are. We just love doing the same things. Not so my daughter.

'No,' she says. 'Don't get drunk. Please. For once, let's not go straight to the bar. Please can we just go in there and introduce ourselves to the chairman and say hi to people?'

'I guess,' says Dean as we arrive in the club's entrance hall, but by the look on his face he thinks it's as weird an idea as I do. 'I can't even remember the guy's name, can you?'

'I know his wife's name is Sian Doyle. The kids are called Maia, Morgan and Hana. How about that for a memory?'

'Blimey,' says Dean. 'Is that the first time you've remembered anything useful?'

'No,' I say defensively, but he might be right. Memory for anything but shoes and clothing is not my strong point. We walk up to the reception desk.

'Chuck,' says Dean all of a sudden.

'Go to the loos quickly then,' I say. 'You don't want to go puking all over reception on your first day in the club.'

'No, the chairman's name is Chuck,' says Dean.

'Oh, I see.'

We smile at the pretty, wide-eyed receptionist and introduce ourselves.

'Welcome,' she says with a sugary smile and a flash of her unfeasibly large blue eyes. 'We're glad you're here. Would you like to go up to the main clubroom? Follow the signs. I'll tell Chuck you're here.'

I can't believe how squeaky clean it all is. It's like the club has just been built, as if the world of football is just arriving in this place, and my Dean will be there at the start of it. He'll be there to lead these men as they battle to make it in this special sport that produces such joy, passion and fabulously dressed women. The stadium apparently seats 25,000 people which isn't exactly Wembley but, as Dean says, 'It's more than big enough.' They usually only get around 6,000 watching.

'Oh my, oh my,' Paskia-Rose keeps saying as she peers out of the window. 'I think I'm going to completely die of excitement. Just look at those pitches down there, Mum. Imagine! Me! Out! There!'

'Mmmm, lovely,' I hear myself saying, because it's not lovely, is it? Pask is twelve, for God's sake. She's nearly a teenager. How many twelve-year-old girls do you know who think they're going to die of excitement at the sight of bloody grass?

'Hello there,' says a man with a loud voice and an even louder shirt. He is swaggering towards us sporting a pair of horrible, slightly too tight, old-fashioned tennis shorts with a moss-green shirt covered in large red flowers on top. The shirt hangs loosely over the shorts, almost covering them. He's wearing naff aviator sunglasses and has on lace-up black shoes and black ankle socks that would be better paired with a nylon suit, by a man going to work in the regional branch of an estate agent. He's striding through the clubhouse towards us.

'You guys!' he exclaims, going for a high five, then realizing that Dean is standing there with his hand out, so he jumps back a little, makes a ridiculous face, then eventually he puts his own hand out.

'Nice to meet you. I'm Dean Martin,' says my husband, but instead of actually shaking hands Chuck pulls it away at the last minute, pokes his tongue out, puts his thumb on his nose and waggles his fingers like a ten year old.

'Give us a song!' he says. 'Come on, Dean Martin, you big crooner you. Give us one of the old ones.'

There's a small silence before the man collapses with mirth at his own joke. 'Only joking. Sorry, I'm a bit mad, I am. A bit crazy. You'll get used to me. I'm Chuck.'

Oh Lord.

Dean and Chuck eventually shake hands and slap each others backs in a manly fashion, with Chuck making several hilarious jokes about Dean's name. 'Not brought the Rat Pack with you then? Ha ha ha . . . sorry – I did warn you. I'm the funny guy in this place. Now then, what have we here?' he says, looking me up and down, and adopting a style of eyebrow-raising rarely seen outside a *Carry On* film or an episode of *Benny Hill*. 'Tracie, Tracie. As fresh and lovely as a summer rose. What is someone as gorgeous and, may I say, sexy as you doing with this rascal Dean, then?'

'Oh, I'm just using him for sex,' I say, and I'm pleased to say that it floors Chuck completely.

He looks from my stunning orange face to Dean's shocking red face, and then over at my daughter's pale freckly one.

'Well, hello there,' he says, and off go the eyebrows again.

'I'm Paskia-Rose. It's nice to meet you,' she says firmly, shaking his hand with a vigour that he's clearly not used to. He clutches his hand to his chest in mock pain, then starts laughing again, slapping his thigh.

'Fooled ya!' he says, pointing at Pask.

Oh God. How much time will we have to spend in this man's company? He's driving me nuts already. All three of us are standing there, looking from one to the other. I know that Dean, Pask and I are all thinking 'What a complete knob.' I have no idea what he's thinking, though, except that he's staring unashamedly at my baps. I feel as if I ought to say something to break the tension seeping out of the silence.

'I've got a whole dressing area for my clothes, you know. Not a wardrobe, but this whole area . . .'

'Maybe you could show us round,' interrupts Dean, cutting me off in my prime. Dean does that a lot, as you'll see.

'OK,' says a slightly bewildered-looking Chuck. 'Let's all head on outside and have a look at the pitches. Dean, perhaps you could sing as we go. Ha ha ha! I did warn you. I did, didn't I?'

OK, so I have three immediate problems to deal with – first, Chuck's unbearable. Second – no sign of Jamie anywhere. Third problem . . . outside . . . pitches? How the hell am I supposed to walk across grassy pitches in these clothes? I'm wearing a lime-green knitted mini-dress with a huge white belt that's pulled so tight it's stretched the wool and made the whole thing see-through. Happily I predicted this outcome, so to avoid unsightly underwear show-through I have worn nothing under-neath. I have on massively high white patent boots, and am sporting more gold round my neck than Jimmy Saville.

We walk outside and the men stride ahead of me, with Paskia-Rose skipping behind. She's wearing her Arsenal shirt now and it strikes me that she's always clad in nylon. Can that be healthy? One day she's going to rub her legs together, cause a spark and whoosh – she'll spontaneously combust. There'll be nothing left behind bar smoke and a puddle of liquid nylon in the Arsenal club colours. As she walks, Paskia swings her foot to launch an imaginary ball across the beautiful lush green pitches in front of us. I teeter along behind them all on tippy-toes, hoping that I don't fall over but being self-aware enough to realize that it will be a miracle if I don't.

'Over there is the baseball pitch,' explains Chuck with an accompanying swing of his arm which narrowly misses

Paskia's head, while Dean nods and looks around, and I try to do faster tippy-toe running to catch up with them. 'You guys ever heard of baseball?' he asks. 'It's different from your damned cricket. They manage to finish on the same day as they started, and they never blame the weather! Ha ha.'

'And what's that?' I ask when I arrive next to them, elated that I'm still upright. I'm pointing to a large concrete outhouse tucked in behind the row of trees that separate the baseball and soccer areas.

'This was part of the old club, before we had the major renovation installation completion,' explains Chuck, opening the unlocked outer door and taking a key from a small hook near a shelf on the right. He opens the white inner door and leads us inside. The place is set out like a small office with an old-fashioned typewriter on an ancient wooden desk. 'Ah,' he says, wistfully. 'This is how things were.'

Paskia hovers in the doorway, still looking longingly at the football pitches while Chuck walks round, mumbling to himself. 'There is simply no point working to a launch and then finding a house of cards, is there?' he says.

'No, no point at all,' says Dean, out of politeness more than agreement.

We walk back to the main building and Chuck starts telling Dean how he made his fortune in the canned food business.

'Once I'd got all my ducks in a row it was fairly smooth running to my first mill,' he's saying. 'I'm not claiming it was easy – there were some major cows on the line which could have derailed the whole project, but I did it. I mean, if anyone can put a pig in a dress and call it grandma, I can!'

What the fuck is he on about? I'm listening to his talk of how he had to do a lot of blue-sky thinking, while picking my way through the mud, feeling a lot like Margo out of *The Good Life* (Dean loves that programme) only better-dressed, obviously.

'So what do you actually do, Chuck?' Dean asks. 'Is it the cans you make, or the food that goes in them?'

'That's right,' says Chuck. 'Bang on.'

'Oh, OK,' says Dean. 'So is it all canned food or just particular sorts of food, like fruit or vegetables or meat or something?'

'Dean, I've done them all and I'd be lying if I didn't say that I've had to jump through a few hoops along the way. Luncheon-meat-related issues are particularly tough right now, whereas corned beef is just an exercise in box ticking. Personally I sense that a great future in cans is set to cascade down, then we can all play in the corporate waterfall.'

'Yeah, cool,' says Dean.

We arrive back and I'm so busy thinking about waterfalls and cans cascading down that I simply don't see the boot scraper that the others have stepped so elegantly over, and I clatter into it, completely lose my balance and squeal pathetically for the duration of my fall to the floor.

I'm lying flat on my face, half in and half out of the door. My dress is up by my waist, giving the Raiders Club chairman and LA's hottest canned foods magnate a bird's eye view of the 'Other Way Round' tattoo on my bottom. Why do things like this always happen?

'Whoops. Cheeky,' says Chuck, lifting me up and

putting me onto me feet. Dean has his head in his hands and Pask doesn't know where to look. Honestly, it's not that bad – it's only a bottom.

'Are you trying to embarrass me?' asks Dean quietly.

'No,' I assure him. I'm not trying; I'm managing to do it with no effort whatsoever. If I tried, imagine how embarrassing I could be!

Dean, Paskia and Chuck have gone up the metal spiral staircase leading to the side entrance to the main club room. I follow them, clinging onto the handrails and hoping that no one comes in below me.

'Here comes the lovely little lady,' says Chuck when I appear at the top. I have mud on my legs, covering my boots and smeared across my face, but other than that I've survived the walk perfectly well.

'Ah, darling, you're here!' trills a voice from a distant room, then in walks an astonishingly thin woman – all bones, huge unblinking eyes and a smile that stretches the width of her face. She has long blonde hair with a thick, almost child-like fringe.

'Woooah,' says Chuck, flailing his arms around as the woman gives him a kiss. 'I've never seen you before. Who are you?'

Both Chuck and the woman collapse into hysterical fits of laughter.

'Isn't he a card? God, twelve years of marriage and he still makes me howl with laughter every day. I'm Sian.'

Goodness. She's so thin it's scary. I never realized before that it was possible to be too thin, but here we are – proof that it is. 'Nice to meet you,' I say, putting out my heavily bejewelled hand, but instead of shaking it she clutches me in a massive bear-hug and squeezes me into her skeleton. I'm terrified she's going to snap in half. Then she pushes herself away and scrutinizes me closely.

'Wow, but look at you!' she squeals. 'Wow, wow, wow. Why do you have such a funny outfit on?'

Funny? Jeeeezz . . . The lady's got a nerve. Sian, let me tell you, gentle readers, appears to be wearing no makeup at all! *None!* I know – it's offensive. She has great skin but, really, no makeup? I do my makeup before getting in the shower, before I go to bed, washing my hair or putting on a face mask. How could she leave the house without makeup?

'Let's get juice,' she says, still staring me up and down.

'Pask, are you coming?' I ask, but when I look round my daughter is staring wistfully out of the window.

'Come on, Dean,' says Chuck. 'Let's brainstorm the dynamics and interpersonal relationships in this team. We need to look behind the power curve and throw up some thought showers that we can circle back on next week.'

'Yeah, OK,' says Dean. 'But it would be quite handy to have a chat with you about coaching.'

'Yes,' says Chuck, patting my husband on the back. 'That's what I just said.'

Sian marches me towards a room further away, as fast as my mud-covered platform stiletto boots can take me. I know I'm going to like her, even though she's thinner than me. I don't normally take to people who are thinner than I am. Come to think of it, I don't think I've ever met someone who's skinnier than me before.

'I have a couple of questions for you,' she says. 'First up, will you let me host a party for you on Wednesday night? Please say I can. There'll just be a few of us there.'

'Oh, thanks, that would be lovely,' I say, meaning it. I love a good party.

'Great. You'll meet Poppy and Macey – two girls from the club. Poppy's going out with one of the players – Rock Lyon. Do you know him? He was a great player in his day. Macey's lovely, too. She's an artist who paints the best watercolours ever. You'll love them. She's been doing portraits of the players for an exhibition. She did a portrait of Van Dooley – do you know him? Great American writer.'

'I know a writer!' I exclaim, glad to be able to contribute something to the conversation. 'He's called Simon. He's the guy who helped me write my columns in England. He's coming over on Sunday and staying for a few weeks to do research for a novel he's writing, set in LA.'

'Wow, honey, I love English writers,' she says. 'Dickens, Austen, Archer. Is he a good guy?'

A good guy? I wonder to myself. I don't know how to answer that. How do you explain the qualities of someone like Simon – a man who's become the third most important person in my life in such a short period of time? How do I explain that this is the person who guided me when my mother turned on me and started selling stories to the tabloid papers; the man who sat next to me and listened patiently to my pain and anguish after Dean's nan passed away? How do I go about explaining that?

'Yeah,' I say. 'He's a good guy. The best. After Dean.' It almost feels as if any attempt to explain our relationship will somehow diminish it.

'Well, then, I need to make the most of you before he comes and takes up all your time, don't I?' she says. 'We can do yoga together and go for runs and swim and ...'

'Are you mad?' I say. 'What do we want to do all that shit for when we could just be getting pissed?'

'Oh, Tracie, you don't drink alcohol, do you? You know it's terribly bad for you.'

'Drinking's just great. I hate being sober, to be honest.'

Sian almost chokes with laughter.

'You're so funny. Look, anything you want – you just call me. I want you to feel at home here in our lovely country.'

'Oooo,' I say, seizing the moment. 'One thing I'd really like would be if you could re-employ Jamie at the club. I met him yesterday and he seems such a nice guy. I know he's worried about where he's going to work. I'd love it if you could keep him on.'

Sian looks quite taken aback. 'Well, he just helped out from time to time when we needed a driver but in the end we had to let him go,' she says.

'Oh, that's a shame. Can't you offer him more work?'

'No, Tracie, I'm sorry. There are reasons why the club can't employ him.'

'Is this about money?' I say.

'Absolutely,' she says, nodding.

So the club has no money. Shit! I thought it was all looking too good to be true. Poor Deany, he's not going to be given the budget to buy any good players. He'll be heartbroken. He's been picking out players he wants since he got the job – a bit like me when the catalogue from Cricket comes through. I think, Oooh, I'd love those patent-leather slingbacks from Dolce & Gabbana, and he thinks, Oooh, I'd love that big, powerful striker from the Ivory Coast. Probably not much difference in the cost, the way the pricing strategy at Cricket works.

I feel as if we were lied to about these money problems. How can there be money problems? I'm a Wag, for heaven's sake. I don't do money problems; I do reckless spending and hedonistic nights out. We were told this was a rich club in a posh area, hoping to make it big time. We were told that money wasn't an issue, that they wanted success and would pay for it.

'Please don't say anything to anyone. Not at the moment, anyway,' says Sian, coyly.

'No,' I say. 'I won't say anything, but I have to say that I feel totally conned.'

'Yes,' she says, nodding. 'We all were.'

How awful. Sian's the chairman's wife and she didn't know about the financial problems either. Her words have got me desperately worried about our future here. I'll have to see whether there's any way I can make some money while I'm out here. I certainly can't cut back. I don't do cheap.

'Hey, come and see this, doll,' shouts Dean, breaking our moment of female solidarity and beckoning me to follow him into the bowels of the club. 'Look,' he says proudly, sweeping his skinny arms before him and indicating the most magnificent spa ever.

'Bloody hell, is this for the players?' I ask.

'Yes,' says Dean, hugging me tightly. 'Isn't this great, doll? I'm working in a brand, spanking new club with loads of money and loads of potential.'

'That's right,' says Chuck, wandering over to join us with a smile on his face. 'Always remember – we're selling the sizzle, not the sausage.'

Tuesday 27 May
10 a.m. New car just arrived.

OK. How do I put this? It's huge!!! I mean, not huge compared to the other cars on the road over here, but a damn sight wider than anything I've driven before. The advantage, of course, is that the width of the seats makes my thighs look much thinner. The only disadvantage is that I don't think I'm going to be able to drive it without crashing. A minor disadvantage really, considering the thigh benefit.

I really wanted a pink Cadillac (of course!) and it had to be manual because I get really confused by the pedal shortage in the automatic ones, but we couldn't find one in the right shade. As far as I'm concerned, cars should be bubblegum pink, not sugary pink, so I said I'd go for the Cadillac wedding car which looked a lovely shade in the picture, but now it's here it's kind of, well, it's way bigger than I was expecting.

It's also all set up wrongly. I'm sitting here and there's no steering wheel in front of me. Next to me, on the passenger side, there's a steering wheel. Now, you tell me how this works. Do passengers have to drive over here? And what if you're a passenger because you can't drive? Do you then have to sit in the driving seat?

'Well, hello there,' says a familiar voice, making me jump and clatter my acrylic nails against the dash board. I look up into big brown eyes staring from beneath small, lightly tinted sunglasses, then glance down at big brown thighs beneath small, tight shorts. Ding-dong!

'Jamie!' I manage to say, delighted by the arrival of my knight in shining leisure wear. 'Have you spoken to Victoria this morning?'

'Er . . . no,' he says. 'I don't necessarily call her every day.'

If I had her number I'd *always* be on the phone to her. She'd have to take out a restraining order to stop me calling and texting a hundred times a day.

'What are you doing here, just sitting in the car?' he asks.

'I can't work it out,' I confess. 'They've gone and sold me one that's all back to front.'

Jamie doesn't stop jogging for so much as a second as he pulls his earplugs out and switches off his iPod. The sun is glaring through the window and I'm having to move my head up and down as I explain the situation with the car, keeping in time with his bouncing frame.

'Say it again, little British lady.'

'This car is broken. Look!'

'No,' he replies, smiling at me. 'It's American. We drive on the other side of the road here, remember.'

He pushes his sunglasses up onto the top of his head and smiles. His eyes sparkle and dance as he looks at me. He has no wrinkles. No sign of age. His skin remains taut and his brow as smooth as a Chloe handbag.

'Oh,' I say. 'Well, how do I drive it? I can't reach that side.'

He's just smiling at me, so I smile back, and I can feel myself going bright red beneath my tangerine skin. I must look like a blood orange.

'You need to move over,' he says, and as I slide across the long pink leather seat that runs the width of the car he jumps into my vacated place and looks straight into my eyes.

'Have you ever been a cheerleader?' he asks.

'No,' I squeal. Then I think, Is that a compliment? I mean, cheerleaders are pretty, young and heavily made up. Then I think, Gosh, is that the greatest compliment a man can pay a woman in LA? Are we talking here about the nicest thing anyone ever said to me? I can feel myself going scarlet, both from the heat of this gorgeous morning in sunny LA, and from sheer embarrassment at having a terrifyingly fit and attractive man telling me that I should be a cheerleader. It's like Simon all over again – only he used to tell me that I'm clever and bright and funny. It's so much nicer to be told you look like a cheerleader.

'Why are you all dressed up like that?' he asks, taking in my simple daywear. (I've gone for head-to-toe Burberry. I'm channelling Daniella Westbrook because I figure when a look's as fabulous as hers is it bears repeating.)

I haven't answered his question because I can't. I'm so hot, flustered and excited that the roof of my mouth and my tongue are stuck together. I reach into my bag for a bottle of vodka and take a large slug of it.

'Don't make me guess,' he says playfully. 'Surely you're not going to a party at this hour in the morning? I know you're a bit of a party girl.'

I hear myself giggle stupidly. It's a side of myself I've

not met before. When did I turn into a girl who giggles at men?

'I'm not going to a party,' I laugh. 'I'm going shopping.'

'Shopping?' he says wisely. 'Spending all your millions, eh?'

I giggle stupidly again, then kind of grimace at myself because I don't know where the giggles are coming from.

'Would you like me to accompany you? You know – show you around.'

Shit. I feel a wave of panic rise inside me. The fact is that I take shopping very seriously, and don't know whether I want the distraction of Mr Suntanned Legs when I'm doing something vital like trying on shoes.

'It was just an idea. If you'd rather go on your own, that's fine. I just thought you might fancy company. It's up to you. I won't be in the least offended if you'd prefer to go alone.'

'No, I'd like that,' I say, because he's friends with the Beckhams, and I can easily shop another time if I don't get it all done.

'I have to shower first. Why don't I meet you at a restaurant called Koi a bit later? Around 12?'

'OK,' I say.

'It should be marked on your little LA map, but call me if you get lost. Do you still have my number?'

I've learnt it off by heart and written it down in three places. It's logged into my home phone and it's stored in my mobile. 'Yep, I think I've got it here somewhere,' I say.

'See you later then,' and off he goes, jogging down the street – his buttock cheeks moving behind him like two large grapefruits in the back of his Lycra shorts.

So, was that a wise thing to do? Arrange to have lunch

with a strange and terrifyingly attractive man? I guess it was. I'm sure it's fine because I'm happily married, no harm can come. Really . . . just fine . . . and even though I feel myself lean over and sniff the seat he's just been sitting on without realizing quite what I'm doing, there's no problem. Any minute now I'll be able to get a grip on the dizzy feeling in my tummy, and drive this damn car.

12.29 p.m.

I'm a teensy bit late for meeting Jamie but, truly, it doesn't matter because today is the greatest day of my life *ever*. This is better than my wedding day and more thrilling than the day I gave birth to Pask (I knew she was coming out eventually – but I never dreamt that this might happen). The feeling I have running through me is like liquid gold. 'Yeeeeessssss!!!' I squeal. I can't help myself. 'Yes, yes and yes again,' almost crying with joy and relief; like the fans at Luton Town used to do whenever Dean was subbed off.

I'm in remarkably good cheer for a woman who is standing half naked in a ladies clothes shop on Rodeo Drive. And shall I tell you why I am in such good cheer? Shall I? OK – I have dropped two whole dress sizes. I was a size 6 in Luton sizing, and here, I'm size 2!!! Whooah!

'I want to take everything in the shop,' I squeal, thinking of my dressing area packed with clothes in a size 2. Imagine what Mum would say? Despite everything that's happened between my mum and me in the past year I still feel a need to impress her – to show that I'm OK, and worthy, and that she might, yet, think about loving me.

I slip into a lovely gold dress. It's skin-tight, and my

heavily spray-tanned breasts are bursting out of the top of it. It looks as if I've shaved and boot-polished two large coconuts and shoved them down the front. In other words, it's perfect. Outside, I can hear the assistants running around to help customers. I wish one of them would come and help me. I have tons of clothes that I want to buy. I remove the dress, slip back into the salmon pink Juicy playsuit and white ankle boots, the first thing I tried on in the shop, and wander back out.

'I'll take all the items in there, and I'll wear this,' I say, indicating my luxurious outfit.

They don't even look up.

'Excuse me,' I try. 'I want buy all those clothes in there.'

Still nothing. I feel like Julia Roberts in that film. She was Pretty Woman; right now I feel like Shitty Woman.

Eventually a woman dressed in subtle shades of cream and beige comes over to me and looks me up and down. 'Are you sure you wouldn't prefer to shop somewhere else . . . somewhere less classy,' she says. 'I mean, this shop may not be right for you. That playsuit's meant for a child, and I certainly wouldn't wear it with those boots. It's very tight, very short and very pink.'

'But I like very tight, very short and very pink things. I'm a Wag!' I declare. My voice comes out like a little girl's and tears sting the backs of my eyes. Why do they have to be so nasty? It doesn't make me a bad person that I want to look like Jordan's little sister, not Hillary Clinton's elder sister.

Two other members of staff have come over to join the soldier-like creature before me. They stand there in a line, like a mini Nazi regiment – all looking me up and down and smirking to themselves.

'We have standards,' says a woman who is so thin that

she really looks as if she might crack. I think she's thinner than Sian. Perhaps I'm too fat here? My heart almost stops. Is that why they don't like me? I love thin, but I genuinely fear for these women. This shop assistant has such a big head for her body, I'm surprised her scrawny neck doesn't snap under the weight. Her face is so heavily plumped out that it reminds me of a satellite dish. Her eyes don't seem quite symmetrical, and I find it very hard not to stare at her.

'Did you hear me?' she asks, eventually, as I struggle to work out why it is that her lips look as if they have a life of their own. They move and shake on the front of her face as if they're not quite connected and might slide and wriggle off at any time. Surely that's not lip pumping? Mine are pumped out about as far as a UK surgeon will allow, but these are jelly-filled to an extraordinary new level. I'm slightly appalled, slightly impressed and ever so slightly jealous, all at the same time. I've never been out-Waged before, but these LA ladies are right up there. Except when it comes to clothes. In the wardrobe department they lag a long way behind.

A woman with her blonde hair tied at the nape of her neck, wearing simple black trousers and a black sleeveless top, steps forward.

'Do you understand English?' she asks me. 'English?'

'Yes,' I say. They know very well that I'm English. Behind her I hear the door open and I hope that all three will rush off and attend to the next customer and stop being so horrible. Sadly, the only person to move is the 'Do you understand English?' lady.

In front of me the two remaining women have their hands on the parts of their body where most people have hips.

'You need to change out of those clothes,' says the first lady – she's wearing a cream shirt and beige trousers with sunglasses and large earrings. I think her earrings may be wider than her torso, which makes me strangely predisposed to like her, but her manner nips any such feelings in the bud. 'Now,' she howls in a voice heavy with nastiness.

'Is there a problem?' a familiar male voice asks, and the two women spin round to see my extraordinarily handsome new friend in the doorway. He's wearing a white shirt and his dark hair is glistening beautifully in the midday sun. It looks as if it's still wet, and the very thought of Jamie in the shower makes me feel quite dizzy. As he walks in he removes his sunglasses and holds them while he stands there, glowering in front of us. I feel embarrassed that he's seeing me being treated so badly. I hope he doesn't think I've done anything to annoy them.

'No problem at all,' says huge earrings lady. 'How can we help you?'

'You could help me by treating this lady with a bit of respect.'

I feel my heart leap up so hard that it almost knocks itself out on my throat.

'Of course!' she cries innocently, looking at me. 'I'm doing all I can.'

Jamie walks over and stands right next to me, draping his arm across my shoulders.

'This is Victoria Beckham's sister,' he says. 'Be very, very nice to her.'

Oh. My. God. I am no longer Shitty Woman.

The shop assistant's face registers all the amazement it can, given the buckets of Botox that have been injected into it.

'I'll go and get all your things from in the changing room, shall I, Madam?' says hair at the nape of the neck woman.

'Yes please. Thank you very much.'

'You look adorable, by the way,' she says, as she scuttles past me. I look at Jamie and he winks. I'll never forget this moment, and how special he's making me feel. I knew my life would change completely if I lost two dress sizes.

'Thank you so much,' I say, as we walk up the road together, Jamie carrying my bags and me recalling the terrified looks on their faces when they thought I might be Victoria Beckham's sister.

'Imagine if I were,' I say. 'Imagine that! I used to fantasize, when I was younger, that I was part of a nice, normal family – you know, with a mum and dad who loved me and maybe a brother or sister. I used to go to bed and dream that there'd be a knock on the door and someone would say, "I'm sorry, there's been a terrible mistake. Tracie Martin, you shouldn't be with your mad mother who leaves you on your own all the time and really hates you, you should be with this kind and loving family where there's a mum and a dad and they both like you." Well, imagine if that family was Victoria's? Imagine!'

Jamie's looking at me, his head tilted sideways. 'So – bad childhood, hey?'

'Not great,' I confess.

'I'm a good listener,' he says.

'Thanks. I'm OK, though. I keep going. This trip to LA is a fresh start for us all. Things are going to be good from now on, I can just feel it.'

'I hope so,' says Jamie. 'LA's a fun place. I'm sure you'll

love it when you get to know it. Now, would you like to shop?'

'Like to shop? Me? Jamie, you have no idea. I live to shop.'

We wander in and out of shops all morning – me spending, Jamie carrying.

Versace is my favourite visit of the day. It's bustling with the most fabulous dresses, including one made entirely from lime green goose feathers, with large ostrich feathers trailing down the back.

'Look!' I cry. 'Isn't it adorable?'

'It's different,' says Jamie. 'Where on earth would you wear something like that?'

'Everywhere!' I say as I spin and twirl in the mirror. It's the most beautiful dress I've ever seen. I *have* to have it.

We bundle out of the shop with my flamboyant purchase carefully wrapped in tissue paper and nestling in the bottom of a shiny new black carrier bag. I swing the bag by my side, just like the girls in *Sex and the City* do whenever they've bought anything. I'm excited and delighted and . . . oh, shit. 'Sorry.'

I've whacked some poor guy and sent the stash of leaflets in his hand flying into the air. Jamie drops down to pick them up while the man stares at me.

'Wow!' he says. 'You'd be perfect. We're looking for people for a film being shot by Sunset-Naidoo Pictures. Have you ever done any acting?'

All my life, I think. 'No,' I say. 'I'd like to, though.'

'Well, we'd have to give you a screen test, but if you could come along on Wednesday – say 1.30 – we could do it then. How does that sound? Do you wanna be in a film? You could make a bit of money if things go well.'

'Yeah!' I say, looking over at Jamie, who's nodding his encouragement. The idea of making money is appealing, given that Raiders are practically bankrupt and could stop paying my husband at any time, and I've just spent more on clothes than most people earn in a year.

They take my details and the guy hands me a card. 'See you Wednesday,' he says. 'Come to the main reception desk at 1224 Sunset Boulevard. The details are all on the card.'

'Wow. Thanks!' I say, and inside I'm thinking . . . if only Mum could see me now.

3 p.m., Koi

My 550 bags of shopping are safely stored away in a cloakroom, taken away by a meaty bouncer with the unusual distinction of having a small bolt of lightning tattooed on his knuckles, I have a glass of champagne in my hand; and if it weren't for the scary wooden carvings of snakes all over the walls I'd be feeling quite relaxed about everything.

'I'm going to be in a film!' I blurt out. 'Imagine having a screen test! Dean will piss himself.'

'You'd make a great film star. I bet you get spotted and become the next Catherine Zeta-Jones,' says Jamie.

'Oooh, imagine that!' I say. Though I'd rather be Marilyn Monroe. She was the very first Wag ever and my ultimate icon. Apart from Victoria and Jordan who are better role models because they are thinner, have longer hair, breast implants and children with daft names – all the attributes one looks for in an icon.

'Cheers,' says Jamie, raising his glass of freshly squeezed orange juice.

'Cheers!' I raise my champagne flute and we clink them together. He catches my eye, and I swear a huge electric shock just ran through me.

'You know what you should do? If you're going to be an international superstar actress you should log your credit card details here, then you'll be given a password and you can phone up any time you want and get priority booking.'

It's a great idea, but I'm not sure.

'Dean doesn't like me doing things like that,' I say, flinching as I catch sight of the snakes. Are they really necessary?

Jamie clicks his fingers to call the waiter. 'I know that a lot of journalists do it, then whenever someone famous comes in, they get a call from the doorman. All part of the LA service. Victoria comes here, you know.'

'Really?' Maybe that's something I should consider. Would they really call me and tell me?

The waiter hasn't responded to Jamie's clicking fingers, so he claps loudly and, if I'm honest, quite embarrassingly. A waiter scurries across and my credit card's handed over in the blink of an eye. They log the details and ask me for a password to quote when I call.

'Paskia-Rose,' I say. That's a password I'll never forget.

'Certainly,' says the waiter.

'I'll order for both of us,' Jamie declares, pointing out various items on the menu. The waiter smiles and bows away from us. He returns minutes later with a collection of candles for the middle of the table. Jamie's face is immediately lit up so he looks like a model from one of the billboards liberally dotted down Rodeo Drive.

'Sushi,' he says, when the food arrives. 'Go on. Try it.'

He gives me these little sticks to eat with. You know the

ones. Dean always sends them straight back, saying, 'We're in England, love. Give us a couple of knives and forks.'

As I try to pick up the rice with the sticks I realize why Dean's never taken to them. It's virtually impossible. If I don't push hard enough the rice doesn't lift off the plate at all, and if I push too hard the small bundle breaks and the rice falls away, leaving me gripping with all my might onto one lonely little grain.

Meanwhile Jamie, next to me, is having no problems at all. 'Try the fish,' he suggests, indicating the pink-coloured jellyfish thing in the centre of the rice bundle.

'Good idea,' I say, stabbing at the fish in an effort to spear it into my mouth. Yeeesss . . . finally I catch it and begin to chew. And chew. And chew. I try to eat it, I really do, but it's like rubber.

'Nice?' asks Jamie, and I just smile back at him. 'Is this your first time with sushi?'

'Yes,' I say, thinking – and the bloody last time. Eventually I have to take it out of my mouth. 'I could do with it being cooked properly,' I explain, and Jamie roars with laughter.

'Very funny,' he says. 'Very, very funny. I'll tell the waiter, shall I? "Make sure you cook your sushi properly for my friend in future." Ha! Very good.'

I take a large gulp of champagne, then a larger one, and laugh back as if I know what the hell I've just said to cause such merriment.

'Right, tell me something about you that I don't know,' he says.

Silence. Well, what am I supposed to tell him?

'OK,' he says, when the silence becomes unbearable. 'You're obviously not used to talking about yourself.

People in LA tend to open up all the time because they've had so much therapy. Tell me a little bit about your dad. You mentioned your horrible mother, but you've not said anything about your dad.'

'Well, I've never met my dad,' I say. 'Mum told me that he really hated me, then I discovered that Mum hadn't passed on any of his letters or presents or anything over the years, and that he did like me after all, and was very keen to meet me. He'd sent loads of money for me that Mum kept for herself.'

There's a silence as I tail off and just stare into the bottom of my empty glass.

'That's awful,' says Jamie. 'I am sorry, Tracie. Terrible.'

'It's not so bad,' I say. 'They'll fill it up soon.'

'No, not the empty glass, the thing with your mum and dad.'

'Yes,' I say, lifting my glass to my mouth and tapping the bottom to make sure I'm getting every last drop.

'I don't think they're used to speed drinkers in here,' says Jamie, seeing my plight. 'I think perhaps LA women and Luton women have a different attitude to alcohol.'

'I think they do,' I reply, looking around for the waiter. He comes running over.

'Why don't you just leave the bottle where I can reach it?' I suggest.

'Would you like to meet your dad one day?'

This is a difficult question to answer. There's no question that I do want to meet him, but I'm absolutely terrified that he won't like me. That's why I never made any effort to contact him while I was in England. I'm scared that he'll take one look at me and run away, or that Mum was right all along. I try to tell Jamie this, but I don't expect him to understand. How could he?

'There's no way he's going to hate you,' says Jamie. 'No way on earth. If you can face it, go and visit him. It could change your whole outlook on life if you meet him and the two of you get on.'

'Yes, you're right,' I say, and we sink into a companionable silence.

'This is nice,' says Jamie, leaning across and holding my hand. He's right. It is nice.

9 p.m.

I can't believe how late it is when Dean finally gets home.

'You're a football coach,' I say when he comes through the door clutching piles of notes and folders. 'Stop making like you've got a proper job.'

'I can turn this team round, you know,' he says, placing the notes down carefully and leaning casually against one of the furiously expensive leopardskin-covered bar stools in the kitchen. 'You know Chuck made an interesting point. He was saying today that there's no "I" in team.'

'No, but there is in "Piss off!",' I say under my breath. Please God don't let him start talking like Cheesy Chuck.

'I can make them good,' Dean is saying. 'If they pull their fingers out they can get through to the play-offs, and then who knows what could happen.'

'Drink?' I say, in the absence of anything more helpful to contribute on the subject of skill improvement in American soccer.

'Actually I won't, love, thanks,' he says. 'I've got a few

DVDs to watch and some player analyses to run through. I'll be in my office if you need me.'

'Dean, are you OK? Why don't you want a drink? Is it something I said?'

'No, love, I've just got quite a lot of work to do, and I've been thinking that I probably drink too much. You know, we should both cut back a bit. People out here don't drink.'

'People out here are *mad*!' I exclaim. 'Dean, don't go all LA on me, will you?'

'Of course not, babes. Look, give me a couple of hours to finish this work and give myself a bit of a stretch out, and I'll be right with you.'

Stretch out? Stretch out? Oh God, Dean's been infected by these people. It's horrible.

'You watch yourself,' I say. 'They'll have you doing yoga positions if you're not careful.'

Dean walks away to his office, with me shouting after him.'Lycra . . . they'll have you in Lycra, doing dog to the moon and ankles in your ears and all that. You watch it, Deany . . .'

Email to: Michaela & Suzzi

From: Tracie

Hi girlies, how are you? It's me – Tracie – speaking to you all the way from Los Angeles. Thanks so much for your email, Mich. It was so nice to hear from someone nice and normal after these mad, healthy and fit loonies over here, for ever worrying about what they put in their bodies and whether they've done their state minimum of 25 yoga classes every day. Hope you're feeling better after the stomach pump. Great that it was the same doctor as last time. Perhaps they'll give you one of those cards, like they hand out in coffee shops, and after your sixth pump you get one free!

Suz, thanks for your email too. I don't think your tongue's supposed to grow to twice its natural size when you have your lips plumped – mine never has. Perhaps they accidentally injected some of the plumper into your tongue? I can't see how else it would happen. If I were you I'd get a truck load more filler chucked into your lips to compensate, then hopefully no one will notice that you're tongue's turned into a swollen nasty lump of gristle? Just a thought!

Life here is really peculiar because hardly anyone drinks. They're just not interested in locking themselves away in dimly lit bars and getting off their faces. They want to run in the sunlight (is that even good for you?) and be all energetic all the time.

When I first got here and people talked about not drinking, I just pissed myself, obviously thinking they were joking, but I swear to God they just don't get off their tits. They always wake up in the morning on first-name terms with the guy lying next to them (Mich . . . imagine that! Have you ever known the name of the guy whose bed you wake up in?) and they stretch and do pilates and all that crap. I've not seen a kebab shop since I've been here, they prefer raw food restaurants. (I know what you're thinking Suz . . . that kebab shop on Luton High Street serves half-raw food anyway!)

All in all, it's taking a bit of getting used to. The very worst part of it is that bloody Dean seems to be getting the bug! He was mumbling on about cutting back on alcohol. Can you believe it? My Deany. For the first five years of our marriage I hadn't seen him sober. Now he's saying we drink too much, and crap like 'I'm going for a stretch.' What's that all about?

Anyway, the really good news is that I'm all set to become an international film star of staggeringly large proportions (not that my physical proportions will be staggeringly large – it's the international star bit that will be staggeringly large proportion-wise. My proportions are smaller if anything because I've gone down two dress sizes!!!). Will write soon, Trace xx

Wednesday 28 May
8 a.m.

Neither Dean nor Paskia-Rose believes me.

'Why would I make something like that up?' I say.

'It's not that we think you're making it up,' says Dean.
'It just seems so unlikely.'

'Thanks. You think it's unlikely that anyone would
consider me for their film, do you?'

'No, love. All I mean is that you've just arrived, it's
your first time on Rodeo Drive and you get asked to be
in a movie. Come on, that only happens in films.'

'Well, it happened to me.'

I show Dean the card the guy in the street gave me,
with the time of my screen test on the back.

'I'm coming with you,' he says. 'It sounds dodgy. We'll
go when we get back from St Benedict's.'

'Fine.'

9 a.m.

The driveway to Paskia-Rose's new school is long and
winding; it takes us past playing fields, a small lake and
smartly dressed young ladies enjoying a morning stroll.

'Fuck me, it's like Eton,' I say.

67

'Please don't talk like that when we're in the school, Mum,' says Pask, rubbing her little button nose with the back of her hand. She's got a pretty nose – it's a pity it's covered in loads of freckles. It's a pity, too, that she's got such piggy eyes. I've frequently offered her the use of a pair of false eyelashes, or even just mascara, but she won't have any of it.

Despite my real fears about Paskia-Rose's dowdy and unbecoming appearance, I do love her enormously, and I feel rocked to the core by the thought of her starting a strange new school. It's nice having her around the place. I've even got used to waking up in the morning to the incessant thump of a football against the wall.

'There,' she screeches all of a sudden, pointing madly to the far side of the imposing building ahead of us.

'What is it?' I ask, veering slightly off the driveway onto the grass and nearly taking out a group of four girls sitting on a rug, reading Shakespeare.

'Muuum . . . you just concentrate on driving. Dad, have you seen what's over there?'

'Yeeeeeaaahhhhh!!!!' says Dean. 'Goal posts.'

Is that what all the fuss is about? The two of them have seen some goal posts . . . big wow! It's not that I really object to her love of football, it's more that I hate the fact that it's a difference between us. I hate the fact that she has a passion that I can't share and craves a world that I can't inhabit. She wants to be a successful footballer and I'd love her to marry a rich and successful footballer. I'd like her to enjoy a wonderful, happy marriage like mine, and be able to enjoy her life knowing that she has someone special who loves her.

I want her to be happy, but because happiness for me

is dressing up, piling on the makeup and funnelling champagne down my throat I guess that's what I want for her, too. I want us to love the same things, and go clothes shopping together, gossiping over the latest copy of *Heat*. I want her to rush in and squeal with excitement at a boy she's met or a sparkly blue eye shadow she's discovered. I want us to dress the same way and act the same way. I thought we'd be like sisters and have pamper parties and snuggly girls' nights in.

I wanted to be as similar to her as my mum was different to me. I want her to know how much I love her. It's hard to show her that when she's more interested in Steven Gerrard's foot work than Alex Curran's footwear.

'Who are we seeing today?' I ask.

'Muuuummmm, *you're* not seeing anyone,' she says. 'You're just dropping me off and collecting me later. I'm spending the day here.'

'Can't I spend the day here too?' I ask.

'I'd rather die,' says Pask.

'Just speak your mind, love. Don't sit on the fence,' I mutter, peculiarly hurt. I'd love to think she wanted me to be here.

We walk up the steps towards the school's reception area, Dean and Pask jogging up two at a time in their matching LA City Raiders shirts, me going one at a time and sideways because my skirt's too tight to negotiate them in any other way.

'You could wait in the car,' says Pask as I'm hitching up the tight plastic pink skirt in order to try and catch up with them.

'Don't worry. I'll be fine.'

Finally I'm at the top, and Pask points at my thighs.

'Do you want to pull the skirt down a bit before we go in?'

'Sure,' I say. She's a funny one, is Pask. She says she has no interest in clothes, but seems always to notice what mine are doing. I inch the skirt down so it covers my knickers. 'Happy now?'

'Happier,' she says.

We walk into the intimidating school with its dark oak walls and that faint smell of cabbage that curses every large building. It's very English-looking inside, designed to appeal to those Americans who still believe that to be truly sophisticated you have to have had a British education. A smartly dressed girl approaches with a wide, welcoming grin.

'Pleasure to receive you here at St Benedict's English School for Girls. How may I help?' she says.

'This is Paskia-Rose Martin,' I say, as if Pask's about two years old and unable to speak for herself. 'We'd like to see the school principal.'

The girl shuffles off in her silly grey pleated skirt and long grey socks. I look over at Pask and shake my head miserably. It's not exactly what I had in mind when I was thinking about LA schools. I thought they were all full of cool kids in funky clothes getting off with each other and getting shit-faced.

'Welcome, welcome,' says a man in his forties, wearing a crumpled beige linen suit. 'I'm Mr Barkett. Principal Cooper's just tied up at the minute, but she'll join us for coffee later. Would you like to follow me?'

He leads us through the school, pointing out the various rooms and corridors along the way.

'This is the science block,' he says, and I howl with laughter. 'Everything OK?'

70

'Yes, sorry, I'm just remembering something that happened to me in the science block once,' I say, and there's a pause while everyone waits for me to tell them. 'His name was John Harrison and he used to keep porno magazines in his desk. One day, when the teacher was out of the room, all the girls took their bras off and —'

'What sciences do the girls do?' asks Dean through gritted teeth, glaring at me with eyes that scream 'Shut up, Tracie.'

'Obviously we do computer science and earth and natural sciences, but we make a point of focusing on integrated curriculum teaching and not on individual subject areas. We explore areas like interdisciplinary teaching, thematic teaching and synergistic teaching. Are you with me?'

'Tracie,' says Dean. 'Tell us what happened when you all took your bras off.'

Principal Cooper comes to join us for coffee. She's a bloody fearsome-looking woman. Reminds me of Margaret Thatcher, but without any of the former Prime Minister's softer, more sensitive and humane characteristics. She's English and she insists that this school produces ladies in the very British understanding of the word.

'The girls here will behave properly, and dress properly,' she insists, with a passing, and rather obvious, glance at my attire. 'This is a school that excels in all areas and is peerless in sport. We do all the classic school sports for girls as well as soccer.'

'Excellent,' says Paskia-Rose.

'Talk in sentences, dear,' says the Principal.

'Sure,' says Paskia.

'Sentences,' bellows the Principal, and I have to bite my tongue not to point out that the terrifying Mrs Cooper isn't talking in sentences.

'This is a deeply religious school and we operate by a strict moral code,' she continues, and Dean and I just nod. 'We believe that God was sacrificed for man and that each man should be willing to sacrifice himself for his brothers. We won't tolerate selfish behaviour or bad community spirit.'

'That's right,' says Dean. 'Like in football – if a player keeps the ball too long, and doesn't pass it, he's not gonna score too often.'

'Quite,' says the Principal. 'Now, do you have any questions?'

We don't. Well, we do. I have tons of questions, but I'm too scared to ask them. Instead we're offered the chance to take a walk around the grounds on our own.

'If you can get back here by 11 a.m., that will assist us greatly,' says Principal Cooper in a voice which indicates strongly that failure to arrive back by the allotted time will be punishable by death.

'What do you think?' I ask Pask when we get outside.

''s OK,' she says, and I can't resist it.

'Sentences, Paskia-Rose, sentences,' I say.

She gives me a half-smile and Dean gives her a hug.

'Bit of a monster,' says Dean.

'Yes,' we all agree.

The grass outside is now littered with girls playing, reading and talking intelligently to one another. Everyone looks rich and sophisticated but desperately dull. On Paskia's instruction we walk towards the football pitches so she can have a look. We take the route round the side of the school where there's a pavement and thus I won't sink into the grass in my high heels. When the path runs out at the back of the school Pask and Dean head off to the pitch while I wait on solid ground.

That's when I see them, like a dream – the school's bad girls. There are three of them standing round the side of the building using a mobile phone (banned), wearing makeup (banned), with their skirts shortened (banned) and wearing high-heeled shoes (banned). They look amazing. I find myself transported back in time to my own schooldays when I was desperate to be friends with girls like these.

'Here,' I say, handing them a bottle from my bag. 'It's champagne. Enjoy it.'

'Wow, thanks,' they say. 'That's awesome.'

I hear the cork pop and I rush off, desperate to reach Dean and Pask despite the heel/mud situation. I need to tell Pask about the great girls I've just seen. 'Sweetheart, I've found some lovely friends for you. They're great. You'll love them. Come and see,' I shriek.

If I can get Paskia in with these girls, she'll be sorted. Gosh how I longed to be one of the tough girls when I was at school. 'You're too soppy,' they always told me. 'Look at you, with your silly pink, frilly clothes and your mad mother.'

I tried so hard to be accepted into that group, but never was. Now Paskia has a real chance to live the dream. She's not soppy – she's tough and talented and lovely. She has to meet them.

I shout over again, but Pask and Dean don't hear me at all – they remain where they are, locked away from the world as they talk about Arsenal's performance last season and whether Cristiano Ronaldo is better than George Best, or some such nonsense.

'Come on,' I shout over, wishing that, just once, I could impress my daughter as much as Dean does.

The two of them begin walking. 'Quickly,' I cry. 'I've found some lovely friends for you. Look!'

The three girls are slouching against the wall, necking the champagne. One of them is even running her heavily glossed lips up and down the neck of the bottle in a gesture which has the two other girls choking with laughter.

I march Paskia over to them in a whirl of excitement. Imagine if Pask could get herself in with the cool girls? She'd start accessorizing properly and having fun. I just want to see her happy, dressed up and made up like a prom queen. Maybe one day she too will perform fellatio on a champagne bottle, but let's not run before we can walk. Such a hope remains a dim and distant wish.

'This is my daughter, Paskia-Rose,' I say, pushing Pask towards the girls entirely against her will, but knowing it's in her best interests.

'I'm Cecily-Sue,' says the dark-haired girl. 'Call me Cecil.'

'Natasha-May,' says the least groomed of the girls. She has long auburn hair that would benefit from a little glitter and a lot of bleach.

'I'm Carrie-Ann,' says the third girl, who's perfect. She stands, menacingly, with her short skirt and her long legs. She's tanned and has lovely blonde hair that hangs like a thick curtain across her face. She makes no eye contact, chews gum and drinks champagne at the same time. She's got 'troublemaker' written all over her. I want to adopt her.

'Come on,' says Dean. 'Let's carry on having a look round.'

'OK, but Pask, why don't you stay here with the nice girls, and we'll come back and get you later?'

The girls stand there, scowling and exuding menace through every pore. How I wish I were a teenager again. What fun they're having!

'I'll come with you and Dad,' says Pask, moving off towards the other side of Dean.

I say my goodbyes and tell the girls they're all beautiful, and we walk off round the back of the school where there are tennis courts dotted around a huge athletics track. Across the courts, all dressed in white and bashing a little ball backwards and forwards to each other, are girls of all shapes and sizes. Why would they do that?

'I can't wait to start,' Pask is saying as she takes in all the sports facilities. 'This school is awesome.'

'And you've already made some nice friends,' I say. 'Those girls seemed lovely.'

'I think they were troublemakers,' insists Pask. 'You know – the way they were hanging around the back, wearing makeup and stuff. And drinking! Did you see that? I can't believe they sneaked alcohol into school.'

'They're just having fun,' I say, but my lovely, perfect, sports-mad daughter's having none of it. She shakes her head and we wander off towards the pool block where she gets more excited than is appropriate at the thought of making it onto the swim team.

'I think my times will be good enough,' she says with

glee as she studies the noticeboard. 'I'm definitely going to the trials.'

We hurry back to the Principal's office, Paskia and Dean delighted with the sports facilities and me feeling more hope than I've felt in a long time that my beautiful child may grow into the sort of teenager I can be proud of.

'Principal Cooper please,' we ask of the smartly dressed girl in reception, but it's Mr Barkett who comes out to see us.

'Sorry, Principal's tied up at the moment. There's been some very uncustomary and deeply regrettable behaviour that she needs to deal with immediately.'

'Oh,' we chorus because it doesn't seem like the sort of school where deeply regrettable behaviour takes place. I'm tempted to ask what sort of behaviour we're talking about here, when he volunteers the information.

'Three girls. Caught drinking,' he mouths. 'Terrible. We've called their mothers to the school. Dreadful business.'

1.30 p.m.

'The rain in Spain falls mainly in the plain,' I say, pronouncing each word as clearly as my Luton-laced accent will allow. We're on Sunset Boulevard and all that stands between me and a stunning career as a glittering leading actress is Gareth managing to find the right building and me passing a simple audition. As far as I can see, the Oscar's practically mine.

'That's it,' I say, just as Gareth's beginning to lose the will to live. The non-sequential numbering coupled with the fact that it's the longest road in the world and I didn't know which part of it we had to go to was making him very irate. His green eyes were blazing and, frankly, I feared for the life of the cab driver who cut him up.

Gareth pulls over, almost taking out a cyclist in the process, and I gather my things together. 'Do you think I should portray myself as the new Marilyn?' I ask. I suddenly feel nervous. I don't know how to act.

'What do you think, Dean? Marilyn?'

'I don't know,' he says. 'I only know about football. You decide.'

'You don't think they'll want me to recite Shakespeare or anything, do you?'

'I wouldn't have thought so, Candyfloss,' he says. 'But you never know with these people. Film people love books and stuff, don't they?'

He's very wise, is Dean. 'Does my makeup look OK?' I ask. I redid it in the loos at Pask's school so that it now stands about three inches off my face. They'll expect me to be camera-ready. I don't want to let myself down.

'Yeah,' says Dean without looking, and we jump out of the car and head to the building. The reception area is painted a bright, glossy orange. Dean says that if I put my head back against it, it looks as if my features are painted onto the wall, so similar is the painted interior's colour to that of my foundation.

'Tracie Martin?' asks a rather scruffy guy with khaki shorts and a baggy grey T-shirt that's seen better days. 'Follow me for the screen test.' He's not what I was expecting at all, but I wave goodbye to Dean and teeter off after the man.

'Through there,' he says dismissively, signalling towards

a large, messy room with four men standing in it, surrounded by technical-looking equipment

'Tracie Martin?' asks one.

'That's me,' I say with confidence, giving them my best smile.

'Great. Glad you could make it. Are you ready to get going?'

'Absolutely,' I say, with a shake of my blonde mane.

The room has rugged wooded floorboards and bits of white masking tape all over the place. It's not very LA at all. More like the sort of place you'd find in Camden High Street than on Sunset Boulevard. There's peeling paint and piles of cables lying all over the floor – knotted and twisted together. I'll need to recall this when people ask me about the audition. I need to remember the moment when my acting career began.

If things take off the way I want them to, I may refer to this moment in my Oscar acceptance speech. I'll thank Dean and Paskia for their support and Victoria for her inspiration. 'And, you know, as I stand before you today, as the most successful and most dearly loved actress in the world, dressed in £100 million worth of diamonds, I should tell you about how it all started – in a messy studio just a few months ago.'

I'll dedicate the Oscar to Dean's late grandmother Nell and I'll make sure I mention every one of my friends. I'll also thank my mum and tell her I forgive her. Forgiveness is important, and I think I could find it in me to be forgiving, especially while covered in Tiffany sparklers.

'Do you want me to say anything?' I ask the guys. They seem to be just standing there, looking down at a pile of equipment.

One guy looks up from where he's fiddling with the camera. 'Wow. Your voice is amazing,' he says. 'You'd never know. I think we'll have to make a feature of that. Can we mike her up, John?'

An amazing voice, eh? That's what being born and bred in Luton does for you.

I stand still while a microphone is attached to the collar of my pale pink jacket.

'OK. First thing I need you to look into the camera and read this. I'll give you a few moments to learn it,' says the cameraman.

I take the piece of paper that he hands me, hoping that I'm going to be playing a beautiful, fragile princess, waiting for her knight in shining armour to return from battle. The men are still looking over at me, so I smile back and think to myself that I'll try and mention as many of them as I can in my Oscar-winning speech – it's only fair.

OK, here we go. What have I got to read out? 'Hi, my name's Tracie Martin, and though I may look like a woman, take a closer look and you'll see I'm a man. Welcome to *Tranny Town* – the new film about Transvestites in the City.'

'Why do you want me to say this?' I ask.

'Screen test,' mutters the guy.

'For a film about transvestites? I'm not a transvestite.'

'Aren't you?'

'No!' I howl. 'Of course not. How could you even think that?'

'Well – the piles of badly applied makeup, the trannie clothes and really skinny legs. Sorry. Simple misunderstanding.'

I tear off the microphone as theatrically as I can, and turn on my heels with a level of drama that these fools can only dream of injecting into their films, then I charge out of the room – away from my dreams of becoming a film star. The Oscar will have to wait. The friendship with Keira and the affair with Brad are on ice for now, I'm off back to Deany.

5 p.m.

Paskia's tucking into a big cheese sandwich when I walk into the kitchen, and almost crash into the door because I'm so busy looking at my reflection in the stainless steel fridge. They do not look like the legs of a man. Why would anyone think I was a transvestite? Is my jaw too square or something?

'How did the screen test go?' asks Pask, and I feel my heart sink. 'Dad says you won't talk about it.'

'There's nothing to talk about,' I say, giving her a little hug. 'I just decided that being an international superstar wasn't all it was cracked up to be. I decided that my main job was being a good mum to you, and a good wife to your dad.'

Paskia looks confused. 'But you are a good mum. I thought you wanted to be a film star, too.'

I'm a good mum.

'I'm not really bothered about a life of fame, wealth, free clothes and global adoration.'

Did she really say I was a good mum?

'So you didn't do the audition?' she asks.

'No. In the end I walked away from it,' I say, but all the time her words are ricocheting round my mind, bubbling up and busting into silky, rainbow-coloured happy thoughts as they glide around my head. I'm a good mum!

'In what ways am I a good mum, Pask?' I ask gently, sitting down next to her and stroking her hair in a way that she clearly finds very irritating.

'I dunno,' she says, between chews. 'I know you love me and care about me.'

'I do, Pask,' I say. 'I really do. I worry that you don't realize how much I care about you.'

'Course I realize,' she says. 'Even when you're being mad I know you mean well. It's like Dad's always saying – you look for the best in people. I've never heard you say a bad word about anyone. You're the nicest person I've ever met. Stuff like that.'

'Pask, that's lovely,' I say, and suddenly it doesn't matter that all the movie-makers in LA think I look like a bloke in a skirt. What do I care about them? Paskia loves me and Dean loves me. Nothing else matters.

'How was school?' I ask her.

'Man, it was unbelievable,' she says, her eyes sparkling as she recalls her day. 'I wish I could start straight away. Do I have to wait until Monday?'

'It's only a few days,' I say. 'I'm sure you can last until then.'

'I guess,' she says. 'I'll practise some maths, and read as much as I can between now and then.'

That's when I have to bite my tongue. Why does she want to go to school? She's twelve! What girl her age wants to practise maths? It's not natural. I worry for her. The girl hasn't had so much as a pregnancy scare. She has no intimate piercings or tattoos, and despite my many searches I've never found any illegal drugs in her room. Now she's desperate to go to school. What horrors have I got lurking round the corner? University? PhDs?

But I don't say a negative word. Not now I know that I am super mum. I smile sweetly and try to interest her in my world.

'Would you like to get your makeup done before the party tonight?' I ask. 'The beauticians are setting things out upstairs.'

'Er . . . like . . . how do I say this? Er . . . no! I don't even want to go to the party. I want to watch TV. There's a match on.'

'You have to come. Oh, Paskia, go on, sweetheart. Mummy would love to get you all dressed up and show you off. Please let me turn you into a little princess.'

'No,' she says definitively.

'Please,' I try. 'It could be fun!'

'No! I'll come, but I'm not dressing up like a fairy. Leave me alone.'

'OK then, love,' I say, 'I'll be upstairs if you need me.' Then I sashay out of the kitchen, glancing once again at my reflection before heading upstairs to where a team of LA's hottest facialists, waxers, hairdressers and nail technicians await.

'What look are you after?' they ask.

'Mainly, I would like not to look like a transvestite,' I say. 'That's my overriding aim.'

'Lady, you look nothing like a transvestite,' says a woman stirring a pot of warm wax and chuckling to herself. 'I don't think I ain't ever met someone who looks less like a transvestite.'

She has no idea how big a tip she just earned herself.

Sian and Chuck's house, 8.30 p.m.

PARTY TIME!!! But we're hovering in the cloakroom.

'Don't bend down, love,' says Dean, again. I know he means well, but – honestly – I can't go through the entire party standing bolt upright.

'You'll have to,' he insists. 'Honestly, love. Every time you bend down to reach for the Bacardi you moon the whole party through the cloakroom door.'

'And?' I say, rather petulantly. 'What's the problem with that?'

Dean shrugs and says nothing's wrong with it, but we don't know these people and they might not want to see a lady's bottom before the watershed. It seems unlikely, but I'm not in the mood for an argument, so I move the Bacardi up so I can reach it without any indecent exposure and promise I won't bend down.

'No, not there,' he says, quickly putting the alcohol back on the floor.

'What are you doing?' I ask.

'No one here drinks,' he says. 'Keep it hidden.'

'Oh God. This is mad,' says Paskia-Rose. 'Can't we just go into the party like normal people? Why do we have to hide away in the cloakroom, drinking alcohol like naughty schoolchildren?'

'Pask's right. Come on, love. Why don't you try and have a night when you don't get drunk? I haven't touched a drop.'

God, he's become dull. What is it with these LA people? It's like there's some sort of bizarre abstinence cult they've all joined. It's no way to live. I grab a large beaker and fill it to the top with Bacardi to keep me going.

'Come on then,' I say. 'Let's go in. After all, they're throwing the party for us.'

Throwing a party for us . . . imagine that! I've been thrown out of parties in the past, and I've thrown up at parties, but never had a party thrown *for* me.

We walk into the main room and, I have to be honest, it's weird. Big time weird. You know how you walk into a party and the first thing you do is look around the room to check what everyone's wearing, and that no one's wearing the same as you?

Ha! Well, no one is! Not by a fucking long, long way, because no one has bothered to dress up for this party at all. I mean – not-at-all! They're in flip-flops, for God's sake. They have great bodies and everything, but their taste in clothes leaves so much to be desired that I can barely speak as I look around the huge open-plan house. There are people everywhere, and as far as the eye can see they have all stopped what they are doing, and they're staring at me. Have they never seen a Bacardi-drinking Wag in a skin-tight gold lamé mini-dress with matching thigh-length gold boots before?

Let me describe what the scene is like. In many ways it's like a Barbie convention – a veritable feast of brown, plastic-looking skin, yellow hair and great big enormous knockers. To that extent they all look like me, and walking into the room is like walking into the hall of mirrors at the funfair, and seeing your image reflected back at you from all sides. Except for the clothes.

And the thing I don't get is, why would you bother starving yourself, eating cotton wool and taking pills to suppress your appetite if you're then going to just stick a T-shirt and flat (I *hate* that word) shoes on? What's the point? Why would you suffer the pain and indignity of having great big jelly mould tits stuck on your chest if you're just going to cover them up? It's a mystery. You can say what you like about me, but I do get my bangers out at every possible opportunity. In fact, with the falsies I've used you can see my nipples approaching you roughly ten minutes before the rest of me wiggles into view.

Dean's shuffling from foot to foot next to me when Sian approaches, wearing a white cheesecloth kaftan and loose-fitting jersey trousers. 'Well, look at you two,' she squeals, and I'm not sure whether she's talking to my chest or to me and Dean. 'Our lovely British friends.' I'm once again enveloped in a rather painful hug and subjected to kissing and hair stroking. 'My God, but you're wonderful,' she says. 'Look at you!'

Behind her strides Chuck. His hair has a parting so neat it looks like it's been done with a ruler, and his hair is all gelled to one side like he's in the Great Gatsby or something. He's wearing white trousers that are ever-so-slightly too tight and way too short. He's got them pulled up high and I can see every lump and bump on his groin. For the sake of absolute clarity: this is a *bad* thing. Chuck is not a man with lumps and bumps that any sane girl would want to admire. His light blue, short-sleeved shirt is ironed to within an inch of its life, and even from this distance I can see that he has huge, round sweat marks under his arms. His belt is elasticated and stripy light and dark blue, and his light blue socks, visible because the trousers are so bloody short, match the shirt exactly. He looks, as Dean so accurately observes, like 'a complete fucking ponce'.

He's on the phone as he walks over, and Sian apologizes before he even arrives.

'Sorry, guys, it's a business thing. He had to take the call.'

'Ya,' Chuck is saying into his state-of-the-art mobile. 'I like where you're coming from on that. We should diarize and book in a hook-up to discuss ballpark figures.' He puts his hand over the receiver and apologizes. 'It's all gone crazy in the world of canned meats. Be with you in five,' then he's back to his conversation. 'It's time for everyone to step up to the plate and stretch the envelope,' he says, raising his voice a little. 'But let's not forget – keep everything swimming in lanes, then we can take a helicopter view of the situation.'

He clips his phone shut and puts it into the front pocket of his shirt.

'Our lovely guests are here. What an honour,' he says, kissing my hand without breaking eye contact. 'Truly. We are thrilled that you could join us.'

He goes to hug Dean but Dean's too British to cope. He knows that when a man gets that close to you in England it means he's either gay or about to beat you up. I can see Dean hoping and praying that he's going to get punched.

'Let's introduce these children to one another,' says Sian, heading off to collect her offspring. Paskia-Rose has run off to the far side of the sitting room and is admiring all the football pictures and signed photos on the wall. Sian's twin girls are the same age as Pask but could not be more different from my daughter. They are, I have to say, among the most perfect girls that I have ever seen. They're dressed in pink and they're all small and delicate, like little dolls. If they piled the makeup on and stuffed a pair of socks down their bras, they'd be almost as lovely as the three girls we met today. Pask runs back over and stands next to Dean. She towers over the twins and looks ungainly next to them in her daft football shirt, baggy jeans and trainers.

'I love soccer,' I hear her say, as the twins look at each other in astonishment. 'I'm going to this fantastic school with the best football pitches I've ever seen!'

'Come on,' says Sian. 'Let me show you three girls what I've got in the kitchen. Frozen fat-free yoghurt!'

'Yummy!' shout the twins.

'Whooppee!' says Paskia, her voice weighed down by sarcasm. 'I thought you were going to say pizza and chips.'

I'm not sure whether the 'p' word or the 'c' word has ever been used in this house before. I can see Sian fighting to regain her composure before leaving the children to their 'treat' and marching back towards me.

'Tracie, can I introduce you to Poppy and Macey?' she says, indicating two women standing to my left. One has plain dark hair and the other has plain blonde hair, and neither is wearing makeup. They stare at me as if I've been beamed down from outer space.

'Great to meet you,' says Macey, flicking her natural locks away from her face like the girl in the Timotei advert. She's wearing a long white cotton skirt and a white crop top which, I'll grant her, does display her large breasts to their best advantage, and gives you a peek at a flat, tanned stomach, but it's not right. She needs a belly-button piercing at the very least.

Poppy's incredibly sweet-looking, with her long dark hair and the way she tilts her head to one side, like Snow White. I expect bunnies to come hopping through the sitting room at any minute. She's wearing a sun dress in an emerald green colour with simple kitten-heeled shoes. It's shameful the way these women dress. I must work with them and try and inject a little of Luton into their wardrobes.

'We'll all get the chance to chat later,' says Sian, dragging me away from them and over to one of the many huge cream sofas in her sitting room. Happily, our journey takes us right past the drinks – all laid out neatly in the kitchen.

'Ooooh,' I say as we pass, my glass now a desperate, Bacardi-free zone.

'A little juice?' asks Sian, picking up a glass, inspecting it, and handing it to one of the women on drinks patrol. 'How does celery and carrot suit you?'

I laugh madly at this. Why the holy fuck would I want a glass full of mashed-up celery? 'You're funny!' I say, minutes before realizing that she isn't joking. I glance around the room. Dean's right. No one appears to be drinking alcohol.

'I'd prefer something a bit stronger . . . if you don't mind.'

'Wheat grass?' she suggests, and I realize that it's time to stop being subtle.

'Alcohol, please,' I say. 'I'd prefer champagne, vodka or Bacardi, but really any alcohol at all would be great. Absolutely anything. I've even got my own bottle with me – it's hidden in the cloakroom if you want me to go and get it.'

'No, no, I've got some somewhere,' she says, looking quite thrown by my confession. 'And you're right. We should allow ourselves a little taste tonight, shouldn't we? We are celebrating, after all. Goodness, I should have thought of that – let's have a little treat.'

Weird, weird, weird. I have alcohol because it's Wednesday, because it's 8.40 p.m., because my name is Tracie, because the sky is blue. Who needs an excuse to get mullered?

'Right, take a seat,' she says, handing me a glass that's got so little in it, it'll probably all evaporate before I get to it. 'Now, tell me all about your screen test. Dean mentioned it to Chuck. Sounds very exciting.'

Oh God. Do we have to talk about this?

'I decided not to do it,' I say. 'I don't really have the time for it right now. I told them to give the role to Nicole Kidman or J-Lo or someone. Just one second.' Sian looks on all confused as I clip-clop across to the kitchen, pull out a large beaker and fill it with champagne, then I tip vodka in the top and walk back to my seat with the glass in one hand and the bottle of champagne in the other. 'Cheers,' I say, and 'Cheers,' she replies. But her eyes don't say cheers; her eyes say, 'Your body is a temple. How could you do this to yourself?' My eyes say, 'How I'd love to take you out in Luton for the night.'

'Tracie, I'm sorry you didn't do the audition. You'd have been great as a film star. What was the role? Did they tell you?'

'They didn't,' I lie. 'They just said it was about life in the city.'

'You'd be great in that,' says Sian. 'Look at you! You were made to be a film star. Can't you call them and tell them you can do it after all?'

I feel I ought to tell her the truth but what if she says, 'Yes, I can see their point. You do look like a bloke.'

'I didn't do it because I thought I might not be attract-ive enough,' I say.

'What are you talking about?' she says. 'Tracie, you're stunning. You'd look better without so much makeup, but you're very attractive indeed. Why would you think otherwise?'

'So you don't think I look like a man?'

'You don't look a bit like a man, Tracie. I'd never realized you were so self-critical. Promise me that every morning you will look in the mirror and say, "My name is Tracie Martin and I am a beautiful person, inside and out."'

'Yeah, right,' I say.

'This is important,' says Sian, deadly serious now. 'Our thoughts define our actions. Self-love is vital for a happy life, and affirmations are part of that. Maybe you should think about seeing someone. My psychoanalyst is very good.'

She hands me a card and I take it gratefully, but I don't think the woman will be getting my business. As long as people keep reassuring me that I don't look like a transvestite, everything will be fine.

10.30 p.m.

I'm off my tiny trolley. Whey-hey! Bring it on. I just wanna dance, but the music isn't really dancing music. It's all whale sounds and seagulls and shit like that – the sort of stuff they play while you're having a massage that drives you up the bloody wall.

'Someone shoot that dolphin!' I shout, and Dean falls about laughing. He's not drinking very much, but at least he's entering into the spirit of things. Any minute now he's going to start singing 'Ingerland, Ingerland, Ingerland'.

To be fair to the other guests, they've had a few, too. I don't think they wanted to, but in the end I just went round and poured vodka into their drinks, and they all thought it would be easier to get pissed than to keep saying no. Pester power! The thing is, cos they don't normally drink very much, just a couple of half pints of neat vodka and some of them have really let their hair down. Three have vomited in the garden, which is always nice to see at a party. Even Chuck's managed to take his phone away from his ear, which is a clear sign that he's pissed. There's some terribly respectable, middle-aged director of the club shagging one of the cheerleaders in the corner.

'This is more like it!' I cry, full of genuine enthusiasm for the happy turn that the party has taken. 'Let's all dance!'

'Yehhhhh!!!' they all chorus back. Trouble is, none of us is sober enough to use the stereo, so I start them off on a sing-song.

'There's only one Deany Martin . . . There's only one Deany Ma-a-artin,' I shout punching up into the air. Soon they're all joining in. We're in a circle in this lovely, sophisticated house, knocking back the champers and punching the air like we were in the Bobbers stand back at Luton. 'Deany, Deany, Deany, Deany . . .'

Fucking marvellous. *Now* we're having a party.

Thursday 29 May

Oh God, oh God. Head bad, bad head. Not good head.
Phone ringing, head hurting. Bad drinking has happened.
Phone ringing. Need staff. Ooooh . . . hurting.

'Mmmm,' I slobber into the mouthpiece.

'Morning, darling. How are you?' comes a bright and
breezy voice. 'Wondered whether you fancied coming
jogging?'

'No. Fuck off,' I say, throwing the phone down. What
sort of weirdo makes crank calls like that at this time in
the morning?

The phone rings again and I lift the receiver angrily,
but before I have chance to howl abuse the same perky
voice insists, 'Darling, it's Sian. Don't hang up.'

'Sian,' I say. 'Oh. Sorry. What are you doing up at this
time in the morning after the party last night?'

'It's 11 a.m.,' she says, as if that makes it all right.
'Come on, up you get. You're in LA now. Time for a jog.'

'Sian,' I say patiently, 'my feet were made for slipping
into colossally high shoes. They were made for staggering
out of nightclubs at 4 a.m. They were made for pedi-
cures and toe rings. They were not, I repeat *not*, made
for jogging.'

The pain and fear at the mere thought of putting on trainers, let alone jogging in them, runs through me like money through my hands, like Cristal through a Wag.

'Oh,' she says. 'Deary me, are you always like this in the morning? Are you an evening jogger? Have you taken your supplements yet?'

'Yes, no, no,' I say, and she laughs so loudly I almost drop the phone. What is it with these enthusiastic Californians? Why are they all so cheery and full of life? It must be the weather.

'Well, I've been for a run along the beach and a swim If you don't fancy coming out I may just warm down, get a stretch and some yoga done, then come over and see you. How about that?'

'As long as you do it quietly,' I say, and she's gone . . . off to throw her legs round her neck and push her shoulders between her knees. God, I need a drink.

Noon

Sian's enthusiasm, healthy glow and general positive attitude are starting to make me feel quite queasy. She's sitting bolt upright, legs crossed, beautiful soft blonde hair falling down her back and hands upturned. As she breathes she emphasizes every breath out. 'It's pilates breathing,' she says. 'It makes you feel centred. Would you like me to show you?'

'No thanks,' I say sulkily.

'It was so lovely to have a little drink last night. I haven't had a drink for years, but I measured three whole teaspoons of vodka into my fresh cranberry and Goji Berry drink.'

Ah, that's how she looks so much more healthy than me – she was using a teaspoon to measure out her alcohol while I was using a bucket.

'I hope I wasn't too drunk,' I say. I'm being polite. The truth is that I don't think there's any such thing as 'too drunk'.

'Not at all. You were fabulous, Tracie,' she enthuses. 'You really made the party swing.'

Oh, good. I didn't make a fool of myself. That's a relief, and a pleasant change.

'Were you OK after the fall?' she asks.

Oh, no.

'Fall?'

'Yes, you know – when you went flying across the kitchen floor while showing us your Pussy Cat Dolls impression.'

'I did what?'

'Do you not remember? I guess you must have tripped on one of your shoes when you got up after the back spin.'

Oh God. Back spin. Why?

The news of my little performance certainly helps me to understand why my hair's so matted. I don't remember anything after about 11 p.m. It was all one big, happy blur as far as I was concerned.

I move my hand to my hair, and subconsciously comb my fingers through as Sian chats on, reminding me of the 'fun' party guest that I was. 'Then you climbed onto his shoulders and started singing a Kylie Minogue song!'

A large clump of hair comes off in my hand.

'Oh my God,' shrieks Sian. 'Do you have alopecia or something?'

'No. Just the extensions,' I say. 'I must have been sick in my hair last night. I do that quite a lot, then the acid eats through the glue holding them in, and they start to come loose. No big deal.'

'Oh my God. You were sick? Have you taken supplements? Why were you sick? Let's take you to the ER.'

'Because I was off my trolley,' I say gaily, adding, 'A champagne chuck. The very worst kind of sick!'

'You drank so much last night that it made you sick? You need to be more careful,' she says, stretching so far backwards I think she's going to topple off the chair.

'Whooah,' I say, leaping up to save her.

'I am totally balanced. I have a strong core.'

And I think, Sian, I really, really like you, but you don't half talk some bollocks at times. I mean, if she lived anywhere but LA they'd be locking her up.

'Do you not ever think, Sod it, I'm just going to drink all night and sleep all day, and sod the exercise?'

'No!' she says. 'Your physical and spiritual well-being must be your primary concern as a responsible adult. If you don't look after yourself, no one will.'

I kind of see what she means, but it's all so boring having to exercise and take herbs and stuff. This whole hippy world reminds me of Mum too much. She went off to live in LA for ten years, but even before that she was obsessed with anti-ageing remedies and covering herself in absurd potions. I grew up in a house with a kitchen that had thousands of pounds worth of supplements in the cupboards, and no bread. There were all sorts of lotions and potions in the fridge, but no milk. I'd wake up to the sound of chanting and go to sleep at night to the sound of the treadmill. Mum's spiritual and physical well-being was perfect. Trouble is, she never smiled. I'd take a bundle of good times and loads of happy drinking over daily yoga and soya bean soufflé any day.

3 p.m.

Paskia-Rose has gone out all excited because she's meeting up with the LA City Raiders Ladies team for the first time. Meanwhile, Dean's come back in from the club and he's all fed up. He says that everything's going really well, and he's confident that he can turn around their fortunes very quickly with some simple adjustments (don't ask me what they are – I have neither interest in nor understanding of what he does), but what he's finding hard is the fact that everyone drives in LA. Everything's so far away from everywhere else that there isn't even the same cab mentality that you get in London or New York. Or Luton. For Dean, who can't drive and has never driven, it's proving a bit of a strain.

'You've got Gareth,' I remind him.

'I know, but I wanted him to take Paskia-Rose to the Ladies' training session, and there'll be times when you need him. No, the truth is that I need to be able to drive myself, then I can just come and go as I please.'

'OK,' I say, reaching for my keys. 'Then, my lover, I shall teach you.'

5 p.m.

Ladies and gentlemen, praise be to God, for I am not the worst driver in the world. Oh, no – that honour goes to my dear husband. He's useless! In fact he's so useless that I'm in fits of laughter all the time, and that, of course, is not making things go any more smoothly.

'I'd be able to do it if you weren't here,' he says angrily. I try desperately to choke back the laughter as the car hops down the street like a great metal bunny rabbit. I'm doing that terrible schoolgirl thing of trying not to laugh and thus snorting and crying and jamming my fist into my mouth, which makes me laugh all the more.

'I don't understand why it's bouncing like that,' he says, looking all confused.

'Are you in the right gear?' I manage to say, leaning over to check.

'Tracie, it's got nothing to do with clothes,' he says. 'The gear I'm wearing is fine.'

'The gear that the car's in, you doughnut. Look, it's in third, that's why it's bouncing around like a fucking kangaroo.'

I tell him to pull over, and he kind of lurches to a stop, right in the middle of the road.

'You can't stop here. Go to the side,' I instruct. I want to run through the gear thing with him again.

He turns the key and the car pounces forward like it's on springs.

'It's in third,' I squeal.

'I don't know what to do,' he howls back. 'I don't even know what 'it's in third' means.'

I move the gear stick for him and he turns the key in the ignition. Then, for reasons that I'll never understand, he slams his foot down on the accelerator and zooms across the street faster than Michael Schumacher. The car mounts the kerb the other side and, just when I'm thinking that things can't get any worse, it heads onto the plush green lawn in front of us, accompanied by screams from Dean, who is by now entirely out of control. Eventually I manage to do the only practical thing I've done in my life, and I yank on the handbrake, forcing the car to skid and come to a stop just before hitting the small fountain in the middle of the grass.

'Phew, that was close,' he says, as we stare up into the genitals of a little boy who is fashioned entirely from marble. He's weeing into the fountain as we sit there.

'Don't worry,' I say to my depressed-looking husband. 'We'll get you some lessons.'

'Yes,' he says despondently, and we decide that's enough for one day, and I'll drive back. We slip out of our seats and walk silently past one another on the grass. Then, as I'm approaching the driver's seat, the sprinkler system kicks into operation, showering us both with a gentle spray of water containing some sort of foul-smelling weedkiller.

It's all too much for Dean.

'This is not meant to be,' he says, his spiky hair horribly flat and wet. He has an unfortunate mixture of weedkiller and Brylcreem sliding down his forehead and dripping into his eyes, and I feel like running round to the other side of the car and wrapping him up in my arms and holding him tightly. But I also feel like jumping into the car, out of the wet, and driving away as quickly as possible before the owners of this house come out and arrest me.

'Let's go,' I say, starting the engine and reversing off the grass. I zoom down the road at top speed, with Dean mumbling, 'It looks so easy when you do it, but I just couldn't stop it jumping.'

'Wake up, doll. Wake up,' says Dean.

'Mmmmm . . .'

'You're asleep on the sofa love,' he says, as I lift my head and look around. I was dreaming of Spangles – my favourite nightclub in Luton. It was karaoke night, and me and Michaela had just been singing 'I will survive' at the tops of our voices. Now I open my eyes I can see that I'm in LA – a whole new country that isn't Luton at all. A feeling of homesickness washes over me. 'How was training this evening?' I ask.

Raiders have started doing extra training sessions in the evening because Dean wants them to spend more time on the pitch and less time in the spa. They must think he's a right miserable sod. 'Oh my God, training was perfect!' he says. 'Let me get a soya milk, banana and walnut smoothie and I'll tell you all about it.'

'A what? Bloody hell, Dean. Are you pissed?'

'No,' he says, mashing up banana into this glass bowl and sprinkling nuts on. 'I told you, I'm not drinking any more.'

'Loser,' I say, making an 'L' sign with my fingers.

'I'm going to get fit and healthy and I'm going to turn this club round. I've got my first game in charge on Saturday and we're gonna win it. I swear. Everyone says we're set to come bottom, but we won't, love. You wait till we play Galaxy. We'll beat them hands down.'

OK, now he's got me.

'Galaxy?' I enquire. 'You mean LA Galaxy? David Beckham's team?'

'That's right, Candyfloss,' he says, tipping sunflower

seeds and goat's milk yoghurt into a bowl. 'Where are the pumpkin seeds?' he asks.

'Pumpkin seeds? How the hell do I know? I didn't know pumpkins *had* seeds. What's going on, Dean? Where did all the food come from?' I've not been near the kitchen except to get glasses for champagne.

'I bought it,' he says, and I think to myself how remarkable my man is. Most of all, though, I think, When are they playing LA Galaxy? When will I meet David? Will Posh be there?

'When are the matches against LA Galaxy?' I ask. I'm only vaguely aware of how this American soccer thing works (you can't call it football here, or they automatically think you're talking about a game like rugby in which they wear helmets). I know that the Raiders are new into the league, which contains fourteen other teams, so now there are fifteen of them, and they play each other team twice during the season. That's all I know. That's all I want to know. The only really interesting thing about any of it is that David Beckham plays for LA Galaxy. I think that Dean should be calling David and making friends with him, but he thinks that would be too 'gay' and that we'll bump into them eventually. I think that this approach, to steal Dean's language, is thoroughly 'gay'.

'When do you play LA Galaxy?' I ask.

'I've marked them on the calendar in the kitchen,' he says.

We have nuts, seeds, yoghurt and a calendar? Who knew? I jump up and rush into the kitchen.

'There we are, dear,' he says, pointing out the dates over my shoulder. 'We play them at home on 21 June, then on 9 August, away. Both MLS games.'

'MSL?'

'Major League Soccer. That's what we're playing in.'

Oh, right. I'm guessing that's the American equivalent of the Premiership, and what it means is that there are two formal occasions on which I'll meet Victoria, and all the possibilities that will arise through Jamie's friendship with her as well as the fact that I'll be tipped off every time she goes into Koi. So many chances to meet my heroine. Soon-to-be best friend. Ooooooooh, it's so exciting. I give Dean a great big hug. 'I love you,' I say, and he hugs me back.

'Come on, Tracie, let's explore.'

'Explore?' I ask, concern ricocheting through me. Why on earth would we ever want to do that? I've never heard Dean use such a word before. 'Go out?' I say. 'Is there an opening of a bar or restaurant somewhere, or are there photographers around? A film première? Why else would I want to go out?'

'Nah, silly,' he says with a loud guffaw. 'Not out and explore. I meant explore the TV. There are loads of chan-nels on it, you know. Most of them are American, but there are some brill cartoons and that. I can't find *Midsomer Murders* yet, but it must be on here somewhere. Come on, love, let's get some telly watched. You've been in Los Angeles for over four days and you haven't sat in front of the goggle box for more than an hour at a time.'

'You're right, love,' I say as we snuggle together on the sofa in this strange foreign country where the sun always shines. Dean is flicking through the channels with a smile on his face and I'm dreaming of shopping, pampering and getting rat-arsed with Victoria. We're on the other side of the world, but nothing, really, has changed at all. Phew.

Email to: Mich & Suzzi

From: Tracie in LA

Hi, girlies. Thanks for the email and the gossip update. I can't believe Mum's back in Luton! When did she get there? It's so weird. I thought she was loving life in Spain and about to settle down with the twenty year old.

I know that nothing Angie does should surprise me any more, but turning up at Luton and announcing that she wants to adopt three African babies? Does she think she's going to attract someone who looks like Brad Pitt if she acts like Angelina Jolie? Someone ought to tell her that it doesn't work like that! Poor thing – I hope she's OK. Do you think I should write to her? All the letters I sent to her in Spain were sent back marked 'Return to the bitch' so Dean told me to stop writing. Let me know what you think, and remember to keep me updated on what she's up to.

I'll have a look for the chewing gum you mentioned – the stuff that you chew three times and it makes your skin look ten years younger. I have to confess that I haven't seen any over here, and I certainly couldn't find those sweets that you mentioned – the ones that make your hair blonder. You know, I'm starting to think that a lot of the things that appear in magazines about LA simply aren't true.

Will write again soon, Trace

PS. I can't believe someone's smashed the statue of the Boy David in our garden. Who would do that? Didn't anyone hear anything? Must be the same person who cut the heads off all the flowers. Kids, no doubt. Thanks for getting it all fixed. x

Friday 30 May (22 days until LA Galaxy game)
6 a.m.

'Bye, love you,' says Dean. I peel back my eye mask and look at the clock. Six a.m.?

'What the hell are you doing up at this hour?' I ask.

'I'm so psyched up about the match tomorrow that I can't sleep,' he says. 'I'm off for yoga on the beach.'

'Yoda's on the beach? What's he doing there?'

'Ha. Ha. Very funny. See you later.'

'Watch out for Darth Vader,' I shout, as Dean heads down the stairs. 'He'll be the one dressed all in black.'

9 a.m.

I couldn't get back to sleep after Dean left. I kept thinking of him and Yoda on the beach together, fighting against the forces of darkness. Now I'm wide awake, so I slip on my pink, spangly mules and my sparkly pink négligé and click, clack, click my way down the stairs, wandering into Dean's office overlooking the front of the house. The postman cycles past and manages to shove our letters into the box with barely a slow-down, then he's off to a house further down the road. We don't really have neighbours here because the houses are so far apart and all protected by big gates that rather inhibit that quaint English custom of popping round for a cup of sugar.

I remember when we moved into the house in Luton, the first thing we did was to invite all the neighbours round for a good old knees-up. They'd always be popping over to see how I was when Dean was away playing football. It tended to be the men who came. I guess that's because the women were at home looking after the children. It was nice that they cared. Sometimes they cared too much, though, and it was hard to get them to go home! I remember one time when Louis from over the road came over – he'd always pop in when Dean was away. On this occasion it was gone midnight and still he wouldn't leave. Even when I put my nightie on and said I was going to bed he just sat there with a funny smile on his little fat face! Ah, they were a nice bunch, our neighbours. They're keeping an eye on the house for us while we're away.

I walk down the path and out to our box (on a long post, just by the gate), and pull out a letter in Simon's handwriting. He must be the only man in the world who still sends handwritten notes. The rest of them look like formal letters that I never deal with – you know, bills and stuff. There are loads for Dean: one from an organization called 'The Positive Life Company' and a whole pile from fitness companies, healthy-living companies and yoga organizations. I'll shove them in the bin when I get inside – don't want him getting any ideas. There's nothing from our new bank, which is annoying. They've only sent one cheque book for our account – with just Dean's name on it. I'm sure he did it on purpose in the hope of keeping me out of the shops . . . like *that* was ever going to happen!

It turns out the account's in his name only because he's the one with a green card to work over here. 'It won't make any difference,' he said when we heard. 'I think the only difference is that you won't be able to take out loans or mortgages or anything on it. Not that you'd want to do that, would you?'

'I wouldn't know the first thing about taking out a loan,' I say. 'To be honest, if I need more money, I'll just ask you.'

I grab the letter from Simon and start to tear it open as I see Jamie running across the road towards me, like he's running along the beach in *Baywatch*. I swear the birds start singing and the world turns brighter whenever he hoves into view. 'You want to cover yourself, young lady,' he says. 'You'll cause an accident with that lovely body on show.'

I smile at the compliment and subconsciously fuss with my hair, wishing I'd checked my makeup before leaving the house. 'What are you doing here?' I ask.

'Just passing,' he says. 'You know – going on my morning run. Listen, can I come in and have a quick chat to you?'

'Sure. Follow me,' I say, and he walks behind me as I wriggle for all my worth, like Marilyn Monroe only without the large hips and with less natural-looking hair and more makeup.

Into the house, and I go straight over to open a bottle. The sound of the cork popping lifts my spirits and I smile as I lift the glasses out of the cupboard and turn to Jamie.

'Not for me,' he says. 'I'm not big on drinking at break-fast. You go ahead, though. We LA types are wimps when it comes to alcohol.'

'Yep, so I'm beginning to realize,' I say. 'Orange juice?'

'Is it fresh?' he asks.

For God's sake, man. What do you want? Blood? It's not fresh – far from it. To be honest, I think it's probably off, but I can only go so far in pandering to the madness and insecurities of these people, so I say yes, and he tips the whole lot of it down his throat.

'Right – do you remember yesterday I mentioned I had a business idea that I promised to run through with you some time?'

I don't remember, to be honest, but then again I don't remember much about lunch. I have a vague recollection of us deciding that Jamie should take some photographs of me in case I ever get a column on a newspaper over here and they ask for a picture, and then of me being so drunk that we gave up, but I don't remember anything else.

'A business?' I say. 'I'm not sure.'

'Never mind,' he says. 'It's just that something's happened this morning that makes me think that this business really will work, and I thought of you straight away.'

'What is it?' I ask, and Jamie pulls his T-shirt out of his shorts, revealing a taut, tanned torso which I try desperately hard not to stare at, but fail miserably. From his shorts he pulls a rolled-up piece of paper and proceeds to flatten it out on the counter.

'Alcohol-less alcohol!' he exclaims. 'What do you think?'

'Well, my first thought is – why would anyone buy that?' I say, looking at the picture on the paper of an attractive-looking bottle with 'alcohol-less' printed on it.

To be honest, the bottle looks lovely – it's very feminine looking, with little white elderflowers running round the edge. It's the sort of wine I'd go for, but I wouldn't go for it if it didn't have alcohol in it. 'Isn't the point of alcohol the fact that it has alcohol in it?'

'Yes,' he says. 'For many people that's the case, but think about it – there are lots of people in LA who don't like to do themselves any harm through alcohol, but they enjoy the taste. Imagine if we could devise a drink that tasted exactly like alcohol but had hardly any calories in it and didn't get you drunk? Imagine how much money we'd make.'

Money! That would be good. I need to start making some money in case things get really nasty at the Raiders and they stop paying Dean or something.

'We'd make loads, Tracie, honestly. People are crying out for this. Guys in LA are not interested in drinking alcohol because of what it does to them. They enjoy a healthy lifestyle.'

'That's true enough,' I say. 'Even my Deany says he's not drinking again and he was eating bloody seeds and bananas last night. The only thing I've seen him eat in front of the telly before are pork scratchings and crisps with ketchup on. Now it's all goat's milk and soya beans. I'm the only drinker in LA. I hate drinking on my own.'

'I'll start drinking to keep you company,' says Jamie.

'Would you do that? For me?' I say. I'm impressed, relieved and flattered in equal measure.

'Of course,' he says. 'Now go and pour me a glass of champagne. I could do with something to take away the sour taste of that orange juice. Are you sure it was fresh?'

He has his glass in his hand, and his promotional

pictures laid out before him. 'Now, the good news. Are you ready for this?'

'Yes,' I say, and he insists on pausing dramatically before saying . . .

'Victoria Beckham wants to be involved.'

I gasp at the sound of her name.

'Really?'

'Yes, David called and said she's looking for something new to throw herself into now the Spice Girls tour is over. They both love the idea of this project. With her involved it would work, wouldn't it?'

I grip onto the table to prevent my legs from collapsing beneath me. 'Yes,' I mutter. 'Gosh, yes, yes and double yes. Jamie, this is amazing.'

'I know,' he says. He looks all excited, like a little boy who's been given a puppy on Christmas morning. 'I'm trying to stay calm because there's a long way to go. I mean, even if Victoria commits to it, I still have to raise funding for it, but I bet with her involved it will be so much easier to get people to commit financially.'

'They'll be queuing up,' I say. 'I mean – really, everyone will want to be involved. This is unbelievable. Completely unbelievable. You're going into business with the most wonderful and famous person in the world!'

Jamie smiles and hugs me. 'I'd like you to be involved, Tracie,' he says. 'Can you be in charge of liaising with Victoria or something? It'll be so much fun if we're both involved.'

'Yes, yes, yes,' I cry, clapping my hands together. We're both smiling madly and jumping up and down in the middle of the kitchen. This is a great, great day. I'll make some money which will save us if Raiders goes bankrupt, and I'll get to be business partner and best mates with Victoria. I want to tell everyone. I want to scream to the whole world.

'Don't tell anyone about this, will you?' he says.

Oh.

'We need to keep it secret until I've copyrighted the whole thing, and got Victoria properly on board.'

'No, of course I won't,' I promise. 'I won't tell a soul. It'll be our special little secret.'

'Thanks,' he says. 'Oh, and did you go for that film audition?'

'No,' I say. 'I changed my mind. I decided I'm a bit too busy to become an internationally recognized film star right now, and with this business opportunity on the horizon it's a good job.'

I can picture myself in a power suit, striding through corporate America. I'll be demanding and efficient, firm but fair. There'll be trips to the White House for me and Victoria, and regular conference calls with London and China. Oh, yes, my future is as a business tycoon. I'll be breakfasting with Donald Trump and Victoria and I will start talking the same language as Chuck.

'Jamie, we're gonna need to touch base soon over this,' I hear myself say. 'The only way we'll hit the ground running is by pushing the needle. Everyone's going to have to eat frogs.'

'You OK?' he asks, as he gathers his things and prepares to leave.

'No, I don't think I am,' I say. 'I'll go and lie down now.'

11 a.m.

'Sian,' I say, when the happy, vibrant voice of the chairman's wife comes bursting through the phone and practically shatters my eardrums. She's obviously been doing aerobics or acrobatics or something involving Lycra and sweat. 'Would you buy a bottle of drink that tasted just like wine but had no alcohol in it, all natural ingredients and very few calories?' I ask.

'Wow!' she says.

'It's a very healthy drink, fat-free, and it tastes just like wine,' I continue.

'I'd buy truck loads,' she says. 'Show me where I can get it.'

'Nowhere yet,' I say. 'But maybe soon.'

Saturday 31 May (21 days to go)
6 p.m.

LA City Raiders beat Houston Dynamo today. Hoorah! Yeah, I know, I know, it means nothing to me either. But a win's a win, and everyone here seems to think it's the greatest thing since St Tropez started doing their tanning cream in spray bottles, so I'll just cheer along with everyone else and pretend I understand what the hell they're all so excited about.

'First victory in Major League Soccer for LA City Raiders,' Dean says. Actually he says it more than once – he repeats it over, and over, and over. So I plainly can see that this is a very good thing. Well worth celebrating raucously and extensively.

Yep – my husband has guided them to victory in his first game in charge, and now we're on the dance floor, stumbling around to Celine Dion, and Dean is singing into my ear in a rather tuneless and annoying manner. Every time we smooch past one of the players, they tap Dean on the back and say 'Good work, big guy', or something like that. The players at the club seem decent enough and they obviously think Dean is great. They're a funny bunch, though, because they're not really footballers in the same way we think of them in Luton. I mean they all 'work out' and are much fitter looking than our guys. They don't really have earrings. (No wonder they've never won anything before. You've got to look the part!) They're not dressed like our guys either – no £500 shirts and £300 jeans. These guys are just in shorts and T-shirts and fitness wear. When I suggest to one of them that you'd never, ever catch a footballer at a disco in beach shorts back home, he says he has to wear them because it's roasting here. I tell him straight away that the term 'roasting' has entirely different connotations in England and we both shrug. He says that's the lovely thing about travel – it broadens the mind and allows you to experience other cultures. I smile and agree with him but I'm wondering whether men in cheap shirts and sandals is a culture that I can ever come to terms with. I think my Dean has spent more money on hair products in advance of tonight's celebratory party than any of these guys have spent on their entire wardrobes. But they seem like nice people . . . Dean likes them – which is the main thing, I guess.

When it comes to the women, I think we had a small breakthrough earlier. I arrived for the match today at the usual time – four hours before kick-off – and there was no sign of anyone. Sian had arranged to meet me to introduce me to the girls, but she was nowhere to be seen. When I called, she was out running.

'You're there already!' she exclaimed.

'Of course!' I exclaimed back. 'I've got my drinking boots on.'

'Oh Lord,' said Sian. 'OK. I'll get back as quickly as I can, and get down there. If you go up into the bar, someone should be there and can get you a drink.'

To be fair to Sian, she came as quickly as humanly possible, and we sat and had a nice little drink – me knocking back the bubbly while she drank snot (OK, it's wheatgrass, but it looks like it came out of someone's nose). Then in came Poppy - the girl that I met at the party. In the cold light of day I could see that she was pretty enough but – shit – her clothes were unbelievable. It was as if she'd come for an afternoon on the beach. She was wearing cut-off Capri pants and a plain white shirt!!!! To the football!!!! I couldn't help staring.

'Hi,' Poppy said, smiling through lipstick-less lips and offering me a hand which was strangely devoid of jewellery. 'Lovely to meet you again. Sorry we didn't have much chance to chat at the party.'

I smiled at Poppy and told her it was nice to see her again too, but I couldn't resist offering her a little advice on her hair. You see Poppy has brown hair, Lord help us. Brown hair! Not yellow like sunshine and flowers, but brown like shit and mud.

'Poppy, what are you thinking of?' I said, pointing towards her head and to her shoulders where the thick dark hair fell in soft curls, framing her pretty, childlike face.

'What's the matter?'

'Your hair isn't blonde,' I said.

'Should it be?' she asked.

Is this a joke? 'Er, yes, Poppy. A Wag's hair should be blonde.'

I don't mean to be rude, but it's a basic error. Victoria can get away with being dark because she has a blonde soul and because we all know that it's only a matter of time before she goes long and blonde again, but Poppy's not in the blonde soul league, so she needs blonde hair. Clear? Not to Poppy it wasn't.

She looked me up and down as I sat there, drinking

champagne from a lager glass to save filling it up all the time. I confess I liked the feeling of being looked at. Oh, yeah – Queen Wag's in town, I thought. The stakes just rose, ladies. This is how Victoria must feel when she turns up at matches – more dressed up than everyone else. If only I had a celebrity Hollywood friend with me, we'd be virtually indistinguishable. The bubblegum-coloured PVC leggings clinging to my skinny thighs (size two, remember, ladies and gentlemen . . . size two) were a real find, and the way the ra-ra skirt matches it exactly (except it's got white lace on it) is just brilliant. I know they're dying to ask where I got it, but I'll just keep that to myself. I don't want to be out-Wagged. I've got a lace-up corset top on. Unfortunately I couldn't find exactly the right shade of pink for that, so the pinks all clash a bit, which is a shame, and not very VB, but I figure that I've pulled it together with the heavy white bondage shoes and created a look that screams 'Wag! Attention! Gorgeous! Sexy!' (See how I did that: all the letters from Wags making up a sentence that describes Wags!)

'Are you always so dressed up for matches, or did you make a special effort today?' asked Poppy, as Macey arrived looking equally young and beautiful, but equally inappropriately dressed. The girls are incredibly attractive, but did no one teach them how to dress? Macey wore a simple black cashmere cardigan over a knee-length shift dress in white linen. She'd pushed her dark sunglasses up into her blonde hair and smiled a lot. I guess they both looked nice, but in an understated way.

'I love to dress up,' I explained. 'I can't leave the house without being dressed up. I can't. I'm a Wag, you see. And proper Wags, no offence, like to look nice. Take Victoria

– she always looks fantastic. Did you know it's just twenty-one days until Galaxy play here? Twenty-one days. Can I get cosmetic surgery done that quickly?'

'I'm not really sure,' said Macey, brushing an imaginary speck of dust off her long, glossy legs in quite a dismissive fashion. 'I guess it kinda depends what surgery you want.'

'Mmmm . . . good point,' I said, following her gaze down her lovely tanned legs. That's when I saw something truly amazing: she was wearing plimsolls! It must be as some sort of joke. 'Ha!' I screeched, laughing hysterically. 'Whoever said LA women had no sense of humour was definitely joking. Look at those shoes!'

Sian turned scarlet and looked down while Macey and Poppy were utterly perplexed. 'Children's gym shoes,' I said. 'For a joke? No?'

'They're comfortable,' said Macey. 'Is that a problem?'

God, that's when I absolutely died laughing. Comfortable! I thought I'd split the back of my leggings I was laughing so much – really choking, howling with it.

'Come on, you guys, let me get you all drinks,' I said.

'OK,' they both replied, looking slightly shell-shocked by my outburst. 'We'll have the same.'

'Sian?'

'I'll have the same too,' she responded.

Good girls, I thought, as I walked up to the bar and ordered four bottles of champagne. But when the bottles came it appeared I'd made an error. They wanted the same as Sian (a pint of snot with a stick of celery poking out of the top of it), not the same as me.

'Oh, just drink up,' I said, and to their credit they did!

In half an hour they were so drunk that Poppy even let me do her makeup for her. She's nice, actually. I mean

– I don't think we'll ever be the best friends in the world, but she's a lovely girl. We went out to watch the match with our faces, at least, looking like Wags, and attracting a proper amount of staring, walking into walls and comment.

So, here we are now . . . me and my man slow dancing, and Dean is holding me close and still singing like a girl.

Behind me, Poppy and Sian are holding champagne bottles like microphones and singing the words to a completely different tune to that being belted out by Celine. They wave frantically when they see me looking. Marvellous – they're back on it! Good for them. I wonder where Macey's got to.

'We love you,' they shout, tripping over each other to come and give me a hug. Poppy almost lands on her face. That's the problem with flat shoes, I advise her. I definitely need to get these girls out on a shopping trip.

'We've had so much fun,' says Sian, swaying through the couples romantically embraced all around us. 'Everything's so much fun when you're around.'

'Yeah,' they all chorus, and Dean pulls me closer to him and whispers how proud he is of me. Everything feels wonderful. It's a bit odd that Dean's sober, but I'm far enough off my trolley for both of us. Gosh, I'm so lucky. To make it all even better, Simon's coming out tomorrow to do his research, and we're going to try and get an American column for my book while he's here. One day soon, when I'm a bit more settled, I'll get to meet my father for the first time. Things have never looked so good. I don't think I've ever been so happy. Nothing can go wrong now. Everything is absolutely perfect. Nothing can possibly go wrong . . .

Sunday 1 June (20 days to go)

Flippin' heck. Someone's banging on the door so loudly it sounds as if the whole front of the bloody house is going to collapse.

'Dean, Dean,' I try. 'Door.' Bang. 'Now. Go.'

'Bang, bang, bang,' goes the door. There's not a movement from the other side of the bed. Is he dead? I peel back the covers to reveal an empty space where once my husband lay.

The housekeeper starts work tomorrow and, to be frank, she can't start soon enough. I wasn't made for answering doors this early in the morning. It's just not me. I stagger out of bed, tripping over the exquisitely designed bedside rug with its tiger's head and almost breaking my ankle on the white bondage shoes and the pink PVC leggings, still lying by the door.

Fumbling around, I reach for my négligé and open the bedroom door. There's a post-it note on the outside of it saying 'Gone for a run. Dean X'. Bloody hell.

Holy moly, it's bright out here. In the bedroom we've got black silk under-curtains which cut out all the light. It's marvellous when you're in the room because it's lovely and dark and cosy and sort of English, but when you come out the LA sunshine attacks you, screams at you and sends you reeling back into the darkness. Dean says I look like a small woodland creature emerging from its burrow when I leave that room. Cute, but not quite the look I've been striving for all these years. Given the choice, I'd prefer he thought that I looked like Jordan, not some bloody ferret.

Bang, bang, bang. I can hear a voice shouting, 'Anyone there? Anyone there?' through the door. Bollocks. What's going on? Can anything be so important that you would force a Wag to rise from her beauty sleep?

This is not a good start to a day that I have been looking forward to since I first came to LA. Simon arrives at 9 a.m. He's staying for three weeks. Frankly, I can't wait to see him again.

'Coming!' I yell down through the large, spacious corridors. 'Just on my way.' I'm shuffling along in my high-heeled mules, barely able to see properly. I think I probably need glasses but I'd rather cut off my head than wear them, so I just avoid going to the opticians and keep staggering.

OK. Négligé closed, no naked flesh showing. Open door.

Oh. There he is. My little mate. Looking all scruffy and unkempt and as if he's just got off a long-haul flight in a strange country with no one there to greet him.

He stands on the step, with the Californian sunlight surrounding him like a halo making him look ever so ethereal, and I can't stop thinking about the moment in *Ghost* when Patrick Swayze walks away from Demi for the last time, his ghostly form heading off to heaven. The difference is that Simon has a pile of bags at his feet, a puzzled look on his face, shaking hands and wild eyes.

'Where were you? Where were you?' he asks in a very un-Hollywood fashion, and the Swayze-filled bubble pops in the air before me. He sounds like he's going to burst into tears.

'Simon!!' I say with genuine enthusiasm and a little confusion. What's he doing here now? I'm picking him up later. 'Did you get an earlier flight?'

'No,' he says. 'It's midday. I landed at 9 a.m. Tracie, I hate flying so much. It was really scary.'

'I'm sorry,' I say. 'Big night last night. I was going to come and pick you up and drive you past the Beckhams' house on the way back and everything. Sorry, Simon. Now, come in and tell me everything. How's Luton? Have you seen the girls?'

'Yes, I've seen the girls and they've given me a present to give to you. I'll get it out in a minute.'

Simon lifts up his bags and walks into the house.

'Bloody hell!!' he exclaims, as soon as he's through the door. 'Some corner of a foreign field that is forever Luton.'

Simon does that from time to time. He says things which are entirely meaningless and totally incomprehensible but which have a poetic ring to them so you suspect there's a lost meaning encased in the words. I just smile, and he explains that this house looks exactly like the one in Luton.

'I know what I like, and I like what I know,' I tell him, and I swing open the fridge door.

'I'm so glad to be here,' he says as I pour drinks into glasses. 'You're the only person I know who likes a drink as much as I do.'

'Cheers!'

Simon takes a huge gulp of his champagne so the glass is half empty. Gosh, I've missed him. The two of us have nothing in common really – what with me being a perma-tanned Wag with a clothes and makeup obsession and tattoos on my bum; and him being a rather serious journalist from the *Guardian* with no interest in his appearance and not the slightest concern for shoes or handbags. I like *Desperate Housewives* and he likes *Newsnight*. We'd never have come across each other if I hadn't made a complete arse of myself one time, and we quickly needed to get some good publicity to counter the damage I'd done. Simon was working on *Luton Life* maga-zine at the time, and he came to interview me for a feature. He says he fell in love with my honesty and simplicity. I told him that I wanted to write words that would help teach Wags around the world how to behave, and he stepped in and offered to help. The result was a series of columns, national acclaim and a great, though unlikely, friendship.

'Come on then. Where's the gift from the girls?' I say.

He goes scarlet as he pulls out a bright pink bodysuit. It's nippleless, crotchless and covered in sequins. 'These go with it,' he says, handing me little bunny ears, a bunny tail and tassels for my breasts. 'I think it's supposed to be a joke,' he says.

'No,' I cry, leaping to my feet. 'It's gorgeous. I love it. It's perfect! I'll try it on now.'

'No!' shouts Simon, jumping to his feet. 'That would be terribly inappropriate.'

Behind us, the sun streams through the glass wall, lighting up Paskia as she runs through the garden with a ball at her feet. It's funny how the light is so bright, so clear, somehow, that it appears to attach itself to people.

It's a light that is wholly different to the sort of light we had in Luton.

Simon raises his glass. 'Cheers!' he exclaims. 'How's the new life?'

I try to explain about the way they all do yoga and running and swimming and drink snot and wear sports clothing. 'Even Dean!' I say. Simon laughs as I talk, and says that he and I will stay proudly British through all this madness.

'The Empire was not built on wheatgrass and crushed rhododendron buds!' he says. 'The Empire was built by men who were complete strangers to the world of high-protein supplements and yogic posturing. We will continue to drink and we shall do it proudly and in their honour.'

Thank God he's here. He may spout a whole bunch of tosh at times, but he likes a drink and he's always up for a party.

'Cheers!' we both say again, as Paskia-Rose spots us and comes running in from the garden to greet Simon.

'Hey stranger, welcome to LA!' she says, and she sounds so grown up and cosmopolitan that I feel all proud and quite tearful all of a sudden. I try not to think about the fact that she starts school tomorrow. If I did I'd be crying my eyes out.

'Dad told me to say that he might do an extra training session with the guys later following the win yesterday, also he's playing squash after training so he won't be back till this evening.'

Simon looks impressed. 'Blimey! Dean has changed!' he says. 'What do they put in the water here? And Raiders won, did they? I thought the team had never won anything before.'

'They hadn't,' I say triumphantly. 'Not until Dean came along. He's doing brilliantly now. I just hope they appreciate him.' More than anything I hope they carry on paying him.

'I've made some friends here,' I say, and I tell Simon all about Sian, Poppy and Macey. 'And a great male friend, too,' I add. 'His name's Jamie. He's so cool. You'll love him.'

'Seen anyone else?' asks Simon.

'I've met loads of new people, but those guys are the ones I'm friendliest with,' I explain.

'So you haven't met up with your dad yet?'

'No,' I say, and I feel my stomach twist and turn itself into a huge knot at the thought. 'Come on,' I say to Simon as I grab my keys. 'It's about time I showed you the *very* best thing about living in LA.'

1 p.m.

'Not far now,' I tell Simon. 'We'll be there any minute. Are you excited?'

'Nope,' he replies.

'What's the matter? Are you ill or something?'

'Nope. I just don't understand what could be so exciting about going to sit outside someone's house.'

'Someone's house? This is not someone's house – this is the Beckhams' house.'

'It's still just a house.'

'Simon, Simon, Simon,' I say, boiling over with frustration. 'Everything associated with the Beckhams is wonderful, special and gorgeous and . . . ooooo . . . here it is. That's it, there. Do you recognize it?'

'No. Why would I recognize it?'

'Because it's been in all the glossy magazines and it was featured on *That's My Crib*.'

Simon's silent. It's clearer than ever that his narrow reading and viewing habits are depriving him of valuable information about the world's most important people.

'Do you never think to yourself, "I know, I'll stop being a complete tosser who reads nothing but the bloody *Guardian*, and I'll read something that's interesting instead, so that I can talk to people and contribute something when I'm out in public"?'

'Nope,' he says. 'I'm quite happy being a complete tosser, thank you very much. Anyway, you and I are different creatures. We should celebrate the diversity, not try to make ourselves the same –'

'Duuuuuuuuuccccckk!!!!!!' I scream as I throw myself down into the footwell and cover my face with my hands. The security officer standing outside the house is walking over to the car. Holy fuck.

'What?' asks Simon, crouching down, but it's too late.

'Hi, everything OK?' asks the officer.

'Fine,' I say, lifting my head and smiling inanely.

'Do you want to come in now? I can open the gates.'

'No, we're –' Simon begins, but I'm straight in there before he can turn down the greatest offer since the half-price jewellery sale at Cricket.

'Yes. We're ready. We'd love to come in,' I say.

'Just drive straight through the gates, you'll come to a barrier that will be lifted, then go straight out to the back. You know where to go after that, don't you? You've been before, right?'

'Yes, all fine,' I say, reversing and swinging the car round for the fastest three-point turn in the history of motor cars. The barrier lifts and I glide through as quickly as I can in case he changes his mind.

'This is madness,' says Simon. 'He clearly thinks we're someone else.'

'No, Simon, this is fucking brilliant. It's the chance of a lifetime. I think I'm going to cry with happiness. Now please don't speak any more, you're ruining the moment for me.'

I drive past the house and notice caramel-coloured blinds. I'm going to get some of those tomorrow. There's a cream vase with beautiful white flowers in it. I'm getting some of those tomorrow. There's a small garage on the right, and there are children's bikes and go-karts outside it.

'Look!' I squeal. 'Bikes belonging to the baby Beckhams. I think I'm going to faint. I can't believe this is happening.'

I continue past the garage to a wall with a door in it.

'Shall I park here?' I ask Simon.

'I think we should just leave right now before we get arrested,' he says.

'I'm not leaving. Let them arrest me. I don't care.'

'Oh Lord,' says Simon, dropping his face into his hands. 'I should be at home in my nice little house reading my books and writing articles. I shouldn't be entering the house of two of the most famous people in the world, uninvited. There are laws against this, you know, especially in LA where there are so many celebrities. Do you know how many people get arrested every year for breaking into the homes of celebrities?'

'Nope. Do you?' I say, as I get out of the car and walk over to the door.

'I don't know the exact number, but I bet it's a lot,' he says. He hasn't moved from his seat

'Hurry up, you might miss something.'

'Does it not bother you that you're trespassing?' he says, finally getting out of the car and walking over to me with all the enthusiasm of a teenage boy being taken to a pottery museum for the day. 'I don't want to do this,' he mumbles. 'Can't I stay in the car?'

'How does this gate open then?' I ask, as I push and pull and shake it vigorously. I'm going in whether the gate's open or not. 'If it won't budge I'll just have to climb over.'

'No!!' says Simon, lifting a simple latch on the top of the door and swinging it open for me.

Holy fuck . . . it's the Beckhams' garden.

Before us sits an utterly immaculate lawn with a big rectangular pool lying longways at the bottom. There are stepping stones through the lawn to the pool, and at the top of the garden, next to the house, there's a lovely terrace with a big table and chairs. Down both sides of the lawn there are flowers growing. Every flower is in white or cream.

'I've never seen anything so beautiful,' I sigh.

'Right, now you've seen their garden, we should go,' he says.

Is he out of his fucking mind?

'Do you think the windows are locked?' I ask.

'No, no, no, no, no,' he says. 'We are not breaking into their house. We're going home now.'

As we stand there, in complete disagreement about

whether it's OK to smash your way into a celebrity's house if you really love that celebrity dearly, a female voice calls out to us.

'Hi there, come in,' says a middle-aged woman with short dark hair. She's dressed in terrible scruffy sports clothes that don't do anything for her figure.

'Hi,' I say, wandering into the garden to shake hands with her.

'You two didn't come last time, did you?'

'No,' I say. I figure that if I keep the answers short I won't mess up and get chucked out.

'Well, it's all fairly straightforward. The equipment's by the side of the pool. It needs to be cleaned out, the water changed, filters changed – all the usual stuff. They like a tiny splash of blue dye in the water at the end, so it looks like the sea.'

'No problem,' I say, and I can feel Simon's elbow digging into my ribs as I speak.

'Well, I'll leave you to it,' she says, closing the garden gate behind us. 'I'll be inside cleaning the play room if you need me.'

'I'm sure we'll be fine,' I say, and she walks off towards the house.

'Well, this is bloody wonderful,' says Simon. 'You're not really suggesting that we clean the pool, are you?'

'It can't be that hard.'

'Yes it can be. Neither of us has the first clue what we're doing.'

'Come on. You're intelligent. We must be able to work it out.'

'Great,' he says, mournfully.

Soooo . . . uummmm . . . turns out there are lots of

different solutions and equipment for pool cleaning, and it's not at all clear how you get the water out of the pool.

'There are buckets here,' I say. 'Perhaps we have to just bucket the water out.'

'And put it where?' asks Simon.

'On the grass?'

'But the chemicals will kill the grass.'

'Mmmm, good point. I know – let's just put the chemicals straight in the water, and not worry about throwing that water away. I'm sure it's clean enough.'

'Tracie, we can't do that. We don't know what the chemicals even do.'

Aaagghhh. He can be infuriating sometimes. I read the label on the first bottle but it's no help at all. I don't understand. Maybe if I smell it I'll be able to work out what it is. I unscrew the top and sniff inside. It smells of nothing. 'This stuff's harmless,' I say with great confidence. 'I think we should just chuck it in.'

But Simon's not listening any more. He's gone over to the other side of the pool and is sitting down, in the shade, with his back against the wall. Fuck it. I'm sure it'll be OK. I lift the bottle and tip the entire contents into the water, which immediately starts to turn a deep navy blue colour. The pool looks as if it's full of ink.

'What the hell have you done?' says Simon. 'Why've you thrown all the dye in?'

'I didn't know it was dye.'

By now the colour's so dark that the pool looks like it's full of coal. It's completely black.

'She might like it,' I say, unconvincingly.

'Yeah, right,' says Simon. 'Until she gets in and comes

out dark blue. She won't be so impressed then, will she?'

'No,' I concede. Then I have a great idea. If I bucket a load of the water out, we can refill the pool from the hose, until the blue is lighter. Brilliant!

I begin my task, speeding up with every bucket, until I'm just chucking the water behind me without thought for where it's landing.

'Tracie!' squeals Simon. 'The flowers!'

I look round and the Beckhams' immaculate white floral display is now half blue. The fence at the side is blue and half the grass is blue.

'We'd better get out of here,' says Simon and, despite my absolute desire to stay for the rest of my life, I realize he's right, so he sprints up the garden, with me hobbling behind as my stilettos sink into the lawn with every move. We jump in the car and zoom off towards the barrier.

'Going already?' asks the security officer.

'No, we've forgotten the ZX67 solution,' I say. 'We'll be right back.'

'OK, you guys, see you later,' he says, adding, 'Are your arms OK, lady?'

I look down and see that they're the brightest blue from my fingertips to my elbows.

As we speed out through the gates, a pink car that looks remarkably like mine turns into the road, and as it goes past us I notice the sign on its door. 'Pool People: the best cleaners in LA.'

'Let's fucking hope they are,' I say to Simon, with a chuckle.

To: Mich and Suzzi

From: Tracie Martin

Hi girls, Thanks for all the emails. In answer to your question, Suzzi – er – no! Definitely not. Tell John Cooper thanks for the kind invitation but I won't be able to travel back from LA to present the awards at the Under 7s 5-a-side tournament, and as for refereeing the final, is he insane?

I appreciate that he's been dropped in it since Miss Woolworths (Luton branch) dropped out at the last minute, but I'm sure he'll find someone else. Like he says, the girl who works on the fish counter in Waitrose might do it, if she can get someone to cover her shift. I'm sure he'll be fine.

Now Mich – your news was very exciting. Fancy you finally finding yourself a footballing boyfriend! When you say Arthur used to play football, though – how long ago? I mean, as far as I'm concerned, if he played football, that makes you a Wag, but purists might want to clarify which decade this was in. He sounds a bit old, if you don't mind me saying.

If he was too old to make the World Cup squad in the year that England won, he must be getting on a bit now. I mean, that was 1966. So that's . . . oh God, hang on . . . take away 1966 from 2008. How do you do this? Um . . . I think you take the 19 from the 20 to give a '1' in the hundreds column, then take the 8 away from 66 so that's – shit – 158!!

Mich, how much too old was he in 1966? He must be pushing 190 years old. Can that be right? Wow. Send me a picture for a laugh. I'm dying to have a look at him. Has he got one of those little mobility cars that you can drive on the pavement in? I've always really fancied one. Imagine how lovely you would keep your shoes looking if you never walked anywhere. Ask him if I can have a go when we come back, will you?

Love you both, T x

PS. Am glad Angie has abandoned the African baby adoption plans but I agree that Luton Town would be mad to employ her as their new fitness coach. She'd have them all out on the pitch doing star jumps in Lycra. Her fitness knowledge starts and ends with Jane Fonda. Please tell me it's not going to happen. I hate the idea of her being back in Luton, let alone working for the club.

PPS. Is he really 190 years old? Isn't that, like, really old? Probably the oldest person in the world.

Monday 2 June (19 days to go)

Today is the day that Pask starts at St Benedict's. It's also the day when my housekeeper starts. She's Spanish and is called Alina. Dean thinks this is hysterical and has already nicknamed her Alina the Cleaner. She's been here since 6 a.m. Along with Gareth the driver, Peter the gardener and Mark the DIY man, we're now fully staffed up.

Simon's gone by the time I get out of bed. He said last night that he wants to walk around and take in the sights and sounds of the place so he can make some notes for this novel he's writing, so that must be where he is.

I sit and watch Alina as she helps Paskia to sort out her school bag.

'Mum,' says Pask, 'you know, Simon was checking the paper this morning, and kept mumbling about wanting to be sure that the police weren't looking for bogus, blue-armed pool cleaners. Is he OK, Mum?'

'A bit jet-lagged love. He'll be fine.'

Pask is absolutely insistent that she doesn't want me to go to the school with her. Gareth's going to drive her. 'You'll have a great time, love,' I say, and I know she will. I bet it's like St Trinian's in there when they all get going.

* * *

I'm in the kitchen when Simon finally returns, pink-faced and breathing fast from his exertions.

'You been running?' I ask, accusingly. The last thing I need is someone else sucked into the mad LA-lifestyle thing.

'No, sit down,' he instructs. 'I've got something to tell you.'

I grab my glass and wander over to the sofas.

'I've just been past,' he says. 'Don't tell me off – I just wanted to have a look at where he lives.'

'Again?' I say. But I'm glad that Simon's so impressed that he went back there. 'It's fab, isn't it! Why didn't you say? I'd have come with you. Perhaps we could have knocked on the door to see whether we could get in to meet him.'

'You know where the house is then, do you?'

'Er . . . yes,' I respond. Has he forgotten that it was me who drove him there yesterday?

'And are you going to make an appointment to go and see him?'

'An appointment? Can you make an appointment?'

'Yes. There's an agency that you can go to. They'll contact him on your behalf and even come with you to the first few meetings to smooth things over if you want.'

'Fuck me!' I say, because this is a fantastic idea. I had no idea that there were agencies that would helpfully arrange for you to meet David Beckham.

'How about his wife? What if I say I really want to meet her?'

'I guess that will come in time, Trace. It'll be up to you and your dad to discuss it.'

'My dad? Why would he be interested in me going to see the Beckhams? I've never even met my dad.'

'Sorry, you've completely lost me. I don't understand what the Beckhams have got to do with anything. I was saying that I've just been to see where your father lives. It's only twenty minutes away.'

'My father? Oh. I thought you were talking about David and Victoria.'

'No, Tracie. Your father. I know his name, his address and where he lives.'

Shit. What's Simon doing? He's been here about five minutes and he's meddling in something that's really complicated and difficult for me.

'Can't we just have fun for a few days and spy on the Beckhams and stuff?' I say.

'I think you should go and meet your father.'

'Not yet.'

'Come on, Tracie. It's easy. I've got all the information you need.'

'Easy?' I say. I can't believe what I'm hearing. Does he really believe that it's easy to meet up with the father you've never met before? Does he think that if he waves his magic wand and produces an address then all the problems of growing up without a father are going to magically disappear? 'It's not "easy", Simon. None of this is easy. It may be simple enough to find out where he lives, but for me this is really fucking hard.'

Simon looks as if he's been shot. 'I didn't mean it like that. I'm just trying to help.'

'But you said you thought it was easy. It's not. I can't just turn up there. Meeting up with my father is going to throw my whole life off balance.'

The mere mention of meeting up with my father has hurled me into an almighty panic. It's so terrifying to think that he's just getting on with his life, with no idea that I'm here in LA. What if he doesn't want to meet me? What if we meet up and he doesn't like me? What if Mum was right all along and he takes one look at me and thinks I'm just a pointless waste of space? I couldn't bear that.

'What if he's like Mum? I really can't handle it yet. I've only been here a week, I've only just settled in. I don't want to see him. I want to see Beckham instead. He won't hate me. I know he won't. He'll like me and want to introduce me to Victoria and we'll become such great mates. You know, it's nineteen days till Raiders play them and I haven't even started getting ready.'

'Tracie, there's nothing scary about meeting your dad. If you're worried, there's this agency called Reunited based in LA who will contact him on your behalf, then come with you to meet him. I've spoken to a woman there called Sheila. She sounds lovely. I think you should contact her.'

'I will when I'm ready.'

'No, I think you should contact her today.'

'Haven't you been listening to a word I've been saying about how terrifying all this is for me?'

'Yes, but I'm not talking about meeting your father. I'm saying that, in the first instance, it would be good to meet up with Sheila and talk through how you feel.'

'Later,' I say.

'Do it now,' he insists.

'No,' I say. 'No, I won't do it now because it suits you, Simon. I'll do it when I'm ready and not before. Why is this so difficult for you to understand?'

I don't need a violent kick in the teeth from my dad

when I've been smacked around a boxing ring by my mum for the past thirty-odd years.

Simon's shaking his head, and I've had enough, so I walk away, unable to find the words to properly explain to him what rejection from a parent is like, and how hard it was for me to feel like I was worth something. Mum said Dad hated me. Mum hated me too. I was always alone, all the time, then I met the girls at Luton and I became one of them. I felt part of something. I belonged – at last. And I loved it at Luton. I was a Wag and it was great.

Now, suddenly I'm on the other side of the world and I don't have anyone all over again. Mum's trying to get back in with everyone at Luton again, from what Mich and Suzzi say. It's horrible. I feel isolated from everything and everyone. Dean's doing brilliantly with the team and is totally into this whole LA-lifestyle nonsense. Paskia's gone to her school. And I'm here – on my own. I'm good at covering up my feelings by having a few glasses, putting on the lippy and smiling at everyone, but the truth is that this morning I feel bereft. Simon's chosen the wrong time to bring up the subject of my father. I feel too lost and vulnerable to even contemplate setting myself up for heartache.

I wish Nell were here. She'd know what to do. Nell was Dean's nan, and though she was completely batty and very old lady-ish, she was also one of the wisest people I've ever met; able to slice through a problem with a simplicity and level of common sense that can only come with age. I'd say she was the one person in my life (besides Dean, obviously) who loved me unconditionally. Nell died at the end of last year, at around the same time as I was having all the problems with Mum turning on me and selling stories to the papers. It was heartbreaking. I loved Nell so much it hurts to even think about it. She was like an anchor – always supporting me when I was worried or under pressure. She was the complete opposite to Mum, and I adored her. When she died it left a massive hole in my life, one that I'm not sure I can ever fill. The thought of trying to fill it by forcing myself to go and meet my father before I'm ready feels all wrong. Meeting Dad will have to wait until I'm much stronger, and if Simon doesn't understand that then he's not the man I thought he was.

'I'm popping out for a while,' I tell him, walking out of the door and jumping into my car. He runs after me, and I feel so bad about the way I'm treating him because none of this is Simon's fault – he's just trying to help – but I don't want to have to explain myself any more. I pretend I haven't seen him and I drive round the corner, pull over and wonder what on earth to do next.

'Hi,' says a familiar voice. 'You OK?' Jamie runs over to the car and jumps into the passenger seat. 'You look really sad.'

'No, I'm fine,' I reassure him, but I clearly don't look fine.

'Come on. Let's go for breakfast and tell me all about it. My treat! I'll take you to this lovely little place where the Beckhams always go.'

Thank God I always carry loads and loads of makeup with me.

11 a.m.

This is nice. We're at a lovely, casual, family-run restaurant in West Hollywood and I don't feel half as stressed as I did earlier. Jamie has this ability to calm me down. I have so much makeup on that when we arrived the waiter thought I was the clown who'd come to entertain the children.

'Over there,' he said, pointing to the games area. When I turned to look, three of the children burst into tears and two of them started screaming for their mothers. That's when you know you've got your makeup exactly right.

Unfortunately the Beckhams aren't here. Jamie thinks we might have just missed them, so we sit down, and I tell him all about Simon and the fight we just had.

'You can't be rushed. You need to give yourself time,' he says. 'It's a bit silly of Simon to go off like that and try and push you into doing this.'

'He was just being kind,' I say.

'Oh, sure,' says Jamie. 'I didn't mean to criticize, but perhaps he doesn't understand what it's like for you. He might not be the best person to help you through this if he's going to be too heavy-handed. It was very brave of you to stand up to him. You need to do this in your own way, and in your own time. Just repeat that to yourself, "My way, my time".'

I smile at Jamie.

'Say it,' he insists.

'My way, my time,' I say.

'Louder,' he instructs.

'MY WAY, MY TIME,' I shout, and I have to say that I feel a weight lifting from my shoulders. I won't see Dad until I am ready. I'll do it MY WAY and it'll be in MY TIME. Blimey, Sian would be proud of me. Jamie seems to understand me in a way that Simon doesn't.

'I can't imagine what it must have been like to grow up with a mother who hated you and a father who wasn't there. Have you ever thought of getting therapy or anything?'

'Yeah. I did talk to someone in England, but it never really worked for me.'

'The therapists in LA are fantastic,' says Jamie. 'I went to talk to this woman called Jasmine once and she really helped. I could give you her number if you want.'

I shrug because I don't fancy going through the process again. It's hard enough to talk about the situation with people I know, let alone some stranger who's charging by the hour.

'Alternatively,' says Jamie, 'just talk to me when things are getting you down and I'll do all I can to help.'

'Thanks,' I say. 'Why did you end up having therapy? You don't strike me as someone who has loads of issues and problems to deal with.'

'No, I'm not. I've been lucky. I had both my parents, though Mum died just before Christmas last year and that hit me hard. Really hard.'

He screws his hands together in his lap as he recoils at the memory.

'Losing her was dreadful. I kind of lost Dad at the same time because he was never the same again. He's still mourning her every minute of every day. He hardly leaves the house. I go round a lot and see him, but it's as if the spark's gone from him. You know? It's like he's sitting there, waiting to die, so he can be with Mum again.'

I feel a tear escaping from my eye and begin to roll down my cheek.

'That's so sad,' I say. 'What was her name?'

'Nancy,' he says, with a smile to himself, presumably at the memory of the happy times they shared. 'I know this is going to sound terrible, but I've almost got to the stage of wanting him to die, just so he can be with Mum and be happy again. Nothing on earth, without her, is going to make him smile. She was everything to him. To me, as well.'

There's a silence between us when he finishes talking, but it's a comfortable one. We're both lost in our own thoughts.

'I lost someone special just before Christmas, too,' I tell him. 'Dean's nan Nell. She and I were so close. She was the only adult who'd ever loved and respected me and treated me properly. I used to tell her everything. Everything. Losing her was horrific.'

'Tell me about her,' says Jamie, and before I can stop myself I've launched into the stories that still make me laugh. I tell him about how I'd take Nell and her two little mates called Gladys and Ethel to the crematorium and they'd run around, putting flowers on all the graves and talking to fallen friends.

'She always said that she knew more people in there than she did in the living world,' I explain. 'When I get sad I think about that, and I decide that she's happy now – with all those people she thought so dearly of. She's with her husband Tom, and they're having a lovely time, catching up on life and wandering around Heaven together, meeting up with old friends.'

I pause and look at Jamie. His eyes have filled.

'Perhaps she's made friends with your mum,' I say. 'Wouldn't that be lovely?'

'It would,' says Jamie, nodding enthusiastically and

smiling properly for the first time. 'What a lovely thought. Gosh, you've really made me happy saying that.'

'Good,' I say, and I must admit I feel cheered by the thought of all these dead people that we love so much, all up there having a laugh. We raise our glasses. 'Nell and Nancy,' I say.

'To Nell and Nancy,' he confirms, and we wrap our little fingers together before knocking our drinks back.

The food arrives, and I push the plate away. I can't remember what I ordered; it's irrelevant when you don't eat. Instead I sit back, drinking champagne and watching Jamie sip his.

'See – I promised I'd be your drinking buddy, didn't I?' he says, when he sees me staring. 'Now, more about Nell. If she was Dean's nan, how did you end up getting to know her so well?'

'I think it was because when I first met Dean I didn't want to burden him with my problems, so I'd sit there with Nell, drinking stuff that was so weak and tepid that it seems inaccurate to call it tea. We'd chat for hours and hours while Dean was training. He played for Arsenal at the time.

'"More sugar?" Nell would ask. As it was, you could barely turn the teaspoon in the cloudy, whiteish liquid because it was packed with sugar.

'"No thanks," I'd say, then I'd tell her everything, and with every word I spoke I'd feel myself becoming more and more unburdened. At the end of it all we'd both have a nice sweet sherry and she'd start mumbling on about the war. You know, the way old people do. Do American old people mumble on about the war when they're drunk?' I ask.

'Oh, yes. And when they're sober, and probably when they're sleeping.'

Then he bites into a large prawn, and as he chews all the muscles in his jaw move like the legs of a sprinter. With every chew they go up and down like pistons and I'm just mesmerized, hypnotized.

'Tracie,' he says. 'Tracie?'

'Er . . . yes. What?'

'Can you hear that? It's a Spice Girls song I think. Is it your phone?'

I rummage around in my handbag, and pull out my mobile. I miss the call, but there's a text from Simon. 'I've made you an appointment with Sheila from Reunited at 8 p.m. tonight,' it says. 'Please will you just go and talk to them. Simon xx'

'OK,' I text back, and I switch off the phone.

7.30 p.m.

I'm not going to the meeting with Reunited tonight. I know everyone thinks I should, but I'm not ready yet. I tried to explain this to Simon but he just went on and on about how important it was, asking me again and again why I didn't want to go, as if he were Jeremy Paxman and I was some wayward government minister hiding the facts about donations to my party's funds. In the end I told him I would go, just to stop him going on and on. Simon then phoned Dean at the club, and when they'd tracked him down to a pilates class on the beach, he told him. Dean was so chuffed he phoned after his Thai massage to say how proud he was of me. Shit. Why can't they all back off a bit? Instead of going to the agency,

I'm going out to a party with Jamie because – get this – the Beckhams will be there! Also, Jamie will be there, and I like talking to him. Now I know about his personal tragedies, I feel closer to him. I know he understands me.

1 a.m.

Oh, dear. No Victoria, and I'm a v sad, v drunk Tracie. Oh, dear. Sshhhhhh . . . must be sshhhh quiet.

I open the door and creep into the house, crashing into the wall twice before stumbling into the kitchen and falling into a heap. Oh, dear.

When I met Jamie at the party he said Victoria had just called to say that she and David couldn't make it. I told him what I'd done – how I'd lied to Dean and Simon and not been to the Reunited agency at all.

'Don't worry,' he told me. 'Stop feeling guilty. This is a hard thing to do – do it on your own terms, and when you feel ready. They'll all understand in the end, but right now you've got to put yourself first. OK?'

'OK,' I said, giving him a big hug, and after that we had an absolutely brilliant night. Not brilliant in the Luton way of things – I mean we didn't get off our trolleys, dance, have fun, laugh, drink some more and get a kebab on the way home, but we did chat a lot, and I got pissed, which was nice. Jamie drank loads, too, though he didn't seem drunk. I have to say that I do love the way all the other women look at me with such envy when I'm out with him.

Now I'm home, and desperate for a drink . . . drink . . . where's the fridge? It's gone. Has someone moved it? Oh, no – there it is. It's dark but I don't want to put on the light in case I wake people up. Ssshhhh . . .

'Tracie?' Dean appears in the kitchen doorway in his Luton pyjamas. He looks all worried.

'Want a drink?' I offer. 'Something to eat for my little Sugar Lump?'

'No, I don't want a drink. You know I don't drink any more, and I don't touch carbs after midday. I want to know where you've been.'

'Out,' I say, because I can't remember the name of the agency woman that I was supposed to be going to see, and I don't even remember the name of the place where the party was held. 'Am I not allowed out any more?'

'Out where?'

'To see a woman about meeting my dad.'

'No you haven't, Tracie. Sheila from Reunited phoned here. She was expecting you but you didn't turn up.'

Fancy ringing on the home number, silly cow. She could have called my mobile.

'So where were you? Why didn't you answer your phone?'

My phone hasn't rung all night. I look at Dean quizzically as I pull it out of my handbag and see that it's switched off. Shit. I have dozens of missed calls. Oh God. They've all been so worried about me. There are messages from Sheila, from Simon telling me he's got us a meeting with an agent called Cindy tomorrow, and loads from Dean, getting increasingly anxious.

'Sorry,' I say.

'Where did you go?'

I can't bring myself to lie to Dean any more.

'I went to a party because I thought the Beckhams would be there, but they weren't. I didn't want to do this whole thing with my dad.'

Then, for some reason, I burst into tears, and Dean

144

holds me tightly while I sob on his shoulder and try to explain that I have to do this in my own time.

'OK, love,' he says. 'I understand, now come to bed. I was just worried about you, that's all. Why don't you come with me tomorrow to Ashtanga? We're going to study the Yoga Sutras of Patanjali.'

'Yeah, I might,' I say. 'Or, alternatively, I might stay at home and eat my own arm. Not sure which thought is the more appealing.'

Tuesday 3 June

Up to the fourth floor we go. Simon and I get into the glass lifts in the marble reception area in 2008 and step out into the 1980s. I swear. Cindy Deloitte's offices are straight out of *Dallas* and her clothing is straight out of *Dynasty*. She has the tiniest little shoulders you could ever imagine, but the biggest shoulder pads. She's the sort of woman that you could trust to get you a good book deal because I can't imagine anyone messing with her. I'm sure her lipstick's made from blood.

You look at her large, large hair and fabulous large earrings and know that she's the sort of person who would bang on newspaper executives' desks and scream, 'My client does not get out of bed for less than three Gucci handbags, a pair of Prada shoes and a Chanel jacket.' In other words, she's just perfect. The name, of course, is the most perfect thing of all. Cindy. Cindy? How great is that. And I know she's successful because she simply wouldn't be able to afford all that hair spray if she wasn't. Those flicks at the side of her head must have set her back three cans a go.

'Hi, I'm Tracie,' I say. 'This is Simon.'

'Well fuck me,' she replies. 'Look at you.'

I'm glad I made the effort now, as I always am. Getting into the gold, crinkly puffball dress with its matching long gold socks wasn't easy, but worth every minute, as was the time I spent liberally covering myself in glitter.

'Everyone in this town will have heard of you by the time I've finished,' she says.

'I'd like to write a column that genuinely helps Wags abroad to come to terms with what life's like for them,' I say. 'And to help women who don't have the great fortune to live in Luton to understand how to look and dress like a proper Wag. By proper, I mean an English Wag, and by English, I mean Luton.'

She looks slightly bamboozled but she takes it in her stride. Anyway, Simon's there to step in and talk right over me when the meeting needs it. I'm chatting on about feeling like an angel breathing Wag-dust down upon the world, and he's saying, 'What Tracie means is . . .' as if I'm a fifteen year old up for looting, being prevented from hanging myself in front of the police by a wise old solicitor.

'Tracie means that she's an expert in this area, and that I'm a writing expert, and that jointly we feel capable of producing a series of columns that will be funny, illuminating and entertaining. If you look through this cuttings file, and this manuscript of the first book we did, I think you'll understand what we're talking about.'

See. He's so cool. Pity he goes on so much about my father at the moment.

'Give me a few examples of the sort of thing you're thinking of,' she says.

'Ummm . . .' I say, so she thrusts a piece of paper in my hand.

147

'Jot something down there – some advice you'd give wannabe Wags in LA. I've got to go and find someone who knows my home phone number – I can't for the life of me remember it. You write that while I'm away. Make it good.'

'I don't want to do this,' I say to Simon. 'This is no fun at all now.'

'Let's just do it,' he says, grabbing the pen. He's been aggressive with me all morning just because I missed his stupid meeting with stupid Reunited last night. 'Come on. Think – just a couple of pieces of advice. Think of the sort of questions people always ask you.'

'Mmmm . . .'

Five minutes later the door swings open and Cindy comes striding back into the room, demanding to know what we've got. I push the piece of paper over the table to her and watch as she reads my advice.

How should I do my makeup if I want to be a Wag?
The first thing to remember is that you should ALWAYS wear makeup. In fact, it would be accurate to say that the makeup should wear you. Every Wag should be so heavily made up that her colossally mascaraed false eyelashes enter the room up to five minutes before the rest of her. You should be coated in the stuff – it should be dripping off you and sliding down your face. You should leave orangey-brown streaks on any towel you use, and anything you touch, wear or hold. When you wash your hands after applying your makeup, the water should run like cocoa off your fingers for a good twenty minutes. The collars of everything you wear will be stained as surely as if you had applied a liberal layer of Cuprinol to them.

Wags love makeup more than anything. You can never wear too much. It is easy to make the mistake of wearing too little.

How do I know which shoes to buy if I want to look like a Wag?
The basic rule is to look for shoes that would not look out of place on a lap-dancer. Perspex platforms are ideal. White is great. Expensive patent white leather is perfect, especially the stuff that sits tightly on the skin and combines being extraordinarily expensive with looking violently cheap. Bling is good too – the more the better.

You should take your lead when choosing shoes – as in so many respects when it comes to Wag dressing – from the likes of former soap stars and singers like Jennifer Ellison, Kerry Katona and Daniella Westbrook.

'Um, well . . .,' she says enigmatically, before revealing that it's not quite what she expected. 'They liked all this stuff in the UK, did they? Beats me. Well, let's give it a go then.'

She starts mumbling on about the sort of people she'll probably contact on my behalf, but I get totally distracted when my phone bleeps and I can't help looking at it.

'Hi. Hope u r feeling OK. Will arrange dinner with V&D soon. Let me know when u r free 4 us 2 go and get pissed. Jx.'

'Is that something you'd like to share?' asks Cindy, as though I'm a ten year old who's been caught passing a note in class.

'No,' I say, with surprising assertiveness. 'Do you need anything else from us?'

I have to get out of there, have to call Jamie. Dinner with the Beckhams is at stake, as is a night on the lash with the only man in LA who seems to drink any more.

'I don't think so,' she says, clicking her fingers for some poor minion to arrive and show us out of the building. 'I'll make a few calls and get back to you guys on Friday. I'll talk to newspapers and magazines. The *LA Star* might be good. Any questions?'

'Yes,' I say. If I'm going to be having dinner with the Beckhams, I need to sort myself out. I can't risk going there and being mistaken for a transvestite, can I? 'Who's the best cosmetic surgeon in LA?'

'Oh,' she laughs. 'That's easy. You need to go and see Dr Johns. Here, I'll write his number down.'

As she scribbles a number on a piece of paper, without having to look it up, I feel a whole new respect for this woman. Fancy knowing the cosmetic surgeon's number off by heart when you don't know your own phone number. Respect, lady. Big respect!

Simon and I get back into the lift and he turns to face me. 'So where were you last night?'

'Actually Simon, I was out at a party. Is it any of your business?'

'Yes, Tracie, it's my business when I go out of my way to locate your father for you, to find an agency that will help you to meet him, and to fix up a meeting with them, for you to then decide not to turn up. That's not to mention how concerned Dean was about you. He'd just had his chakras balanced and they were all thrown out of line again with the worry of it all.'

'I just couldn't face it.'

'And rather than tell me that, you went to a party?'

'Yes, because I can't tell you, Simon, because you're just not listening. I need you to stop going on about my father. I can't do this on your terms or because you think it's the right thing. I have to do it when I'm ready.'

'You're making no sense, Tracie,' says Simon. 'No sense at all.'

Why is he making me justify myself to him? He's supposed to be my friend. Christ, I've been looking forward to seeing Simon for weeks and now he's turned up and gone on and on and on at me.

'If it doesn't make sense it's because you don't understand what I'm going through. Stop trying to push me all the time. Just leave me alone.'

'OK then, I will,' he says. 'You won't hear another word out of me. I'll go down the club and have a look at what Dean's doing.'

2 p.m.

To: Mich and Suzzi

From: Tracie

Yes, sorry about that – adding up and taking away aren't exactly my greatest strengths. I'm glad Arthur's only 82 and not 190. That's obviously much better but it still seems old so I'm wondering whether he does actually have one of those drive-anywhere mobility cars, because I'd really like a go in it, if he doesn't mind.

T x

PS. Fuck, fuck, fuck. I can't believe Angie's been appointed fitness instructor at Luton Town. What did she have to do to get that job?

Wednesday 4 June (17 days to go)
11 a.m.

The street before me is long and wide, with a row of immaculate gardens leading towards modern-looking houses in shades of cream and white. There are no huge bubblegum pink cars behind ornate gates here, no statues or pink marble furniture in the gardens, not even fancy house names or rhinestone-encrusted front-door bells.

The houses are large without being ostentatious, which seems a shame. If you're going to spend the money getting a nice pad, you might as well do it up properly. I got Mark to paint our gates pink yesterday and put fairy lights all over them. They look beautiful – like the gates leading to a Barbie palace. But there are no such little personal touches here.

One thing that is nice, though, is the fact that so many of the houses don't have fences or gates at all, and they have only short paths leading up to the front doors, so people don't seem quite so locked away in their own little worlds as they do on my road. It lends this place a community air that I find strangely and unexpectedly attractive. It's the sort of place where children play in the streets, and the cars slow down for the driver to wave affectionately as he passes. In my area, the sunglasses-wearing drivers would speed up and try to hit the children as they played.

'OK?' says Sheila, as we stand there.

I went to see Sheila last night in the end. It was the oddest thing, but when I received that email yesterday from Mich and Suzzi saying that Mum's now working at Luton Town, it made me start thinking about her and Dad and everything. I picked up the phone and dialled the last mobile number I had for Mum. It rang and I heard my mother's high-pitched voice bursting through the airwaves. 'Angie here.'

'Mum, it's me,' I said.

Silence.

'Can you hear me?'

I could almost hear the silence, it was so loaded with hatred. She said nothing, nothing at all.

'Talk to me,' I begged. 'I'm going to go and see Dad. I want to talk to you about everything.'

The phone went dead then. She wouldn't say a word to me.

I rolled over onto my back and let the tears slip across my face and down my neck. Not one single word. So, what now? Continue to try and convince my mum to talk to me, while shutting my dad out of my life because of fear? Or take a step towards trying to develop a relationship? In the end, it wasn't Simon's nagging or even my own curiosity that had me picking up the phone to Sheila, but Mum's coldness.

'I need your help,' I told Sheila, through pitiful sobs. 'Can you help me? I'd like to meet my father.'

Sheila was extraordinarily kind and helpful. When she approached my father he was desperate to meet me. So that's what we're doing. Sheila and I are standing here and she's preparing me for the first step on one of the most complex journeys of my life. We're entirely inconspicuous on this street except for the fact that I'm wearing a short, white, plastic mini-skirt, long patent boots in a deep raspberry colour, a white sequinned boob tube and white-framed sunglasses. No one else seems to be dressed like me, but as my time in LA stretches into its second week I'm learning that this will always be the case when it comes to fashion. I am truly a trailblazer.

Sheila is dressed elegantly and discreetly, and has an aura of calm about her. She's the sort of woman who looks as if she's got her life completely under control. I bet she's never shown her gusset at the football or been mistaken for a transvestite. I bet she doesn't shriek and dance on tables at parties. She probably doesn't drink. She looks as if she glides around, dispensing wise words and calm thoughts. Her gentleness and serenity are reflected in her outfit, and for the first time in my life I am jealous of its simplicity. Her clothing gives her the sort of anonymity that I find myself yearning for right now.

I'm the woman who gets every party started and encourages everyone to drink and have fun. I love to be seen. I'm proud of who I am, but right now I'm thinking that it would be much nicer to feel proud a little more quietly, and without the driver of every car that passes screeching to a halt and staring unashamedly.

'I don't think I can do this,' I say, sweeping my hand in front of me. We parked at the end of the road because Sheila felt that the walk down would calm my nerves. The woman clearly knows nothing about walking in six-inch heels, because there is absolutely nothing nerve-calming about it, I can tell you. Every step has been utterly stressful and now we're standing here and I know his house is a few doors away. The man I've wanted to meet all my life is waiting for me, and all I want to do is run for the hills.

'There's no rush. We'll go to see him in your own time,' says Sheila, kindly. I'm so glad she's here. I know I wouldn't have come this far without her. The trouble is, I feel stuck, rooted to the spot. If I don't go in and see my father, nothing bad will happen. Life will carry on as usual. I'll still be surrounded by friends who care, and most importantly, I'll still have Paskia-Rose and Dean. If I go in and see him, so much could go wrong. My whole world could come crashing down. He could be as nasty and deceitful as Mum. He might lie to me, sponge off me and talk about me behind my back. I couldn't bear to be let down by him as I have been by Mum. What sort of person would I be if *both* my parents hated me?

I keep thinking of all the things that Mum told me about Dad: about how much he loathed me, how awful he thought I was, and how much he resented the fact that he had a daughter. In other words, how he wished he'd never had me.

'Shall we walk towards the house?' asks Sheila, and I feel my feet moving along even as my mind, my spirit and everything else about me is desperate not to get any closer. I'm trembling. I've never felt so scared.

'There's no need to stay any longer than you want to. You can change your mind and leave at any time,' says Sheila.

'I think I want to change my mind,' I say. But I don't even know whether that's true. What I want is to protect myself from harm. But as we're standing there, and I'm shuffling from pink PVC-clad foot to pink PVC-clad foot and rubbing my fingertips together anxiously, the door opens to reveal a chunky middle-aged man. He doesn't look like the LA type I was expecting at all. He looks more like a retired history lecturer than the long-lost father of a Wag. He has a beard and hair that is not curly and not straight – kind of wiry, but worn short on his head where it sits in no particular style. I bet his wife cuts it for him. He walks out towards us with his hands pushed deep down into his pockets, and smiles nervously.

'Hey,' he says.

If I were in a great romantic movie – like the kind they make in this city – I'd go 'Daddy!' and rush into his arms, but it's not like that at all. I just feel really scared and awkward. I look at Sheila for guidance and she moves closer to me. It's a tiny movement but designed to illustrate that she's there for me, and it works. I feel reassured and protected.

'Raiders play Galaxy in seventeen days and Victoria's coming to watch,' I hear myself mumble. Shit. What did I say that for?

'How interesting. You must tell me all about it. Shall we go inside?' says the man – *Dad* – and in we go. As I walk past him I notice that he's rubbing his fingertips together, just like I do when I'm scared. I give him a little smile and as his eyes light up I suddenly realize that he's as nervous as me, and that my small gesture has reassured him immeasurably. All I can think from that second onwards is 'Please like me, please like me.'

The truth is that we're not going to be running along

a sunlit path towards one another, but slowly edging along a tightrope, both worried about messing up and falling off, both terrified about how painful the fall could be, and both thinking deep within ourselves that we really didn't have to walk along this tightrope, so why did we?

Inside, the house is very homely, very English somehow. It's not ultra-modern like my house. It doesn't sparkle and dazzle, but it's clean, comfortable and has that feeling of a well-loved home. The sofas are soft and squishy, and as I sit down and feel my skirt riding up to somewhere near my belly button it takes a serious amount of correction, using leg muscles that haven't been taxed for over a decade, to stop myself from flashing my father. Even I know that wouldn't be the done thing.

A woman in her mid to late fifties comes in and shakes my hand. She turns awkwardly on high heels that she's clearly not used to wearing, and apologizes to Sheila.

'I know I'm not supposed to be here,' she says, then she looks at me. 'I just wanted to say that I'm so glad you got in touch. Keith has been desperate to see you, to know that you're all right. Thank you for making the effort. We tried so hard to find you, but with no luck.'

Sheila looks at me. 'Are you OK with this?' she asks. It was supposed to be just me, my father and Sheila, but my father's wife (My stepmother? What a thought!) is now exuding such a feeling of warmth and generosity that I find myself feeling glad she's here. Her relaxed and affectionate manner is like Sheila's and is a vast contrast to the rather awkward, prickly feeling emanating from me and the man who is my father.

'It's fine,' I say, looking up at her and smiling. She smiles back, revealing lipstick on her teeth. Her shimmering blue eye shadow is so badly applied that on one eye it extends up into her eyebrow, and on the other it stays within the creases and folds of her eyelid. This woman's clearly not a natural with the foam applicators. Nice that she's made the effort, though.

'Lady Grey tea?' she asks.

She clearly doesn't know me very well. 'Do you have anything stronger?'

'Of course. Earl Grey?'

'Um . . . anything alcoholic?'

The woman looks a bit worried. 'Do we, dear?' she asks Keith. 'Or shall I go and buy some?'

Keith excuses himself and heads off in search of booze, and Sheila touches my arm lightly. 'It might not be a good idea to drink,' she says.

I, on the other hand, think it would be a very good idea to drink. The very thought of sitting here for an hour not drinking seems to me to be by far the most ludicrous suggestion ever.

'I need one,' I say. 'I am the sort of woman who needs a quick tipple by this time of the day at the best of times, and this, I'm afraid, is not the best of times.'

'OK,' says Sheila, and to her credit she winks and says, 'You're doing really, really well, Tracie. I know this is hard. You're a star. Well done.'

I'm not big on words. People say my columns are funny and make them feel nice, but I've always been more into appearances than words. But those words . . . well, I guess they made me feel as good as any Fendi mini-skirt ever has.

Keith – I still can't imagine ever calling him Dad – comes back into the room clutching a bottle of vintage champagne.

'We've got some put by for a special occasion,' he says, wrinkling his nose a little in a way that reminds me so much of Paskia. It's then that I realize the magnitude of what I'm doing. He's not just my father, he's Paskia's grandfather and Dean's father-in-law.

I glance at the label and smile. It's Pol Roger, Simon's favourite champagne. He says that Winston Churchill drank it. A wave of guilt washes over me. I wish I'd told Simon I was coming, he'd have been so pleased that I was taking this step, but I couldn't handle the pressure and endless questions from him. In the end I thought it would be better for me to sneak off and see Dad for the first time without the whole world knowing about it.

'I don't think occasions get any better than this,' says Keith with a tear in his eye. It's almost too much for me to bear.

'I wish we'd met years ago,' I blurt out, as the tear escapes and runs slowly down my father's ageing, rugged face. 'I wish you'd been there when I was growing up, to catch me when I fell over, and to teach me to ride a bike. I never learnt to ride a bike, you know. I really wanted to but Mum wouldn't teach me. She said she didn't have time. All the other children played on their bikes and I just sat and watched them. I really, really wanted a bike. A pink one – with a bell on it, just like Sharron Webster had. I used to dream about that bike every night.'

6 p.m.

I'm armed and dangerous when Pask comes home from school. She walks through the door, takes one look at me brandishing cooking utensils, and gasps. There's a flicker of terror in her little eyes.

'What are you doing?' she asks.

'I'm preparing supper,' I say brightly, and I see her eyebrows rise and her expectations fall. 'It'll be lovely. Don't worry. I know what I'm doing.'

Actually, that last statement's an out-and-out lie, but I got back from Dad's feeling rejuvenated, happy and ready to take on the world. I wanted to do something domesticated and life-enhancing. Cooking was the only thing I could think of, and since the last time I did any cooking I nearly burnt down the kitchen I decided to prepare a barbecue instead.

'I didn't know we had a barbecue,' says Paskia.

'Aha!' I say. 'I adapted the drinking fountain.'

'Oh God,' she says, running through the house and out into the smoke-filled garden.

There's a huge fire raging in the drinking fountain and various meats forming a small mountain on the table.

'You know you have to wait for the flames to go down, don't you?' she says.

'Yes,' I lie. 'Now come and tell me all about school.'

'It's brilliant,' says Paskia, smiling as she speaks. 'The football standard is excellent and the teachers seem lovely. I could do all the work really easily. I think I was one of the best.'

'Great,' I say. 'What about friends? Did you meet any nice girls to play with?'

'Yes, I did,' she enthuses. 'There are these three girls – they're not in my class but I met them at break time and they're so cool. I really like them.'

'That's wonderful, darling,' I say, and it is, because

161

I know exactly which three girls she's talking about. This is brilliant news. Absolutely brilliant. They'll bring Paskia-Rose out of her shell, I know they will. It'll be the best thing ever to happen to her.

'Why don't you invite them over on Friday night?' I say. It's the one night of the week when she gets home at 3.30 p.m. because she doesn't have late football training. 'We'll have a little tea party and I'll drive them all home afterwards.'

'Can I, Mum?' asks Pask. I'm usually a bit funny about her bringing friends home because of those bloody lesbian footballer types she used to hang around with in Luton. I banned them all from the house.

'Of course you can, hon. Let me just check, though – they're not footballers are they?'

'No!' she squeals, with a little giggle. 'I can't think of anything funnier than them playing football. They keep saying that Sunday mornings were not designed for kicking a ball around.'

'Absolutely right,' I say, thinking of Sunday mornings when I was twelve – I'd be lying in bed, clutching my head after a night drinking Merrydown cider in the parks of Luton. 'Abso-bloody-lutely right.'

7 p.m.

Alina's in the kitchen making supper and Mark's in the garden repairing the drinking fountain. Oh, dear. Things didn't really go according to plan on the barbecue front. Paskia thinks it's because I didn't use any charcoal. I just put firelighters in there and it kind of burned and burned until the thing became so hot that it started to come away from the wall. That's when Gareth piled in with the fire extinguisher and I realized we weren't having barbecued sausages for tea after all.

Luckily Alina's a brilliant cook. I knew she would be as soon as I laid eyes on her. She's such a matronly-looking woman with an alarmingly large bottom that seems to overlap at her sides and make her round and cuddly all over, like one of those Russian dolls that goes inside another Russian doll, then another one goes on top. Well, Alina looks like the big one that goes on the outside. It looks as if she's got a bean bag shoved down the back of her skirt. She has light brown hair that's greying at the temples and she has a soft, round face that looks as if it's been moulded from uncooked pastry. I bet she was pretty when she was younger, but her features have all but disappeared into her puffy face now, all except her eyes which remain lovely. They're a deep, dark brown, like chocolate. Only a good person could have such rich, expressive, soulful eyes. She'd look miles better if she made them up properly, of course.

Simon's been at the club with Dean all day. I know he's there mainly to get away from me because I was so horrible to him when he went on and on about Dad.

I feel a frisson of guilt that I haven't told either Simon or Dean about my exploits today, but I also feel that no one can understand what it was like growing up with a mother like Angie, whose sole aim was to look good and attract men. No matter how much I tell them about my childhood they won't truly understand. No one who hasn't been there can know what it's like when you grow up believing that both of your parents hate you. Most kids grow up knowing, if they know nothing else, that there'll be someone there for them. I grew up dreading the nights when Mum would go out and leave me in the house on my own. I grew up feeling unwanted and uncared for. My father had left and had no desire to get to know me, and Mum told me on a daily basis what a burden I was to her and how much she wished she'd never had me. Looking back, I don't know how I had the self-confidence to go out with someone like Dean who was a young football star when I met him. He came into the hairdresser where I was working wanting to get his ear pierced, and after a few mechanical problems with the gun which created a hole in his ear big enough for a pencil to go through, we bonded while sitting in grey plastic seats in accident and emergency. We've been together ever since.

It's around ten past seven when I hear Simon and Dean approaching, chatting together in a way that I'd never thought I'd hear. It's what I'd love to have seen when we lived in Luton, but now it's happening I have to confess that I feel a little excluded. Dean's like a new man since we came to live here. He's much less blokeish, if you know what I mean. He's started reading stuff and watching what's going on in the world. He never much liked Simon before because Simon's too gay (generally speaking, if someone does not play football, spit in public or do that thing when you snort out through one nostril while holding the other, then you are gay). Now, though – now they're best buddies.

As they walk into the room Simon's laughing and telling Deany about an opera singer whose angelic voice is so beguiling, so light and delicate that it floats across to you, then passes through you like liquid, making the hairs on the back of your neck stand up. Or something like that.

'Yeah, mate. I know what you mean,' Dean is saying, enthusiastically. 'Not with the opera singer, but with some footballers. They're so talented, they make you go all goose-pimply when you see them play.'

'The question is, Can you teach that? And if not, how do you find it, improve it, channel it and make it work for you?'

'I do think you can coach it,' Dean says thoughtfully.

'Mmmm,' Simon says, taking the fruit juice offered by Dean and plonking himself down next to his new best mate on the high stools surrounding the 'island' in the middle of our kitchen. 'You know, there are some great books on leadership and management – nothing to do with football at all, but it would be interesting to see whether the lessons contained in them are worth learning. I'll go to the library tomorrow morning and get Dale Carnegie's book out, perhaps *Good to Great* by Jim Collins as well. I think you'd find that useful.'

'Cool. Library. Yeah, mate. Good idea. Thanks.'

Now I know the world's gone completely stark, staring mad.

'Anyone going to talk to me today?' I ask, looking up from my position on the squashy sofa where I've disappeared into the cushions so completely that clearly no one can see me at all.

'Sweetheart. What are you doing there?' says Dean, leaping up and coming over to give me a hug.

'Having a lie down. Stressful day!' I say.

'Oh, dear,' says Dean, turning to face Simon. 'That sounds expensive.'

I told him I was going shopping. Happily, Dean would never in a million years ask me what I bought. Instead he gets me a glass of champagne and I sit, flicking through a magazine without reading it, while the men continue to debate the merits of business leaders I've never heard of.

As I flick, I'm not concentrating on Britney's latest meltdown or looking at the pictures of Katie Holmes, I'm lost in thoughts about my father, and how difficult it's going to be to tell these two about what I really did today. To tell them will involve too much explaining and justifying of myself. No, I'll tell Dean when I'm ready. He's got enough on his plate right now, in any case.

'Just going up for a bath,' I say. Dean tops up my glass and gives me an affectionate kiss on the head.

'OK, love,' he mumbles – his mouth full of vitamin supplements. He returns quickly to Simon, and to the most important issue of the day. 'So, as a coach, should I be concentrating on individuals and making them better, or working on the team as a whole?'

'The difficult thing for you,' says Simon, with a scratch of his beard, 'is that it's about both. Dean, this is fascinating, isn't it? I think I'm going to base my novel in the world of top-level sport.'

'Great idea,' says Dean with a smile.

Christ, I think I preferred those two when they didn't get on.

Upstairs, with the bath running to lend credence to my story, I lie on the bed talking to Jamie. He texted four times to see if I was OK, and to reiterate that if I needed anything at all just to call him.

So, while foam gathers under the hot tap and my

husband chatters about the management strategies pertinent to success in American soccer, I'm pouring my heart out to Jamie.

'Tell me everything,' he says, kindly. 'There's no rush. I've got all the time in the world. Just relax and tell me all about it. I'll meet you if you want to have a few drinks. Would you like that? I'm your big drinking mate now, aren't I?'

I decide it would be way too complicated to meet him, so I unburden myself to him on the phone instead, and he listens quietly.

'I ended up blurting out all this tosh about how much I wanted a pink bike when I was a little girl, and how no one was ever there to teach me how to ride a bike,' I say. 'I just wanted him to know how much I desperately missed him, and how wrong it was for him not to be there when I was growing up. I needed him to know that what Mum did took away so much of my childhood.'

Jamie is silent on the other end of the phone, so I carry on.

'Do you think that was a bit too over-emotional of me? You know – with it being the first meeting?'

It's still silent.

'Jamie, are you there?'

'I am,' he says quietly, sniffling.

'Are you OK?'

'I'm fine, sorry,' he says, composing himself. 'That was so moving. I'm really sorry. Let me just get a tissue.'

'I'm seeing him again next week,' I say.

'Tell me if you want me to come with you,' says Jamie. 'You know, if you're worried about things getting too intense.'

'Let me think about it,' I reply, with unusual restraint.

I'm the sort of person to go piling in with 'Yes please, do come', but it's different with this. My relationship with my dad is something I'm desperate to make work now we've both taken the first step. And I need to do it alone.

'Talk to you in the morning,' I say, and we do this thing we've started doing where we touch our fingers to the phone, as if our fingers are making contact down the phone line. 'Nell and Nancy,' we say, in honour of our departed relatives. 'Rest in Peace.' I find it so comforting talking to Jamie. He's just wonderful. By 9 p.m. I'm fast asleep, mentally drained and sober!! My first sober night since I arrived in this city.

Thursday 5 June (16 days to go)

I may not have the 'Go get 'em, running along the beach and taking forty-eight supplements a day' mentality that some LA women have, and I'm certainly not part of their bizarre teetotal club, but in one respect I am an LA girl at heart, because today I am visiting Dr Johns, Hollywood's most celebrated cosmetic surgeon. His surgery is at the International Beverly Hills Beauty Clinic. Fucking hell! You don't have to read *Hello* for very long to realize that the IBHB Clinic is where everyone who's anyone has their essential repair work done.

'Tracie Martin to see Dr Johns,' I say, and not for the first time I wish he had a more exotic-sounding name. I'm struggling to take him seriously. Dr Johns – he sounds like an ageing GP from a small surgery in the Cotswolds, not the man who's going to turn me into an even more fabulous version of myself.

'A new patient. Welcome! I'm Didi,' the lady beams, revealing immaculate teeth – bright, fluorescent white and gleaming so much that I'm temporarily blinded.

'Would you take a seat over there, and fill out this form for me? Dr Johns will be with you right away.'

'Sure,' I say, walking across the polished wooden floor

towards the brown leather armchairs. There's a grand piano in the reception area, with the most magnificent bowl of exotic flowers on top of it, with all these stalks and kind of bamboo things bursting out of the top. The whole thing must be about three feet high. It's quite magnificent, but all I can think of is the time I took Nell out for lunch in this posh hotel, and she'd never been anywhere like it before. There was a piano in the room, and after a couple of sweet sherries she decided to start playing it. Trouble was, she can't play the piano, so she pretty much just bashed away on the keys like a mad woman, while singing in a terrifyingly loud voice. 'It's a long way to Tipperary' has never sounded quite the same again for me, nor I suspect for anyone else in the restaurant that day. We had to leave, of course. At the time I was mortified, but looking back now it's those moments I remember most fondly. God, I miss her. She'd be coming along for a bit of Botox now if she were still here.

Dotted around the room are small wooden coffee tables, each with a large vase of white lilies on it. It gives the place a most wonderful smell. There are also glossy magazines dotted around, but only magazines with white covers, I notice. Do they wait for a white magazine cover, and then display them? What if there's a great copy of a glossy magazine but with a purple cover? Do they display it? No, probably not in this world where appearances are what count most.

It's a lovely sunny room, with rays of light streaming through the windows and skating across the flawless surfaces. On the walls are signed pictures of various film stars who've presumably passed through and been treated by this famous doctor. The only thing that annoys me is the sight of a velvet rope separating a VIP area. Surely one of the main reasons for coming to a surgery like this is to have a look at which famous people are here. What's the point in hiding them away? This seems particularly strange since their pictures are all over the wall.

I need to have a look in the VIP area. Imagine if there's a celebrity in there? Perhaps it's Madonna or the Pussycat Dolls! Maybe that's why the piano's there, just in case they find themselves unable to go on without bashing out a quick rendition of 'Like a Virgin' or 'Doncha' or something.

I stand up and wander nonchalantly past the velvet rope, peering inside in a manner that couldn't really be described as subtle. There's someone there! There's only someone in there!!! I *have* to know who it is. Right, I walk past again but this time lose the nonchalance completely. I'm now standing and staring into the VIP area. It's bloody dark in there, though. What's the use of that? I wish I had a torch or something. The woman in there has bandages round the top of her head and a plaster across her nose.

I lean right over, squinting into the semi-darkness, desperate to take a look. She's not moving or turning away from me, so she can't mind too much.

'Hello. Who are you?' I ask, but there's no reply. I lean forward a bit further. I think I recognize the face from somewhere, but where? Perhaps if I lean over just a little bit mo— ahhhhhhh.

I go tumbling arse over tit over the top of the velvet rope – spinning right round like I'm a performer from the Cirque du Soleil show that Nell took me to see years ago. Unlike the acrobats in that, though, I land flat on my back with my legs in the air. Shit. How am I going to explain this?

'Ma'am, are you OK?' asks Didi, rushing across the slippy floor to me. 'You know you can't go in there, don't you? That's a private area, I'm afraid.'

'Oh, sorry, I didn't realize,' I say, like I hadn't noticed the three-metre-high signs and the bloody great big rope. She guides me back to my seat.

'How are you getting on? Have you filled out the form?'

'No, I'm just about to,' I say.

'Would you like me to help you?'

Does she think I can't write or something? Still, it would be handy if she filled it out instead of me.

'Yes please,' I say, and she takes the piece of paper and begins running through questions about my address, my doctor's name and my contact number.

'Any previous surgery?' she asks.

'Who's that in the VIP area?' I ask.

'Sorry, I can't divulge such information. Previous surgery?'

'I've had my breasts done,' I say. 'Is it Madonna?'

'No, it's not Madonna. So, is that all the surgery?'

'No!' I say. 'I also had a bit of liposuction on my stomach after my baby. Is it the girl out of Pussycat Dolls? You know, the really minxy one?'

'No. Any more surgery?'

'Lipo on my thighs.'

'Anything else?'

'My bum . . . and my arms.'

'Right, is that it?'

'Yes,' I say. 'Unless you count the laser treatments on an Arsenal tattoo that had to be removed when they sacked my Dean – does that count as treatment? It was an emergency. Then there was the nose job, and then the second operation I had on my bust to make it a bit bigger. But that's all. It's one of the women from *Desperate Housewives*, isn't it?'

'No,' she says, turning the page and scribbling frantically. 'Is that it for previous surgery?'

'I had my lips plumped up, too. Does that count as surgery?'

'I'll just write it down, shall I?'

'Yes. OK. Is it one of the women from *Sex and the City*?'

'No.'

I decide to try a change of tack. Perhaps if I befriend her she'll tell me.

'Your teeth are beautiful. Can I ask you where you got them done?'

'Sure you can,' she says, beaming and radiating relief that I've stopped quizzing her. 'It was Mr Johns, Dr Johns's brother. Shall I make you an appointment right now? I have his diary on reception.'

'Er . . . OK,' I say, and before I can draw breath I'm in the diary for shiny white veneers.

'You can come through now,' says a young girl with the most perfect skin I've ever seen. 'My name's Annie.' She's pencil-thin and her hair glosses, glows and gleams as she walks.

'Thank you,' I say, adding, 'You know, that woman in the VIP room – it's Jennifer Aniston, isn't it?'

'There's no one in the VIP room,' says Annie.

'There is,' I insist, dragging poor Annie to the velvet rope and pointing out the woman in there.

'No, that's just a plastic dummy. We use it to show clients what sort of bandaging they can expect when they have a treatment done. Now, come and meet the doctor.'

'Tracie Martin. How lovely to meet you,' says Dr Johns, and again I find that I'm struggling to hide my disappointment. I thought he'd look like a hot doctor from *ER*, but he's wearing glasses, he's skinny and pale and looks like the guy who always got beaten up when he was a boy.

'Hi,' I say.

'Right, take a seat and tell me what I can do for you.'

I dig into my bag and pull out a picture of Victoria. 'I'd like to look like that, please,' I say. 'I need to be much, much thinner and I think my face needs to be smaller. I'm not sure how you'd do that, but you're the expert. I'm sure you know exactly what to do.'

'Right. OK. Well, Tracie. I have to say that you are already a very beautiful woman. I would say that you are much prettier than the lady in this picture.'

'Get away!!' I say.

'No, I'm being serious. You have perfectly symmetrical, high cheekbones and a pretty heart-shaped face. You have lovely big eyes. The lady in this picture is very attractive but she has a narrow face. I couldn't give you the same face shape as her, even if I thought it was a good idea.'

'I thought you were supposed to be a brilliant surgeon!' I say.

'I am,' he replies. 'I'm the best in the business, and part of my success comes from not giving people unreal expectations, not lying to them.'

Lie to me, I think. Just lie to me.

'I need to be thinner,' I say. 'Even if I can't have her face I need to be as thin as her. Everyone in LA is *so* skinny.'

Dr Johns asks me to remove my long boots and my dress and lie on his couch.

'Aren't you even going to buy me a drink first?' I ask, but he's not the sort of man you make jokes with, so I just shut up and do as I'm told.

'Tracie, you are already incredibly thin,' he says. 'I would say you were desperately undernourished. You most certainly do not need to lose weight. I think you could do with putting some on, in fact.'

'Don't be so ridiculous,' I gasp. 'I'm the fattest person in LA.'

'No, you're not, Tracie. This is all in your head. You're one of the thinnest people I've ever seen.'

'Well, can you just do your best to make absolutely sure that I look nothing like a transvestite?'

'You look nothing like a transvestite, Tracie. Nothing at all. What you look like is a very beautiful woman.'

This doctor is crap. But I'm not leaving empty-handed.

'What can you do to make me look better, then? You must be able to do something. I've got a crucial meeting in a few weeks I have to look perfect for it. Lip plumping? Botox?'

He looks at my face, frowns and tells me to smile. 'Raise your eyebrows,' he instructs. 'Now, wrinkle your nose up. Now, I wonder . . .'

'Hi. I'm home!' I shout, walking into the house.

'Hello, Mrs Aaaaaaaaahhhhhhhhhh,' howls Alina. 'Is

terrible. Oh, Mrs Martin. How has happened here? It is terrible. What has happened? Somebody is chewed your face off?'

'What?'

Alina's holding her hands over her face as if the sight of me is too much for her to bear, and she's moving constantly, as if she can't shake the image of me from her mind. Her whole large body rolls in time with her as she moves from foot to foot.

Paskia-Rose comes racing out. 'What is it?' she cries. 'Oh my God. Mum. What happened? Were you in a car crash or something?'

'I'm fine,' I reassure them. 'I just had a bit of work done. It looks a bit sore right now, but it'll calm down and I'll look more beautiful than ever.'

But Paskia's not convinced. She bursts into tears, saying that her friends are coming to tea tomorrow night and I look like something out of a horror film. She's sobbing while Alina looks from her to me and back again and is clearly wondering what on earth she set herself up for when she agreed to be our live-in housekeeper. One thing I find comical about Alina is her permanent look of confusion, regardless of the circumstances. She has every right to look confused now, but she wears this dazed expression even when she opens the fridge to take out the cheese, as if the fridge is quite the most ridiculous place in which to keep it.

'I had no choice!' I try to explain to Dean, when he stares at me as if I've grown three heads. 'I was the only woman in LA who hadn't had her skin resurfaced.'

'Is that what you've had done? Is that what the scabs are? You promised you'd stop having these extreme treatments after the mix-up with the face cream and the hot wax.'

'Yeah,' I say, but all I can think is, scabs? What does he mean, scabs?

'Excuse me,' I say, and I rush out to look in the mirror.

'Aaaaahhhhhhhhhhhh,' I howl. It's like someone has taken a potato peeler to my face. It's red raw, bleeding in parts and forming blisters and scabs on my cheeks. Perhaps I should have left those bandages on after all, but I felt like such a fool so I tore them off in the car. I also had what Dr Johns described as a 'staggering' amount of Botox that will kick in over the next few days, and my lips have been heavily plumped up. I've got my dental appointment tomorrow, so I'm going to look bloody amazing by the time the match comes round. No one will *ever* confuse me with a transvestite again.

I look up again, into the mirror, and see Simon standing behind me.

'Are you OK?' he asks.

'Yeah. This is nothing,' I say.

'Why does someone as lovely as you feel the need to do this to herself?' he asks. He looks desperately upset. 'When will you stop trying to be perfect and realize that we all love you just the way you are, Tracie? I love you, Dean loves you, Paskia loves you. Everyone who meets you loves you. If you took the time to go and see your dad I think you'd realize that he loves you too, whatever your skin looks like. But maybe not today.'

Friday 6 June (15 days to go)

There's a real buzz in the house as soon as I wake up, as there tends to be these days with Dean, still in the throes of excitement after the victory, jumping out of bed, throwing back the curtain and jogging manically on the spot like some sort of deranged cartoon character whose legs turn into spinning wheels when chased by a baddie. Dean slows down and jumps gently on the spot, letting his head fall from side to side as he breathes deeply, in through his nose and sharply out through his mouth, like an athlete preparing for a race or a boxer gearing up for a fight. 'We're gonna win this league,' he says, repeating it over and over to himself. 'Positive thinking, positive thinking.'

He does some sort of bizarre knee bends which he tells me are called squats. His knees crack every time he bends them and I struggle not to smile because if I do my face will really, really hurt.

'What are you doing?' I ask.

'I'm preparing for the day,' comes the reply. 'Getting myself ready to take on the world. Fancy an energy shake for breakfast? I picked up some Gingko berries on the way back last night; if you crush them up and whisk them up with soya milk they taste wonderful.'

'No, it's OK,' I say. 'No Gingko berries for me, thank you very much.'

'Simon bought us a smoothie-maker yesterday,' says Dean, and honestly, he's got such a straight face that I can't tell whether he's taking the piss. Except, of course, that he must be because Simon has solemnly promised me that he will not be sucked into the health and fitness sect.

'Alina's downstairs. She'll do you a nice fry-up,' I say, hoping to tempt him back from their world and into mine.

Alina's proved to be fabulous since she started. Even though she always looks dazed and slightly confused and as if she's no idea what she's doing, the truth is that she knows exactly what to do, and she works tirelessly. She tidies up, organizes all my clothes, cleans the house from top to bottom and bows courteously when I walk past her. She's just brilliant. Honestly. Never known anyone like her. All the staff I had in England don't begin to compare. I mean, I needed about four English girls to do what she does in half the time. But then again, as I discovered later, this was probably because they were spending half their time having parties and trying on my clothes. I came home unexpectedly one day to see them dancing around the sitting room, dressed in my jewels and drinking my champagne.

Meanwhile, Dean is still putting himself through an entirely unnecessary degree of pain in pursuit of some higher level of thinking. He's now trying to put his head through his legs but is about as far from his knees as I am. 'That needs a bit of work,' he says, and he stretches up to the ceiling and urges me to meet him in the kitchen.

Paskia's up and dressed with greater speed than she ever was in Luton. She needs no reminding to brush her hair or remember her bag.

'Don't forget that my three friends are coming back tonight for tea,' she says.

'I won't,' I promise.

'You won't embarrass me, will you, Mum?'

'Of course not,' I say, as I kiss her goodbye and close the door behind her. As if!

In the kitchen, the world has truly changed beyond all recognition. Simon and Dean are sitting there, sipping glasses full of what looks like blood.

'Is this some sort of strange vampire club?' I ask, because I can't imagine what other reason there can be for two grown men to drink such a concoction in the morning. They're chatting quietly and occasionally looking closely at one another.

'You should try some of this,' Simon offers, pushing his glass of revolting-looking red slime towards me and looking closely at the state of my face. 'It's very good for you. We've just noticed how our skins have improved since we stopped drinking so much, haven't we, Dean?'

To Dean's credit, he realizes how gay this is all sounding, and goes a delicate shade of red which matches his drink perfectly.

'I'll stick with champagne, thanks.' I pour myself a large glass. 'I'm not giving up alcohol for breakfast – it's one of the things that most fundamentally defines me as a Wag.'

They both nod their understanding and go back to their muted chatter about oxygen capacity and body, spirit and mind. For fuck's sake.

'And,' I add, rather aggressively, pointing at Simon to give emphasis to my words, 'I thought you were going to drink with me. I thought we decided that the British Empire was not built on hand-picked loganberries.'

'I just think this LA lifestyle thing has a lot to commend it,' is his feeble response. 'I feel more alert and alive than I have in ages.'

Bloody hell. I'm going to need something stronger than champagne to get through this. 'Anyone seen the Smirnoff?'

The crushed fruit drinkers eventually finish up and go jogging towards the door, telling me to be careful today and not, under any circumstances, to indulge in any more painful surgical procedures.

'Trace, there's something here for you,' shouts Simon as he and Dean open the front door. 'A great big box in the hallway. Clothes, no doubt!'

I walk out to see a box big enough to hold an adult. It's addressed to me, which is exciting, but quite how I get it open without breaking my nails is a mystery.

'Alina,' I shout. 'Can you help me?'

Armed with knives, scissors and the stubby fingers and brute strength of Alina, we begin our battle to get into the box. Staples are pulled out, cardboard is torn and plastic sheeting is removed. I rip off a layer of paper and gasp. 'Oh my God.'

Alina leaps back. 'God?' she says. 'Is a gift from God? Oh mercy.'

'No, I was just saying "Oh God",' I say, but Alina's expression has changed from looking dazed and confused to stunned and amazed as she tears away at the cardboard to see what the Lord has sent us.

Tucked inside the box is a beautiful pink girl's bike. It has a pink hooter on the front, a pink basket and a pink bell. Tucked inside the basket is a note.

'Tracie,' it says. 'Meeting you yesterday was one of the best things that has ever happened to me. I can't change the past, but I can help make the future as wonderful as possible. All my love, Dad xx.'

'Is for Paskia from the Lord?' asks Alina, while I sit down on the floor, clutching the note to my chest and sobbing helplessly.

'Is bad bike?' she asks, confusion spreading across her face as my wails get louder. 'The Lord he sent bad bike? What is happening in family if the Lord he sends bad bike?'

'No, Alina, is very good bike,' I say, smiling through my tears. 'Is very good bike from the Lord.'

It's amazing what the receipt of a bright pink little girl's bike can do to a woman. I feel as if I could take on the world today. My face may look like I've had a fight with a cheese grater (and lost), but my spirit is unbroken. I keep looking at the note, and at the bike, still sitting in the hallway, gleaning and shining and looking like every girl's dream.

'Perfect for Paskia,' Alina keeps saying. 'Just perfect present from the Lord.'

The note is incredible. I'm going to keep it for ever and ever. I've already learnt it off by heart, but there's one bit that I don't agree with – when Dad says that we can't change the past. It may sound funny, but I think we can. In fact, as far as I'm concerned the past has already been changed. My childhood is no longer a cruel place in which I was hated and despised by everyone. It isn't a place in which I had no one who cared for me; it is a place in which there was one person who loved me but was kept from me, like a fairy-tale, and that changes everything.

11 a.m.

Right, before going back into the surgery for my dental work I have to put the bandages back onto my face, or I'll be in big trouble. The problem is that my face hurts so much that the thought of touching it fills me with complete and utter horror. I've been given all these painkillers that I've been shovelling down my throat, and this cream to put on my face, but I don't want to put it on because it's so painful.

OK. Come on, Tracie, you can do this. I'll have to put the bandages on without the cream, something that I was expressly advised not to do, because they'll stick into the pus on my skin and it will be agony to take them off. I'll just have to worry about that later. I take a large gulp of my drink and wrap the bandages around my red, raw and desperately tender mush of a swollen face.

With my sunglasses and the bandages on I look quite ridiculous.

'Tracie Martin to see Mr Johns,' I mumble, before sitting down in the seat the furthest from the door. I don't even peep into the VIP area – I'm too concerned with the fact that I'm suffering a quite unbelievable amount of pain. There are four other women in the reception area. They're filling out their forms. New clients, obviously. They look up and stare when I walk in, and who can blame them?

'I only had my eyebrows plucked,' I say.

They continue to stare and I remember that LA is not the sort of place where people say jokey things.

'Mrs Martin, Mr Johns will see you now.'

While I pull off my shades and head off in pursuit of shiny white teeth, I can hear the girls behind me whispering and mumbling, and clearly worrying about what they're going to look like if a simple eyebrow reshape has rendered me looking like a burns victim.

It turns out that Mr Johns was at the front of the queue when the good looks were shared between the two brothers. Blimey, how Dr Johns must hate this guy.

'Call me Dominic,' he says, looking straight into my eyes. He reminds me of Jamie, with his square jaw and well-proportioned features. He's beefy, unlike his brother, and sports the fabulous LA tan that I'd thought was compulsory until I met his pale, insipid butcher of a brother.

'Sit down,' he says. 'Now, let's have a look here. Why do you have all these bandages on?'

'Dr Death gave me a facial resurfacing yesterday,' I explain.

'Right, well, I'll be as gentle as I can with you then,' he says, and my mind's filled with thoughts of this big strong man throwing me onto the bed and being all gentle with me.

'Open wide,' he says, and it honestly takes me a few

minutes to work out that he's talking about my teeth and not my legs.

It's decided that veneers are the best way forward, and I select the most blindingly white ones on the cards he shows me.

'Are you sure?' he asks. 'We don't do many in that shade, it's quite unnatural-looking when they're first put on. The dazzle fades a bit after a while, but they really are quite arrestingly bright for the first few days.'

'Ideal!' I say, so he takes a mould of my mouth and says that if I come back on Sunday morning the veneers will be in, and I'll be able to get them fitted. They're called number ones, apparently, and he's only ever fitted them once before – into the mouth of a famous lap-dancer called Juicy. On the way out I ask bright white shiny teeth lady what number her veneers are. 'Four', she says.

'Four? Why didn't you go for ones?'

'Because they're insanely bright, and every time you smile it looks like a searchlight's gone on in your mouth.'

'Cool.'

2 p.m.

I'm back home and have ordered in the most fabulous collection of exquisite foods for Paskia's little tea party this evening, and pulled out some vintage champagne. The girls are bound to fancy a little drink, aren't they?

I've also had quite a productive day. As well as my visit to the dishy dentist I've had a long chat to Sheila and she told me how much my dad enjoyed meeting me, and that he'd like to see me again. I told her about the bike, and how sweet his note was, and she seemed quite alarmed at first. Apparently he's not to make any unsolicited contact with me.

'But it was lovely!' I say. 'It was the nicest bike in the world.'

We've arranged for my father and me to get together again on Wednesday afternoon. This time, though, I'll go on my own. There are things that happened in my childhood that I need to talk to Dad about and, nice as Sheila is, I don't feel I can speak about them in front of her.

'I understand,' she says, adding, 'Remember, though, if you change your mind just call me and I'll come with you.'

'Thanks,' I say, and as soon as I put the receiver down I'm filled with massive, mind-blowing doubt. What if it's different this time? What if Dad says, when I'm on my own, that he really hates me? Shit! What if he's spoken to Mum and she's told him terribly things about me? And yet every time I look up and see the shiny bike with its beautiful pink seat I think, no, he must love me. No one could buy a perfect bike like that without loving the person they were buying it for.

My thoughts are silenced by the shrill of the phone, followed by Cindy's voice. 'You've been offered a column in the *LA Times*,' she declares, sounding wholly surprised that I should have been offered anything. I expected her to follow up the statement with 'God knows why'. Happily, she doesn't, and I thank her for calling, adding, 'It's lovely of you to ring when you said you would.'

'That's what we do in this town. It's called good manners. It's more important than good etiquette, which is what you Brits seem obsessed with.'

I once read that good etiquette is telling the girl next to you that she's drinking out of the finger bowl, good manners is drinking from yours too, so she doesn't feel bad. I quite like that. I like that having good manners means making other people feel comfortable and happy.

'Make this column good,' barks Cindy with less pleasing manners, and rather more aggression than is strictly necessary. 'This is the land of the writer. There are a million writers who want this gig. *Don't* let me down. You'll only get one chance. If they don't like the piece they won't take another one from you.'

'I'll do my best,' I say, and realize instantly that was the wrong thing to say.

'*Always* do your best,' she says, 'but this time do better than your best. Do what it takes to get it right.'

People don't talk like that in England, do they? It's a peculiarly LA sort of thing to say. Over here they seem to delight in success, but they also expect it. I've seen that with the way Dean is at the club. There's a pressure on him to be successful. They want him to reinvent the club and make it different, better, and adopt more creative strategies. They want him to be more assertive. It's not all 'make do and mend' like in England. I guess that's the downside of living in a city where everyone wants to be famous.

I pick up the phone to call Dean and tell him about the conversation I've just had. I want someone to laugh along with me, but I stop myself before I've dialled. For some reason it doesn't feel right. I feel like I'd be wasting my time. He's wholly bought into this 'work hard, achieve, be someone' mentality and I know he'll be way too busy to take a call from his batty wife.

In Luton we spent every minute that Dean wasn't at the club together. We'd snuggle up on the sofa, with Dean eating crisps with tomato sauce on the top, and get off our trolleys while watching *The Bill* and *Casualty*, and stuff like that. I'd tell him everything about my day, and he'd tell me all about his. It was brilliant.

But since we've been in LA I've felt like I can't talk to him about anything at all because my problems seem trivial when he spends all day with Chuck who's full of non-stop business bullshit. The other day he left a message on the answerphone saying: 'Dean. Hi teammate, it's Big C. Just to say that we really need to get the monkey off our back this season, bite the bullet and hit the ground running so we can belly up to the bar, whilst all swinging from the same branch. If we do that, we'll create synergistic win-wins that positively impact the bottom line.'

I mean – what the fuck is that? It's not English and I don't think it's American. But Dean listened to it, nodded enthusiastically and called him back to say, 'I hear you, I hear you.'

I call Simon to tell him that we've got a deal, but he sounds so busy in Dean's office, putting all the corporate literature together and checking their press releases, that I don't bore him with the details either. It just seems that everyone's out there getting on with their lives and with no real interest in what I'm doing, stuck at home.

I sit there, holding the phone, thinking of how much I want to ring Jamie. I don't call, though, because there's this voice inside my head saying it's wrong to. I'm leaning on him too much. It's not fair on him – he's got so much on his plate, what with finding a job, developing the business and getting his portfolio together as well as looking after his poor dad who's grieving so terribly for Nancy.

I can't expect him to drop everything and look after me, especially when I've got nothing to offer him. I'm a married woman and I definitely don't want him to think I'm interested in an affair or anything. No, it's best that I only call him when I really have to. I'll just sit here and console myself with the thought that the *LA Times* column will mean I get to earn some money to help Dean out if things go wrong at the club.

3 p.m.

The house looks fabulous, even if my face doesn't. I'm wearing my bandages covering every spare inch of face flesh, and I have to confess I've had a little bit of a drink. Alina's cleaned the place until it gleams and now she's in the kitchen, singing what sounds like the Spanish version of 'Onward Christian Soldiers' as she sorts out the food I ordered. She marches across the kitchen in the chorus, before standing still for verses. Whatever she's doing with the food, though – marching or no marching – it smells divine. If I were the sort of woman who ate, I'd be getting stuck right into it.

I remember back in the days when I used to eat, before Dean was made captain of Luton and thus I became Queen of all the Wags there. Nell would cook a roast dinner on Sundays and I'd go round there and have peas and carrots, sometimes I'd have a little piece of chicken, and one time I had half a roast potato, but my weight ballooned up to nine stone so I soon stopped that.

I manage to exist without really eating now. The rule

for Wags is that 99.8 per cent of your calories should come through alcohol, and I'm happy to report that I do regularly hit that target. I certainly will today. I've drunk half a bottle of champagne and have had just a couple of champagne cocktails and a few large Bacardis. All that's left to sort out now is the bike – still sitting there in the hallway, in all its girly pink glory. I need to move it out of the way until I think of a half-decent reason to explain its sudden arrival to Dean.

I hitch my skirt up and swing my leg over the handle-bars, almost doing myself a nasty injury what with the relatively small seat and me not having any knickers on. I tinkle the little bell, then try to put my feet onto the pedals to have a little cycle around. Oooo . . . it's quite easy. It has stabilizers on (pink, of course) which makes it easier to stay upright. There's even room in the pink straw basket for my bottle of Bacardi, which is an unforeseen bonus. Yee-ha! Amazing what fun you can have cycling around and ringing your little pink bell while swigging Bacardi. I cycle into the kitchen and terrify the living daylights out of Alina.

'Mrs Martin, Mrs Martin. Is dangerous for cycling and drinking in kitchens with bandages on face. Be careful of stove is hot.'

'Like me, Alina,' I say. 'Hot. Just like me.' I'm feeling kind of rebellious and thrill-seeking and I really wish Sharron Webster could see me now looking so damn cool. Out of the kitchen I go with a small yee-ha! But when I hit the slippy hall floor at speed, the bike goes skidding off, heading for the wall at terrifying speed. I rescue my precious Bacardi from the basket just before a full-speed head-on collision.

'Good save!' I say, applauding myself loudly. 'Good save.'

That's when I see Paskia-Rose standing in the doorway with three dumb-looking friends, staring at me as if this is a strange scenario. I kind of accept that it is a little odd to see a grown woman with her head all bandaged up cycling round on a children's pink bicycle while showing her fanny to the world and drinking Bacardi. Alina is in the kitchen door almost shaking with relief that I'm OK. 'Is no good to cycle child bike when pissed like this,' she says, sounding strangely knowledgeable about such matters. 'Always not to pissed cycle. Always. Is law.'

Wait a minute – who are those girls?

'Pask,' I say. My daughter and her new pals have been standing there in stunned silence since arriving. 'What happened to the nice friends you were going to bring back?'

'These are my nice friends,' she says defensively. 'This is Sarah, this is Mary and this is Molly.'

'Hi, Mrs Martin,' they say in unison.

Not a double-barrelled name, a stiletto heel or a scrap of makeup between them. Two of them are wearing glasses and the other one has bright ginger hair and bloody awful freckles.

'Drink, anyone?' I ask, clambering off the bike in a rather inelegant way, and raising the bottle in front of me.

'No thanks,' says Pask, looking close to tears. 'None of us drinks.'

The foursome head upstairs, with Paskia stomping rather more than is strictly necessary – at least she's acting like a proper teenager for once, though *what* a disappointment that school has turned out to be. I was expecting plastic mini-skirts and sunglasses, not plastic bags and reading glasses. I thought Pask would befriend the cool girls and become one of them. That's what I always wanted when I was at school. It didn't happen for me; now, sadly, it looks as if it's not going to happen for my only daughter.

'What time I prepare food?' asks Alina, looking at me with those big brown, puppy-dog eyes. I feel like patting her head and giving her some chocolate buttons when she does that scared face with the wide eyes. But what shall I do about food? I have to confess that I don't feel half so eager to feed these dowdy girls now.

'I'll find out,' I tell Alina, as I walk upstairs to Paskia-Rose's room. They're chatting away in there, and it's not so much that I decided to eavesdrop by pushing my bandages away and shoving my ear up against the door, as I happened to overhear (while my ear was pushed up against the door).

'I don't want to say his name,' Paskia-Rose is saying. 'You might laugh at me.'

Ooooo . . . what's all this then?

'We won't,' says one of the girls. 'Go on, tell us what letter his name starts with.'

'OK,' says Paskia. 'It begins with J.'

'I knew it, I knew it,' says one of the girls. 'You fancy my brother, don't you?'

Hello. This is getting interesting.

'Is that really awful, Mary?' asks Paskia. 'Is it?'

'I think it's quite cool actually,' says Mary.

'But how do I get him to notice me?' asks Pask. 'I bet he doesn't even know I exist.'

'You've just got to be yourself,' says Mary.

'Yes,' chorus the others in agreement. It's more than I can stand. I open the door and push my way in to the room.

'Be yourself?' I say. 'Are you all mad? What sort of advice is that?'

'Um, don't know,' they mumble.

'I'll tell you what sort of advice that is – the very worst sort of advice,' I say.

They're all sitting there in shocked silence.

'Do you like Mary's brother?' I ask Pask. 'The boy J – do you like him?'

'Yes,' says Paskia, looking around the room, mortified with embarrassment as the contents of her very worst nightmare are played out before her.

'Well, we'd better get you some pulling clothes then, hadn't we?' I say.

The girls look doubtfully from one to another.

'OK,' says Mary eventually, but as I drag them to their feet and lead the way out of the room I swear I heard her say, 'What are pulling clothes?' to one of the others.

'Follow me. We're going shopping.'

'But, Mrs Martin, wait. What about food?' says Alina, emerging at the bottom of the stairs in a fluster. She couldn't look more concerned if her kitchen was being taken over by alien hijackers.

'No need for food. These girls are much plumper than I thought they'd be. They could do without the calories. You eat it, Alina. Have a glass of champagne while you're at it. The bike's there, if you feel the urge. Just make sure you look out for the wall.'

'Come on,' I cajole them. 'It's my treat.'

'Mum, none us wants a makeover,' whines Paskia-Rose.

We've been up and down the escalators in this massive mall, in and out of shops, entirely against the wishes of the girls, and they're now dressed beautifully – in tiny pink mini-dresses and long white boots. They look like mini versions of me!

All they need is the makeup to go with their outfits and a little accessorizing to bring the clothes to life. Candyfloss pink doesn't work on natural skin colour, especially the sort of pale skin these podgy tweenies have.

'But the four of you look absolutely beautiful, spectacular,' I declare. 'Please let me give you the proper makeup to go with it, or the whole outfit will be ruined.'

'OK,' they concede, more because they're well brought up young ladies and are reluctant to argue with an adult than because they have any interest in being plucked, preened and painted. They'll learn.

We troop into Makeup World and over to the Painted Faces Department where a host of girls in white overalls are poised ready to do complete makeovers on unsuspecting youngsters.

The girls smile when they see me coming. It's amazing how well I'm being treated by the shop assistants this time. It helps that I'm not on Rodeo Drive, but it also helps that my face is bandaged. It's like a badge of honour in these parts. People treat me as if I'm a pregnant woman – giving me a seat, regarding me with a certain amount of envy and a considerable amount of kindness. They ask when it's due.

'When what's due?' I reply, baffled.

'The bandage removal. The unveiling.'

'Just a week,' I say, and they say how excited I must be.

'Now, makeup. We need completely drop-dead, all-out glamour for these four,' I say.

'Sure,' one of the assistants replies, examining the four girls and calling for help. 'Were you thinking sparkly, pretty, pouty, glossy?' she asks. 'Kind of Britney before the crash?'

'Yes!' I say. Perfect.

The girls emerge just twenty minutes later and they look quite stunning – really cool and sexy. I've never seen Paskia-Rose look so utterly beautiful. The others as well. It's the most magnificent transformation I've ever witnessed.

'You four look amazing. I'm going to buy you all the makeup they used,' I say. There's not much response from the girls, who continue to stare at the carpet and avoid looking at each other. When we leave they drag their heels and Paskia moans about how 'slaggy' they all feel.

For God's sake.

'Girls, you look wonderful. Before you looked like dweebs but now you look like starlets. Pask – if you want to bag this boy, this is how you're going to have to start looking.'

'My mum will have a fit,' mumbles Mary as we walk away from the store. 'She'll be really cross.'

'No she won't,' I say, alarmed. 'She'll be thrilled, delighted and overcome with emotion at the transformation that's taken place. Mark my words – she'll love it. Get her to call me and I'll make her over too.'

OK, so it turned out that Mary was right. Her mother really did hate her new look. Weird, it was. The four of us led her proudly into her house, expecting tears of joy, but when her mother saw us she screamed and started crying.

'You look like a prostitute! A hooker!' she kept saying. 'It's appalling. I've never been so offended. My beautiful, perfect daughter turned into a whore.'

The crying was getting louder and louder so I suggested to the others that we leave. Paskia stood there, mortified.

'Come on, let's go.'

The other girls lived just down the road. We dropped off Sarah and I'm sad to say that her mother was equally dismayed at her daughter's new look, especially since Sarah had her glasses in her pocket, so kept crashing into things. Her mother screamed when she saw my bandaged face and nearly collapsed with the shock when she saw Sarah.

'We'll just go then, shall we?' I said to Paskia and Molly.

When it came to dropping off Molly I didn't even get out of the car. I was tempted to slow down outside and make her jump as we drove past the door, so I wouldn't have to stop. In the end I did, but not for long. As soon as Molly was out and on the path I put my foot down and away we sped to the screams of her mother.

The worse thing of all is that the reaction of the parents means that my plan to help Pask has completely back-fired. She's now upstairs, crying and saying she hates me and all her friends will hate her because they're in trouble. Pask will be banned from playing with them, and she'll be all alone.

'Don't worry about that,' I say. 'Look at the surprise I've got for you.'

I indicate the pink bike and give her a demonstration of its little bell and pretty basket.

'And that's supposed to compensate for the fact that you've just wrecked my life, is it?' she says.

I just shrug.

'Mary's brother is going to think I'm a complete slag,' she adds. 'He'll want nothing to do with me.'

Paskia slams the door and is gone before I can say that, on the contrary, if Mary's brother thinks she's a slag he'll want *everything* to do with her.

9 p.m.

It's late when Simon and Dean come in and drop two sports bags down on the kitchen floor.

'I thought you'd be back earlier,' I say.

'We had a game of squash,' replies Dean, swinging his arm as if he's going to hit a baseball or something.

'Squash?' I say, fearing that my husband is now involved in an even more weird spiritual activity. Has he joined some infamous squash cult? Scientology while carrying a small cup of orange squash?

'It's like tennis, only you hit it against a wall instead of to each other,' explains Dean. Oh. Fascinating. I think my explanation was more fun.

'Except when we play,' adds Simon. 'Then Dean hits it against the wall and I fall over my shoelaces trying to get to it, then don't manage to hit it anywhere near the wall. I'm rubbish at sports.'

'Well, I'm rubbish at writing,' says Dean, very nobly.

'Thanks for all your help with the corporate literature and press releases. I couldn't have done it without you.'

'No problem,' says Simon. 'Glad to help. I don't know who on earth wrote them in the first place. The writing was hysterical. You know, in one of the sentences the word football was spelt wrong three times!'

'Oh,' says Dean.

'I mean, you wouldn't have thought you could come up with three different ways to spell "football", would you? It's mad.'

'Yeah,' says Dean quietly. 'Anyway, it's all fixed now. Did I tell you I read through the books you got me?'

'Oh, great. How did you find them?'

Dean puts a plate of blueberries and raspberries in front of himself and Simon and the two men start to discuss leadership styles. It's a whole different language to me. They might as well be speaking Hebrew. When did Dean learn to speak Hebrew? Should I learn? I fear that if I don't start learning about management, leadership and team dynamics, we'll have nothing to talk about at all.

'Can I borrow the book when you've finished?' I ask Dean, and he looks at me as if I've just ask whether I can wear all my clothes back to front from now on.

'Why?' he asks. I shrug and tell him that I want to be able to join in his conversations.

'Don't worry about that,' says Dean. 'Why don't you plan a nice day out shopping for yourself tomorrow instead?'

Saturday 7 June (Two weeks to go!)
10 a.m.

Paskia says she hates me and is leaving home.

'Don't do that, love,' I say. 'You know how much I love you and how much it hurts when you talk like that.'

'I know you love me but you don't act as if you like me very much. You don't think about me, it's always about you. You're the most selfish person I've ever met.'

'Paskia, that's horrible,' I say. Her words have really stung me. I can feel tears rising as I stand there looking at her.

'I want Alina to be my mother,' she says, much to the surprise of Alina who drops her brush and holds her head in her hands, muttering something about the child being with the mother always.

'Come on now, Paskia,' says Simon. 'Your mum was just trying to help.'

'Yeah, right,' says Pask. 'Help who? She wanted to help herself by making me and my friends look like the sort of people she wants to be associated with. Nothing's ever about me and the way I am. It's all about Mum and the way she wishes I was. She's just like Grannie Angie sometimes.'

'Pask!' I shout. 'How can you say that? You know I love you. Yesterday was a mistake, but I was just trying

199

to help, that's all.' How things change in the mind of a child. It wasn't that long ago that I was supermum.

Paskia opens her mouth to hurl more abuse at me, but Simon puts his hand up to stop her. 'I know it's difficult when you're growing up,' he says. 'But your mum really loves you, Pask.'

'Simon,' she says. 'Will you be my mum instead?'

7 p.m.

OK, what's wrong with this scene? We're at a football club. Nothing wrong with that. We're sitting in the bar – everything right with that. There are six of us – all women, and we're chatting. The team has just lost – that's all fine. I'm used to the smell of failure in the air – it was the only smell I knew at Luton, and it's a strangely familiar feeling to be sitting here getting steadily pissed while the players look as if they're on death row.

No, that's all OK. What's really wrong here is that the women I'm talking to are, in effect, Wags. I mean they're married to the footballers who've just come off the pitch so they should be Wags. But look at them! For fuck's sake. I spent all last night thinking about where LA women go wrong, for my article, and I've come to the conclusion that it takes more to be a Wag than to be consorting with a footballer, and these women just do not have what it takes. We have nothing in common.

Take Sian and Poppy – I like those two a lot, but how can I take either of them seriously when neither of them has even put on the false eyelashes I gave them? It's sick. Honestly, absolutely sick. I'm sitting here with three pairs of eyelashes on top of each other, deep brown lip-liner round my now very, very, very full lips (the lip plumper kicked in at last!), and a light pink sparkly colour in the middle. And that's with the rest of my face bandaged up! Imagine how made up I'd be if I had any flesh on show to put the damn makeup on!

Opposite me I've got Sian with naked lips! Naked! I wouldn't sit here butt-naked, would I? Yet as far as I'm concerned it's as offensive to show naked facial and lip skin as it is to show naked lady bits. I'd sooner flash my bare breasts at the paparazzi than I would show my un-made-up face, and the same can be said for everyone I've ever met in Wag world. But these women . . . these women . . . I can't imagine what Lady Victoria will make of them when she comes here in *two weeks' time*!!

'Look!' I say, bursting with enthusiasm as I thrust a copy of *Heat* across the table. 'There's Jordan. Look at her makeup. Isn't it fabulous?'

'Oh, no!' cries Poppy, as if her favourite puppy has been shot. Then she relaxes. 'You're joking, aren't you?' she says. 'Oh my gawd! You English with your funny sense of humour. I thought you were serious. I looked at that dreadful woman with her piles of makeup and her horrible bright clothes and such silly high heels, and I thought you were serious. You'll be saying next that you think Victoria Beckham has class.'

'*Don't knock Posh!*' I growl. 'You can insult my religion, insult my name, my family and my honour, but *do not insult Posh.*'

It's fair to say that I'm shouting at this point, and I should probably add that I have stood up, causing a considerable scene.

'I just don't think Posh Spice is very –'

'*Don't*.'

'She's not at all –'

'*Don't!*'

OK, so I'm yelling now but I'm very defensive about my friends. I won't sit around while my friends are insulted, and though she might not know it, and might not like it particularly, there's not doubt that, in my mind at least, Posh is my bestest of friends. Which is just as well as I don't have too many around here at the moment.

10 p.m.

'Breathe,' says Simon. 'Just breathe and relax.'

'I can't help getting all uptight,' I say. 'These women, they just don't get me at all.'

'This is a different country. People behave differently. Isn't it quite fun learning about new people and new things?'

'Would you think I was awful if I said "No"? I like things the way they were in Luton. I miss it madly.'

'Oh, Tracie. Why don't you pop back for a break, and see all the girls? Or invite them out here?'

'I was thinking about getting them out here in the summer,' I say.

'That's a great idea,' says Simon. 'I bet by then you'll be a real LA girl.'

'I bloody hope not,' I say, but with my newly resurfaced face and my teeth being done first thing tomorrow morning, who knows? I could yet look like perfect Sian, perfect Poppy and the other perfect wives at the club.

Sunday 8 June

Email to: Suzzi and Mich

From: Tracie Martin

Hi,

I'm a proper LA type now! I have bright, shiny white teeth that dazzle every time I smile. Dean's banned me from so much as parting my lips while driving because he's convinced I've caused a couple of crashes due to the substantial glare that my teeth now give off. This morning a small plane crash landed in one of the gardens near us, and Dean's certain it's because I looked up and smiled a little too broadly.

We're managing to cope in the house by everyone wearing sunglasses. I'm sure that's why so many people in LA wear them, day and night. I bet if we did a research paper into sunglass usage and grade one white veneer purchasing, there would be a direct correlation. Alina the cleaner (yes, that's her name, honestly!) is finding it more difficult than most and has these blinkers that she wears because she's convinced that when I smile to the side of her it strikes her in the corner of her eye and renders her completely blind for a couple of minutes.

They've told me that I'll blind myself if I smile into a mirror, so I've taken to putting on my makeup while wearing a very surly expression. My attempts to do my makeup while wearing my sunglasses were very disappointing. I looked like I'd just got back from a skiing trip or something, with a sunglasses-shaped strip missing from my foundation.

Anyway, must go now. Pask has got her first match this afternoon, so we're all going to watch.
Bye for now. Write soon,

Tracie x

PS. I need a full update on Angie . . . you didn't mention her in your last email. What's happening?

3 p.m.

Dean, Simon and I are threatening to cheer loudly and make complete fools of ourselves at Pask's match today.

'You won't miss us – we'll be the noisy ones,' says Dean. 'We'll make sure we stand out.'

'Just for a change,' says Paskia, staring straight at me. 'You *always* stand out. I think you do it just to make me look silly.'

She's been unbearably miserable since the whole drunk

on the kids' bike/dressing them like little fairies thing. Honestly, get over it.

She's captain today, though, which is brilliant – it should cheer her up. She's also the striker, which is the same position that she played in Luton when she scored loads of goals, so we're all full of confidence that she'll be the star of the team again.

I see Sarah, Mary and Molly as soon as we get to the ground. Standing in a huddle, talking quietly, and not wearing their lovely clothes.

'They're Pask's friends,' I say to Dean and Simon. 'I'm going over to say hi.'

'Don't embarrass her,' warns Simon.

As I approach, I'm trying to work out which is which. Mary's the one with long sandy-coloured hair (kind of gingery, but not quite). It's got that slightly wiry texture to it which means it never looks nice. She has tons of big, thick freckles covering her nose and forehead.

Molly and Sarah both have glasses and dark hair, and I think it's Sarah who's the bigger of the two and the jollier. She smiles and seems happy, whereas the other one's completely morose and severe looking, with sharp features and a pinched mouth.

'Hello, girls,' I say as I approach, making sure I keep my lips as tightly shut as possible so as not to blind them. It's quite hard to do, and I reckon if I keep this up I'll be able to take on a secondary job as a ventriloquist.

'Hi, Mrs Martin,' they say politely, and I decide to behave like a proper respectable mother.

'I'm sorry if those clothes I bought you got you into trouble the other night. I thought they were quite fun. You girls are young, it's nice to have party clothes.'

'Yes, Mrs Martin.'

'So were your mothers very cross?'

'A little,' they say.

'Will you wear them again?'

'I don't think so,' they confess.

I'm starting to feel that I've conversed all I can with these girls, and I'm hearing the distinct sound of the bar calling, when two young men walk towards us. One of them is very attractive. He's clean-shaven, with very short hair and a muscular frame. He oozes confidence as he strides towards us.

'These are my brothers,' says Mary.

'Hello, I'm Jacob, nice to meet you,' says the strong, handsome one. Jacob, eh? If my alphabetical skills are correct – and they're not always – then Jacob begins with a J. Ding-dong. Get in there, Pask.

'Are you a soccer fan?' I ask in a polite, future mother-in-law sort of way.

'I love all sports, ma'am,' he says. 'I'm in the US Marine Corps. We do lots of sports there. Not much soccer, though.'

Oooo . . . the thought of this man in his uniform throws me right off balance, and he has to catch me as I, literally, swoon.

My Pask has excellent taste but this kid must be eighteen. A young man like him will want a girl with sophistication and style, not some little girl with freckles and puppy fat. I need to get Paskia sorted out if she's to have a chance of being friends with him. I hope he's decent and will treat her properly. I'd love Paskia to have a lovely, gentle introduction to the world of men.

'Here they come!' shouts Molly, I think, or perhaps the other one, as Paskia leads her team out onto the pitch.

'See you later,' says Jacob, and he and his mousy little friend wander off to the other side of the pitch.

6 p.m.

'I didn't smile on purpose, Paskia.'

'You did, Mum.'

'I didn't.'

'Mum, I saw you running round the pitch every time I got the ball, smiling madly at the opposition defence.'

'Paskia, you're being daft. Of course I didn't do that. What must you think of me if you imagine for a minute that I'd do that?'

'Well done, young lady,' says Jacob, striding over with the mousy guy to shake Paskia's hand. Both boys give her a kiss on the cheek and she starts giggling and behaving in an unexpectedly girly fashion. This boy's having a tremendous effect on her. It's so sweet!

'I've never known of someone scoring eight goals before,' says Jacob.

'No, it was amazing,' says the mousy one. 'It was like all the defenders just dropped to their knees whenever you got the ball. They just couldn't cope, Pask. You were excellent.'

'Yes, amazing, wasn't it?' says Paskia, scowling at me.

Monday 9 June (12 days to go)
8 a.m.

Her name's Cristelle, and Simon is convinced that we should be meeting her for breakfast because she's an agent who buys in books that might make good films. Like everyone else in this God-forsaken place, she does enjoy her early mornings.

'Hey, let's do breakfast,' she said to Simon when he called her. 'How's Monday?'

Simon agreed that Monday would be great, and said he'd make sure I was there too. So here we are – in a crap place, having breakfast.

Cristelle's arrived, and is fascinated by Simon, but has no interest at all in me. She took one quick look at me, wrapped in bandages, and she said something about the curse of cosmetic surgery, and turned her attentions to Simon, quoting bits of his articles to him. He seemed quite taken with her too.

I have to say that I do not understand why he would be. She has dark hair. Now I know Posh has dark hair, but at least it's blonde sometimes. This woman has the look of someone who's never been blonde. That, to me, is utterly unforgivable.

I've been blonde for as long as I can remember. At

school I sprayed my hair with Sun-in until it was soaking wet, then I held the hair-dryer so close to it that I had burn marks on my scalp, and a vile, sickly-sweet, acrid smell wafted through the bedroom. Smoke billowed off my head, and the hair-dryer inevitably cut out due to the colossal heat.

'You doin' that bloody Sun-in on your hair?' Mum would shout. 'Are you?'

But nothing would stop me. I'd just turn up the stereo and pretend I couldn't hear her through the sounds of Spandau Ballet.

Once the hair was dry, three lemons would be squeezed onto it, aggravating my red raw scalp. The whole lot would then be subjected to more drying at thermonuclear temperatures until the desired shade had been reached.

'Bloody hell,' Mum would say when I walked downstairs. 'Your hair's turned to bright yellow cotton wool.'

'Thanks,' I'd say. They were the only kind words she ever said to me.

'You'd look much better blonde,' I say to Cristelle now.

'No, I wouldn't,' she replies. 'I'm naturally dark.'

Naturally dark. What the hell's that got to do with anything? Does she think my breasts and lips are naturally this size? Or that my hair is naturally the colour of a dandelion? Am I naturally brightest orange? No, of course not. Just because you weren't born blonde doesn't mean you shouldn't *be* blonde. Jeez. You're not born with a law degree – does that mean you can't be a lawyer? Women who wish to become Wags (presumably all women?) adopt the same philosophy and they change their natural state, be it hair colouring, breast size or skin colour.

'Dye it,' I say.

'No,' she replies.

'I think you should dye it. I'll dye it for you.'

'Tracie, please. Stop it,' says Simon. 'Just eat your breakfast.'

'Eat it? How can I eat it?'

Let me explain. To me, breakfast is something you can chew on. I don't think I'm the only person in the world who believes this. I think, in fact, that most of the world's population would agree that having something substantial enough to sink your teeth into would be the defining factor of food as opposed to, say, spittle.

Not here in the land of the mad. They have breakfasts like nowhere on earth. It's all about the bloody 'shakes' again. When they say 'breakfast meeting' they don't mean a nice table in a fab London hotel, sipping champagne and playing around with smoked salmon and scrambled eggs. What they mean is being confronted by an insane waiter who looks like he hasn't eaten for three and a half years, who's holding a menu of weird and wonderful shakes and smoothies. You can choose between those that promise to make you more alert, stronger, with improved memory, better skin, sleep better or lose fat. Great. I don't want any of them. I don't want food either, but I do want to be given the opportunity to turn food down. I want to be able to put on bold public displays of abstemiousness like some sort of Mother Teresa. If no one's eating, it takes the edge off refusing it. I'm almost tempted to eat just to be difficult. Almost.

'Just champagne for me, thanks,' I tell the waiter.

'We don't serve alcohol in here,' he says. 'How about trying the dried pumpkin seed and ground ginger infused lime squeeze in an immune system boosting wide-awaker? It's awesome.'

I don't think I've ever felt more like punching someone in my life.

'That'll be just fine,' I say, rising from my seat. 'Do excuse me, everyone. I just have something to do.'

I leave the table with Cristelle busily ordering a smoothie with this wheat, that grass, these supplements and absolutely no essence of grapefruit, and with Simon mouthing 'Where are you going?' in an angry fashion. I just shrug and continue to skitter across the shiny floor in the direction of the door.

By the time I return, the two of them are discussing body improvement strategies. Simon is waxing lyrical as if he were an expert, based entirely on knowledge of the subject gleaned from chatting to the fitness guys down at Raiders.

In fact, so engrossed are they in the conversation that neither of them notices me chucking half a bottle of vodka into the vile-looking 'breakfast' before me. 'Cheers!' I say, my spirits restored. I take a sip and there are two things that I'm immediately sure of – that this is definitely the worst taste ever to pass my lips, and that it would have tasted a hell of a lot worse without the vodka. At least I'm making a protest – however silent and thus useless – about the impeccable behaviour in LA. At least I'm being a bit naughty, and that's what life's about, isn't it? Having a bit of fun and breaking a few rules.

Simon is doing no such thing, though. In fact, he's badly letting me down. 'Mmmmm,' he says. 'The immune-boosting ginger essence is lovely.'

We only stay in the meeting for about half an hour, then Simon and Cristelle exchange cards.

'Oooo, have one of mine too,' I say, handing over a bright pink card with 'Tracie Martin' in gold embossed letters. Beneath it, in deep pink glittery letters, it says Super Wag.

'What's a Wig?' asks Cristelle.

'Wag,' I say. Silly cow.

'It says Wig on this card.'

I grab the card back from her and look at the writing. Bollocks. It says Super Wig. What a nightmare. These are going to have to go straight back. 'I'll send my card on to you,' I say, grabbing Simon's arm. 'Come on, we're going,' I tell him firmly, and we march out of the restaurant.

'What a waste of time,' I say when we're standing on the street.

'At least I'm trying to make something of my time here,' he says. 'At least I'm making an effort. What are you doing, Tracie, except sitting at home all day moaning that there are no Wags here and that no one drinks? Can't you just try the lifestyle? Have a go at yoga; make friends with the girls at the club.'

'I am,' I say. 'Look at my bloody face. I've got right stuck into the LA lifestyle.'

'Tracie, why do you have to embrace all the destructive elements of life? Why do you have to do things to hurt yourself all the time? I'd love to see you do something healthy, something that was life-affirming and positive, fun and good for you.'

'This *is* good for me. It's going to make me look better.'

'When will you allow yourself to just be? Tracie, no one wants you to change. Stop fighting so hard to be perfect. You can't change the past, and nothing you do will change the way Angie treated you as a child.'

'This isn't about Mum, it's about me,' I say.

'I really wish it was,' said Simon sadly. 'But nothing you ever do is for you – it's all about how you're seen and what people think of you. Don't you sometimes think that it really doesn't matter what people think?'

'I often think that,' I say, and it's true. I've lost count of the number of times I've been told that my skirt's too short or my top's too tight, but I never take any notice.

'So why are you standing there in agony having inflicted the worst sort of injury on your face?'

'I don't know,' I mutter. 'I just want to look like Victoria. If I was like her, everything would be fine.'

'No, it wouldn't,' says Simon.

'OK then, next time you go down to the club I'll come with you. I'll get involved more.'

'Come on Thursday,' he says cheerfully. 'There's a big team meeting at 3 p.m. Come and sit in on it. It's fascinating.'

'Mmmmm . . . sounds riveting. Today we could write the article in a coffee shop later. I've see a lot of these LA people doing that,' I say.

'That's a great idea,' says Simon. 'I have to go and read through a couple of press releases that Dean's drafted. Shall I do that and meet you down there late afternoon? How about that one with the pink frill on the outside? It's got wi-fi.'

I know about pink frills. Not sure about wi-fi. 'OK, see you there about four.'

4 p.m.

Clip, clip, clip . . . off I go. I have my fabulous new pink laptop (I bought it in my extreme shopping frenzy at

213

Heathrow) in a rather swish carrying bag, and I'm off to think of some ideas for my column while sitting in a coffee shop. Oh, yeah . . . we're in LA now. This is what they all do. If it's good enough for these LA types then it must be worth a try. OK. Here we are, pink frills outside, and it's called 'The LA Coffee Bean'. As I look through the window I can see dozens of like-minded people bashing away on their computers. This is the place for me. A writer's retreat.

'What can I get you, ma'am?'

'Two glass of Cristal please,' I say, then I rethink. 'No, hang on – just give me the bottle.'

'Cristal?' asks the confused assistant. 'I don't think we do that. But we have all these types of beans on the board up here.'

He points to the huge blackboard behind him.

'No,' I say, realising where the confusion comes from. 'I don't want coffee, I want champagne.'

'Ma'am, I'm sorry, we don't have that.'

'Oh, OK, I'll have vodka then.'

'No vodka, sorry.'

'Bacardi Breezer?'

'Sorry, ma'am, we just don't sell liquor in here.'

'What's liquor?'

'Alcohol.'

'Whaat?? How am I supposed to get any creative inspiration?'

'I can't help you with that, ma'am. I can only serve you coffee. Do you want one?'

I'm aware of the huge queue growing behind me and of the deep sighs of those waiting for their drinks.

'Yeah, coffee,' I say.

'What type?'

'Tia Maria coffee? With extra Tia Maria and hold the coffee and cream.'

'Lady, they don't have no alcohol here,' says the man who's next in the queue. 'You're gonna have to go to a liquor store for that. Do you wanna coffee or not? There are lots of people waiting.'

'Sorry,' I mumble, and I feel an enormous pressure to order quickly, and to order the right thing.

'Well, OK, what coffee do most people have?'

'Soya latte.'

'I'll have that then but without the soya, I'll have proper milk. From cows. I'm not even sure how they milk a soya bean. How would then do that? Does it have little udders or something?'

'OK, so it's a normal latte. Any add-ons?'

'Add-ons?'

'Ice cream, fudge, toffee, whipped cream, fondant, flavourings like caramel, almond, hazelnut or fruit, chocolate, sprinkles, candies, honey, maple syrup, sparklers, birthday candles . . .'

'Yes, OK then.'

'Which ones?'

'All those ones you just mentioned.'

'Take a seat and we'll bring it over,' he says.

Right, where to sit? Maybe in the window so that Simon can see me when he arrives. That would be good.

OK . . . Now then, how do I switch the laptop on? I look around but everyone seems to be really busy, bashing away on theirs. I push a few buttons and try to prise it apart with a teaspoon but I'm not having any luck at all.

I turn round to look for help, and see the waiter

approaching with what looks like an enormous ice cream – it's got whipped cream and chocolate bars sticking out, and chocolate and jelly sweets sprinkled all over the top. There are sparklers sticking out at the side and candles all over the top. As he approaches me, everyone in the Coffee Bean stops what they're doing and starts singing happy birthday. They begin to chant for me to blow out the candles just as Simon walks in.

'Hooray!' they all cheer when the flames are extinguished. I take a small bow.

'Everything OK?' asks Simon as I smile and thank them for their impromptu and entirely unexpected serenade.

'Yep, let's go,' I say.

'Where to? I thought you wanted to be in a coffee shop to be like everyone else in LA.'

'Nope. I don't want to be like everyone else in LA. Look at this fucking coffee they gave me. We're going to find a bar,' I say, and I teeter out of there, leaving the world's biggest, most expensive and most undrinkable coffee behind.

Finally, I have a drink in my hand. Aahhhhhh . . .

'Want to tell me why everyone was singing happy birthday?' asks Simon.

'Oh, that. Simple misunderstanding,' I say.

'Right,' says Simon, unconvinced. 'Let's get going on this article then. You need to tell me what you want me to say. I'm not a Wag. You're the Wag.'

'I don't know,' I say. 'This is so much harder than when we wrote the columns in England because we're starting from a lower base. These women know nothing,' I say mournfully.

'Maybe you should start at the beginning,' says Simon, clicking on his computer.

'I know,' I say. 'I'll write a call to arms. Urging the women of LA to change their mindsets and think like Wags. That would be good, wouldn't it?'

'OK,' says Simon. 'That sounds like a great idea.'

Wednesday 11 June

AN OPEN, KIND AND HELPFUL LETTER TO THE RESIDENTS OF LA
From: Your friend from Luton, Tracie Martin

Holy bollocks, ladies – what are you doing? I have not seen anyone, not anyone since I arrived in this funny little town who would even begin to qualify as a Wag. Now I hope that's not too hard for you all to take. I know that here, as in Luton, indeed across the globe, it remains the primary wish of all women to be one day married to a footballer. (That's football, the game in which you kick the ball . . . with your foot . . . that's why it's called football. You need another name for that thing you do where a bunch of blokes in helmets lob the ball across the field, then crash into one another.)

Now, being a Wag is as much about joining an elite group of ladies as it is about finding a footballer whose bad habits you can put up with. The doors to that elite group are not easily broken down. It takes more than a gentle knock.

Sure, I've seen some perfect bodies out here (pretty much the thinner the better as far as being a Wag is concerned, although I'm still wondering whether it's possible to be too thin after some of the bones I've seen sticking out of women over the last couple of weeks). But being thin is just a knock on the door. Being tanned is just a knock on the door (especially if you're brown instead of orange. What are you all thinking of?). If you want to be a Wag you need to charge the door down. You need to be pissed, for starters. If you're sober, you're out. Sobriety is completely over-rated. Get hammered and get dancing, show your bits off (I have never seen an LA woman flashing her bits in nightclubs . . . no wonder you're all struggling to attract the elusive Wag badge). You need to be raucous and uncouth – if you're not always drunk, then you need to be seen getting into fights. You need the sort of boyfriend who'll come along, clutching a lager can, and say 'Leave it', and march you off faster than you can possibly go in your high heels, forcing you to fall over, flashing everyone once again and looking generally undignified. Look at the first few pages of a British tabloid newspaper any day of the week, and you'll see what I mean.

I think it's only through being drunk that you can touch upon the heart and soul of what it is to be a Wag. It is only through being pissed, also, that you can cope with the down-side of the role like the fact that he's away all the time playing footie and when he's home would rather be on the Playstation than talking to you. There's also that horror moment when you open the newspaper pages and see that yet another footballer has been caught in an embrace with a busty blonde or a tempting brunette. Every time you think – there, but for the grace of cosmetic enhancement, go I – have a vodka. It is really the only way through it. Have a drink and you won't give a flying toss whose rear end he's playing blow football on.

Yes, ladies of LA – get pissed, get undignified, get the right colour of tanning done, add a few wire wool extensions into your hair, pile on the makeup and you, too, can join the greatest club in the world.

8.30 a.m.

'Go away, go away,' I feel like screaming. It's barely dawn and outside the house I can hear voices. It sounds like a load of people chanting something.

It's like there's some sort of mass yoga ritual taking place right outside the gates to *my* house! Can they not go and meditate somewhere else? Preferably more quietly?

I sit up in bed, peel off my eye mask and begin to step out of bed. As I do, Simon comes hurtling in without knocking, sees me wearing nothing but my very short babydoll nightie, screams and hurtles back out again.

A second later there's a knock on the door. 'Can I come in?' he asks.

'Yes, Simon,' I say. 'Since you've already been in and seen me in all my morning glory, you might as well come back again.'

He shuffles through the door without looking at me. He just stares at the carpet.

'Oh, for goodness' sake,' I say, throwing a silk dressing gown over my nightdress. 'Happy now?'

He looks up and is clearly relieved that he can no longer see any of my womanly bits.

'Tracie, there's a problem,' he says.

'What sort of problem?'

'Look out of the window.'

I push the blackout curtain aside and peer through the slats in the blinds. There are about twenty people out there, all holding banners and chanting something.

'What are they doing out there?' I ask. 'Campaigning for equal rights for tofu or insisting that the soya bean has the right to vote?'

'They're holding a protest about your article this morning.'

'Why would they do that?'

'They think it's sexist nonsense and that your views are old-fashioned and designed to keep women constrained. They also think –'

'OK, OK. That's enough abuse, thanks, Simon. I think I get the picture. Are they all lesbians or something?'

'No. Just women who object to your article. There are a few men there too.'

'There are men campaigning against me because I said that women should get drunk and wear lots of makeup?'

'Yes,' he replies.

'Come on. Follow me.'

I slip my feet into some fabulous feather-covered mules and storm out of the bedroom as fast as can be expected of a woman in five-inch heels.

'Where are we going?' asks Simon as I gallop down the stairs, taking them two at a time, less by choice than because I stumbled over the first one and have a momentum that is entirely out of control.

'Slow down,' he says, sprinting after me. 'You can't go out there like that. Can't you put some cargo pants and a T-shirt on or something? You know, a leather jacket, flat boots? Anything that's less feminine. You'll just rile them if you go out there like that. They won't take you seriously.'

I stop in my tracks and turn to Simon. 'These people out here are protesting about the fact that I'm telling them to behave in a girly way. Right?'

'Right,' he says. 'They don't think you should be dictating to them to dress like a fairy – their words, not mine.'

'But you think I should dress like a bloody action man to go and talk to them because they won't take me seriously unless I dress in the way that they think is appropriate. Right?'

'Well, yes.'

'So, what you're saying is that they're allowed to dictate to me, but I'm not allowed to dictate to them.'

'Well, no, I'm not saying that, Tracie. I'm just trying to make it easier for you.'

'Come on, sunshine,' I say. 'Follow me.'

Out we go, into the lions' den, with me leading the way, bolstered by a confidence that I can't explain. Outside the people are chanting things like: 'No to Wags' and 'Go back home'.

There are banners with high-heeled shoes on and a red line through them. It's a shame really because the shoes look lovely – all pink and glittery.

'Is there a problem?'

A woman with bright red hair steps forward. She's a well-built girl, bless her, and her face wasn't one of nature's better attempts. Given her appearance, I can see how she might object to the beautification process. 'The article this morning was sexist rubbish,' she says. 'We won't sit back and take this nonsense. Go back to England.'

'Go Back Home! Go Back Home!' the others start chanting too.

'Oh, for God's sake, get a grip,' I say. 'Have you got nothing better to do? If you're so liberated, go away and be liberated. I'm me and I'm very happy being me. I've got a lovely house, a lovely family and remarkably slender legs. If you want to fight wars and be a politician, do that, and don't wake me up in the mornings when I'm trying to get some sleep.'

'No. We will not be moved,' says the red-haired girl. 'What you're doing is destroying hundreds of years of women's fight for freedom and acceptance.'

'Oh, go and pluck the hairs out of your chin and leave me alone. If hundreds of years of freedom is going to collapse because of one article from me, then it wasn't worth fighting for in the first place, was it? Now you, madam,' I say, pointing at the red-haired girl's face. 'You would look much better as a blonde. You can have that advice for nothing.'

I spin round on my heels and storm back into the house, dragging Simon out from his hiding place in the bushes.

'There,' I say when we're back inside. 'Fancy a glass of something?'

'No thanks,' he says, and I notice his hands are trembling.

'What are you worried about?' I ask. 'Surely you're not scared of the lesbians.'

'No, not really,' he says. 'I was worried that they might hurt you, that's all.'

The phone rings, and I reach to pick it up before Alina can get there. She looks heart-broken when she realizes that I've taken the call myself.

'Alina too slow!' she admonishes herself. 'Alina must run.'

'Tracie Martin speaking,' I say into the mouthpiece.

'What the ****?' comes an angry voice.

'Is this the red-haired lesbian?' I ask. 'Because if it is you can piss off before I call the police.'

'It's Cindy,' says the caller. 'Just what the **** was that article this morning?'

'Fuck?' I offer, kindly.

'Exactly,' she replies. 'Are you trying to make people look stupid? Why would you write that?'

'That's what Wags need to look like,' I say. 'I'm not trying to make people look stupid at all.'

'But what were those ridiculous pictures with the article? Surely you're not suggesting people should dress like that?'

I can barely breathe.

'They were pictures of some of the greatest Wags in the world,' I declare, a mixture of disbelief and defensiveness creeping into my voice.

'They don't seem terribly stylish.'

'What?? Those girls are super, super cool. They have a style that is all their own, and which is highly sought after. If you're expecting me to write about how to look like Nicole Kidman or Grace Kelly then you've come to the wrong place.'

I've impressed myself but, as is so often the case, though my words are strong and my attitude is bold, deep inside I feel weak and vulnerable. In truth, I feel like crying. It's like the time I was told off by the headmistress at school for wearing glittery eyeshadow. 'I'm causing no harm,' I told her confidently. 'I don't see why I should remove it.' My friends thought I was amazing, but deep down I was churning up. I was terrified that the headmistress would take offence, and that would be yet another person who didn't like me.

'Sorry,' I say, rather ruining my earlier stance. 'I didn't mean to be rude but I wrote a long-running series of articles like that for the *Daily Mail* in England and everyone loved them. I got loads of fan mail and they're making them into a book. The book's out in October.'

'I'm aware of that,' says Cindy, and I can picture her, in her office, with her feet up on the back of some poor office assistant whose role is to crawl around on his hands and knees all day.

There's a silence.

'Look, the newspaper editor thinks you need to be more upbeat and LA about things. Can you do that? If you can, then we're OK.'

'I'll try,' I say.

'Good,' says Cindy dismissively. 'Just make it live.'

Make it live? What the fuck does that mean?

'Oi,' I shout over to Simon who's lying on the floor peering up over the window ledge to see whether the protesters have dispersed yet. I'm not terribly bothered whether they have or haven't. They're quiet now, which is all I care about. 'Cindy wants me to make the articles "live". How do I do that?'

'Shall we have a chat about it over breakfast or lunch?' he suggests.

Shit. I can't do either. I need to start getting ready for brunch with Jamie soon. He texted last night and suggested we meet up. He said he needed a bit of Tracie Therapy because he went to see his dad last night and was feeling quite low about his mum. I assumed that Simon would be tied up at the club, so I said I'd meet him.

'How about having a chat later this afternoon?' I suggest.

'Where are you going this morning then? Have you got plans?'

'Yes. I'm seeing Jamie,' I say. 'We're just going to hang out.'

'OK,' he says, standing up like a sad old man raising

himself off a park bench, and walking towards the door. 'I might as well go down the club then, and help Dean out.'

'You're more than welcome to come to brunch.'

'No, it's OK,' he says, wandering away, and I find myself glad that he's not coming. I love Simon to death, but he's not Jamie. I can talk openly with Jamie. I'm seeing Dad this afternoon and I'm more nervous than I was the first time because now it's starting to mean something. A nice lunch with Jamie and a relaxing drink will be the perfect preparation.

I get to the restaurant before Jamie, and make a quick call to the cosmetic surgeon to book an appointment to have the bandages removed tomorrow. Frankly, I can't wait. I'm dying to see what I look like underneath. Then I sit a while, looking out at all the people bustling in and out, drinking coffee and reading the paper. We're at Koi, where we came before, and the same bouncer's there – standing at the door, nodding at people when they walk in. He's got his hands clenched in front of him, as bouncers often do, ready for a fight at any minute. I can see the bolt of lightning across his knuckles from here.

Besides Mr Lightning on the door, the restaurant's got quite a different feel to it this time. Everyone seems much more friendly, especially when I tell them what name the table's booked under. On the table next to me sits a middle-aged man in a stripy sports top and khaki shorts. He's with his daughter, who looks about thirteen or fourteen. She has braces right across her teeth and is wearing a purple T-shirt and red cut-off trousers with trainers. They're sitting in silence while she sucks a strawberry-coloured milkshake through a straw and he watches her, clearly wanting to talk to her but struggling for something to say.

They've probably seen each other every day for thirteen years, but they can't communicate at all. It's like they've got nothing in common except that she's his daughter.

Oh God, what chance has my relationship with my father got? How can I meet a strange man when I'm in my – um – thirties and start having a relationship that should have been developing slowly since the day I was born? It's impossible, surely, to catch up on thirty years. It can only end in heartbreak.

Shit. I'm suddenly having a real panic attack about going over there this afternoon. I don't want to go. Or do I? It was fine last time, but . . . Oh God. I'm usually so clear on what I want and don't want; what is good and what is bad. For example – makeup is good, therefore the more of it you ladle on the better. High shoes are good, therefore the higher the better. Fake tan is good, therefore the more orange the better. When it fades and you start to turn the colour of Homer Simpson, just get back down there and spray it all back on again. My head's a simple place, really.

But Dad? Dad's different. I feel happier for having met him, but the prospect of seeing him again and trying to form a relationship with him is terrifying. It turns out that meeting your long-lost father for the first time is a far more complex thing that getting a spray tan done, and I just didn't expect that at all.

The whole thing makes me feel vulnerable. There's so much difficult, painful stuff that we haven't even mentioned. I just wonder whether, now I've met him, I should let it all lie, and not see him again. That way I could move on with my life in the knowledge that I have a father who is very nice and very normal and likes me, without having to build a new relationship.

Jamie arrives and the waiters dash to greet him. 'Hello, hello,' they say. They clearly adore him. 'So lovely to see you again.' They rush over offering menus and good tidings, slapping him on the back in a manly fashion.

'What have you had done?' he asks, when he sees my mummified face.

'A resurfacing,' I say.

'Wow, how cool. I bet it'll look fantastic. Well done, Tracie.'

'Thanks,' I say, and I can't help compare his total understanding of my actions with the questioning and condemnation offered by Simon. He's changed.

'So, why the sad eyes then? You've had some brilliant surgery done, I'd have thought you'd be bowled over with happiness.'

'Oh, it's nothing,' I say. 'I just feel so confused at the moment. This whole thing with Dad is just like . . .'

That's when I burst into tears. Not in a Hillary Clinton, moist-eye, delicate-sniffle sort of way, but in a whole crazy waterworks, howling, dribbling, runny nose, unpleasant sort of way that has all the diners turning to look and the waiters rushing to help.

'Napkins,' Jamie is saying. 'Just napkins.'

'And more champagne,' I blub through tears. 'More champagne too.'

The pain of the salt tears soaking through the bandages and stinging my sore skin is quite unbearable.

The waiters scurry, and the murmuring in the restaurant makes it clear that I'm one of the most exciting things to happen in here in a *long* time.

'Perhaps she just caught a glance in a mirror,' I hear a lady say cattily to her companion. That sort of comment wouldn't normally bother me, particularly since she's wearing a cream suit and white silk blouse with just the smallest gold earrings.

Her sartorial restraint makes her no judge of Wag style.

Still, today I find myself unduly affected by the comment and the blubbing starts again. This time it can't be contained until I've finished the bottle and ordered another one. My anaesthetic, I mumble to myself, as the tears dry up.

'There. Where were we?'

'You were about to explain to me why you're upset,' says Jamie, taking a sip from his glass. It's lovely that he's drinking with me. He's the only person in LA who does.

'I don't know,' I say. 'I'm scared of getting close to him because I don't want him to end up leaving me. I feel so alone out here sometimes. I thought when Simon came out that things would be different and we'd have adventures – going round LA laughing at everything and everyone, but I've hardly seen him. It's like everyone's busy and there's no role for me. I've got no one to talk to. If it weren't for you I'd have gone nuts. You're the only friend I've got.'

'I'm the only friend you need,' says Jamie. 'Good job we found each other. Now, when are you due to see your dad?'

'At 3 p.m.,' I venture. 'I'm dreading it more than ever because I look so ridiculous.'

'Why don't I come with you to see your father? If I'm there too, things can't get too intense. You'll feel safer. We'll just say that I'm accompanying you because you feel a bit weak after your surgery.'

Suddenly that doesn't seem like such a bad idea.

'There's no need to rush this process of getting to know your father, Tracie. You've got the rest of your life. Take it easy. Take the pressure off yourself. I'll drive you there and stay with you. I'll come with you every time until you feel comfortable.'

'Thanks,' I say. 'But I don't want to put you out.'

'You're not,' he says. 'We're friends, remember. I've been feeling so low about Mum that it would help take my mind off everything.' He raises his glass. 'Nell'n'Nancy,' he says, and I smile and raise mine, too.

'Now, anything else troubling you?' he says, leaning forwards like he's a psychoanalyst being paid to make me open up and talk through my problems.

'Did you see my article in the paper?' I ask.

'Yes,' he says. 'Didn't I text you? I thought I had. It was brilliant. I really enjoyed it.'

'The editor didn't think so. Apparently it's not lively and "LA" enough,' I say.

'What's that supposed to mean?'

'I wondered whether it's because it wasn't about LA *per se*, but I wasn't trying to do a column about LA. I'm not an expert on LA. I'm an expert on Wags.'

'OK,' says Jamie. 'I have a plan. You haven't seen anything of this town yet, have you?'

'No,' I say. 'Not really.'

'Well, I think what she means is that she wants more of your very English, Wag style but about LA. Next week I'll take you on a tour of Hollywood – to a different place every day. You can see how LA people live and include that in your articles. How does that sound?'

'Thanks, Jamie,' I say. 'You're one of the kindest people I've ever met. Thank you so much.'

'That's all right. You can stop worrying now. I'll show you the sights and I'll come with you to see your father this afternoon. Remember – friends forever.'

'Friends forever,' I say, feeling much happier about the meeting ahead of me.

3 p.m.

I see Dad and instantly feel all warm and happy inside. What was I worried about? I feel a bit silly for dragging poor Jamie along. There was no need at all.

'Oh, Tracie, what's happened?' asks Dad. I can see the worry on his face and in his eyes.

'Just a facial treatment,' I say. 'The bandages come off soon, and I'll be fine.'

'But Tracie, you had perfect skin. You didn't need to put yourself through all that.'

'Honestly, I'm fine. Don't worry,' I say.

We walk inside – Dad leading the way in his brown, knee-length shorts revealing chunky old man's legs with that scarcity of hair – on limbs as well as his head – that comes with age. It's hard, looking at him, to imagine him with Angie – my super-glamorous mum. Perhaps he was super-glamorous too back when they were young things, living life to the full in the Swinging Sixties in London.

'Look, I hope you don't mind, but I brought someone with me,' I say.

'Of course I don't mind. Good to meet you,' says Dad, shaking Jamie's hand enthusiastically.

Then he turns towards the kitchen.

'Sylvia,' he shouts. 'Come and see who's here. It's Tracie and she's brought her husband Dean.'

231

'Oh, Tracie,' says Sylvia, before I can correct the mistake. 'What on earth happened to your face?'

'Nothing, honestly, just a little treatment. It'll all be fine soon.'

'Oh, good,' she says. 'And how lovely to meet Dean.' Sylvia smiles and looks up adoringly at Jamie. 'You can see you were a professional soccer player just by looking at you. Very athletic! You know, we looked up the results of the match in the paper and saw that your team won their first match under you. Well done. They were all saying how good you were.'

'Thank you,' says Jamie, charmingly, looking over at me for guidance.

I stand there rooted to the spot, unsure what to say next. What do I do? Say to these lovely people that this isn't Dean – it's a random taxi driver that I picked up on my travels?

If I correct the error I'll make everyone feel uncomfortable and make Jamie look ridiculous, and I don't want to do that. That would be bad manners when Jamie's only here to help me out. We all walk through and sit down on the sofa. I look at Jamie and he looks at me and shrugs. He doesn't know how to get us out of this either. In different circumstances it could be quite funny.

I look over at my father, who's smiling adoringly, and at Sylvia, who looks as if she's about to burst with pride at the situation, and I know that I don't have the strength to correct this illusion. Not now.

'Drink?' he offers, and Jamie jumps up.

'I almost forgot,' he says. 'I have a gift for you.'

He produces a bottle of vintage champagne from the inside pocket of his jacket, and hands it to Sylvia.

'How very kind,' she says, turning scarlet as Jamie kisses her on the cheek. 'Oh, it's from Koi. How lovely. I've always wanted to go there.'

'Shall I open that?' asks Keith, and Jamie smiles.

'Yes, please. Tracie and I like a drink, don't we, Trace?'

'We do,' I say, a little bit startled at the English accent that Jamie has adopted.

As Keith enters the kitchen, Jamie goes to join him and I hear the sound of manly laughter as my make-believe, fake-accented husband and my newly discovered father chat amiably. They emerge clutching glasses, smiling and flushed with the success of their manly bonding over a bottle of $600 champers.

'I suggested to Dean that we play tennis some time,' says my father.

Silence.

'Would you like that, Tracie?' he asks.

'Me?'

'Yes.'

I'd rather boil my bandaged head in olive oil. They can't be serious. 'Me? Tennis?'

'I'm not much of a one for tennis either,' says Sylvia. 'But it might be fun to try, don't you think?'

'Sure,' I find myself saying, simply because everyone else seems to think it's such a marvellous idea, and I'd hate to be the one who put a dampener on things, but I've never held a tennis racket in my life.

'Right, that's agreed on then.'

'OK,' I say meekly, and I can feel myself pulled along by this mad situation. I want everything to go smoothly. I was always like that with Mum, too. Even when she was vicious and cruel I'd smile and tell her that everything was OK because I was terrified of alienating her. If she left me – what then?

'Thanks for the bike,' I say, and my dad looks really embarrassed.

'Probably a bit of a silly idea,' he says. 'Don't worry if you end up giving it to charity or something. I just wanted to do something after hearing your story. It really touched me.'

'I'll never, ever, ever give it to charity. I'm going to keep it all my life. It's brilliant.'

As I'm enthusing over the bike, which isn't really enthusiasm over the bike at all, but over the wonderful gesture, Sylvia bursts into tears.

'I can't believe Angie was so cruel to you,' she says. 'I wish it were possible to change things. Honestly, Tracie, it sounds like you went through hell with that woman.'

'No. It was fine,' I say. 'I just felt different from other children. I didn't really understand happiness until I met Dean.' I look up at Jamie and he smiles warmly. 'As a child, I was a real dreamer – I'd imagine this handsome man coming along and sweeping me off to a life of love and luxury. That's what Dean did. But it didn't make everything right. I'm so glad I've come to see you now. I'm so glad this is all happening.'

Jamie puts his arm round me and holds me tightly.

'I'm going to make it up to you,' says Dad. 'And you, Dean,' he adds, patting Jamie on the knee. 'The two of you – you're welcome in my house any time you want. Anything you need – you just ask.'

Thursday 12 June (9 days to go!!!)

'My bandages come off at lunchtime and I'll look lovely. You won't recognize me!' I tell Jamie.

We're at a small wooden coffee shop tucked away in the Hollywood Hills, roughly half-way between my house and the Raiders clubhouse. We're here because we've called a meeting to work out what to do about the situation with my father.

'Your dad is lovely,' says Jamie. 'I really like him – I think he's a thoroughly decent person. I'm so relieved.'

'Yes, he's nice, isn't he?' I say, feeling all tingly inside.

'I was quite worried in some ways,' confesses Jamie. 'I mean, if he'd been horrible I think I'd have ended up belting him because no one's going to upset you or use you, or make you miserable again. Not if I can help it.'

'Thank you,' I say, touched. 'That means a lot.'

'Nancy'n'Nell,' he says, with a raise of his glass, and we drink and we smile. Then I remember.

'But I can't play tennis.'

'No, and I can't pretend to be Dean for much longer either, but I think we're going to have to just this once, then the next time we'd better front up and tell him the truth. I'm sure he'll see the funny side of it.'

'Yeah, I guess,' I say, unsure. It feels wrong to pretend another man is my husband. Like I'm being unfaithful or something.

He smiles, and we both look out at the long trucks pulling up on the forecourt as the drivers come in for huge American breakfasts.

'Do you want anything to eat?' he asks, seeing a waitress walk by with plates of pancakes and waffles.

'No, silly,' I shudder. There must be enough calories in that lot to feed an army. 'I'd better head off in a minute. I promised Simon I'd go down to the club.'

'OK, sweetheart. You're very special, you know.' Jamie reaches over and holds my hand so delicately I feel like crying. 'And you have such beautiful hands. Do you mind if I photograph them – for my portfolio? Say if you do. I'm just trying to build it up, and add to it whenever I see something truly beautiful.'

'I'd be honoured,' I say. 'Then when you're a world-famous photographer my hands will be talked about all over the world.'

Jamie snaps away, holding my fingers gently as he moves them across the table, catching light and avoiding shadows.

I look down at my bright pink six-inch talons and I have to agree with him. The eye-watering contrast between the flame-orange of my skin and the pinky-purple acrylic nail can only be accurately summed up by the word 'beautiful'.

'Thanks,' he says. 'I just figure that if I take a few every day I'll soon have a portfolio to be proud of.'

1.30 p.m.

'What do I look like?' I say to Dr Johns. I'm so excited, I can hardly breathe.

'Well, it's still a bit red, and will be sore for a couple of days, but it'll be fine. It's worked well. I think you'll be very pleased.'

He tells me that my face must be covered in a thick, white, antiseptic barrier cream for a couple of days, then after that I have to wear a high sun protection cream and treat it gently. He hands me the mirror and I look into it. I almost scream. Noooo! I look worse than ever. My face is completely white. I look like I'm a Japanese Geisha.

'I can't go out like this,' I plead, but Dr Johns is insistent. 'If you take the barrier cream off there's a very high chance of infection which will lead to scarring.' I think I'd rather be scarred than white but reluctantly agree. Marvellous . . .

3 p.m., LA City Raiders clubhouse

I'm supposed to be in a bloody meeting with the senior coaches of the LA City Raiders right now. Persuading Dean to allow me to sit in on it so I can better understand how the club works took Simon about three hours yesterday. You'd think they were debating matters of national security or something.

'Where's it held?' I asked. 'In a bunker somewhere?'

'No,' said Dean. 'It's in the meeting room behind the away team's changing room.'

OK.

He tells me that I mustn't take any notes, tape the meeting or take any photographs.

'What the fuck would I want to do that for?' I asked, genuinely perplexed.

'That's OK then,' he says. 'The meeting starts at 3 p.m.'

The thing is, though, now I'm at the clubhouse I'm wholly distracted by a sign on the spa door saying that auditions for cheerleaders are taking place today at 3 p.m. I think of the bunch of old blokes sitting round discussing the offside law and penalties and shit like that, and I think how much more fun it would be to be in here, watching the cheerleader auditions. I can hear Pussycat Dolls being played, and the sound of female voices. I have to investigate.

There's a long trestle table just inside the door, and two ladies wearing cowboy hats, spangly bikini tops and sequined mini-skirts.

'Hi!!' I say. 'You two look fantastic. With a bit more makeup and shorter skirts, you could be like me!'

'Thanks,' they say apprehensively. 'Can we take your name and address?'

'Sure. I'm Tracie Martin,' I say, and I give her my address.

'OK. Synchronized acrobatics, aerobics, baton twirling, trampoline display or all?'

'Sorry?'

'The cheerleading. Just asking what you're interested in.'

'Oh, all of it,' I say, because I quite fancy having a look at everything that's going on here.

'Cool. Well, you're obviously all ready in your stage gear, so head inside and have fun.'

'Sure,' I say, wandering down into the big aerobics

studio which has 'auditions' written on the door. They've given me a name badge so I stick it on my chest, push open the door and enter. The room is full of leggy sixteen-year-old girls with ponytails like liquid gold. They're all standing, facing the front, where a man in jazz pants and a T-shirt saying 'Go Raiders' is marking out a routine for them to follow.

It doesn't look half as exciting as I thought it would be. I imagined they'd have pom-poms and be running around and lifting each other up and stuff. I turn to leave, but Mr Jazz-pants has spotted me.

'Ah, Tracie, come in,' he says, seeing my name badge. 'Wow – fancy costume. Love the white face – nice touch.' He takes my bag off me and shepherds me so I'm in the middle at the front.

I'm surrounded by kids in braces and plimsolls. What the fuck's going on?

'After three. One, two, three . . . to the left and clap, and up and down, and shake your booty. No – left, Tracie. Let's try that again.'

'But I only wanted to –'

'One and two, and – clap, clap, step, step, *left*, Tracie. We're all going *left*, and bend and kick and everyone – *splits!*'

The girls are all in splits in the left-hand corner of the room and I'm sitting on the floor on the right-hand side, having smacked my head on the wall and ripped my lime-green PVC mini-skirt, which clearly wasn't designed with kicking in mind.

'Right. Thank you, ladies. You'll hear from us in due course. Those down for trampoline, come with me. Tracie – don't go. That's you. Follow me.'

I learn lots of things about trampolining. First of all you have to take your shoes off, which I'm not overly thrilled about. I don't throw these outfits together, you know – they're carefully planned to coordinate and complement. I can't just go kicking off shoes – the whole look's ruined. As it turns out, the whole look's ruined even further because you have to wear ankle socks. The second lesson I learn is that you jump up and down a lot when you're trampolining, and if you have no knickers on everyone can see everything . . . especially when you're doing the star jumps and the back drops. Third, it's hard to do front drops when you have breasts the size of mine. Finally, I learn that the whole thing is much harder than it looks. You'd have thought that just jumping up and down would be easy, but no – I was jumping about an inch off the canvas and waving my arms around like a demented orchestral conductor, while the other girls all twirled and spiralled in the air, roughly eight feet above my head. Every time I jumped I felt my mouth fall open and my eyes widen so much I thought they were going to pop out of my head. Everyone was laughing like mad and pointing at me the whole time, which was a bit off-putting. Quite how those girls manage to jump so high is beyond me.

I clamber off and fall to the floor with my dignity in tatters, my skirt ruined, my hair matted, tangled and standing up vertically, and my makeup mainly on the bed of the trampoline, but also all over my plunging white top.

'OK, girls, we'll let you know,' says Mr Jazz-pants. 'Next, acrobatics. Ah, Tracie – I see you're down for this one as well as juggling and baton twirling.'

With that, I grab my shoes and go racing out of the room, down the corridor, past the trestle tables and to the door of the spa. I'm still wearing my ankle socks, and my skirt, now severely ripped, is flapping open with every step I take.

'Have a nice day,' say the cowboy-hat-wearing women as I skid past them at about 400 miles per hour.

I hurl myself out of the spa and land in a pile at some passing man's feet.

'My, my. It's my lucky day,' says a voice.

I look up and it's Chuck, clutching his mobile phone to his ear while he looks down at me on the floor.

'Listen, Jack. I'll have to park this call and put the issues on ice but I do think we need to cut to the chase here, and ring-fence the concerns. I'll ping you later and see you at the face-to-face.'

He clicks his phone off and looks down at me.

'You OK, little lady?' he asks

I nod, but I'm not really. The ground's still going up and down, my legs are sore from the high kicks and my head still hurts from when I fell into the wall. 'I only wanted to watch them with their pom-poms,' I say to a bemused Chuck. 'That's all I wanted.'

To: Mich and Suzzi

From: Tracie

God, that sounds like it was fun, Suze. How many police cars had to come? You just don't expect people to get drunk and disorderly at a christening, do you? But that's Luton for you. I really miss it!

The thing is, though, how did you end up having so many uninvited guests? Did they all end up coming along just because you mentioned it on that Facebook thing? It's not ideal, really, is it?

I'm sorry the vicar got so funny about it all but I guess he's not used to seeing twenty burly gate-crashers trying to get into the font. I think it would be a good idea to offer to pay for the damage and give a contribution to the church roof fund. (Why are churches always frantically raising money to repair the roof? What are they up to that's wrecking the ones they've got?)

Anyway, hope the second attempt at a christening goes well. I think it's a good idea to make it an all-ticket affair with bouncers and a no-trainers rule. That's what they always do at Spangles and there aren't half so many fights there.

Love you, T x

PS. Why did Mum have them running around the edge of the pitch holding long red ribbons in the air? How is that ever going to turn them into fit and healthy players?

Friday 13 June (8 days to go)

The phone rings and I'm sure Cindy's squawk can be heard all the way over in Luton. 'The weirdest thing is happening,' she squeals.

'Oh,' I reply. I'm slightly too nervous to ask what.

'The *Daily Mail* in England have rung and said that they want to run the pieces the day after the *LA Times* run them. Apparently everyone in England is writing in and saying how much they miss you. A features editor there looked on the web to see what you were up to and downloaded your article. They're going to rebrand you as the Wag on the West Coast.'

'Oh,' I say. 'Does that mean the *LA Times* are happy now then?'

'No,' says Cindy, before tempering this assessment with, 'not really.'

'Why not?'

'Well, they love the controversy it's causing – their website has had more hits than any previous article – mainly with liberated and enlightened women complaining. They love the fact that your pieces offer a platform to other writers to pen columns about the cultural differences between the two countries. In short

– they're happy with the impact the articles are having, even though they don't like the articles themselves.'

'Oh. Well, when I wrote them in England everyone loved them and thought they were funny.'

'Yes, the British sense of humour is a wonderful thing. The nation's delight in sarcasm, in particular, is quite marvellous to behold,' says Cindy, sarcastically (ironically).

'So what do I do now?'

'Next article's due for next Wednesday's paper. File it to them and we'll see what happens after that. I'm not making any promises.'

1 p.m.

How do I get myself into such ridiculous situations? How do I find myself in a sports shop, surrounded by packaging, boxing, and half a dozen assistants who are eager to help me because Jamie (who's also here) has just told them that I'm Lindsay Lohan's older sister. I'm buying tennis gear because I'm off to my father's house to play tennis at 2 p.m. and I possess no flat shoes, let alone trainers, and whilst I have plenty of short, frilly white skirts Jamie says they're not right for tennis, and I need to get the whole kit. While we're here, Jamie's going to get a new racket.

In the end I choose a 'tennis dress'. It needs taking up a bit (the ladies in the shop don't think so but, as I explained, the ladies in the shop won't have to wear it). There's nothing here in the way of footwear that is anything like appropriate, so we head next door to an excellent shoe shop where they sell those fab high-heeled baseball boots that Lady Vic wore one time. I'm all set.

Jamie's all set. We stop for a quick glass, then we're off to Dad's house (he has a court in the garden, apparently) for me to make my début.

2.20 p.m.

Whose life am I living here? Sylvia is dancing around, excited beyond all reasonable behaviour by the prospect of mixed doubles. She's wearing a tennis skirt and top, with pink piping around the edges and a matching pink headband. She wears no makeup and is swinging her racket around as if she actually knows what she's doing.

My lovely blonde hair is cascading over my bare shoulders (I ditched the tennis dress and am wearing a white boob tube and hotpants instead).

Jamie makes us all stand together for a photograph – me, my dad with his arm round me and Sylvia. Then he puts the camera onto the post holding up the net and rushes round to join us, grabbing me and pulling me into his arms because I'm not smiling enough.

'Say cheese!' he says, and we all grin inanely until the camera clicks.

'Perfect,' says Jamie, pulling his racket out of his bag.

'A new racket?' says Dad.

'A-ha,' says Jamie, before picking up a ball and smashing it into the far corner. 'Shall we get started?'

'Sure,' says my dad, running (that's a generous description of what he was doing actually) to the base line. He kind of shuffles from one foot to the other like they do on Wimbledon, but when they do it on the telly it looks as if they're preparing to whack the ball back, whereas when Dad does it he just looks like he needs the toilet.

I move down to the far side of the pitch to stand next to Jamie. He's explained that when the ball comes to me I have to hit it so it lands on the other side. It mustn't go into the net and it mustn't go over the line or they get the points (fifteen of them!) I'm thinking that this is all very useful advice but if I so much as hit the ball I'll be celebrating for the next twenty-five years, regardless of whether it's in, out, over or under.

'Rough or smooth?' asks Jamie. My dad says 'Smooth' straight away but I need a bit longer to think. I like Beckham when he's looking all rough, stubbly and manly, but I also like him when he's smooth-shaven and more boyish.

'Rough, I think,' I say, then Jamie spins the tennis racket round on its head and lets it fall onto the ground. 'Rough,' he declares, patting me on the back and saying well done. It seems to mean that we're in charge of serving.

'Let's get this tennis game out of the way first,' I suggest kindly. 'We'll serve the drinks later but now I'm all dressed up like a weirdo we might as well play tennis.'

'Serving's part of tennis,' explains Jamie, and I smile and tell that I knew that, I was just being funny. He asks me if I want to serve first and since I don't actually know what that is I suggest that it might be better if he did it.

'Sure,' he says, bouncing the ball up and down on the white line. I'm standing right next to him but he tells me to go and stand by the net.

'No, other side,' he says.

I begin to clamber over the net.

'No, this side of the net,' he says.

Make up your bloody mind.

He runs over to me. 'Over here.' He manhandles me

into position. 'Face the other way. There, we're ready. Don't worry, you'll soon get the hang of it, angel.'

I'm not sure what I'm supposed to get the hang of, but at least I'm in the right place and I figure that I can just stand here until it's all over, waving my racket around occasionally.

Then, just as I'm thinking about whether I should get longer extensions next time, or get wavy ones instead, the ball comes whistling over my head and bounces in the court in front of me.

'Bloody hell!' I exclaim, hitting the deck, but no one else seems bothered. While I've thrown myself to safety, my dad has whacked it back, and Jamie has run the width of the field to return it – belting it over my head as I lie on the ground. Sylvia then swings at it, and the ball comes flying so close to me that I have to lie completely flat to avoid it.

'Love-fifteen,' shouts Jamie, then he moves me to the other side of the court and we do the whole thing all over again. After five minutes of this nonsense I've had enough, and I sit down to keep out of the way of the balls and pull my mobile phone out from the front of my hotpants.

'I'm playing tennis,' I text to Michaela and Suzzi in Luton.

Michaela is first back. 'What the fuck?' is all she says. Suzzi has just one word: 'Why?'

I text back to ask them what they're doing, and have a moment of complete longing for the place of my birth when they type that they're absolutely hammered at Café de Parisienne in Luton.

'I've smoked a box of fags, drunk eight bottles of champagne and the way things are looking I'm gonna get a shag tonight,' reports Mich. Suzzi says she's dying for a kebab and chips on the way home, and will just have to get stuck into the laxatives tomorrow to compensate.

Home sweet home, I think longingly.

I'm starting to feel a mild depression sweeping over me. Here I am, in LA, miles from Luton, sitting on the floor while people blast balls at me. What's more, my hotpants have gone orange from the stuff all over the pitch. They're ruined and I . . . oh, hang on. I look again at the colour that my hotpants have turned and realize instantly why so many cool-looking girls love tennis. The pitch makes you go the absolute proper colour for a Wag. I rub my hands against the ground and start to rub the dark orange colour into my arms and legs. With increasing fury I'm rubbing it over my face and my hands, and lifting my boob tube to rub it all over my stomach. In fact, why don't I take this boob tube off? I'm just about to lift it up when my dad walks towards me, sweat rolling down his forehead. He leans on his racket like a walking stick.

'You OK?' he asks, and he sounds genuinely concerned.

'Yeah,' I say, looking up. 'I'm fine. I'm just not much of a sportswoman. Sorry – it's just not my thing. I don't understand it and I don't enjoy it. I'm really sorry.'

'Hey, no problem. It's my fault for insisting. Next time we'll do something that you enjoy. OK?'

'OK,' I say, feeling all nice and snugly and warm inside. 'Thanks, Dad.'

My dad smiles, and looks over to smile at Jamie.

'You should have told me Dean was such a demon player,' he says. 'I had a terrible shock yesterday and I still haven't recovered. That's my excuse for today – still recovering from yesterday.'

Eh?

'I've got some home-made lemonade here if anyone fancies it,' says Sylvia.

'Marvellous idea,' says my dad, and we all troop off towards the side of the court, but I'm not really thinking about the lemonade, I'm still thinking 'Eh?'.

'Did you play tennis with Dad yesterday?' I ask Jamie.

'Yeah. Just kind of bumped into him, you know. He said did I fancy a quick knock-up, so I said yes. It seemed rude not to.'

I take a long gulp of the drink I'm offered, and look over at Jamie. I still don't really understand this. Why would he be coming over to see my dad without me?

'We had a good morning yesterday,' my dad says to me. 'Thanks for letting him get away. He's quite the businessman, isn't he? He wanted to know all about the company's merger last year. You know, Dean, you have the same fascination with the market as I do. I'll show you how we redesigned the company in preparation for the merger later, if you want. If the ladies can bear it.'

I look over at Jamie but he's too busy smiling at my father and making smalltalk with Sylvia to catch my eye. The question still hovers above me, niggling at me. Why would my make-believe husband be grilling my new father about his stocks and shares, and how on earth does he know anything about company mergers?

'I know nothing about the market actually,' says Jamie as if he can read my mind. 'I envy you your understanding of it.'

'They talked business all the time, Tracie,' groans Sylvia. 'I was bored to tears. I was glad when they went outside to play tennis.'

'Yes,' I reply, looking over at Jamie, who's got his head down, doing up his tennis shoes.

6 p.m.

'Why didn't you tell me you saw Dad?' I ask. We're in the car, on the way home and I'm mystified and not a little pissed off.

'Because I got myself in a complete mess,' says Jamie. 'It was awful. I was out for a run with some friends when your dad drove past and saw me. He started chatting to me through the window. He was calling me Dean and asking about the football. It was a nightmare. I didn't know what to do. My friends were saying, "Dean? Who's Dean?" and your dad looked really confused, so I just blurted out, "Fancy a game of tennis? Shall I meet you back at yours?" so that he'd leave before anyone said anything. I was then stuck with having to play bloody tennis, so I tried to get out of it by chatting to him instead, about his businesses. It was a nightmare, but I didn't know what else to do. I didn't want to mess everything up between you and your dad, so I did the only thing I could think of. I'm sorry.'

8 p.m.

I'm sitting on the bed, thinking about how ridiculous this situation with Dad and Jamie is, and wondering what to do about it. I'll feel such an idiot saying to Dad that Jamie's not really Dean, especially when Dad doesn't know me that well. He'll think I'm a lunatic. Should I call Sheila and explain everything to her? She might be able to help. I feel such a lemon, though. How have I got myself into

250

this mess? As I'm pondering the madness of things there's a gentle knock on the door.

'Not now, Alina,' I say.

'It's me,' says Paskia-Rose.

My daughter and I have hardly spoken since the football match. She ignores me and walks away whenever I try to talk to her. I still feel very upset about her comment that I act like Angie. She can't mean it, surely? If there was one goal I had for the upbringing of Paskia, it was to make it as different as possible from the way I was brought up.

'Come in, sweetheart!' I say, enthusiastically. 'Is everything OK? What's the matter?'

'Nothing's the matter. I just wanted to say that I'm going out with Mary's brother on Sunday night, just to the cinema or something, and we won't be back late. He says I have to check with you that it's all right first.'

'All right? All right?' I say. 'I'm delighted.'

'Great,' says Paskia, walking away. 'Just don't get so delighted that you start smiling at people.'

All my fears about my daughter being a raving lezzer were unfounded after all. That's a relief. At least that's one thing I don't have to worry about.

'Hey,' I shout after her. 'Anything you want to borrow from my wardrobe, you just say. OK? I've got loads of stuff in pink PVC that would be perfect for the cinema, or feather boas and skin-tight leopardskin Lycra dresses – you just say the word, sweetheart. You can borrow whatever you like.'

'I'll be all right, thanks,' she says.

Saturday 14 June (One week to go!!!!!!!!!!!!!!!!!!)

One more week to go, one more week to go . . . I'm so bloody excited about the match between Raiders and Galaxy. So excited. Even though Jamie has been fantastic at trying to introduce me to the Beckhams, as he's always saying, he can't guarantee anything, it just depends on their diaries whether they turn up. He's seeing Victoria next week about the Alcohol-less Alcohol project though, so that should come together soon. Yipppeeee! The lovely thing about this match – *in one week's time* – is that I absolutely know that the Beckhams will be there because David will be on the pitch. It's the one date in the diary when I know, with all certainty, that the great meeting of the world's two premier Wags will take place. Like a G8 meeting, according to Simon.

This week, though, things aren't going so well. I'm with my real husband today – imagine that? Simon, Paskia-Rose, Dean and I have been watching Raiders playing away at some rough old ground. It makes the Raiders clubhouse look perfect. To make it all worse, Raiders didn't win so Dean is all sad and miserable.

'If we don't win the games the players aren't going to want to do all the extra training,' says Dean morosely.

'It's very hard to get them there as it is, but without the results there's no way they'll come.'

Simon shakes his head, pats Dean's back and tells him that he's sorry.

'Mate, the work you're doing will pay off in the end. The players'll have to be a bit more patient. You're a brilliant coach, but you're not a miracle worker.'

'No,' says Dean. 'Thanks, mate.'

'No problem,' says Simon. 'Look, if I can do anything, just give me a shout.'

'Will do,' says Dean. 'You've been a fantastic help to me already. Did you manage to pick up the Swiss ball, the weights, yoga mat and power plate?'

'All ordered,' says Simon.

'Spiky balls?'

'Yes, I have those.'

'You have what?' I ask, alarmed. 'Spiky balls? Is that some terrible venereal disease?'

'Pilates, you fool,' says Simon, giving me a hug.

'What are we doing later?' I ask, tiring of hearing about the latest fitness crazes to sweep through my husband's life, and fearing that I'm going to have to suffer these two analysing player formation and attacking ploys all evening.

'I'm going to take the players back for some video analysis and to try and restore their self-esteem, and I think I might try and take in a kick-boxing class and a thalassotherapy session,' says Dean.

'Oh, Jamie, please,' I say, then I stop myself suddenly. Shit. I called him Jamie.

'What did you just call me?' he asks.

'Jaynie?' I say. 'How weird is that? I called you Jaynie – that's my agent's assistant.'

253

'Is it?' asks Simon suspiciously.

'Why don't you and Simon go out somewhere tonight?' suggests Dean.

Oh God. If I go out with Simon I'll just be lectured all evening about my father and my unwillingness to embrace the LA lifestyle.

'Let's just go home,' I say morosely.

'I thought you were fed up of being at home. I thought you wanted to go out,' protests Simon.

'Yes, but . . . is there any point? Will we have any fun? I mean – do you want to go out with me?'

'Always,' he replies, astonishingly chivalrously. 'What man wouldn't?'

10 p.m.

Simon and I are, officially, proper friends again. We've had a rather splendid night, actually, with Simon even persuaded to dance with me. He's a bit like a mad uncle at a wedding when he dances – clicking his fingers out of time and smiling a lot while he moves his shoulders from side to side in a manner which suggests he's not listening to the music at all. I even got him to request a Madonna song for me, and when 'Like a Virgin' burst into the room I thought he was having a fit of some sort the way he was leaping around. His arms flailed in the air and we even had a few unlikely hip thrusts in the choruses. He also did that thing when you start to mime along, then realize half-way through a sentence that you don't know what the rest of the words are, so have to just mime the wrong words and hope no one notices. Simon covered this up by shouting 'Woo-woo' frequently.

It's not long before the hilarity of watching Simon's dancing has worn off, and it's time for us to head back over to the bar.

'You OK?' I ask. Simon's gone an alarming shade of tomato-red and is sweating so much it looks as if he's just stepped out of the shower.

'I'm just fine,' he says with a wink, still clicking his fingers and shrugging his shoulders. 'You seem in a much better mood tonight.'

'I'm always in a good mood,' I say. 'You're just never there to see it, that's all. You've practically moved into the club with Dean. Are you two gay or something?'

'I haven't moved into the club,' he says, still moving his shoulders out of time with the music. 'I'm just there because Dean needs some help, and I've decided to use the club at the centre of my novel.'

With that he twirls round, knocking two drinks off the bar and whacking some poor unsuspecting woman across the head.

'Ah, sorry,' he cries, and there's a small fuss while he attempts to wipe the bar and apologize to the woman, while paying for replacement drinks.

'I wish you were at home with me more,' I tell Simon. 'I get quite lonely during the day.'

'Why don't you call Sian, or Poppy and Macey? They seem like really nice girls. They were at the match today, and you didn't even talk to them.'

The trouble is, I feel as if I have nothing in common with them. They wear hardly any makeup and even though I can see they're nice people, and I try not to hold their fresh-faced look against them, I do find it difficult to take them seriously.

'Take them shopping then,' says Simon. 'Show them how a Wag shops. That would be a good piece for the paper.'

'Yes, I could,' I say. 'The trouble is that I just want to be back with my Luton friends.' As the words come out, I realize this is true. I'm desperately homesick. 'I think I just want to go home,' I tell Simon tearily, and he gives me the most enormous hug.

'You need to tell Dean how fed up you are,' he says.

'I can't. He's got so much on his plate at the moment. The team aren't doing well, he's working like mad, and did you know the club has financial problems?'

'No,' says Simon, concerned. 'I had no idea.'

'Yes, they're in real trouble. Sian told me when I first came over here. Don't mention it to Dean, will you, but I'm terrified that if he doesn't start achieving something with the team soon they'll sack him.'

'They won't do that,' says Simon. 'He's achieving great things. He's transformed them.'

'But they don't win all the time. Won't he be sacked if the team doesn't start winning?'

Simon goes quiet for a moment. 'You've been worrying about this all on your own, haven't you?' he says.

'Yes,' I say.

'Listen, Tracie. Dean's doing a brilliant job, and it's not going unnoticed. It may not seem to you that the team is being terribly successful but they've improved phenomenally since he arrived, and the players are all about twice as fit, so the results should get better and better now. My friends on newspapers back in the UK have been emailing to say that there has been loads of coverage of his work in the papers at home. You should see how many interviews he does every day. He's becoming a real star.'

'I had no idea,' I say. 'I feel so out of it, I'm not involved in the club at all. At Luton I felt like I was part of it all, but here it all takes place without me.'

'Only because you don't want to be involved. What about that day I invited you to come to a meeting and then you went cheerleading instead? It's hard to help you if you won't help yourself.'

'Now you're sounding exactly like one of Paskia's teachers,' I tell him.

'Yeah, sorry,' he concedes, giving me a big hug. 'That was a bit preachy. Look, I've got a week left before I leave. Let's spend loads of time together, shall we? We can go out somewhere every day, can't we? I haven't been spending half as much time with you as I'd like to. Shall we explore this town next week?'

'Yeah!' I say, thinking – shit, I've already agreed to do just that with Jamie every morning, and I've got beauty treatments booked every afternoon – essential if I'm going to meet Victoria in a week.

'OK. I'll make a plan, and we'll go and explore every morning!' he says, looking absolutely chuffed with his suggestion.

'How about every afternoon?' I suggest.

I'll have to see Jamie in the morning, Simon in the afternoon and have the beauty treatments in between, and in the evenings. Blimey. I've gone from having nothing to do to being manic.

'OK,' he says. 'Whatever you want.'

It's not ideal, but at least I'll know this town inside out and back to front by the end of the week. Great for the columns.

Midnight

We've been dancing, chatting, drinking and having a great time. I feel relaxed, happy and at peace with Simon for the first time in ages. I'm drunk and loving it.

I feel a vibration from my bag, and realize my phone's ringing. I can barely hear it above the vast noise in the beachfront nightclub, but when I open my pink Marc Jacobs I see the flashing light and wander out onto the beach to take the call.

'Candyfloss, it's me,' says Dean.

'Hi, how's it going?' I reply, trying hard not to walk into the boardwalk, the sea or any of the many courting couples lying along the sand.

'It's going fine here, but it didn't go so well in LA Galaxy's match,' he says. 'David's injured. He won't be playing next week.'

I bite down hard on my lip to stop the tears. How could he? How could he get injured?

'Perhaps he and Victoria will come and watch anyway,' I venture, brightening a little at the thought.

'No, I don't think so,' says my husband. 'The club have announced that he's going to Germany for a couple of weeks to see a doctor there who's an expert in knee injuries.'

Oh God, will it never happen? Will I never get to meet her? I need Jamie more than ever now. Only he can get me a precious meeting with the Special One.

Sunday 15 June

Paskia-Rose only scored two goals today, and we all know why that is, don't we? I was banned from going to the ground. Imagine that.

'See, we managed to win without you cheating,' she says.

'It wasn't cheating, Paskia,' I say. 'Where in the rules does it say that the team captain's mother must not smile during the match? Where does it say that?'

'So you admit you were doing it,' she says accusingly.

'I may have offered a gentle grin, but nothing much. Anyway, hadn't you better start getting ready for your hot date?'

'It's not a hot date. We're just meeting outside the cinema at 7 p.m. It's nothing.'

'Nothing? You haven't begun getting ready. Have you waxed your bits?'

'What? I'm not waxing *anything*. Mum, I'm just going as I am.'

Paskia is wearing these pale blue jeans and a white blouse that she must have stolen from somewhere because I certainly wouldn't have bought it for her. She's got trainers on (or 'sneakers' as she's now taken to calling them).

'You can't go like that,' I say. 'You look awful.'

'Thanks a lot.'

'Sorry, I don't mean awful,' I say (though I do). 'I mean that you could look so much better. Where's the horrid blouse from?'

'Mary lent it to me. She thought it would be perfect for tonight.'

'Mmmm . . . and who do you think can offer you the best style advice, a slightly overweight schoolgirl with plain hair or a super-tanned, gloriously abundant SuperWag?'

'I'm off,' she says, which seems to answer the question. 'Gareth's driving me.'

'Oh, Pask, let me take you.'

'You've been drinking, Mum.'

'Go on, love. Let me take you.'

'No, please, Mum. If you don't let Gareth drive I'm calling the whole thing off.'

'OK then, go. Have a nice time. Use a condom!'

'Muuuuummm,' is the last thing I hear from my daughter as she disappears through the front door and out into the world of men. How lucky she is to be starting out on her dating life. I remember what I was like at her age – saying yes to every boy who asked me on a date, then saying yes to everything they asked of me on the date. I just loved it that they wanted to be with me. The more I let them do, the happier they seemed to be with me. It was great. When I was at home there was nothing I could do to get the affection I craved from my mother; but when I went out with men it was simple and straight-forward to get affection.

I remember going on a date once with a boy I'd arranged to meet at the bus stop. He fumbled and groped me while we were waiting for the bus, and by the time it came he'd had all he came for, so he got on the bus on his own and went off to join his mates. I wasn't bothered, though – he'd told me I was special and lovely and how much he adored me and that's all I really wanted from the whole experience. I can still remember sitting on the bench at the bus stop for hours thinking how lovely it was that he'd wanted to hold me, touch me and be with me. He'd smiled at me and told me I was lovely, then when he realized I was prepared to do everything he wanted he piled on the compliments. I was the most fabulous person he'd ever met. I was wonderful, perfect and the love of his life.

9 p.m.

The sound of the key in the door. Oh, no. I hope the date's not gone wrong for her. I'd hate it if he'd told her that her clothing made it impossible for him to take her seriously, and he'd have to end the date prematurely.

'I'm back. Just off to bed,' says Paskia as soon as she's in the hallway.

'Woooah. Hang on a minute,' I say, rushing out to meet her. 'Not so quickly. Aren't you going to tell us about the date?'

'It was fine,' she says.

'Well, what did you do?'

'We just hung out, really. You wouldn't understand.'

'I think I do understand,' I say, with a roll of my tongue and a twirl of my hips.

'No, not like that, Mum. Everything doesn't have to come down to sex all the time. Why can't you be like other mothers?'

'Oi,' says Dean, joining me at the bottom of the stairs as we look up at our incredibly angry daughter marching up two at a time. 'Don't talk to your mother like that, Paskia-Rose. Show some respect.'

'Respect!' she snarls, before slamming her bedroom door shut. 'Do either of you even understand the word?'

Monday 16 June
8 a.m.

Paskia-Rose is gone by the time I wake up. When I call her on the mobile she says she needs to be left alone. Honestly, you'd think I was the sort of mother that you couldn't talk to. 'Darling, you can tell me everything,' I say. 'You know that. I'm not like these stuffy mothers who don't let their daughters have underage sex or get tattoos done. I'm a cool mummy.'

'That's the problem,' she says, slamming the phone down.

It's so hard being a mother sometimes. It's hard, too, having to go sightseeing with two different men on the same day, especially since I don't even like sightseeing. All that walking . . .

I like people. I love going out and having fun. I'd be happy to go out all week doing things like shopping for party dresses and arranging big nights out. What I'm not good at is looking at buildings and going 'Oooh, interesting brickwork. I wonder who the architect was', or 'Mmmm, fascinating art', when it's just a few splashes of paint on a bit of paper. I'd rather be getting pissed with my mates for hours on end for no good reason.

Still, sightseeing it will have to be. It's all arranged.

'Need a lift to the spa this morning?' asks Gareth, kindly. That's where I've had to tell people I'm going, because I feel so daft about the fact that I'm going sightseeing with Jamie every morning, and Simon every afternoon. I need to stay friends with Jamie more than ever because it's the only way I'm going to meet the Beckhams, and I love the way he talks to me honestly and openly about his mum and dad. But, on the other hand, I'm desperate to see more of Simon before he goes home. I need to build some bridges.

'I'm fine, thanks,' I say. 'Doesn't Dean need you at the club?'

'No, he's out training all day so I thought, instead of wasting time just sitting there, I'd come home and help Peter and Mark. We're gonna see whether we can build a pool for Paskia. Dean thought it would be a nice birthday surprise for her. All the other kids have them, see. Dean said he fancies a pool at home. He's asked for an infinitely one or something. What does that mean?'

'No idea,' I say. 'I'll go and look up infinelity, shall I?'

'That would be great, Tracie, thanks,' he says, so I head up to Paskia's room and take her dictionary down from the shelf. Infinelity? No sign of that word. Infinelity? Mmmmm . . .

I walk downstairs clutching the dictionary.

'Gareth, there's no such word as infinelity. Are you sure that's what he said?'

'That's what it sounded like. The designer's coming this afternoon and I have to discuss with him the building of an infinelity pool.'

'Infidelity?' I suggest. 'There are other words here that sound like it. Shall I leave the dictionary with you?'

'Please,' says Gareth. 'Must have been infidelity. I'll ask the designer if he can make an infidelity pool for Dean. Thanks a lot, Tracie.'

Noon

To: Mich and Suzzi

From: Tracie

Hi, girls. Just a quick email from me today because I'm half-way between dates with two different men, neither of whom is Dean. I'll explain when I see you!

So, Mich – first of all, I'm very sorry to hear about Arthur's gout. It sounds really painful, so I hope it's better soon. (If he has one of those mobility cars that would be perfect. If not, he should definitely get one.)

Suz – I'm glad the christening went ahead without any violent, crack-smoking gate-crashers this time. I'm sure the vicar was relieved.

The cutting you attached from *Luton Life* made me laugh, especially the bit when Angie was talking about her three-point fitness plan for the club. Making the subs sit on Swiss balls while they're waiting to come on, instead of sitting on the bench, is hysterical. Also all that stuff about how she's told the coach not to select anyone who can't walk on his hands. Eh? Her plan to change the team's outfits because the colours aren't healing and giving make me laugh. They'd never let her do that, surely . . .

T x

PS. I keep meaning to say thanks for the fab gift. Simon gave it to me. I absolutely love it xxx

2 p.m.

Here we go . . . I'm heading back off to bloody Hollywood Boulevard again – this time with Simon in tow. He's dressed up like he's about to backpack around Australia, with his binoculars and a knapsack containing enough maps and compasses for us to navigate our way through the Himalayas. I'm sure he'd see the funny side if I told him there was really no need for maps because I'd been there all morning. But, of course, I don't. I just go along with his plans.

Actually, to be fair, I have a much better time with Simon than I had with Jamie this morning. I don't know why, because Simon keeps getting us lost. He then insists that we skip down the street, stopping to say hello to everyone we pass 'for fun'. 'I want them to think I'm an English eccentric,' he says.

'Simon, love, you don't have to stop and smile and wave at everyone for them to think you're a nutter. They already think that.'

Jamie was lovely but our morning was very different from this afternoon. We went into this little museum first of all, and learnt all about the history of movies.

'There's a section on the history of fashion in films,' said Jamie enthusiastically. 'I thought you might like that.'

I liked the idea of it a lot. I thought they might have some of the clothes there from *Legally Blonde*, or even some of the fab PVC clothes that Julia Roberts wore at the beginning of *Pretty Woman* (before she turned into a dork and started dressing like a middle-aged lady). But no! The clothes were from period dramas and they were all horrible ancient garments made of lace and with ruffles and heavy, long skirts. Not my sort of thing at all. We got out and had a glass of champagne, took a little stroll down to have a look at the stars, then it was time to leave.

All very different from Simon, who's thrown himself into the afternoon with gusto and determination.

He's trotting along, his little pink-flushed cheeks burning in the sun, smiling to himself, with his long hair flying out behind him. He's swinging a walking stick by his side like a cane (he doesn't need it – it's all for show, much like the bowler hat and braces he's sporting). He couldn't look more eccentric. He looks like he's just a slug of whisky away from removing his clothing and conducting the traffic wearing nothing but his socks.

I don't think I've laughed so much in ages, though, especially when he starts imitating Chuck.

'Tracie, it's essential that you, like, calibrate yourself to this out-of-the-box process as synergistically as possible. I'm talking about the team dynamics that we face moving forwards and the need to strategize our agenda and challenge the paradigm. Are you hearing, Tracie? Are you hearing?'

'I'm hearing, Chuck,' I say.

'Good, then we have synergy and we'll soon be cooking

on gas. We really need to gather a field of top-down, user-centred, interpersonal solutions.'

'What does it all mean?' I ask Simon. 'Do you understand what he's talking about?'

'No idea at all,' says Simon. 'I just nod and scratch my beard and soon enough he goes away.'

'I think you're an angel for going in to help Dean out,' I say, and I mean it. Simon's just the nicest guy in the world. The reason I met him in the first place was because he offered to help me write my *Wags' Handbook*. It was he who gave me the confidence to have a go. He taught me how to set up my own blog, then fixed up the column with the newspaper. Now he's helping Dean out. I feel so bad for having pushed him away over the past couple of weeks, but at the time I just couldn't cope with the pressure he was putting on me to see Dad.

'OK, lady. Look at these,' he says, as we approach the Walk of Fame, the metallic stars embedded in the ground beneath our feet. 'Fascinating, isn't it?'

'Sure,' I say.

'Let's find Marilyn's handprints,' he suggests. 'You really remind me of her. Where are her prints?'

'There,' I say, pointing them out instantly.

'That's uncanny,' he says. 'Audrey Hepburn's?'

'Oh, they're just up there a bit, on Vine Street.' I point towards them and Simon rushes over to check. When he realizes that I'm right he's too excited for words, jumping up and down clapping his hands. 'How do you do that?' he asks, his face a picture of childlike delight. It's as if he's five years old and has just watched a clown produce a chocolate from his hat. 'Magic!'

Turns out I have quite a memory for glamorous

Hollywood icons. It's far better than my memory for directions or basic mathematics.

A couple of people have stopped to watch us, as Simon explains in his uniquely flamboyant way that this delightful young woman from England who has never been anywhere near this place before can point to celebrity stars with amazing precision.

'Elvis Presley,' he instructs, and I point to the far side of the street like I'm an amazing performing seal or something. There's a spontaneous round of applause and Simon does a mock bow. I'm not sure whether I should clap my flippers together or balance a ball on my nose in response.

'Does she communicate with the dead?' asks an elderly lady in a rather unforgiving pair of shorts.

'We're working on it,' says Simon, as he takes my hand and we go running along, dancing over the stars and handprints of the great and good – me struggling to stay upright in my high heels, Simon still mesmerized by my apparent skill.

'Drink,' he says, and 'Yes,' I say.

'I'll just have one drink, then I'll go on to mango and crushed elderflower beetles,' says Simon. 'So maybe we shouldn't order a bottle.'

I'd forgotten that Simon had been bitten by the venomous LA bug. But then – a most delightful turn of events.

'Aaaahhhhhhh . . .' he says. 'Gotcha!'

'Did you?'

'You didn't really think I'd gone all LA on you, did you?'

'Well, I did, actually. I saw you drinking that vile berry

stuff with Dean the other morning. It was quite upsetting to watch it happen.'

'Yeah, I know. I decided to try not to drink alcohol before lunch, but it's bloody 4 p.m. in the afternoon – nothing wrong with a drop of the hard stuff *now*, is there?'

I jump up and run round the table and give him a hug.

'Thanks for being such a brilliant friend,' I say. 'I wish you weren't going on Saturday. You've only just got here.'

'Me too,' he says. 'But I have to get back. I've only got three weeks off work.'

'Well, I'll definitely take you to the airport.'

'Oh, good,' he says. 'I was dreading going to the airport on my own. Bloody terrified of flying – it's an awful curse. Thanks, Trace, thanks so much.'

Tuesday 17 June

I'm blessed this morning, for when I wake up Dean is lying next to me – he's flat on his back, twiddling his sovereign rings round and playing with the four earrings in his left ear. He looks as if he's miles away, pondering some deep philosophical issue. Probably mentally weighing up the works of the greatest existential thinkers. Possibly trying to remember the words from some Samuel Beckett play or other. It wouldn't surprise me. The once simple workings of his lovely head have become a complete and utter mystery to me.

'You OK?' I ask.

'Just thinking,' he says. 'You know in Tom and Jerry – was Jerry the name of the cat or the mouse?'

'Don't know, love,' I say, secretly delighted. I've missed his quick wits in the mornings – the devilishly complex repartee coupled with his insatiable thirst for knowledge.

'And I can't remember the dog's name at all. Can you?'

No, I can't, especially not since I was drinking champagne with Simon for seven hours yesterday. Oh yes, gentle readers, *seven hours*. Simon may be a bit of a prude at times with his 'no alcohol before midday' bollocks, but at least when he drinks, he drinks.

'The guys have gone to UCLA this morning,' Dean explains, sitting up and stretching to the ceiling. 'That's a university. I've arranged for them to see a biomechanics expert and someone who specializes in homeostasis for sportsmen.'

'Specializes in what?' I retort. 'Are they all gay?'

Dean beats his chest in a bizarre way then breathes out very quickly, closing his eyes before breathing in again. When he's finished his little routine he looks at me rather condescendingly. 'Homeostasis is all about the water levels in the body, it's got nothing to do with being gay,' he tries to explain. 'The body's made up of over 70 per cent water. Making sure the body is properly hydrated is vital.'

'You're telling me. I think I need to see him. My body's made up of about 105 per cent Cristal.'

10 a.m.

I'm at the rendezvous point before Jamie. The sun's beaming down, so I'm clutching a parasol so I don't ruin my recently resurfaced skin. Sun is so bad for you!

I'm looking forward to seeing Jamie today. We didn't get the chance to talk much yesterday, and I do need to remind him of his duty to get me a meeting with the Beckhams.

He told me to dress casually (yeah, right!) but wouldn't say where we were going. 'It's a surprise,' he said, so I've dressed in an attractive all-in-one Juicy couture fluffy pink shorts suit and very high white sandals that have leather ties running up my calf. Dotted along the length of the ties are big, cerise-coloured flowers. I'm buggered if we have to walk anywhere. This is as casual as it gets for me, and I have to confess that I'm not overly happy with letting myself go like this, so I have compensated by putting on my going-out eyelashes – they have diamonds on the end of every lash! Super-cool, eh?

'Hello there, gorgeous,' says Jamie, and as I look up he takes a photo of me. 'Wooah! Are you going to be able to walk in those shoes?' he asks.

'Yeah, of course,' I lie. Don't they have cabs here?

'Great. Well . . . today I thought I'd take you on a trip to Muscle Beach,' he says, and my disappointment is unmistakable.

'I don't like mussels,' I say. 'I tried them once but they just taste like phlegm and sand to me. No matter how much wine and garlic you smother them in, I'm still crunching on the sand and struggling to swallow the spit and it's most unpleasant.'

'No, muscles!' he says, flexing his in order to explain himself.

Gosh, he's got a great body. Dean's looking much better since he started taking care of himself, but this guy is awesome.

'Ohhhh . . . muscles.'

'Yep. It's a fab beach where loads of the guys work out. It's well known in these parts. You'll love it. It's the sort of thing that you could write about in your articles.'

'Sure,' I say, moving to stand up, but Jamie sits me back down again. 'Wait just there,' he says. 'The light's perfect. Tracie, you look lovely. I have to capture this moment.'

He stops a passer-by and pulls out his camera.

'Please,' he says. 'Would you mind taking a photograph of my beautiful wife's face?'

I feel myself blanch at his words. He's taking the married couple thing way too far. A simple mix-up at Dad's house and now he's telling random passers-by that we're husband and wife. But before I can say anything he's grabbed me and is holding my chin in his hand, looking deep into my eyes as the man snaps away.

'Another one,' says Jamie, pulling me close to him and tickling me. I squeal and laugh and beg him to let me go. Finally, he stops and I lay there in his arms thinking that, even though Jamie's very good looking and hunky and everything, lying in his arms is not very pleasant. It's just not right, because he's not Dean.

He lets go of me and intertwines his little finger with mine.

'Friends forever?' he says.

'Friends forever,' I reply, but for the first time, I feel odd saying it. There's something about Jamie that worries me but I can't quite put my finger on what it is.

11 a.m.

We arrive at Muscle Beach and I'm pondering the high shoe, soft sand situation when we spot Macey, walking towards us.

'What do you want me to say?' asks Jamie as we see her approaching, waving furiously.

'Fuck,' I reply. 'Don't say we were together or I'll get into trouble with Dean. He doesn't know I'm with you. I'm supposed to be at the spa.'

'Helllooooo,' screeches Macey, giving me a hug. 'It's so nice to see you. Where've you been hiding? I haven't seen you for ages.'

'Just been getting used to my new life here,' I say.

'This is my lucky morning,' says Jamie. 'I've bumped into two lovely ladies. What are you up to, Mace?'

'Off to do a little shopping,' she says, daintily sitting down on a pile of white rocks, and looking out to sea as she speaks. 'You're more than welcome to come. If you want?'

'Why don't you go, Tracie?' says Jamie. 'You girls go and have some fun.'

'OK,' I say, not needing too much persuasion. I mean Jamie's lovely and everything but he's only a bloke, and this is shopping. I sit down next to Macey while Jamie announces that he's off for a run.

'It's beautiful here, isn't it?' says Macey, looking out across the beach, to the sea beyond. 'I'm going to miss it.'

'Miss it?'

'No, I mean – when I'm not here, by the beach, I really miss it. How about you? Do you like it in LA?'

'Yes,' I say. 'It's lovely – bright and fresh and, well, very different from Luton.'

'Have you been to many different countries?' she asks me.

'No, not really,' I say.

'Ever been to Australia?'

'No, why?'

'I don't know, really, just always thought that it would be quite a cool place to go. Not sure about all those kangaroos, though.'

'No, kangaroos are mad,' I say knowledgeably, thinking of a cartoon I saw once in which a kangaroo stole three babies and kept them in its pouch. 'They have huge great big hairy spiders in Australia too, don't they? I wouldn't like those.'

'No,' she says, absently.

Further down the road there's a sudden clatter of noise as a series of carnival floats begin heading down the seafront. They feature all manner of people in fancy dress – from fairytale characters to political leaders. As it approaches, we both stand up to take a closer look.

'What have you come as?' shouts someone on board, pointing at me. 'Are you a clown?'

'I'm not in fancy dress,' I reply.

'Yes you are,' screams the man. 'You must be. You're not a man, are you?'

'No,' I howl. Bloody hell, what's wrong with these people in LA? Don't they recognize a red-blooded woman when they see one? My jugs are practically hanging out. What more proof do they need of my femininity?

'Sorry!' shouts the guy. They continue their journey along, and we watch as four nuns are similarly accosted.

'Whe-hey, guys, good costumes!' shouts the same man as the carnival floats rattle by. 'Jump up.'

When the nuns turn round it's clear that they're not in fancy dress at all.

Macey collapses with laughter. The nuns, it has to be said, find it less amusing, and I'm too busy looking at my face in the mirror and checking that I haven't grown a moustache or hairs on my chest.

All the way down the seafront there are girls on roller skates who fly past at reckless speeds. You'd never see that in Luton town centre. But here, everywhere I look across this magical place with its azure seas and soft white sand there are women gliding magically along, as if carried by the breeze. Some move so quickly they're just a series of cocoa-coloured streaks with a blaze of sunlight trailing them, as their hair flies out behind.

'Shall we go?' says Macey.

'Yep,' I reply, clambering to my feet.

'Wow, look at your shoes,' she says as she sees me grabbing onto the rocks before I can stand up in them. She's wide-eyed and open-mouthed. That's when I realize. This woman is in awe of my style. She wants me to come shopping with her today because she needs my advice. She wants to be a Wag but she hasn't got the confidence or the basic equipment necessary.

'Come on,' I say, grabbing onto her arm in a manner which suggests sisterly love but also helps me to walk straight. 'Let's get you some new clothes.'

12.30 p.m.

'They're not,' I say.

'They are,' she replies.

'Not!'

'Are.'

'They're not too high, Macey. I'm not actually sure whether the word "too" exists in Wag language because you certainly can't be too thin or blonde. You can't be too heavily spray-tanned or made up, and you can't have a bag or sunglasses that are too big, or a skirt or hotpants that are too short. You certainly can't have shoes that are too high.'

'Listen, Tracie,' she says. 'I can't walk properly in these shoes and I look a tart, so I'm not buying them.'

'But I thought you wanted shoes like mine,' I say. 'I saw you staring at them on the beach.'

'I was staring at them because I couldn't work out how on earth you walked in them,' she says.

Weirdo. I had such high hopes for this shopping trip, not least because our names rhyme. How can two Wags called Tracie and Macey not get on?

'I'm named after my mother's maiden name,' says Macey dismissively. 'It's an unusual name, and I love it.'

'Mine's unusual, too,' I say. 'Especially the way I write it.'

'What do you mean?' asks Macey, having taken off the beautiful marshmallow-coloured stiletto that I recommended and slipped on a stumpy navy court shoe. 'You mean because it's spelt "ie" at the end?'

'No, I mean because I always put a heart over the "I".'

'Are you for real?' she says, and looks in the mirror at the shoe once again.

'Take it off or get a job in a library,' I say. 'It's no good at all.'

While Macey continues to browse in what looks to me like the orthopaedic section of the shop, I sidle up to the assistant.

'Do you have shoe-bombs?' I ask.

'What?'

'Shoe-bombs.'

But no one has ever heard of them. Odd.

When I turn round, Macey has sneaked up to the till and is buying the offensive shoes. Well, frankly, if she won't take my advice then there's nothing I can do. A girl can only do so much to help others see the error of their ways; after that they're on their own. So far today Macey's bought navy linen trousers, navy court shoes, a cream silk blouse and a pair of tailored sand-coloured shorts.

I'm so fed up that I'm dragging behind her, trailing my bags on the floor like a disgruntled teenager, saying, 'I'm bored, I'm bored.'

I perk up when we're in shops selling proper clothes, and I make a few purchases myself. I go for a couple of new pairs of white hotpants because they go orange so quickly, don't they? I bought a sparkly pink bikini top with – get this – matching sparkly pink mini-skirt and knickers, and long sparkly pink boots!!! I also got a white ruffled baby-doll nightie that will look great for going out and some brilliant new lipsticks for my newly pumped-up lips, in four different glossy shades of pink.

Now she's suggesting lunch, and marching me the length of the bloody street to find this particular café she likes. We walk passed a packed, glass-front hotel with a cocktail menu in the window. It looks exactly like my sort of place, but no.

'I want to go to Lentil Delight,' she says.

'Well, I don't.'

And that's when I realize I can't do this any more, so I drop my bags to the floor and stand still, in a complete huff, refusing to move.

'I'm going in here,' I say. 'Join me if you want.'

I walk inside, out of the heat, and delight in the cool interior. When I look over to the doors, Macey is following me.

'Sorry, Macey, I know you want to eat raw beans and shit like that, but I promise you my need for alcohol is greater.'

'OK,' she says, and we both wander over to the bar area, past the brightly attired, brown of face and blonde of hair youngsters, and grab a couple of the bar stools, dropping our bags down by the side.

'A small freshly-squeezed grapefruit juice, please,' she says.

'A large bottle of bubbly for me.'

3 p.m.

'Sorry, sorry, sorry,' I say to Simon as I burst through the door clutching my bags. 'I'm really sorry I'm so late.'

'Good Lord,' he says, when he sees me. 'You're wearing a lot of makeup for someone who's been at a spa all morning.'

'I know,' I reply. 'You know why? I didn't go to the spa. I bumped into Macey and went out for the morning with her instead.'

'Oh, great!' he says. 'I am pleased. She seems like a really nice girl.'

'She is,' I say. 'Crap shopper, though, and appalling at drinking. Ooooh, and guess who I got a text from just now? Paskia! She's got another date tonight with her hot new man.'

'Are you sure she's not too young to have dates with hot young men? She's only twelve.'

'Oh, behave,' I tell him. 'By the time I was her age, I –'

'Yes, Tracie, but just because you did it doesn't make it right. I think you should discourage her.'

'Yeah, whatever. I'm not suggesting she does anything terrible. It's just nice that she's enjoying male company. Now – what are we doing this afternoon, big boy?'

'Well,' he says. 'I kind of had a thought, something that I think might be fun.'

'Yes . . .' I say.

'Let's go on a tour of movie stars' homes and see if we can spot any celebrities.'

'But . . . you'd hate that.'

'Yes, but you'd love it, so I think we should do it. Look.'

He pulls out a load of leaflets and brochures from his bag, and starts flicking through them and showing me the route. There are scribbles and notes on the sides of the glossy pamphlets, and I realize he's been working on this all morning.

'I thought you wouldn't want to be walking anywhere, and I know you'd like to have a drink as we're going, so Gareth has arranged to drive us to the bus stop and pick us up afterwards, and I have two bottles of Cristal in my backpack. You know – the backpack that you mock all the time.'

He spins round to illustrate said pack, and I tap against it. Yep, there's glass in there – all is well with the world.

'Come on, slow coach,' I say. How can it take a man in soft-soled, flat shoes as long to climb up the stairs of a bus as a woman in sky-high heels?

I reach the top and hear the gentle pitter-patter of Simon's feet as he runs up after me. 'I was just asking the guy where we were going to go,' he says.

'No, don't do that. It'll spoil the surprise. Let's just sit back and enjoy.'

'I'd rather know beforehand,' says Simon. 'You know, have a written itinerary, so I can tick them off when I see them. I feel happier that way, so we don't miss anything.'

'Mate, this is an open-top bus ride to see the houses

of the rich and famous in LA. You're not about to take your final exam to become a brain surgeon. Relax.'

'Ladies and gentlemen, welcome to LA. My name's Bob,' shouts a rotund man clutching a microphone.

Everyone on the bus cheers and claps, so I join in, clapping loudly and cheering, 'Go Bob! Go Bob!' standing up and stamping my feet.

'Oh God,' says Simon. 'Not audience participation. You know how much I hate that.'

'Get the drink out then,' I instruct, because Simon is clearly not going to get through this sober.

We both take a large slug as the bus sets off.

'Yee-ha!' I shout, but realize that I'm alone this time. Everyone else is quietly looking out at the city as it rolls passed.

'I need a volunteer,' says Bob, and it was beyond my abilities to resist.

'Simon would like to volunteer,' I say.

'Good man,' says Bob, handing Simon a cape made out of the American flag, a large top hat decorated with the stars and stripes, a whistle and a large rattle. 'You put that on, and I'll tell you what exciting plans I have for you.'

'Thanks a lot,' says Simon, draping the brightly coloured cape over his shoulders. 'Keep the champagne out. I'm going to need it.'

'OK, my man. You are on celebrity look-out,' says Bob. 'If you see any celebrities you must blow your whistle as loudly as you can and twirl your rattle so we can all hear it. Give it a go, just to check that it's all working.'

Simon suffers the indignity of standing on the seat in his absurd costume, blowing the whistle and rattling loudly. He's treated to a generous round of applause and lots of cheering – mainly from me.

'Tracie, I don't know any bloody celebrities,' he says. 'The only celebrities I know are politicians and leading businessmen. If the deputy leader of the Liberal Democrats walks past, or the Trade and Industry Secretary, shall I blow my whistle?'

'No,' I instruct. 'I'll tell you if we see someone famous.'

'This here is the home of Gloria Swanson,' says Bob. Gloria who?

'Oh, wow,' says Simon. 'Gloria Swanson. She was great. You must have heard of her.'

'Was she in *Mean Girls*?'

'*Mean Girls*? No, she was a few years before that.'

'Then I probably haven't heard of her.'

'Anyone who wants to take a picture, do so now,' says Bob, and several people jump up and snap madly at a view of a large gate.

'Now here on the right,' says Bob, when we've moved further up the road, 'this is the house of Al Pacino.'

'Amazing!' declares Simon. 'Scarface himself!'

'Never heard of him,' I say, and I'm wondering when we're going to come across Lindsay Lohan, Alicia Silverstone, Pamela Anderson and cool people like that.

'Next it's Greta Garbo,' says Bob, and this provokes everyone on the bus to say 'I vant to be alone' for some reason.

Even Simon's joining in. 'Lighten up a bit,' he says, when he sees my downcast face. 'This is much better than I thought it would be.'

'OK everyone, prepare yourself. This is the house stayed in by Clark Gable,' says Bob, and the woman in front of me swoons and sits back down on her seat, being fanned all the time by her concerned-looking husband.

'This is fabulous,' says Simon, while I push back my cuticles and wait to hear the name of someone I've heard of.

'When we turn left at the bottom of this road we'll be at the house owned by Dean Martin,' says Bob.

'Ahhhhhhhhhhhh,' I shriek. 'We're home. Are we home, Simon? Oh my God, oh my God. Dean's properly famous.'

I guess things have been going well at the club, and coaches do become famous when their club is doing well, don't they? José Mourinho's dog even made the front page, that's how famous he got. How amazing, though, to be featured on one of these tours! I bet bloody Alex Ferguson isn't.

'Wrong Dean Martin,' says Simon. 'This is Dean Martin the singer – you know, the Rat Pack?'

'Oh, yeah,' I say. I know there was a Dean Martin who sang in a pub called the Rat Pack because Mum thought I was marrying a singer when I told her of my upcoming nuptials to Dean Martin. She was terribly sad when she eventually met him.

9 p.m.

Once again Paskia-Rose returns from her date, and once again she gives a cursory grunt and troops up the stairs, completely unwilling to divulge any of the details of her first experiences of the LA social scene.

'Where did I go wrong?' I ask Simon. 'Why won't she talk to me?'

'She's a kid,' Simon says. 'She shouldn't even be going

on dates, let alone chatting away to you about them after-wards. How old is this boy she's been seeing?'

'He's about eighteen,' I say. 'He's a soldier in the United States Marine Corps, so very trustworthy.'

'Are you sure?' asks Simon. 'She's very young to be going out on dates.'

'It's not really a date, Simon,' I say. 'She's just going out with an escort. I only want her to be popular. Once the girls at school realize that she's getting out and about and seeing something of the town, they'll all want to be her best friend. I want her to be the prom queen, Simon. I want her to be the most popular girl in school.'

'As long as she doesn't get herself into trouble,' he says.

'There's no chance of that. Paskia's too sensible. She's just out having fun.'

Wednesday 18 June

*A QUICK TEST TO SEE IF YOU ARE
A PROPER WAG:*

*You might want to do this test yourself or on your
friends to make sure you, or they, are bona fide Wags.
It takes more than a life-long devotion to the tanning
salons and a penchant for sunglasses the size of dinner
plates to be a Wag, you know. Read on to discover
whether friends who you'd previously considered fine
examples of Wagkind are, in fact, utter fakes. If they
prove to be so, it goes without saying that you should
dump them immediately.*

OK, here goes. This is the test.

Pick up your makeup bag.

Done it? Have you lifted it off the floor? Have you?

*Ha! If you have, I have caught you out! You are
not a proper Wag if your makeup bag is so light that
you can raise it off the floor without the aid of a
mechanical lifting device. If it doesn't take the eight
quarterfinalists from the World's Strongest Man
competition to shift – girl, you are not a Wag. In the
same way that a true princess cannot sleep on*

anything, not even a pea, without feeling extreme discomfort, so a true Wag knows what discomfort would befall her if she attempted to lift the hundred-weight of lipsticks and mascaras that she relies on every day. Put simply, every Wag knows it would be easier to lift her car than her makeup bag.

A true Wag knows that her false eyelashes alone fill a suitcase that's so heavy it needs a twenty-stone bodybuilder to lift it. Her foundation resides in a bucket (a pink bucket, of course). It's the texture of gloss paint and the colour of nuclear waste and, crucially, there's lots of it.

You see, the life of a Wag is a life of excess, and the true Wag understands this. Take me. I get through so many lip liners that I have them delivered every morning with the milk, the hoops through my ears are so big that small children regularly knock at the door asking whether they can borrow them for hoopla, and my fingernails have so many layers of acrylic on them that they are strong enough to cut diamonds. How about you? Are you a Wag or a mere civilian?

9 a.m.

I'm due to see my dad for lunch today and I feel awful. Simon and I ended up getting so drunk after the mad open-topped bus ride that we decided it would be a good idea to keep going, so we found a nightclub where we stayed until they chucked us out. It was brilliant. We kept ringing Dean and asking him to come out and join us. I really missed him last night – I feel like I've hardly seen him these past few weeks. I know it's hard when you move to a new country and take on a whole new job, but I want to spend more time with him. Because I was drunk, I obviously decided that it would be a good idea to ring him and tell him this . . . again . . . and again . . . and again.

It's now 9 a.m. I got in about ten minutes ago, and I'm still drunk. As Simon and I fell through the door, we bumped straight into Dean who was heading out to the club.

'Hello,' I said, staggering into him. 'Sorry we're late. Were you worried?' I'd hate to think of Dean being awake and all worried about me.

'No, I kind of worked out that you were having fun with Simon,' he says. 'You left me about 150 messages. Right, I'm off or I'll miss canoeing class. Catch you guys later. I've got an aromatherapy massage this evening so I'll be back a bit late. Have a nice day.'

I look over at Simon, who trips over his own feet and goes skidding across the shiny floor, landing up in a heap by the sofa.

'Oh. My. God!' I squeal. 'I think I will die laughing.'

I send Jamie a text apologizing but saying I can't make this morning's sightseeing, then I fall into bed for a few hours before going to meet my father. I feel a bit guilty not even mentioning the meeting with Dad to Jamie, but I feel I ought to start untangling things, and that has to start with me seeing Dad on my own so I can bring up the subject of the confused identity of Dean Martin.

1.30 p.m.

We're at a lovely restaurant in Beverly Hills. The sun shines down, the gentle sound of people chatting floats across the warm air, and I feel like I'm about to die. I know when I get this ropey the day after a booze-up that there's only one thing for it – I have to have another drink.

'I'm going to take a strawberry smoothie made with soya milk. What do you fancy, Tracie?' asks my dad.

'I fancy a huge big cocktail packed with things that are really bad for me,' I say.

'Ha, ha, ha,' laughs my father, releasing a big, strong belly laugh. The sort of laugh that a father's supposed to have.

'I mean it,' I say, and he just smiles.

'I know you do. I love that you're willing to do things the way you want to without worrying about conforming. You know – you and I haven't talked all that much since we met up, but we'll get the chance today, and I want to say to you, before anything else, that I think you're just great. I'm so proud of your individuality – the way you dress, drink and behave. Your mother was all about conforming – always wanting to wear the right clothes and look the right shape.

'I remember her picking up magazines. It would say "Wool skirts are the latest thing" and off Angie would go. She'd have to buy exactly the same wool skirt as she saw in the magazine. You're you. I love that!'

It strikes me that I probably do look like a very individual sort of dresser out here. The waitress is still standing there, balancing on these ridiculous roller skate things – like the girls on the seafront yesterday. She's looking at the two of us as if we're stark staring mad.

'What would you like in this cocktail?' she asks.

'Well, champagne, obviously,' I say. 'I'll have a double

vodka in there too, and maybe some gold-dust or something. Just no celery. If there's anything green in my drink, it's going straight back.'

'Sure,' says the woman. 'What about strawberries?'

'No food!' I say.

Dad laughs again then. 'Hey, listen – I'll have the same as my daughter.'

'Sure,' says the waitress, and she zips off on her roller skates.

'You didn't have to do that,' I say. 'You know – order the same as me. I don't mind drinking on my own. I do it all the time.'

'Hey, I thought I'd try it. It sounded nice. Besides, I'm playing tennis later with Sylvia, be quite fun to run about on the tennis court while drunk. Don't you think? Be kinda funny to see how I go.'

'Now you're talkin' my kinda language,' I say, mimicking his accent.

Minutes later the waitress is back with two large glasses. They've put mint in the top, and I'm tempted to howl, 'I said no bloody greenery!' but I manage to keep calm. 'Cheers!' I say, raising my glass and taking a huge slurp.

'Good heavens!' shouts my father. 'It takes like cherry-flavoured methylated spirits.'

To me it tastes wonderful – a bubbly, fizzly, sickly-sweet confection that reminds me of spangles, cherry drops and cherryade. It may be the perfect drink.

'Are you sure you don't want anything to eat?' he asks, and I do that shrug thing that teenagers do when you ask them ridiculous questions like 'Why can't you tidy your room?' or 'Why do you have to play the music so loud?'.

'I might just order some bits and pieces for us to pick at,' he says, taking the menu and scouring through it. He raises his hand and I notice how tight his short-sleeved shirt is around his chest and arms. He's a big man, is my father. Too big to fit in with the LA way of things. He's a rebel in his own sweet way, too.

'Right,' says Dad, looking deep into my eyes. 'How did you cope? How did you get through a childhood with Angie and live to tell the tale?'

'Woo . . . that's a tough opener. I think kids are survivors, aren't they? When you're young you deal with what's in front of you because that's all you know. I mean, I'm not saying it wasn't hard, and I was aware, even when I was very young, of being left on my own a lot, and of not having the fun that other kids have. I felt like I was unwanted.'

'Why did you feel unwanted?' he asks.

'Because she kept telling me I was in the way and that she wanted to pack me off to boarding school so she could live the life she wanted to.'

Dad's shaking his head and looking really upset at what I'm saying, but it's the truth. There's no point in me lying to him now, is there?

'She left for LA when I was sixteen and it was difficult. I was still at school and had no money to support myself. I had to leave as soon as I could, and get a job. I started work as a hairdresser, and after that things slowly improved. When I was eighteen I met Dean and my life was transformed overnight. I felt really loved – not just by Dean, but by his nan, Nell. I haven't really told you about her but she was an incredible woman. She spent hours, days, weeks, months, years being a soul mate. She'd support me, encourage me and tell me I could do anything I wanted. She told me I was beautiful, and no one had ever said that before. I mean, boyfriends did, but not Mum. She would spend all her time telling me how ugly I was.'

'I met up with Angie once when she was in LA,' says Dad. 'She said you needed a lot of money for your wedding, so I gave it to her.'

'Whaaat? I didn't need any money for the wedding. Dean paid for it. He was a Premiership footballer at the time, making a fortune.'

'I'm sorry you had to suffer all this,' he says. 'I feel mortified by the way she treated you. If only I'd tried to contact you directly . . . What's she been like more recently?'

'Once I met Dean, everything changed because I stopped relying on her, so she couldn't let me down. And, of course, Nell was like a surrogate mother. Then there were the Wags. I'd go down to the club and meet the girls, and we'd be like a group of little sisters – all dressing the same and wanting to look the same. We wanted long blonde hair like all fairytale heroines. I felt like they were my surrogate family. The thing that people don't understand about us Wags is that we're living the dream, aren't we? We're girls who start with nothing and end up with the whole fairytale because of the arrival of a handsome prince.'

Dad lays his hand on my arm and squeezes it gently. I stop what I'm saying and look at him. 'Go on,' he says softly.

'Well, this new lifestyle allowed me to cut myself off from the past and all Angie's abuse,' I say. 'But then Angie started to come down to the football, dating boys half her age. It was so embarrassing. She didn't like me being there so she did her evil best to split me and Dean up.'

'That's terrible,' says Dad, moving his chair round a little so he's sitting right next to me. 'I can't imagine why she felt the need to behave so vindictively.'

'I'll probably never know,' I say. 'But it was soon after that that I discovered the letters from you, hidden at her house, and realized that she'd lied to me all my life. She told me you regretted the day I was born and wanted nothing to do with me.'

Dad's got his head bowed over and he's holding his hands over the top of it, as if the horror of what I'm saying threatens to blow it off completely.

'I had over thirty years of being told that you didn't want me until I found those letters that showed you'd been desperate to communicate with me for as long as I'd been alive.'

The tears are flooding down my face now. Dad's crying too, trying to hold back a lifetime's emotion.

'Come here,' he says, and we hug tightly. I'm amazed at my ability to talk about all this with Dad. There must be something in the water here that makes everyone unburden themselves and reveal their innermost pain and angst. Perhaps it's all designed to keep the lucrative therapy business going strong.

'How did you end up in LA?' I ask, sniffing in an inelegant fashion to avoid my nose dripping. Dad offers me a napkin.

'I came out here for a work-related project. I was only supposed to be here for six months, but I met Sylvia and stayed.'

'It's a nice place to live,' I say. 'Though I must admit I miss home and all my friends. I miss not seeing Dean so much as well. He spends all his time at the damned club.'

'He's doing well there, though, isn't he?' says Dad.

'Yes, he is,' I say. 'But, I have to be honest, I haven't been following it all that closely. My friend Simon, who's out here for a few weeks, was saying that he's doing good things, though.'

'Blimey, yes,' says Dad. 'He's transformed the club. There's a real buzz about what he's doing.'

'I should probably pay more attention, shouldn't I?'

'I wouldn't worry. The two of you seem quite happy and content about everything. Was he trying to get hold of me yesterday, by any chance? A neighbour said that some fit-looking young man was knocking on the door.'

'No,' I say, full of confidence that it wasn't Dean, because Dean doesn't know who my father is.

'Ah, must be that Sylvia has taken a lover then.'

The thought is so ridiculous that we both burst out laughing.

'I don't think so,' I say.

'No, I hope not,' he replies. 'I could do without two straying wives.'

Is he going to start telling me about Mum's affairs? I don't think I'm ready for this just yet. It's all been emotionally draining enough for one day.

'Sorry.' He looks sheepish then. To his credit, he doesn't bitch about my mum despite the fact she swindled him for the best part of thirty years.

I lift my drink and take a huge gulp, dribbling half of it down my chin. 'Sorry,' I say, dabbing away with a white napkin and seeing the soft cloth turn a shade of brightest orange.

'I saw your column,' he says.

'Yeah. I don't think my column over here is going to be

294

the hit it was in the UK,' I say. 'People don't get Wags quite the way they do in England. They don't see it at all.'

'I'm sure they will. I thought it was funny,' he says.

'No. I don't think so. There were people protesting about it outside the house the other morning. LA people are so bloody uptight, aren't they?'

'I'm not uptight,' he says.

'That's because you're English,' I reply. All English people seem to find my columns amusing, even though they're not supposed to be funny at all. 'It's supposed to be serious advice for would-be Wags. People in England find it funny, and think I'm taking the mickey, and people in LA just think I'm barmy.'

'Well, for what it's worth I think your column may end up becoming a great cult hit,' he says. 'I bet people start getting into it, and will look for it every week, and before long a movie mogul will come along and offer you several million to buy the rights to a blockbuster film.'

'Ha,' I say. 'It could happen. And cows might fly.'

'It easily could,' he says. 'Very easily. Sylvia and I read through the articles that you wrote for the *Daily Mail* – they're hysterical. I'd be amazed if they didn't make a film of them.'

'Thanks, Dad,' I say, although it's obvious he just doesn't get that my book is a self-help guide, as we sit in this lovely restaurant on this lovely day. In fact, the only thing that's wrong right now is that I'm clean out of cherry-flavoured methylated spirits.

'Waitress,' he calls, and I'm more than delighted that he's noticed. 'Can I order another couple of these drinks, and a selection of nibbles?'

As he reels through some less than delicious-sounding

dishes, including sweet potato and shrimp, I look out over the beach and across the ocean. I'm miles away from home but I feel relaxed and happy. Perhaps home really is where the heart is.

8 p.m.

This is nice. Dean, Simon and I are sitting in the sitting room laughing about the funny way they behave in LA.

'Everything's different, isn't it?' says Dean. 'I mean, at the club the way they do things is so different from England. Everything's so much quicker, not so many meetings, and people really throw themselves into projects. Sometimes I think they're taking the piss with their enthusiasm. But they mean it, don't they, Simon?'

'They do,' he says, with a smile. 'Sian's amazing, isn't she? She's practically running all the team's admin arrangements now – booking hotels, transport and so on. She said she's dying to catch up with you, Tracie. You should give her a call.'

'I will,' I say. I had no idea that Sian was involved so closely with the team. I wonder whether I should get more involved. I'm just about adjusting to the idea that there are no proper Wags in LA but I don't think I can handle the idea of Sian taking on the Queen Wag's role while wearing nylon shorts and flip-flops.

'I'll give her a call now,' I say. I need to find out how involved she is, but then I have a terrible thought. 'But I can't bear it when Cheesy Chuck picks up the phone.'

The men both laugh.

'Cheesy Chuck – great name,' says Dean.

'Ya,' says Simon, adopting Chuck's twangy American

accent. 'You should call him pronto to maximize one-to-one interfaces. Perhaps you could explore non-vertical relationships while implementing synergistic metrics to productize both front and back-end client experiences.'

Dean claps his hands in delight. 'Brilliant, Simon. Spot on,' he says, then he turns to me. 'Call her and put it on loudspeaker. If he answers I'll dash over and speak to him.'

'Ya,' says Simon. 'You two could stir-fry some ideas in each other's mind-woks while you're about it.'

I tell Simon to be quiet and stop making me laugh, and I click the phone onto loudspeaker and prepare to hear Chuck bleating on about mental imagery and corporate visionaries. Instead, though, the sound of my daughter's voice bursts into the room. She's obviously on the upstairs phone.

'J really wanted me to do it,' she is saying. 'I felt I had to do it. I had no choice.'

Simon and Dean look up. 'Who's J?' whispers Dean.

'Her boyfriend,' I mouth back. 'I told you. Mary's brother.'

'I felt really uncomfortable. I've never done anything like that before,' says Paskia.

'He was wrong to make you do it,' comes the voice on the other end.

'That's Mary, I think,' I mouth to Dean.

'I felt horrible,' Paskia is saying, then she starts sobbing. 'When he made me put it in my mouth, I just felt that I didn't know what I was doing. I didn't like it. I wish I hadn't had to do it in front of all those people. I was so embarrassed.'

'In her mouth?' I say.

'In front of people?' says Simon.

'The bastard,' says Dean, rising to his feet. 'Just wait until I get my hands on him.'

Dean strides out of the room..

'Gareth,' he shouts. 'I need you urgently.'

Gareth runs down the stairs while Dean goes to the noticeboard and rips down the class list that Alina has put there in one of her regular 'Let's sort Tracie's life out for her' moments. Mary's address is one of the ones circled by Paskia. Gareth grabs his keys while Dean grimaces and punches the wall. Poor Jacob is in for a visit he'll never forget.

While the men go striding outside, the theme from Rocky no doubt ringing in their ears, on the phone I can hear Paskia saying, 'Dad, Dad? Is that you, Dad? What's going on down there? Hello.'

'Paskia, come down here,' I say. I'm not sure what to do. I feel numb. The thought of this boy making Paskia do sexual things makes me feel quite sick. Oh, sure, I did lots of naughty things when I was her age, but that was different. I was never forced into them. I never felt uncomfortable or used by boys. If I had, I wouldn't have had a father there to intervene and protect my honour.

I have to say I'm proud of my husband for dashing off like that. I think that's the sort of thing Dad would have done for me when I was young if he'd been around. Despite all my toughness and confidence, and my protestations that I knew what I was doing and wanted to mess around at bus stops with boys, I know I'd have loved that protection.

Paskia comes running onto the landing at the top of the stairs.

'What is it, Mum? I'm on the phone.'

'Put the phone down,' I say. 'And come straight down here.'

She gives me her teenage-style raised eyebrows and loud tut and tells Mary she'll call her back.

'What were you just talking about?' I ask.

'It was private,' she says.

'This is important, Paskia-Rose. Your father overheard you saying you'd been forced into oral sex by J, and he's gone round there to have it out with him.'

'What? Oral sex? What are you talking about?'

'He made you put it in your mouth and you didn't like it.'

'Nooooo,' she cries.

'So, what happened then?'

'We went to church. He wanted to teach me about his religion. He belongs to the Church of Jesus Christ of Latterday Saints. He wanted me to try the sacrament – that's when you have to put this piece of bread in your mouth, and I was really embarrassed because everyone was watching and I'd never done anything like that before.'

'Oh, no!' I say. 'Come on, we better go and stop your father.'

Pask and I jump into the car and head off towards Mary's house.

'Dad won't hurt Joseph, will he?' asks Pask.

'Who's Joseph?'

'The boy I went to church with – Mary's brother.'

'I thought that was Jacob.'

'No, Jacob's her older brother who's in the Marines. Joseph's my friend.'

'The mousy one with glasses who looks like he wouldn't hurt a fly?'

'That's him,' she says. 'And he wouldn't hurt a fly. It's part of his religion to protect all of God's creatures.'

I screech to a halt outside Mary's house, and we go running in there like Cagney and Lacey (Dean's favourite cop show).

'Stop!!!' I howl, bursting into the room, expecting to see Dean and Jacob slugging at one another in the middle and blood all over the walls. Instead, there's silence. The family all sit round the table, saying grace. Gareth and Dean, it seems, have joined them.

'Welcome to our home,' says Mary's father. 'Would you like to join us?'

'Sure,' we say, taking the two spare seats. I look up at Dean and he's holding the Book of Mormon in his hands. He looks terrified, and a little disappointed. I think he was quite looking forward to a fight. He used to get into a few scrapes in Luton, but he hasn't had the chance for a scrap since he's been in LA – too busy wrapping his ankles round his neck and looking through the centre of his being with his third eye.

'There's been a huge confusion,' I whisper to Dean, once the religious activities appear to be over.

'I know,' he mouths back. 'We sorted it all out. Mary explained what their conversation was about.'

'Thank God!' I say.

'Indeed,' says Mary's father, head bowed in prayer. 'Thanks be to the Lord Jesus Christ, our master and our saviour.'

Thursday 19 June
8.30 a.m.

Paskia leaves for school without saying a word to any of us this morning. She hates me more than ever now, after last night's little incident. I'm not sure why it's all my fault, but apparently it is. Even when I call her mobile phone she won't answer. 'Pask, it's Mum. I'm sorry you're upset, sweetheart, but it was a simple mix-up. Your father thought the boy had hurt you, that's why he rushed off. There was no harm done in the end. Let's have a chat about it tonight. Love you.'

What else can I do? Paskia can be the most adoring and adorable girl one minute and full of hatred for me the next. She seems to want to blame me for everything that goes wrong in her life.

10 a.m.

I'm in my dressing area, pulling out something fabulous to wear for my sightseeing with Jamie, when the phone rings.

'Can you get that, Alina?' I cry. 'I'm up to my eyeballs in Lycra and PVC at the moment.'

Alina's footsteps can be heard shuffling across the

landing as I throw my clothes selection onto the bed. I fancy going for something a bit different this morning. How about red PVC trousers with the cerise ostrich-feather jacket? I've got a red bra to match the trousers that I could wear under the jacket, and I'll slip my big gold platform shoes onto my feet. Ideal.

'Tracie. Is call,' says Alina, appearing at the doorway with that surprised look on her face which alerts me to the fact that nothing at all out of the ordinary has happened. 'Is Jamie phone calling.'

I pick up the receiver and sit down next to the cerise jacket. 'Hi, how are you doing?' I say.

'Fantastic,' says Jamie, excitement ringing through his voice. 'Something amazing's happened. The Beckhams' people want to meet me about Alcohol-less Alcohol this morning.'

'That's fantastic news,' I say. 'Can I come with you?'

'That might be a bit difficult,' he says. 'But I've got a suggestion. Tomorrow I'm going to take you to a fab restaurant called RawStuff – it's the new place to go in town, and if all goes well this morning the Beckhams will be there to sign on the dotted line with the company and to meet you.'

'Wow, that's wonderful!' I say. 'How exciting. Meeting Victoria at last!'

'I did promise,' he says.

But hang on a minute. 'Aren't the Beckhams in Germany?'

'No, that's why the meetings are all last minute,' he says slowly as if I am an idiot or something. 'They *were* in Germany but it's not working out, so they're coming back early, so they're free to meet.'

'Oh my God,' I say. 'But if I'm going to meet her tomorrow I have to get ready. My extensions aren't right. What about my face?'

'Tracie, please,' says Jamie. 'RawStuff is a very laid-back restaurant and she won't want to attract attention to herself, so just dress down, come casual, no need for a fuss. OK?'

'Yes,' I say.

'Remember – you're a businesswoman now.'

'That's true,' I say.

'So, are you going to wish me luck today?'

'Goooooood luuuuck!' I squeal. 'I'll be thinking of you. Text me after the meeting.'

'Of course I will. See you later. Friends forever.'

'No spa today?' asks Simon when I wander into the sitting room.

'No, not today,' I say.

'Good, then we can go out now?'

'I guess,' I say.

'Let's go then.'

'Where are we going?'

'I thought we'd go and find the best bar we can and just drink and chat,' he says.

'Really?'

'Really,' says Simon, and I find myself overcome with emotion.

'But it's not noon yet.'

'Just this once,' he says. 'I'll break my rule.'

We order champagne and Simon orders something involving goat's cheese and pine nuts. He also orders water, which makes me laugh. If you're thirsty, drink champagne. No one ever got drunk on water.

'There's something I really want to talk to you about,' he says, taking a bigger gulp than normal. 'Your father.'

'What about him?' I ask.

'I was just wondering if you're ever going to make the time to see him,' says Simon. 'I think it's an important thing to do, while you're in LA. I'm not going to go on about it, but I think you'll regret it if you don't make the effort. Your father could be a great support to you while you're here. You've got lots of time on your hands to get to know him properly, and it would stop you feeling so lonely. Tracie, I wouldn't say this unless I thought it was really important. I beg you to go and meet him.'

'I will,' I say. 'I promise I'll see him over the next couple of weeks.'

I've arranged to go round there on Sunday, so I know I can honour that.

'Good,' says Simon. 'Will you take Sheila with you?'

'I guess so,' I reply.

I'm scared to look at him as I'm talking, but he leans across the table and takes my hand.

'I can't believe I'm going back to London on Saturday,' he says.

'Me neither. I'll miss you,' I reply, and I realize that I really mean it. Dean's caught up with the football club, Paskia has loads of new friends and hates me anyway, and Simon's been my light relief this week. I know that I still have Jamie, and that I need to make more of an effort with the girls at the club, but it won't be the same. It's felt a bit like a holiday since Simon's been here. I'll miss having him round.

'Shall the two of us go out for the day tomorrow?' he asks. 'Go to Disneyland? We could kidnap Pask for the day and take her. It might cheer her up after last night. Or we could go to Six Flags Magic Mountain – that would be fun. It's all fun rides – it's got more rides, and bigger rides, than anywhere else in the world.'

'Has it?'

'I don't know. Probably. This is America! It's bound to have!'

I'm seconds away from screeching 'Yeah! Let's do it!' I know funfairs are cool because the England Wags went on the funfair when the players were in Germany for the World Cup. Anything the Queen Wags do is good by me. But I can't go. I'm due to meet Jamie at the raw food place, and it's my big chance to meet Queen Vic, the greatest of them all.

'Oh, no,' I say, and I watch the elation fade from Simon's face as quickly as it arrived. 'I'm really sorry. I've made plans tomorrow.'

'Oh,' he says. 'Oh, well, never mind.'

I feel awful, but I can't tell Simon about the lunch with the Beckhams because then I'll have to mention the business, and Jamie has sworn me to secrecy. Something to do with patents, which had me quite excited for a moment as I thought he meant shoes but apparently it's something legal and deadly dull. Not like shoes at all.

'We'll have loads of time together on Saturday when I take you to the airport,' I say. 'We'll get there early and have a drink before you go.'

'Yes please,' says Simon. 'Even the thought of that flight is making me feel quite ill. I'll have to have a bottle of whisky before I get on the thing.'

'Don't worry,' I promise, grabbing his hand. 'I'll be there.'

My phone bleeps in my pocket. It's Jamie. 'All well with Beckhams meeting. Lunch tomorrow with D & V as discussed. Be there for 1 p.m. Jxx'

Oh my God, Oh my God, Oh my God, Oh my God, Oh my God.

To: Mich and Suzzi

From: Tracie

Hi girls,

Thanks for the email. Mich – only you can decide whether Arthur's too old for you. I guess it must be quite frustrating for you if he keeps referring to people you've never heard of. He wants you to dress like Vera Lynn? I don't know what she looks like, so I can't help you there but I'm guessing that anyone called Vera is not going to be at the cutting edge of fashion. Like you say – with his failing eyesight and all that he probably doesn't have a clue what you're wearing anyway, so just tell him you look like Vera Lynn.

I'm glad you're managing to avoid Angie. It sounds like she's having quite an impact on the team if three of them fainted on the pitch because she wouldn't let them eat anything but pine nuts. I can't imagine what the coach is thinking, but then if what you're saying is right, then she's keeping him very busy and he's not got all that much time for thinking.

T x

PS. I'm keeping my fingers crossed that 'Angie's Amazing Fitness Roadshow – coming to a town near you soon' doesn't come to the Hollywood Hills!

Friday 20 June
8 a.m.

Things are becoming more and more distant between me and Paskia. She left for school without saying a word.

'Have a good day,' I shouted after her as she stomped down the street.

'Whatever,' she replied. Parenting can be so tough.

2.30 p.m.

Where are they? Where are they? I can't contain my excitement any longer. I'm sitting in this awful place surrounded by celery and other horrors where I've arranged to meet Jamie and the Beckhams and there's no sign of them. Our meeting was arranged for 1 p.m. My nerves are jangling with excitement and have been all day. Any minute, the Beckhams are going to walk in. Oh God. But why aren't they here?

Why the delay? Why's Jamie's phone not on? Why doesn't someone call me? I'm terrified that I'm in the wrong restaurant, but I called him last night to check and this is definitely where he said. So where are they????

Despite Jamie's insistence, I didn't dress down – of course I didn't. I'm wearing a Pucci dress with mad swirls all over it, with matching knickers and matching cowboy boots. (Yeeess!!!! Imagine my delight when I found these beauties nestling in the bottom rail in Cricket.) My eye makeup is a lovely mix of blue and lilac and is so liberally applied that Gareth was moved to leap out of his chair and say, protectively, 'Who did that to you? I'll 'ave 'em.'

I keep calling Jamie but every time I ring it goes straight to answerphone, and none of my messages is returned. It's weird, so disappointing and a little bit worrying. I hope he's OK. More than anything, I hope he's not in another restaurant having the meeting and wondering where I am. Perhaps that's why his phone is off . . .

This is a nightmare. I don't want to leave in case he arrives and he's just late and lost his phone or something. I also don't want to go in case Vic comes in, but I don't want to eat any of this crap either. I've been out and bought myself a bottle of Bacardi that I've thrown into one of their mango delight raw food specials (it has a power booster to help with hangovers so I figure the Bacardi and booster will cancel each other out and I'll be OK to drive home).

The only thing I like about restaurants is getting dressed up, chatting, drinking alcohol and watching people. It's not much fun on your own. If you start chatting to yourself people think you're nuts, and if you go over and start chatting away to the people at the table next to you they'll call the police. I can watch people, of course, so that's what I do – starring like a mad old lady at everyone who comes in, wanting to give them advice on makeup application and styling but feeling that my intrusion would be unwelcome. There's only one thing for it.

'Another one of your delicious mango delights,' I request, rummaging in my bag for the Bacardi.

'With the same power booster?' asks the waiter. 'Or would you like to try another one?'

'Look,' I say. 'Let's be really straight with one another here – they don't work. Do they? If achieving fat loss, brain power or a vitamin injection was that easy, we'd all be perfectly proportioned and fighting fit.'

He slouches from one foot to the other and scratches his head. 'I guess they help?' he says, and I feel mean – it's not his fault that Jamie hasn't turned up.

'Sure,' I say. 'Sorry – I'm feeling a bit under the weather.'

'How about an immune system kick-start then? That should help.'

'Perfect!' I say, unscrewing the Bacardi bottle with skill.

4 p.m.

The waiter's taken to popping over and chatting to me every so often and I've taken to having a little fun with him to kill the time until Jamie arrives.

'Mmmm, the immune system thingy's brilliant,' I say. 'I can really taste how it's giving me a kick-start. Here, try some.'

'I've tasted them before,' he says. 'For our training we had to try them all and learn all about the nutritional qualities of the food.'

'Please taste it,' I say. 'I can't believe how wonderful it is.'

The waiter is torn between insisting that he knows full well what all the power boosters taste like, and just bloody tasting it to shut me up. In the end he decides to grant my ludicrous but heart-felt request, probably judging it to be the quickest way to shut me up.

'Wow!' he says. 'Gosh, that's great, isn't it? I'd forgotten completely how powerful that boost is. I might get one myself. Do you mind if I join you? I've got a break now.'

'Please do,' I say. 'I'm bored out of my mind.'

He skips off to get himself a drink that will taste nothing like mine, while I unscrew the bottle of Bacardi again and think how lucky it is that I went for the litre size.

He returns to the table clutching it. I have the bottle open in my bag. 'Would you mind getting me a napkin?' I request.

'Sure.' Down goes the drink and off goes the waiter. Out comes the bottle, in goes the Bacardi, back comes the waiter and down goes the drink.

'Jeeez, that's good,' he says, and I just stop myself from saying thank you, and explaining that I put slightly more in that time because the bottle slipped.

'Tell me then,' he says. 'Why have you been sitting here in this restaurant all day? I assumed you were waiting for someone.'

'I was,' I say. 'I don't think he's coming.'

The waiter takes another slug of his drink and his little face goes pink. 'Lovely,' he says, all wide-eyed. I wonder when was the last time he had a drink. Probably do him the world of good to lighten up and relax a bit. It'll certainly brighten up his afternoon.

'I was due to meet a friend here for a business meeting and he said that the Beckhams would be coming too.'

'David Beckham – the soccer guy from England?' says the waiter, and I'm impressed that he looks genuinely excited by this news. 'I think his wife Victoria is so cool.'

'Me too!' I exclaim. 'I was so hoping to meet her.'

'But the Beckhams are in Germany,' says the waiter. 'They were on Fox this morning.'

Still in Germany? I thought they were back. What's going on?

The waiter heads off, weaving between the tables. He walks straight into the counter and collapses in fits of giggles. It might be time for me to leave: Jamie's not answering his phone, I've drunk the best part of a bottle of Bacardi and consumed more mango in one sitting than I've had in my life before. I stand up, gingerly, and stagger towards the door where Gareth's waiting. Poor bastard's been sitting there all afternoon. I should have invited him to join me here but I kept thinking that Jamie would arrive and I didn't want Gareth to report back to either Dean or Simon because the whole thing's supposed to be hush-hush.

'You OK?' he says, reaching out to help me as I stagger out of the restaurant. 'You seem a bit down.'

'I'll be OK,' I say. 'Just take me home and let's all get pissed.'

I wave goodbye to the waiter, who thinks he's Tom Cruise as he makes raw potato and green bean juice with all the finesse of a cocktail waiter. He waves madly. 'Come back soon, come back soon,' he calls, as if we've been friends all our lives. 'Wow! Cool boots!'

You see – he's really enjoying himself, I've saved him for a day from teetotal boredom, but alcohol's such an unmentionable thing in this town. It's like everyone is either teetotal or in rehab with problems. No one seems to be able to drink it normally and healthily like we do in Luton – you know, a couple of bottles of wine, three bottles of Bacardi, vodka, Bailey's and Malibu and a couple of bottles of Cherry B to finish off the night, then stop before it gets silly. No need to overdo things.

'Take me home, Gareth,' I say.

'Home?' he asks. 'What? Back to Luton?'

And I have to say, it's a lovely thought. But, no.

'Take me to our LA home,' I say, thinking of Simon sitting there on his own. It'll be nice to spend the evening with him. I'm glad I'll be taking him to the airport tomorrow; we'll have time for another chat. Perhaps I'll tell him about meeting Dad.

'Sure thing, ma'am,' he replies.

Saturday 21 June
9 a.m.

Dean comes in to tell me that Paskia-Rose has locked her
door, and insists that she will not talk to anyone in the
family because we don't understand her. She is thinking
of becoming a Mormon.

10 a.m.

The phone rings just as Dean is coming through the door
after his morning run with a personal trainer. 'I'll get it,
Candyfloss,' he shouts.

'Hello, Dean Martin speaking,' I hear Dean say. He
does have a habit of yelling into that phone.

When we got back yesterday afternoon there was no
sign of Simon. He'd gone to join Dean at the club, so
I spent so much of the evening trying to get hold of
Jamie. Leaving messages and sending him texts requires
a level of secrecy that would impress MI5. I never
managed to get hold of him, so at about 6 p.m. I booked
an emergency extensions upheaval and quick spray tan.
Today I'm all Wagalicious but with nothing to do!

'Thanks so much for calling. Great to talk to you, mate.
Brilliant. See you later,' Dean is saying.

Poor Dean must be exhausted. He was in his office for hours this morning before his run. I bet he's watched 350 technical videos, made twenty-five phone calls and run through team strategy for today's match a thousand times. I just know that the call he's been taking is about the match. He's determined to get Raiders winning because his biggest aim in life right now is to get them through to the play-offs, something which everyone at the club, in the Major League Soccer Organization, indeed the world, seems to think is about as likely as Hillary Clinton is to be selected in goal.

I'm aware that this is the big one today because Galaxy are our nearest neighbours and our toughest rivals.

'Babe, babe, babe,' he howls, bursting into the bedroom.

Oh Lord, what now?

'Hold on to your knickers,' he squeals, leaping onto the bed. I peer out from under my eye mask, quickly disappearing back under it again. If he thinks he's having sex he's got it all wrong. I spent yesterday evening having my legs spray tanned and my extensions done. There's no way I'm risking a patchy leg and tangled hair situation just so he can get his end away.

'Take the eye mask off,' he instructs, but I snuggle down under the sheets, pulling them over me protectively. 'I have some sensational news.'

I don't move.

'The best news you could ever hear,' he says.

'Well, unless that call was from David Beckham's manager saying that David and Vic are coming to the game today, and would like to meet us, then I'm afraid you're wrong.'

'It was.'

'It was what?'

'On the phone just now. David's assistant calling to say David's back from Germany and is going to come along and support Galaxy. He wonders whether I, sorry we, fancy meeting them for a drink afterwards.'

'Them is . . . him and . . .'

'Yep – Victoria.'

'NO!' I yelp, removing my eye mask and thanking the Lord that I got my tan topped up and my extensions done yesterday.

'It's true,' says Dean, adding, rather childishly, 'cross my heart and hope to die.'

Fuck!!

'Happy?' he asks.

'Er . . . yes!!!' The truth is that 'happy' doesn't begin to cover it. My whole world is spinning on its axis – tossing and turning and remoulding itself in a new and more fascinating shape. This makes up for all the heartache of not seeing her yesterday. I can't believe it. It's wonderful, truly wonderful.

'I'm off then,' says Dean.

'Tell Paskia,' I say. 'It might cheer her up. Tell her not to become a Mormon yet because they're not allowed to go lusting after people and Beckham's going to be there.'

'I will,' says Dean. 'See you later, Candyfloss.'

'See you later, Sugar Lump.'

Gosh, I can't wait. What time is it now? Ten past ten . . . Maybe I should get dressed now. Shit. Dressed???? Fuck. What am I going to wear? I have to look sensational. I have to look so much better than I've ever looked before in my whole entire life. I need a new outfit. I need to call all the shops on Rodeo Drive and get them to bike over all their outfits for me to try on. Perhaps I should call Jamie? He's good at organizing all that sort of thing. Perhaps I need an emergency stylist. Do I dial 911 for one of those?

No. I know. The green dress!!!! The one I've been saving. Yes – I'll wear that!

I race into my dressing area and start hurling things around in a crazy rush. I pull out a shoe box with complete disregard for the other four sitting on top of it, and feel the full force of a stiletto attack as they come tumbling down. Ow. Shit. I stand up again and start to rummage through the rails. I have a perfect dress here somewhere. When I brought it back from my shopping trip on Rodeo Drive, Dean said I looked like something out of a kids' cartoon in it, but he's the man who's always telling me not to show the tattoo on my bum to everyone – especially if we don't know them – so he's not really the first person I'd consult on the subject of style and sophistication. All I know is that the dress would be perfect with my now very tanned legs, and with white lace-up ankle boots and brightest pink lipstick.

'What are you up to?' asks Simon, leaning into the room as I race around, throwing clothing about with gay abandon.

'Here!' I screech, pulling out the dress. Oh my God, it's even more perfect than I remember it being. Truly – it's wonderful. 'Look,' I say to Simon. 'Don't you think this would be just major for today?'

'Wow,' he says, looking unsure. 'What, for going to the airport?'

'Airport?'

'Yes,' says Simon, then he sees the look of confusion on my face. 'Not now, silly. The flight's not until 3 p.m. Thank God.'

'3 p.m.?'

'Yes. Don't say you've forgotten?'

'Ummm . . . no,' I say. But I'm thinking, Fuck, fuck, fuck. 'I can't believe you're leaving today,' I mutter. What I mean is, I can't believe he's leaving today – the day that I will finally get to meet Victoria. How am I going to get out of this one?

I didn't go and pick him up from the airport when he arrived three weeks ago, I spent hardly any time with him for the first couple of weeks that he was here, I lied to him about my dad, I lied to him about Jamie, I cancelled going out with him yesterday so I could see Jamie, and now I'm going to wimp out of taking him to the airport. Shit! I'm such a bad friend.

Why's the flight at 3 p.m.? What an utterly ridiculous time to send a plane into the sky! Does no one think these things through?

Where is the airport anyway? I've got no sense of where anything is in this town because ever since I arrived I've been going past the Beckhams' house en route to everywhere, so all I know is that everywhere takes an hour minimum to get to. Simon interprets my sudden silence as sadness and moves to console me.

'Don't worry, we'll talk all the time while I'm in England,' he says. 'We'll be talking every Monday night about the articles anyway, won't we?'

'Yes,' I reply, but my mind's wandering. I'm skipping and laughing and dancing down Rodeo Drive with Victoria. We're spending money in obscene quantities and hugging each other.

'We'll have a chat on the phone whenever you're feeling down,' says Simon, intent on being boringly practical while I'm deep into my fantasy. 'Don't worry, Tracie, it'll be fine. I'll be OK once I'm on the plane.'

I'm not worried about Simon's fears of flying. I'm worried about today. Victoria, planes, friendship with Simon versus meeting the woman I adore more than any other. And I'm worried because whilst it may seem that I have a choice, I don't. I *have* to meet Victoria. Asking a Wag to choose between Victoria and a friend is like asking a civilian to choose between her first-born and a friend. Friends are lovely and all that, but this is a completely different level entirely.

'Sure,' I say abstractly, but I'm not really here in this room at all. I'm back on Rodeo Drive with V and the paparazzi have just arrived. 'Oh, no!' shrieks Vic. 'Where shall we hide?' but we can't. We're pictured together on the front of every newspaper in the world, and I look far skinnier than she does and everyone I've ever met sees it, including Mum who's so impressed she can't believe it.

This afternoon I will meet her. It's guaranteed. None of this driving past her house and hoping, or sitting in stupid raw food restaurants all day, just in case. No more cleaning the pool or scraping wood off their gate. This afternoon I will definitely meet the woman who I know is destined to become my very best friend in the world. Anyway, Simon will be fine in a cab – just fine. He'd probably prefer that, to be honest. He hates my driving. I don't think he's ever quite forgiven me for that time in Luton when I drove into that brook and we had to swim for our lives.

'Tis a far, far better thing I do, than I have ever done before.

I couldn't do it in the end. Couldn't let Simon get a cab to the airport, so I drove him, and now here I am in departures, dressed like fucking Orville (or so I heard Gareth mutter) because I thought I'd be able to kiss goodbye to Simon and send him on his merry way at 1 p.m. when he checked in, and get back for the match. What I didn't know was that the plane was going to be soooo delayed. Yep, not only did they manage to plan the flight to coincide with the biggest football match of the year, but then, having gathered everyone at the airport, they've decided to emergency land that flight somewhere in South America, so we're all sitting here, watching the board in the hope that it will tell us when the pilot will be willing to lay down his mohito and fly over here to pick up Simon and the other passengers.

Apparently not just yet. I text through to the club where I've got a hairdresser and makeup artist on stand-by at the committee entrance – all poised and ready for my arrival. Dean has reserved me a room inside where they can top up my makeup, check my hair and make sure I'm perfect for the introduction. The plan is for them to stay for the match, and tend to me at half-time and between glasses of champers, so I always look perfect.

'Slight delay. Don't go ANYWHERE,' I text. 'Will be there ASAP. Will need drink, hairspray and foundation as a matter of absolute urgency.'

'Message received,' comes the text back.

Phew. Now all I've got to worry about is this plane arriving and keeping Simon calm.

'The thing is,' he says again, as he has done all morning, 'the thing is that planes *do* crash. We have to accept that. It's OK saying "You're more likely to get hit by lightning or get bitten by a dog", but they do crash. And, shit, if lightning's that common, what if it hits the plane? What then? We're certain to die. No question.'

It's quarter past two. I'd have to leave now to get back for the start of the match. Simon is sitting on the edge of a long metal bench, shaking like a leaf.

'Drink?' I say.

'God yes.'

We walk over to a small bar in the corner, conscious of being watched every step of the way. One of the things about this outfit is that it does help you to stand out in a crowd. I clearly wanted to stand out in the crowd at Raiders because of my desire that every damn person in that crowd sees that I, Tracie Martin, am sitting next to Lady Vic.

Here, though, I'm not all that keen on the stares and plain astonishment on the faces of everyone who sees me. A man just ran his trolley into the wall because he was watching me so closely, and a bunch of young children came running up to me, wanting to touch my feathers. I didn't want them to touch the dress because I want it to look absolutely perfect for when I see Victoria, so I moved away a little. They followed me. I moved some more. In the end I was running across the concourse being pursued by half a dozen nine-year-old brats. I nearly went flying over in my high-heeled boots, and I left a trail of green feathers behind which the damn kids went and picked up before I could get to them. I could really do without moulting any more feathers before I see VB or I'll have little bald patches which will rather ruin the impact of the outfit.

We buy some champagne and walk over to the seats where I spend the best part of ten minutes trying to sit myself down without squashing the feathers too much. Around us, the gawpers continue to stare. I don't mind, though, because I know the outfit looks good.

When I appeared all dressed up this morning Simon remarked on it straightaway. 'You shouldn't have, you shouldn't have,' he cried.

'My pleasure,' I said with a little curtsey, but he kept on insisting.

'No, Tracie – I mean it, you really shouldn't have.'

The door opens and a lady walks into the bar with two poodles on long gold chains. She's dressed in black and has that haughty demeanour that one associates with French women. The dogs take one look at me and attempt to leap into my lap.

'Down, down,' I shriek, as they rub their stupid noses into the feathers, biting them out and sneezing on them. They're yapping away, clawing at me and growling, while their owner does precious little to restrain them. Lime green feathers and bits of lime green cotton and silk fly up into the air until Simon leans over and pushes the dogs roughly away.

'Be careful,' says the owner.

'No, you be careful,' says Simon, who looks as if he's about to punch the woman in the face. 'How dare your dogs ruin my friend's beautiful dress.'

'Beautiful?' says the woman, looking down at me through eyes shielded by sunglasses.

'Come on, Tracie,' Simon says, pulling my chair out to help me up and nearly sending me flying off it. 'We're going.'

I look down at the mess of gooey fathers plastered over my front and feel like crying. My dress is ruined and the match is about to start. My chance to meet Victoria feels as if it's slipping through my fingers.

'Look,' says Simon, when we get out of the bar. He's pointing at the screen. 'All passengers for flight BA194 are requested to go to through to Departures and to Gate 23 for immediate boarding.'

'Shit,' I say, as Simon flings his arms round me. 'I can't believe you're off. I thought we were going to be here all day.'

'Nope. It would seem not.'

His shaking has started again, and I can feel myself start to shake, too. I might get to meet the Mother of all Wags after all. Oh God, I hope and pray. Please God let me get back in time. Surely now that Paskia is friends with the Mormons God will look kindly upon me and help me in my time of trouble.

I kiss Simon heartily and promise him that the plane won't fall out of the sky, and I'm on my way out to the car park . . . Where the fuck did I leave the car this time?

It's not where I left it – of that much I'm sure. I run round and round, stumbling across the concrete, leaving a little trail of feathers behind. Eventually I see it – my very own coach and horses to take me to meet the fairy-tale princess. It's 3.45 p.m. The match finishes at around 5 p.m. I have time to get back, sort my dress, face, hair and attitude out, and get myself up to the bar to order a bottle of champagne and drink half of it before she gets up there from her seat. No problem.

I head onto the main road out of the airport. I have to say it's much more difficult to do all this without Simon map reading and warning me every few seconds that I'm on the wrong side of the road. I keep swerving from one side to the other.

The thing is – it doesn't matter. Nothing matters now. I'm so excited I want to start singing. I reach over into the glove compartment in search of my Spice Girls CD.

'Wooooaahhhhhh . . . wrong side of the road.'

I wave my fists madly at an approaching car before realizing that it's actually me who's wrong.

There, the Spice Girls are singing to me and I've got plenty of time to get back. Relax. This is all looking good. Right, which way now? Ah, here we go – I recognize this bit here. If I just head down this mighty freeway I'll be there in no time.

'Two Become One' comes onto the stereo and I sing along, swaying gently as the road stretches ahead and the sun shines down, warming my hair in the late afternoon heat, drying out the matted feathers on my dress, and, sadly, making my foundation run. As long as the glue holding my extensions in doesn't melt, we'll be OK.

Oh, no, this is looking wrong now. There are signs for downtown. I know I'm not going there. Damn, I've gone wrong somewhere. I need to be in the Hollywood Hills to find the stadium. Shit, shit, shit. It's 4.40 p.m. Fuck. A sign ahead announces that I'm now in Westlake. Westlake? Where the fuck's that?

I pull over in this deserted urban area and realize for the first time how rough it is, with broken windows and boarded-up shops. I probably shouldn't stop here but I'm running out of time. Given the option between risking attack and risking not seeing Victoria, I know which way I'm leaning. I reach for the map Dean gave me and pull it out, looking at the collection of lines in front of me that make no sense at all. I don't know where Westlake is and I don't know where the Hollywood Hills are, and even if I could find them on this map I know I wouldn't be able to navigate between the two of them. How do people understand maps? It's a mystery.

Ahead three big men are walking towards the car. They look rough, hands in pockets, scowls on their faces and plenty of earrings and tattoos. In other words, they look like they live here. Ideal! They must have an idea which way I have to head to get back on track.

'Excuse me,' I say, staggering towards them as I push the map back into its fabulous gold sheath.

'Wooooaaahhh,' all three of them say when they see me. 'What's this, man? Some kinda fucking joke with the feathers an' all? Are you some sort of fancy decoy? A ho?'

'No, I'm a Wag,' I say. 'I'm lost. I'm trying to get to Hollywood Hills.'

'Who you wiv?' they say aggressively. 'You got someone wiv you?'

'No.'

'Well, what you doin'?'

'I'm lost,' I repeat, lifting the map to show him where I want to go.

'Wooooaaahhh,' says the tallest of the men. He has a shaved head with some sort of tattoo on it. He pulls a gun from his pocket as he sees the flash of gold from the map case. 'No knives, lady!' he yells.

'I'm just going to show you the map,' I say, taking a peek at his gun. Then I realize what sort of gun it is. 'Ooooh,

I thought it looked familiar. I had a gun like that,' I say. 'They took it off me when I left Heathrow Airport. They wouldn't let me bring it onto the plane. I was really upset.'

The men look at one another.

'I bet they fucking wouldn't. What you wanna bring weapons in for?'

'Security.'

'You for real?' asks the smallest of the men. He's extremely muscular – he must be a body-builder or something. One of his eyes doesn't open, and with the scar down his neck and the bashed-up nose he's ended up with a horrible, menacing look about him. He has earrings all the way up his earlobe.

'Of course I'm real,' I say. 'Can you show me how I get to LA City Raiders? They're based in Griffin Park, not far from Hollywood Hills.'

The men look from one to the other and decide that yeh, OK, they'll help me. I hand over the map, wishing my name and address weren't all over it, but thinking that nothing matters more right now than getting to Raiders, and these guys are my best bet. Behind me there's the most terrific noise as a car door slams and a car screams off at reckless speed. I spin round to take a look, just in time to see my beautiful pink car go whizzing past me.

'My carrrrrr,' I howl. The men, to their credit, drop the map and go racing after it, screaming profanities and hurling things at the back windscreen. But it's all to no avail. The car's gone and I'm stuck. By the time they come back it's all too much for me. I collapse in tears, choking and coughing as they stream down my face.

'What's up?' asks the guy with the tattooed head.

'What d'ya thinks up, man?' asks the one who has not spoken before. He is black and has a baseball cap pulled down hard over his face. His voice is deep and melodic and it strikes me that if circumstances had been different he might have made an excellent tenor. 'Jeez, man, you're thick sometimes. They've nicked her car.'

'I have to get to the club,' I say, through cries. 'My husband's there and I'm meeting Victoria Beckham and David and everything.'

'Take her in the van,' says tattoo man.

'Na, can't do that. Too risky, man,' says melodic-voice baseball hat wearer.

'We haven't got it sprayed or nothing,' says shut-eye earrings guy.

'Please take me,' says mad Englishwoman in messed-up green feather dress.

'Take her,' tattoo man repeats.

'I'll pay you,' I say.

'Don't be disrespecting us. We don't want your money, lady.'

Earrings guy and baseball guy head back in the direction from which they've just come, while tattoo man stands there and keeps asking me if I'm OK.

'My bag's in the car and everything,' I say.

'Hey, no sweat. At least you safe, man.'

The van is not ideal. They apologise before bundling me into the back, and explain that they had engines in there earlier, and they had dogs in there yesterday. I figure it's best not to ask. Two of the men are in the front, one of them with my map in his hand while the other drives off at exhilarating speed, pitching me forward so I slide straight into a puddle of oil that I had been studiously avoiding. It's quite dark in the back of the van with its blackened windows, which I can peer through only by putting my eye up against the peeling bit at the bottom.

Baseball hat man sees the state my dress is now in and pulls the peak of his cap over his eyes. I reach for the bars at the side of the van to keep myself still, but just manage to get more oil over me as we lurch from side to side. I can feel the tears running down my face again as I think about my stolen car, and of some nutter driving it around with all my favourite Spice Girls' tracks blaring out. But when I reach up to wipe the tears away, baseball man just mutters, 'Holy shit, lady. Don't do that,' and I realize I've got about three inches of axle grease on my hands from holding onto the side. It makes me cry even more.

'Thank you for your help,' I say through sobs, and baseball hat man says it's no problem. 'I hope you're not coming right out of your way,' I say. 'Were you heading somewhere special?'

'New York City for two days, gonna lie low. Be back then. Gotta find us some place to stay.'

'You must let me take you all out for a drink when you get back,' I say. 'To say thank you. My number's on the map – just call me.'

As soon as I've said it, I regret it, but the men just laugh.

'We ain't gonna be calling you, ma'am.'

'Why not?' I ask. Suddenly I'm offended that they don't want to come out with me. I'm good fun. Everyone tells me that I'm a great socializer.

'I'm thinking that you and us – we different people.

328

We probably don't drink in the same places an' all that. We like the hard stuff mainly, ma'am.'

'Well, I've been looking all over LA for friends who like the hard stuff. Make sure you call me when you're back. Bet I can drink more than any of you.'

The men laugh and the two men in the front introduce themselves for the first time. 'I'm Bob,' says one.

'Bill,' says another.

'Hey, I'm Barry,' says the third. 'I was named after Barry White.'

'You have a lovely voice,' I say. 'My name's Tracie.'

'OK, I think we're almost there, lady,' says tattoo man. 'Do I go down here?'

I look out of the gap in the blackened window and see the familiar sight of the LA City Raiders ground ahead. The road down to the ground is about a mile long.

'Fucking crap!' declares earrings guy. 'Fucking police.'

'Get out,' they howl. 'Get out now.'

I fumble with the door, trying to work it out, while they talk to each other in loud voices which indicate that there are a lot of drugs in the van, it was stolen, yesterday they knocked someone down in it and stole his dog, and previously they've used it to steal a lot of engines.

I climb out while they're swinging the van round, and go flying into a small ditch.

'Don't say nothing,' shouts Barry, as the van disappears at a ferocious speed. 'Don't say nothing about where we's going or our names or nothing.'

Up ahead I can see the police car. I'm sure the police would have had only kind words for these men who rescued a Wag in distress. Besides, I know the car's only there because the policeman's son plays for the Raiders.

But my heroes have gone so I can't explain, and I'm left to pick myself up, dust myself down and begin the long walk to the ground.

My feet hurt, so I remove my boots and walk barefoot, covered in oil, dirt and dust. Half the feathers are missing on the dress and my eye makeup sits around my eyes, making me look like a panda bear, and running down my face in the manner of Alice Cooper.

In front of me I see the police car turn and come tearing up the road. Thank God. He's seen me and he's come to give me a lift to the ground so I don't miss the Beckhams. But as the car gets near to me, the policeman shouts over, 'Do you know the owners of that van?'

'No, they just gave me a lift,' I say, realizing that I have a clump of chewing gum stuck in my feathers at the back along with two cigarette butts.

'Three of them?' he asks, and I nod.

'Fuck me,' he says, screeching off with his sirens wailing. 'They're the most wanted men in the state. They're evil.'

'No, they were really sweet,' I say, but it's no good. He's gone off at a record-breaking speed.

I continue to walk, my excitement mounting now after the drama. Wait till I tell Victoria! The clubhouse is just a few metres away, so I bend down to put on my ankle boots. They're muddy and covered in tar but I've got a phalanx of assistants inside, they'll be able to clean me up.

While I'm doing the ninth buckle on the second boot a car drives towards me – an elegant, long black car. I stand up and peer through the windows. Oh my God – it's her. I bang on the window and wave. Nothing. I bang again. 'Victoria, Victoria,' I squeal, delirious with excitement. 'Victoria, Victoria. Please . . .'

The driver's window opens and my heart skips a beat. I'm going to be invited in and taken back to their mansion for champagne cocktails. But as I move towards the car he closes the window, then he puts his foot down and the car zooms off at top speed, sending litter and dust up into my face and all over my feathers where it sticks in the messy mix of oil, dog spit and fear-induced sweat. I stand there, filthy, tired and sad, with broken dreams scattered all around me.

8 p.m.

Dean's horribly confused, and has asked me five times what happened because the euphoria induced by Raiders beating Galaxy has dulled his senses, and he's not capable of understanding a word I say.

'Did you actually get to meet the Beckhams?' he asks. 'Cos they was really nice.'

'No,' I tell him bluntly. 'I didn't meet the Beckhams because I was in the back of a filthy van with a bunch of renowned criminals. I arrived as the Beckhams were leaving. I've told you this a million times.'

'Oh, yeah,' he says. 'Shit. That's terrible. So why were you so late?'

Oh, for Heaven's sake. I can't do this any more.

I leave Dean with a confused look on his face and wander off towards the middle of the room where people move quickly out of my way. I feel like a tramp who's just walked into a royal garden party.

The police have just arrived back to talk to me, since

my three heroes managed to give them the slip. They need to know everything I can remember about the men.

'So, where were you when you first saw them?' asks a very old policeman who looks like he'd rather be anywhere else in the world.

'Westlake,' I reply.

'Oh my God, Tracie, what were you doing there?' cry the people in the bar. 'It's a terrible place!'

'Why did they come to your aid?'

'Because I approached them and told them I was lost and wanted to get to Hollywood Hills.'

'Holy moly alive!' says Chuck. 'I'm amazed you escaped with your life.'

I look over at the crowd in front of me, all absorbed in every word I'm saying. Everyone except my daughter, that is. Paskia sits looking at the floor, not making eye contact with anyone. She didn't even say hello when I came in. She'll have to snap out of this ridiculous sulk soon or she and I will be having words.

'Were the men vicious?' someone asks.

'No. They were kind to me,' I try to explain. 'Someone stole my car, and they tried to catch him. When they couldn't, they offered me a lift here.'

'These are very violent men,' says the policeman. 'I don't understand why they behaved like that.'

'Maybe because I told them about bringing weapons in through customs and all the trouble I caused. I think they respected me after that.'

'Sure,' says the officer. But he doesn't look like a man who's at all sure. It doesn't really help that a fairly large crowd has gathered round us and that people are randomly hurling in questions.

'I can't believe they tarred and feathered you! Like the Dark Ages!' cries one lady, looking at the feathers matted in oil against my skin. 'Just awful.'

'Do you remember if they said where they were going?' asks the policeman. And I remember with crystal clarity that they were heading for New York and would be back in a few days. Suddenly, though, I don't feel like I want to grass them up. Why should I? They were so nice to me. There's also the niggling feeling that upsetting three of the most renowned criminals in California when they've got my home address would be far from ideal.

'No,' I say, confidently. 'They didn't say. They told me to be careful.'

There's a round of applause from the small crowd, and the officer's had enough.

'OK, this is ridiculous. Show over, people. Can you come to the station tomorrow morning, ma'am?' he asks. 'It's LAPD. I'll send a car if you let me have your address.'

I give him our address, and we arrange that a car will pick me up at 9.30 a.m. I'll go straight from there to my dad's for lunch. At least we'll have something to talk about!

Paskia-Rose has been incredibly quiet since I stumbled into the clubhouse. While everyone else has piled in with their questions, and has been oooing and ahhing over the details of the armed robbers who came to my rescue, my daughter has sat there in silence, still refusing to talk to me or even make eye contact with me.

'Come on,' I say. 'We're going home.'

The two of us jump into a cab and I turn to face her.

'Paskia, I know you're cross because you were embarrassed in front of your friends, but ignoring me is not going to make it any better. You've just sat in the club in complete silence, staring at the floor for an hour. How is that going to change what happened the other night? Is this all about making me feel terrible? If it is, Paskia, then you'll be pleased to hear that it's working. You're making me feel rotten. Happy now?'

Silence.

'Are you, Paskia? I'm talking to you.'

I look at my daughter and see a lone tear trickle down her face.

'I was so worried,' she says, her lip shaking and her voice croaking. 'I've never been so scared in my life. I'd hate it if anything happened to you, Mum. I'm really sorry I've been so horrible, Mum.'

Then she dissolves into tears. Her shoulders are shaking and she's howling in pain as the tears fall into her lap.

'It's OK,' I say. 'Don't worry, sweetheart. Everything's going to be OK. I'm sorry I shouted. Is that why you were so quiet earlier?'

She just nods and I hold her tightly. 'Everything's going to be fine. I'm safe and well and we're friends again. That's all that matters. You know how much I love you, don't you?'

'Yes,' she says, sobbing all over my green feathers. 'I'm never going to be nasty to you ever again.'

We travel all the way home wrapped tightly around one another and I feel closer to my kind and thoughtful daughter than I've ever felt before.

Sunday 22 June
8 a.m.

I'm not sure where I went when I came in last night, but by the look of things – everywhere. I pop into Paskia's room where she's sleeping soundly, a lime-coloured feather resting gently on her lip as she snoozes. She's such a wonderful little girl. I'm so glad we're the best of friends again. There are feathers on the floor, in the bathroom, in the wet room, in my dressing area. Honestly, feathers everywhere you look.

I pass Gareth in the kitchen just as he is muttering, 'Fucking feathers everywhere!' to himself.

Dean's at the club already. It seems that if the team loses, you need to get the players together as soon as possible afterwards in order to rebuild self-esteem and re-bond as a team. You need to learn from your mistakes and move forward. If you win, it's not much different – then you need to get back together again as a team as soon as possible, not to learn from your mistakes but to learn from everything that went right. The positivity of victory must be harnessed, apparently.

It's all bollocks to me, but that's what Dean says and, to be fair to the man, he does seem to know what he's doing when it comes to training football teams. I just wish he hadn't rushed off this morning. After what I went through yesterday, I could have done with having him around to talk to, because while he's down the club breathing in positive vibes and generally being on the edge of international greatness I'm off to the police station to tell them how my car got nicked yesterday while I was driving through the roughest part of LA, and how I then returned to the club in the company of three of America's most wanted criminals in the back of a van full of oil and dog hair, cigarette butts and chewing gum. To say this trip to LA is not turning out exactly as I had hoped would be quite an understatement.

1 p.m.

I arrive at my father's house bang on time, which is entirely an accident. Gareth's driving me. Dean sent him back once Gareth had dropped him at the club this morning, telling him not to leave my side all day, and certainly to make sure that I didn't take lifts from strange men. Especially not armed ones. Perhaps Dean does care after all, then.

The chivalrous gesture is much appreciated, though it has rather complicated things because rather than getting a lift to and from the police station from the officers, as arranged, I have Gareth to take me, thus the sneaky visit to lunch with my father is less sneaky than I'd hoped.

'Listen,' I tell Gareth, 'it's Dean's birthday soon, and I want to get him a suit made by a renowned British tailor living in LA. I'm going spend a few hours talking to him about size, style and cut. I don't want Dean to know anything about it, OK?'

'Sure,' says Gareth. 'I won't say a word. When's his birthday?'

'On Wednesday,' I say, unwisely.

'Will the guy have time to get it all made by then?'

'Yes, he works very quickly.'

Oh God, oh God. This is getting absurd. One little lie – no, not even a lie, more like one momentary lapse of concentration – when I failed to tell my dad that Jamie wasn't Dean, and now I'm buggered. I can't introduce Dean to my father because my father thinks he already knows Dean, so I have to lie when I visit my father or Dean will, understandably, ask why I haven't mentioned these visits before and, indeed, why he's never been invited.

I feel as if I'm layering lie upon lie to avoid having to unpick the first one, but the first one wasn't a lie – it was a simple misunderstanding that got out of hand. This is so unlike me, but I can't work out how to get out of this hole, and I really want to see my father. I actually thought to myself this morning, I can get through all this hassle with the police because at the end of it all I'll see Dad, and that'll be really nice.

'No Dean?' asks Dad when he opens the door and gives me a big hug that dislodges the giant pale pink corsage on the front of my white dress. I shrug and say something about training and skills and how important it is for him to be at the club. Dad nods understandingly. 'Of course,' he says. 'He's doing a remarkable job. Sylvia and I have been following all the matches. What a great win yesterday. We were reading all about it. We both thought Dean came over very well in the quotes.'

'Oh, good,' I say, genuinely pleased. Dean finds dealing with the media very difficult after a couple of incidents last year when my mum sold pictures to the newspapers of Dean training young girls. The newspaper implied that Dean was having affairs with the girls and we ended up suing. We got quite a nice pay-off in the end, actually. I can't remember how much it was exactly, but roughly speaking it was two Chloe handbags, some Versace boots, a pair of Jimmy Choos and a pink and white Marc Jacobs top that I wear as a dress.

'I thought it was slightly unfair of the journalist to call him "thin and mousy-haired", though. Both Sylvia and I felt like phoning in and complaining,' Dad continues. 'He's not like that at all!'

'That's right,' says Sylvia, coming over to give me a hug and dislodging the corsage still further so it's now sitting on my right breast like some giant floral nipple.

'Dean's a lovely big hunk of a man. I don't know why anyone would call him thin,' she says defensively. 'He has the loveliest, thickest, glossy black hair I've ever seen.'

Thank God football's not a big sport over here. If that match had been played in England, Dean's face would have been plastered over the newspapers and television, and poor Keith would have been utterly baffled by how different Dean looked in real life.

'Journalists can be cruel,' I observe.

Sylvia is wearing a white apron today and she looks quite the suburban housewife. Underneath the apron, which is either too narrow for her or she's too large for it, she wears navy tailored shorts and a starched white shirt with patch pockets on the front; in one of them is an imitation spotty blue-and-white handkerchief and on the other is a motif of an anchor. She's wearing navy blue deck shoes to complete the nautical theme.

'Drink?' she asks.

'Yes please,' I say, and I've never felt more desperate for a drink than I do at this moment.

My father and I go and sit in the garden while Sylvia bustles around in the kitchen, clattering dishes and banging doors, and shouting occasional things like:

'Is Mexican OK?'

And:

'Do you like your guacamole garlicky?'

'Yes,' I reply to everything.

'Really?' she exclaims at one point when I say 'Yes, perfect.'

'Are you sure?' asks my dad.

'Yes,' I say nervously.

'Blimey,' he says, adding 'Don't you find they burn your throat?'

'No,' I say. 'It'll be fine.'

I'm wondering what on earth I've said 'yes' to, but since I don't plan to eat I'm confident that I won't suffer.

As we sit there in the sunshine, chatting amiably like any father and daughter anywhere in the world, it occurs to me how much I'm getting to like him, and what a respite these trips here have become. It gives me a grounded kind of feeling that is totally at odds with everything else in my crazy life.

Sylvia walks through with our drinks on a platter. She's made mohitos to complement the Mexican flavours in the lunch she's preparing. The anchor is bouncing around on her ample bosom with every step she takes, and I think how apt that is. Having a dad is like having an anchor – something stable. This house, and these people, well, they're kind of like my . . . '*Holy fuck!*' I squeal. 'Jeeeez.'

Keith laughs as I leap from my chair and dance around the garden, clutching my mouth and swearing in a most unseemly fashion.

'Thought six chillies might be too many,' he says. 'Thought you were being a bit brave.'

'Oh, I am sorry – I should have thought,' says Sylvia. 'Perhaps these are stronger chillies than you're used to?'

I look at the two of them through eyes that are streaming with tears. 'Did you ask me if I wanted chillies in my drink?' I say.

'Yes,' she replies. 'Didn't you hear me?'

'No,' I say, admitting that I didn't hear any of her questions but felt it was rude to keep asking her to repeat herself, so just said 'yes'. I don't tell her that I'm a Wag and thus don't eat, in case she feels offended. After all, she is spending hours cooking for me, so the least I can do is pretend to eat it and hide it in the bushes or in my handbag.

My dad howls with laughter at the thought of me saying 'yes' to everything, and almost falls off his chair with the mirth of it all. Meanwhile Sylvia pats me on the head in an affectionate but slightly uncomfortable way and tells me I'm with friends. 'If you can't understand what I'm saying, just you yell. There's no pretentiousness round here. Shall I repeat the question I asked?'

'Yes please,' I say.

'The question was, "It says in the cocktail book here that authentic mohitos have six chillies in. Do you want that many?".'

'Ah,' I say, as she moves to head back to the kitchen. 'In answer to your question, I don't want any.'

She laughs and I pull the chillies out of my drink one by one and place them on the table.

Cooking smells waft out of the kitchen as Sylvia pulls back the huge French doors to let herself back inside. It occurs to me that I haven't smelt that too much since I've been in LA. People's houses don't smell so much of cooking over here, I guess because they eat out more, and they eat so much raw stuff, it's as if cooking things is tantamount to covering things in lard and sugar and frying them in cat's blood.

'I've brought a photo to show you,' I say, pulling out a picture of Paskia-Rose. It's the only one I have of her without either a football shirt on or a ball at her feet. I feel very strongly that it's far too early for him to know that his young granddaughter is a football fanatic.

'Wow,' he says, clutching the photograph. 'Wow. She's lovely. My other grandchildren are living in England.'

'Really,' I say. 'I never knew that. Tell me about them.'

'I've got two sons – David and Alex,' says Dad. 'David's divorced now, but he sees his ex-wife Nicola and the kids a lot. I made it very clear to him that he was to fight for every moment with those children and make sure he was a proper father to them. To his credit that's what he's done. The children are Andy, who's eleven, and Fraser who's seven. They live in a place called Teddington. Have you ever heard of it?'

I tell him that I haven't but I'll look it up as soon as I get back.

'My other son Alex runs a health club in Manchester. He's got three daughters – Yvonne, Lee and Sally. He's married to Julie, who's a delight. She reminds me of you, actually.'

'Really?' I say, thrilled to the core. I can't believe that I have two half-brothers and that there are all these little people walking around the place who are half related to me. I look over at Dad and notice that he's clutching the picture so tightly that I can see the veins in his hand standing up.

He sees me looking and lays the photo down. He thanks me, telling me how much it means to him.

'Keep it,' I say. 'It's a gift.'

'Thank you, Tracie,' he says. 'You don't know how much this means.'

'You'll meet her soon,' I promise.

'I'll look forward to that,' he says. 'And you shall meet David and Alex very soon. They'll be just blown away when they know we've met.'

'I can't wait,' I say. Imagine that – me, Tracie Martin, with all this family all of a sudden. It's the best news ever.

'There's something I need to tell you,' I say carefully.

Dad looks up.

'I had my car nicked yesterday.'

'Oh, no, Tracie, that's terrible. What happened?'

I run through the whole thing as thoroughly as possible, telling him about the delay at the airport, and my rush to get back because I wanted to meet Posh.

'You know how much I want to meet Victoria, don't you?' I say.

'Yes,' he says. 'You told me before that you kept missing her, and driving past her house and hoping she'd turn up at the same events as you.'

'That's right,' I say, amazed that I told him those things and that he's actually remembered. I've grown to really trust this man.

'What happened when you were asking for directions?' he says, his face a portrait of paternal concern.

I tell him everything. Then I tell him about going to the police station this morning to file a report about the stolen car, and how there were about five officers asking me loads of questions.

'They kept saying that the men were armed and dangerous, but I told them I knew that because one of them pointed a gun at me.'

'*Oh my God!*' shrieks Sylvia, dropping a plate of enchiladas before returning to the kitchen.

'The thing is,' I confess, 'when the police asked me this morning where the men were going next or whether I knew their names I said I didn't. But I do.'

'Why didn't you tell them? These are clearly dangerous men, Tracie. They need to be caught.'

'But they were so nice to me, and they asked me not to say, and I did kind of promise.'

'Still, I do think you should tell the police the truth. Honesty is always the best policy.'

'Yeah, I know,' I say. 'But the criminals have my address and phone number, so I figure I don't want to upset them too much. Not that I think they'd come and hurt me at all. I just think that it would be really unfair to promise them something and not do it. And they did go right out of their way, and wouldn't take any money, and put themselves at such risk. Do you think it was terrible that I didn't tell the police?'

'No, I don't,' says Keith. 'I think in your own sweet way you're being very honourable. I would, though, change the locks and inform the police that these guys have your address. What crimes are they wanted for, in any case?'

'Things like murder, kidnapping, torture, arson, theft, burglary and things like that,' I say.

Sylvia walks back out again and catches the end of our conversation. 'Oh God,' she says, putting the bowl of nachos down quickly before they go the same way as the enchiladas. 'Are you sure everything's OK?'

'Yes, honestly, I'm fine. Just had a bit of a bad day yesterday,' I say.

'Tracie's car was stolen,' says my dad.

'Oh, love, I'm sorry.' Sylvia lays out dips next to the nachos. 'Keith, perhaps Tracie should use some of the money you gave Dean, to buy a new car.'

'Of course, if you want to,' Dad says, turning to me. 'You know, the money I gave Dean was for the business, to set you two up, because I imagine this football management is precarious to say the least. We agreed that I would have a place on the board of the Alcohol-less Alcohol company and have a say in how things are run in return for a large investment, but really, Tracie, the money's all yours. If you need to use some of it to buy a car, that's absolutely fine.'

Money? What money? I can feel my heart start to pound in my chest. Why's Jamie taken money from my dad?

'When did you give Dean some money?' I ask, going white beneath my orange veneer.

'Friday,' says Dad. 'He came round for lunch and told me about all the money problems you were having, and how the club weren't due to pay him until the end of the season, and he needed to invest in the Alchol-less Alcohol now or he'd lose the US franchise. I was always planning to give you some money, Tracie – you know, maybe a trust fund for Paskia-Rose or something – but if things are difficult now, then now's when you should have it. I think starting a business is a good idea.'

I must look completely startled because, well – I am.

What the hell's going on? Why's Jamie lying like this?

'Don't worry,' Sylvia says. 'Dean was right to tell us. Every couple goes through difficult times financially. We wanted to help.'

'I didn't know Dean had been round on Friday lunchtime,' I say. 'How much did you give him?' I can feel my heart beating in my chest. While I was sitting in that raw food restaurant by myself, waiting for him to turn up, Jamie was here asking my father for money. It makes no sense at all.

'Did he not mention it?' asks Dad, sensing my confusion. 'I thought you two would have discussed it.'

'Well, er, no. Because of everything that happened yesterday, I guess we haven't had time to talk.'

'Of course not,' says Dad. 'Well, Dean probably wants to get everything set up first. He's bringing the paperwork round some time this week for me to sign it all. He forgot it on Friday.'

8 p.m.

I get back home and flop onto the bed. Where's Jamie? Why won't he answer my calls? I've been driving round in tears all afternoon. I've been all around the area, hoping to see him out jogging and I've been to some of the places we went together – just in case he's there. I have to find him. He has to call me and help me sort this out.

I hear a noise and look up, glancing in the mirror by my bed and expecting to see a worn and haggard woman looking back at me, but I'm astonished to see how spectacularly clear and fresh my skin looks. The effects of the skin resurfacing are really starting to show now. I have the skin of a twenty-one year old but after the day I've just had, I feel about as lively and energetic as a ninety year old.

I'm peering at my flawless skin when I hear a sound again, coming from the bedroom door. Paskia is standing there.

'Mum, can I have a word?' she says.

'Of course. Come in, love,' I say, making myself smile despite my urge to cry.

'Do you remember those naughty girls that we met when we first went to the school?' she says. 'They wore makeup and high heels and you thought they were really cool.'

'Yes, of course I remember.'

'Well, they keep being horrible to me. They came to watch the match today and were shouting at me and calling me horrible names like "swot" and "potato face". They pronounced "potato" the English way to make sure everyone knew they were talking about me.'

'Did you tell your father?' I ask.

'No, I told Joseph, but when he told them to leave me alone they just started taking the mickey out of him and calling him a "God-squadder" and a "Bible-basher".'

'They don't sound like very friendly girls at all,' I say. I can't believe they've turned on Paskia, especially since I gave them that bottle of champagne. What did they think I gave them that for? For fun? I feel like strangling them, but I don't want to make things any more difficult for Pask.

'I think you should try and forget all about it, and if it happens again I'll sort them out. OK?' I promise, and I will.

'OK,' she says. 'Thanks, Mum. You look really pretty, by the way. Your skin's all shiny and lovely.'

Monday 23 June

I've been up all night fretting and thinking and trying to make sense of things. I think I've finally worked it all out. Jamie wanted my dad's expertise so he asked him to be involved in Alcohol-less Alcohol. Dad insisted on investing so Jamie, in a panic, said 'OK' and took the cheque. He's probably now wondering what to do. The cheque's no good to him, because it's made out to Dean Martin.

Clearly he can't actually get Dad to invest in the business because that would necessitate signing a formal contract with my dad, but he can't do that until I tell Dad that he's not my husband. Blimey! It's hellishly complicated. I feel sorry for poor old Jamie.

I just wish he'd answer his phone so we could chat about it. I haven't been able to get hold of him since before lunchtime on Friday. I suppose I should have guessed there was a problem when he didn't turn up at RawStuff, but I assumed there'd been a last-minute change of plan and he'd forgotten his phone or something. I bet he's trying to sort out all the business plans and contracts, then he'll call me, we'll go and see my dad together, admit our silly pretence and Jamie can then ask him if he's still interested in investing. If so, the paperwork will be all there and ready for Dad to sign. Yep. That's it. I'll keep trying to call him, though, just to reassure him that I understand and everything's going to be OK.

Because I'm thinking about Jamie when the phone rings I automatically think it's going to be him.

'Hello, strange man,' I say. 'How are you doing?'

'I'm neither strange nor male,' comes a very businesslike voice. 'Tracie, is that you?'

'Yes,' I say, feeling disappointment wash over me.

'Cindy here, darling.'

'Oh, hi. Is there a problem?'

'Darling no, not at all. You're the story of the week.'

'Am I?'

'Being car-jacked at gunpoint by the most vicious gang in the history of LA, being thrown into the back of their van, then hurled out into the streets, tarred and feathered and made to walk barefoot across the ground. Darling, this is dynamite.'

'That's not really how it happened,' I mumble.

'Are you in the hospital?' she asks.

'No, I'm fine, thanks.'

'Shit, shit, shit,' says Cindy. 'That's a real shame. Did they hit you? Any bruising?'

'No.'

'Oh, Tracie, well, I can't hide the fact that I'm disappointed. It's still a great story, but it doesn't sound like there'll be great pictures. What a dreadful shame.'

'I just had my car stolen, that's all,' I say. 'Then I was given a lift by these guys who I later found out were big-time criminals.'

'Tracie, don't make the mistake of underselling this story,' says Cindy. 'People wait a lifetime for something like this to happen. Don't just throw it all away. Hype it up and make the most of it.'

'OK,' I say warily, thinking of how sweet baseball hat man was when he warned me not to rub my oil-covered hands all over my face.

'The *LA Times* want you to write this up for their Tuesday column instead of the ridiculous Wag things you've been writing. Tell it big, and they'll pay big. Remember, Tracie – don't throw this gift away.'

'Ok,' I say, replacing the receiver and pulling out a notebook.

I jot down my memories and thoughts from Saturday, starting with the plane being delayed at the airport and ending with the police station on Sunday, and read it through. It makes no sense at all, of course. I'm not a writer; Simon does that. He takes all my thoughts and feelings, views and sentiments and weaves them into these articles that then appear in the paper.

The deal is that we split the money 50/50. I get to spread the word about being a Wag and he gets to earn some money and write for an international newspaper. It suits us both. It does make me think, though, that I'm now going to have to tell Simon all about what happened on Saturday. When he phoned to say that he'd got home safely, his voice full of genuine surprise that the plane had arrived at the right airport, and on its wheels instead of its roof, I told him that everything was fine and I'd got back to the club all right. I know he'll feel guilty for making me come to the airport with him if I tell him that I had my car stolen on the way home.

Still, what choice do I have?

I look through my notes again, weighing up the need to satisfy Cindy's appetite for violence and the need to reassure Simon. I take out some of the more colourful language, describe the three men in less terrifying terms, and generally tone the whole thing down. I write that the men never threatened me, were kind to me and helped me when I was alone and scared. I then type the whole thing into an email and forward it to Simon with a covering note explaining that the *LA Times* have requested a piece about the incident on Saturday and it needs to go in Tuesday's paper. It's 10.54 a.m. here, and London is eight hours behind. I'll expect a frantic call some time later this afternoon.

Tuesday 24 June

Dean's out all day today because the Raiders are playing again tonight and he's now convinced himself that the more time he spends at the club the more chance there is that the team will win. I think what he means is that if he does all he possibly can, then he's done all he possibly can . . . so to speak. He doesn't want to leave anything to chance.

'Sorry, doll,' he says, as he slips into his Raiders tracksuit at 7 a.m. He rushes downstairs and downs a vegetable juice with a raw egg whisked into it, and runs back upstairs to say goodbye. He has a baseball hat on and tells me that the morning is the best part of the day.

'Bollocks,' I say, pulling my eye mask over my face and snuggling back down beneath the covers. I don't want Dean to leave me here alone with my fears and confusion about how on earth to get in touch with Jamie.

'Bye then, sweetheart,' he says, grabbing his shades and a protein drink for later in the day and jogging towards the door, looking for all the world like a bonafide Californian.

In the distance I hear the phone ringing and the sound of footsteps as Alina, having finished with her juicing and egg cracking, moves as fast as she can (slowly) to answer it.

'The LA residence of the Martin household. Alina speaking,' she says in her measured tones, just as I've instructed her. 'One moment please.'

I can hear Alina waddling up the stairs, huffing and puffing. There are phone extensions in every room. I've told her this about twenty times, but still she brings the phone as if it's the only one in the land. Please don't let it be a call for me. Please.

'Tracie, is phone call,' she pants, as she arrives as the room.

Shit.

'Tracie Martin speaking,' I say, as Cindy's voice bellows back.

'I am so ashamed,' she says. 'Mortified. I'm beyond angry.'

'What? Why's that?'

'The *LA Times* have called. They say the article you wrote was nowhere near sensational enough. They wanted the whole drama – the attack at gunpoint, the fear for your life, the trauma of nightmares afterwards . . .'

'But that's not what happened,' I say. 'I wrote what happened in the article.'

Simon and I had a long talk yesterday afternoon, and I know he worked hard to make the piece as fair and accurate as possible. He included all the stuff about the guys being armed but made it clear that I never felt they were going to harm me. Cindy's not happy.

'You're such an amateur,' she says. 'Letting the facts get in the way of a good story is the first mistake of naïve journalists. The second mistake is not making the most of every story you have. You've broken both rules.'

'Cindy,' I say. 'If the *LA Times* don't want to run the

352

story, that's fine by me, but I'm not making a story up to suit them. That's what happened. That's the end of it.'

'Then that, I'm afraid, is the end of your column. It's over. You have only yourself to blame. If you'd tried harder you could have had nightmares and developed a trauma disorder, but oh no, you wouldn't, and now you're paying the ultimate price.'

She puts the phone down and I breathe deeply. 'It's this town that's mad, not me,' I say to myself. Then I try Jamie's number again. No answer.

'It's this town that's mad, not me. It's this town that's mad, not me . . .'

Midnight

I am lying on the thick zebra-print rug on the floor in the sitting room dressed in nothing but a pair of deep-pink marabou-fringed knickers while a woman called Sandra files my toenails and chews gum at a terrifying rate.

It's midnight and I'm being pampered. Now I know why we came to LA. This is great. The ladies are from a company called Emergency Glamor 911, a twenty-four-hour grooming service that I'm totally addicted to.

I've got them swarming around the house. There's Mia painting my fingernails with a glittery pink varnish, and there's Debra who's massaging my face with black soap to detoxify and improve circulation. She's about to wash the soap off with tropical rain-shower water, then she's going to do a lymphatic drainage massage that she promises will have me looking years younger. If I keep going like this I'll look younger than Paskia.

Anya is standing by the microwave in the kitchen

mixing up hot wax for my legs and bikini line, while Sarah-Lou is in the hallway preparing the extensions by laying them out across the wooden floor. There's a rather sultry-looking beautician called Gordana somewhere, setting things up for my spray tan. She seems to have disappeared completely, though.

'Phone is call,' says Alina, waddling into the room with the mobile and almost collapsing with shock when she sees me lying topless on the floor in my little pink knickers. The timing's not great. I can't use my hands, so Alina has to hold the phone to my ear while I speak. The fact that she does this with a look of utter horror on her face doesn't make it any easier.

'Doll, it's me,' says Dean. 'What's going on there?'

'Just got some professionals from the beautification industry in for the night.'

'At midnight, Candyfloss?' he queries.

'Yes,' I say. 'Welcome to the twenty-first century. How was the match?'

'We only fucking won again,' he says. 'Never seen anything like it – this place is on fire, man.'

'On fire?'

'No, I mean it's all alive and buzzy and everything. There's something else. Hang on, let me find somewhere quiet.'

I can hear the sounds of Dean walking along, being heartily congratulated. 'Nice one, Dean', 'Good man', 'All hail, Dean'. 'Thanks, guys, thanks,' he says, as he continues walking. 'You still there?' he asks.

'Yes. What's going on?'

'Right, hang on, I'm in the stationery cupboard in the office. Let me just shut this door. There, can you hear me?'

'Yes. Dean, what is it?'

'A guy just came up to me.'

'Oh, yeah, what guy?'

'An agent. He asked me whether I'd respond positively if I was offered the job as coach of Chelsea.'

'Fuck!!!' I exclaim, swinging my hand up to my mouth and sending poor Mia flying across the room. 'What did you say?'

'Trace, I had no idea what to say, so I said I was open to offers. Does that sound OK?'

'Yes, of course it does. Shit. How exciting.'

'The thing is, if they decide to make me an offer it'll be to start next season, so we'd have to go back in time for pre-season training. We'd have to leave mid-August.'

'Oh,' I say, thinking of my dad and Sylvia and how I'm only just starting to know them, and how nice it is to get up and find it warm and sunny instead of cold and rainy. Then I think of Luton and my friends and how everyone likes to go out and have fun.

'Listen, we'll talk later. I don't know whether they're actually going to offer me anything yet – just wanted to let you know what they said.'

He disappears off the line, and I turn my attentions to the first tranche of beauticians, who are just finishing. My nails and toenails are now a vibrant pink colour with glitter that sparkles in the light. The smell of warm wax reminds me that it's time for the second round of treatments.

'That's perfect,' I say, attempting to stand up despite the tissue paper wedged between my toes. I'm just about on my feet, balancing precariously on my heels and the outside of my feet, when my phone rings again. One of the beauticians reaches for it and holds the phone to my ear. It's Dean again.

'Sweetheart, can you ring Chuck and tell him to come and get me?' he asks, plaintively.

'Get you?' I question. 'Where are you?'

'I'm stuck in the stationery cupboard. The door's closed shut. I can't get it open and it's all dark in here. I've got the photocopier open to give me some light. Trace, you know how much I hate the dark. Hurry!'

To: Mich and Suzzi

From: Tracie

Oh God! Things haven't changed, have they? Is Angie actually in police custody now? What a bizarre thing to do. What made her want to streak across the pitch at half-time? It's not what you expect from a woman who's fast approaching her 60th birthday, is it? (Ignore claims that she's 53. I've seen her birth certificate.) Do you think the streak was prompted by her finding the Luton coach in bed with that girl from Radio Bedfordshire? Bizarre behaviour all the same. Still, like you say – at least she'll get sacked from Luton and hopefully move away.

T x

PS. What was her body like when she streaked? Good boobs? Has she had another op?

Wednesday 25 June

Dean's having a lie-in this morning after yesterday's great victory.

'Unbelievable,' he keeps muttering to himself. 'Unbelievable.'

Now most Wags would assume that when their man is lying naked next to them in bed saying 'unbelievable' it's to do with their body and all-round sexiness.

So that's why I turn onto my side, flick my extensions seductively and pout adoringly at him. 'Unbelievable, you think?' I say in a voice which is intended to come out sounding like Marilyn Monroe but possibly sounds more like Miss Piggy.

'You got a cold, babe?' he asks. 'You should take Echinacea for it.'

What's the bloody point?

'I mean it's just unbelievable that we're winning every match we play now, and the players are getting better all the time. I can genuinely see us making the play-offs and no one thought we'd do that – no one.'

'Is that why the Chelsea agent called?'

'Yeah, he says I'm the talk of the Premiership. Imagine it . . . me, little Dean Martin, being the talk of the

Premiership. David said on Saturday that he'd heard nothing but good things about me. Even Victoria said, "Oh, Dean. I've heard all about you!" I mean they really thought I was a good coach.'

'Yeah, great,' I say, lifting myself up onto my elbows. I mean I'm thrilled for Dean and all that, but do I really need to hear all about how he met Victoria and I didn't?

'Sorry, babes,' he says. 'Look, I'll tell you what. If I get offered this Chelsea job, and we decide to take it, I'll sign David, just so you can play with Victoria.'

'Will you? Really?' I gasp. It's the nicest thing anyone's ever said to me. The nicest present a Wag can be given. Sure, roses are nice, clothes are nicer and diamonds are nicer still – but David? He's going to buy David Beckham for me! 'Thanks so much,' I say, and the look on his face indicates that he fears he may have promised more than he can deliver.

'Well, you know – if I can. I mean, if I get the job and if everyone agrees that we should sign him, and if we can afford him, and if he wants to come and everything.'

Yeah. Not so much a fantastic gift now as an empty promise.

'Listen, Dean – you know that guy Jamie who used to work at the club? He picked us up from the airport.'

'Yes,' says Dean. 'Good-looking bloke.'

'Yes, that's the one. You don't know his second name by any chance, do you?'

'No idea sweetheart,' he says. 'Why?'

'No reason. I just thought I'd seen him on a TV show. Wondered if it was the same guy.'

As we're talking, there's an astonishing amount of noise coming from downstairs. 'What on earth is that?' asks Dean.

We both climb out of bed. Dean slips on a pair of England footie shorts and I wrap my marabou-fringed silk cover-up around myself, then we head downstairs, Dean taking them two at a time in his bizarre footballery way with his knobbly knees out to the side, kind of jigging from foot to foot.

When we reach the bottom of the stairs there's an almighty cheer, and the staff all burst into a chorus of 'Happy Birthday to You'.

'Happy birthday, mate,' says Gareth. 'This is from all of us.'

He hands over a carefully wrapped present, while the others let off firecrackers and throw streamers around.

'I bake cake,' says Alina, bringing in a fabulous chocolate confection with the Raiders' red and white strip fashioned out of marzipan on the top.

'I'm so touched,' says Dean, opening his presents and looking round to me for guidance.

'Tracie told us it was your birthday today so we thought we'd do something special.'

Oh, shit. The trip to Dad's on Sunday . . . me pretending that I was buying a suit for Dad's birthday. Shit, shit, shit.

'They misunderstood,' I whisper to Dean. 'I'm really sorry, and they've gone to all this trouble.'

'OK, let's not disappoint them,' says Dean, playing along with them. 'Happy birthday to me!' he says.

'Thanks,' I whisper. 'That was a really nice thing to do.'

'It's all about manners,' he says. 'I just drank from the fingerbowl to make the girl feel better.'

Christ, I think. He *does* listen to me sometimes.

Sunday 29 June

Dean's gone to a big celebratory lunch at the club. He was desperate for me to come, but I made some excuse about women's problems that had him backing out of the door in no time.

'Eughhhhhh . . .' he said. 'OK, fine. Stay here. Don't tell me about all that stuff. Just let me know when you're feeling better, or if you need a doctor or anything.'

'I will,' I said, clutching a box of tampons pathetically. The minute he closed the door I bolted up the stairs, taking them fifteen at a time, ran into my clothes room and flung on something casual for lunch at Dad's. Just a simple and elegant sequinned boob tube and hotpants with long boots and a feather boa in case it gets cold later. I've ordered a cab to take me there and back because Gareth's at the club with Dean, and I still can't get hold of Jamie, no matter how many times I call. Is he on holiday? I wonder. I'm starting to panic a bit now. I could really do with talking to him. My only hope is that he's gone back to Dad since I last saw him, and put things right somehow.

Dad's in the garden when I arrive. He's flicking through documents, notes and pages, concentrating hard as he frowns to himself, jotting down figures on a large piece of plain white paper with an expensive-looking pen.

'Someone looks as if they mean business,' I say, and he looks up, startled.

'Tracie, sorry. I was miles away. Lovely to see you.'

He removes his glasses, rubs his eyes and looks extremely tired.

'You not feeling well?' I ask.

'Just trying to sort out all my accounts. Did Dean mention the paperwork he was going to bring round? I could really do with it. My accountant wants to check a couple of things out.'

'No, he didn't,' I say. A feeling of uneasiness is clawing through my stomach. 'So he didn't pop in during the week, then?'

'No, he didn't. Would you mind asking him for me? If he's busy just tell him to stick them on a bike over here – I'm happy to pay the driver when he gets here. I'm just eager to sort out the business's finances.'

'Of course,' I say.

Sylvia brings a drink out into the garden for me. 'No chillies this time,' she announces. I thank her, and remove the sprig of mint.

It's odd but there's a strange atmosphere today. We're talking politely and I'm telling them all about the *LA Times* and Cindy the agent, but it's not like last time I came. Some of the closeness has gone. As we relax in the garden it's as if there's something unspoken that needs to be resolved. It's the money, of course.

My father is clearly concerned that Dean has persuaded him to part with a great deal of money, but won't call him, or turn up as he proposed to, to discuss and formalize the investment of it into the business. It must seem inconceivable to my dad that Dean has not spoken to me about it in some way. Perhaps my dad thinks we're both involved in a scam to do him out of loads of cash.

The problem is – what do I do? Admit that Dean is not my husband and send Keith rushing to the police to track Jamie down and retrieve the money, or bide my time in the knowledge that Jamie's for real. He's been talking about this business from the first time I met him. I know he'll come back next week and sort everything out with Dad, we'll organize a meeting with the three of us and Victoria and we'll create a world-famous brand that Dad will be extremely pleased to be associated with.

'It'll all be OK,' I tell my father. 'I'll make sure Dean sorts everything out. He's just been a bit manic recently with loads of mid-week and weekend matches all at once, and I know that incident with me having my car nicked really threw him. I'll get him to call you and come over next week.'

'Thanks, Tracie,' says Dad. 'I'm not worried at all. I've just got these bloody accountants breathing down my neck. You don't know what the company's called, by any chance, do you? My accountant did a search but couldn't find anything listed. Dean told me it was a registered company and that he was the only director of it at the moment, but you would be soon. I can't find Dean listed as a company director. Does he have a middle name that he uses or anything like that?'

'No,' I mumble.

Tuesday 1 July

This is the thing: even though I feel I've got to know Jamie very well, over the past few weeks I've realized that I don't know much about him at all.

I've got no idea where he lives, or what his landline number is. I don't even know what his surname is despite calling everyone I can think of to try and find out. We always used to just keep bumping into each other all the time, but I haven't seen him anywhere recently.

I'm fast running out of ideas. Jamie's mobile number is now not ringing at all. I've called the operator, who says the number's disconnected. I even went to Muscle Beach yesterday and walked around looking for him, in case he was out running. I don't know where else to look. I'm sure he'll be back in touch soon, but I'm worried that in the meantime my dad will think we've stolen his money. He'll think I'm just like Mum. I couldn't bear that.

Perhaps I should call a private detective agency. They do this sort of thing, don't they? But how will I find one? On the internet?

'Mark?' I call into the garden. 'Have you got a minute?'

'Sure,' he says, wiping his hands on a towel and coming

into the house. He and Peter have done all the basic work in the garden for a swimming pool now. They just need to make a few alterations to the designs. You see, there was some sort of confusion in what pool Dean was after. Mark and Peter got the idea that Dean wanted one with pictures of people having sex all over it.

'You said you wanted an infidelity pool,' they told Dean.

'No, an infinity pool,' Dean explained. 'It's a pool in which the water's always right up to the top. Have a look in the brochures. They're in there.'

The guys just need to remove the smutty pictures, the condom fountain and the phallic statues and it'll be fine. Dean told them to take time off after that but they've decided to create a fitness area next to the swimming pool instead.

'How do you go about finding things on the web?' I ask, keeping my request as vague as possible.

He leans over the computer and presses a few buttons until the screen lights up.

'What sort of things?'

'Oh, I don't know – places locally. You know, businesses in the area.'

'Google's your best bet,' he says, typing it in.

'Google?' I say, alarmed. 'Are you sure that's not a porn site?'

'No,' he says, looking alarmed. 'Why would it be?'

'You know, as in "Let's have a look at your googles", or "Get your googlies out for the boys".'

'No, Tracie, nothing like that,' he says, pointing at the screen. 'You just need to write what you're looking for in that box and it'll come up with everything.' As an example he types in 'Shoe shops, Los Angeles' and onto the screen comes a list of shoe shops in the LA area.

'This is perfect,' I say. 'Does anyone else know about this Google thing?'

'Yes,' admits Mark. 'I think a few other people know about it.'

While he disappears into the garden, I call up the main Google page again and begin by typing in 'Searching for someone. Los Angeles'.

A list of names appears on the screen and I glance down it. There's one that looks perfect. Her name's Rose-Clair and she promises to be able to communicate with anyone at all. It says that she can reach people who are out of your life but with whom you'd like to get back in touch. Blimey, this looks perfect. I pick up the phone and dial the number listed on the screen.

'Hello, this is the house of Rose,' says a spooky-sounding voice.

'Ah, well, this is the house of Tracie Martin calling,' I say. 'I'd very much like to come and see you as soon as possible. I'm desperate to get in touch with someone . . .'

'Of course,' says Rose, interrupting me. 'I understand. I feel your pain.'

'Do you?' I say, and she's right – I do feel pain. 'I feel let down and angry. I just want to talk to him so we can sort everything out,' I say.

'Then you must come and see me straight away,' she says. 'I'm sure I can help.'

As we're talking, I hear the doorbell ringing, followed by three loud thumps on the door. I try to ignore it, and concentrate on Detective Rose-Clair.

'Can I come later today?' I ask. 'Say around 4 p.m.?'

'I'll look forward to it,' she says in her spooky voice, and then she's gone, leaving me wondering whether I should have asked more questions, or told her more about the case. I guess I'll get the chance to do that when we meet.

There's still banging going on, as someone hammers on our front door. Who the hell is that? No one knocks on the door here. In Luton people were always popping round, but we don't really know anyone that well in LA yet.

'I coming. I coming,' says Alina, shuffling with her usual tortoise speed towards the door while I finish my clicking.

'Nobody,' I hear Alina say in amazement, before the shuffling starts up again and she appears beside me clutching a scruffy piece of paper with 'Tracie' written in pencil on it. It's sellotaped round the edge and has 'ergent' written on it.

'OUTSYDE,' is all it says on the note.

Shit. What's this all about? I slip my mules onto my feet and head towards the door. Outsyde? Who do I know who spells like that?

I go scampering to the door, popping my head round. Alina is about an inch from me, watching my every move with increasing alarm.

'Everything's fine, Alina,' I say. 'You can go back inside.'

There's no sign of anyone outside, which is unusual to say the least. I walk out a bit further and hear 'Psssssst . . .'

I look behind me, but there's no one there. Just Alina peering out through the windows. She's looking through the slats in the blinds and presumably thinks I can't see her. I knock heavily on the window and see her jump, almost pulling the blinds clean off the wall.

'Pssssssst . . .' I hear again. This time there's a slight shadow movement down the side of the house, so I walk over, tiptoeing over the grass so I don't completely wreck my fancy shoes. As I'm just reaching it a big hand reaches out, grabs me and pulls me roughly behind the house.

'Mmmmmuuuurggghh,' I say.

'Shhhh!' he says.

I look up into the less-than-attractive eyes of Bill. Next to him stand Bob and Barry.

'We got sumut for you,' says Barry, holding up my handbag.

They all stand there, looking at me.

'Aren't you going to say something? We risked our lives to get this back.'

'Mmmmmuuuurggghh,' I say.

'Oh, sorry,' says Bill, releasing his grip.

'Thank you so, so much,' I say. 'That's just brilliant.'

They seem much happier now they've been thanked. Even violent criminals deserve proper courtesies.

'Look,' says Bill, pointing to the road where my old car sits, smashed up, dirty and barely recognizable as the one I was driving around in just over a week ago.

'Wow!' I say. 'Thank you. How did you get it back?'

'Don't ask. It's our job to catch baddies,' says Bill. 'That's kind of what we do. Anyway, we thought we owed yas a favour. That thing what you wrote in the paper, man. You never mentioned our names or nothin'. Never said where we was going.'

'I gave you my word,' I say proudly, and they clench their fists and raise them in a 'solidarity' sort of way, so I do the same but my long fingernails make the creation of a fist impossible, so I just hold it up in an odd claw-like fashion.

'Where are you off to now?' I ask. 'Do you fancy a drink?'

'Man, we're on the run. We can't come in your house.'

'On the run?'

'Yeah, few problems, man.'

'So you've got nowhere to stay?'

'We be fine on the streets, lady. That's where we's at.'

'No, I know somewhere you could stay. It's perfect. No one will find you there.'

'Where?'

'At Dean's club. There's this old outbuilding that used to be used as an office years ago so it has bolts, locks and window bars and everything. It's tucked in the bushes. No one knows it's there. It's derelict now, but a coat of paint, a couple of leopardskin scatter cushions and a few tasteful prints of Dean in his Luton tracksuit or that woman in her tennis skirt scratching her bum on the wall, and it'll be as good as new.'

4 p.m.

Wow, these Los Angeles private detectives are a funny bunch. You should see the outside of their offices. I thought it would be all formal and proper, but the office is in this small wooden building. It looks more like a hut, actually, and there are pictures of stars, angels, moons and planets on the outside of it. Beaded ribbons hang down in the doorway, and as I walk through them into the most bizarre office they clatter against one another.

There's a strong smell inside, like burning perfume, and a woman dressed in ridiculous clothes sits before me.

'Oh, sorry,' I say. 'I'm looking for Rose-Clair, sorry – I mean Detective Voyant.'

'I am Rose,' she says. 'You must be Tracie. Take a seat, my love. Do you have a personal item that I could hold while we talk?'

'Sorry?'

'Any personal item. It will help me to work with you.'

'OK, Detective. How about this?'

I hand over my Versace glittery face powder, and watch as she holds it in the palm of her hand and breathes deeply.

'I'm getting someone,' she says, to my surprise. 'I can picture a lady. She's old but happy.'

'Sorry. I'm all confused now,' I say. 'I'm here because I need to find a guy called Jamie. He's stolen money from my father and I need to get it back urgently.'

'She says she's watching you. The old lady. She's happy and at peace, and she's saying something about a man who's making you happy.'

'What old lady? What man?'

'Nell? Do you know a Nell?'

'Yes. I loved her. She was my rock. I adored her, but she died last year.'

'She's with us, here in this room.'

'What?' I say. 'Detective, how can she be in the room?'

'Her spirit remains with us, and she wants to talk to you. She has something to say. She's talking about a man and a bike. Is that a man on a bike?'

'I don't know what you're talking about,' I say. There's no way that Nell's spirit has come wandering into a detective agency to have a chat to me.

'Is this a gay man or something?' says Rose, but she's not talking to me now, she's talking to an imaginary, ghostly Nell who Rose believes to be in the room with us. It's beyond madness.

'Well, how did I know that?' Rose says, getting aggressive with the empty space by the side of her desk. 'You said a man and a little pink bike and I thought he must be gay.'

'Oh God.' I realize who the ghost of Nell must be talking about. This is really freaky now. How's this happening?

'Dad!' I say.

'What?' says Rose aggressively. 'First you call me Detective, and now you're calling me Dad.'

'No, I think Nell's talking about Dad, and I thought you were a detective.'

With that, Rose falls off her chair and onto the floor. She stands up quickly, looking embarrassed, brushes herself down and takes her seat. 'Yes, I think that's who she's talking about – your Dad. She can be quite rough, your Nell, can't she?'

This is really spooky. Nell was indeed a bit of a tough nut. She didn't tolerate fools easily, and she was exactly the sort of person to push a batty detective off her chair.

'She says that your relationship with him will bring you great joy and happiness. She also says something about your skin looking lovely. Something about a piano, too, and Tipperary – does that make any sense?'

'Oh my God,' I say, collapsing into my chair. 'How do you know these things?'

'It's my job,' she says.

'Your job? Is that what detectives here do?'

It turns out that Rose-Clair Voyant is not a private detective, but is Gypsy Rose – Clairvoyant. She can communicate with the dead, which doesn't make her much use at catching Jamie, but incredible at conversing with Nell.

'Ask her how she is,' I say. 'Tell her I love her and miss her enormously.'

'She's doing well,' says Rose. 'She misses you too but she's looking out for you. She says she's with you every day, in everything you do. She says you should be aware that there's no Nancy with her. Does that make sense?'

'Nancy. Yes – Jamie's mum.'

'There's no Nancy,' repeats Rose.

'Does Nell know where Jamie is?' I try.

Rose drops her head into her hands for a few seconds, then looks up at the ceiling.

'It's no good,' she says. 'I'm not getting anything – there are strikes of lightning across my mind. I can't see anything but lightning . . . oh, and fish. I can see fish too. That's all I'm getting for Jamie. Now – oh wait, hang on. I'm getting something else, something different. "Beware of the angel." Does that mean anything to you?'

'It doesn't,' I say.

'Nell is warning you that someone called Angel will be returning soon and to be very careful. Angel? Angela? Angie?'

'Angie?' I say, and off the chair goes Rose again.

'Careful!' she shrieks. 'That hurt.'

'My mum's called Angie,' I tell her. 'We don't talk any more because she really let me down.'

'I think she's coming back soon,' says Rose, holding out her hand and asking for money. 'Be careful. Be very,

very careful. Don't encourage her, don't return her calls or communicate with her. Your happiness depends on this, my dear.'

8 p.m.

I'm lying on the bed, stroking my Versace sparkly face powder compact in the hope that Nell will come bursting into the room. She doesn't, of course. I just end up spilling it all over the sheets. It means Dean will end up with glittery chest hair in the morning, which he won't be overly impressed with.

As I'm dusting away the worst of it, there's a gentle knock on the door.

'Come in,' I say, and in walks Paskia with tears streaming down her face.

'What on earth's the matter?'

'Do you remember I told you about those horrid girls at school? You know – the ones who were laughing at me for playing football?'

'Yes,' I say.

'Well, they keep putting notes in my bag, being horrible to me because I'm friends with Joseph and saying that being part of the Jesus Christ of Latterday Saints religion means that people can't have sex before marriage and can't have lustful thoughts at all. They say that's why Joseph has chosen me as a friend, because no one could have lustful thoughts about me. They also said they read the articles you write, and they think you're really cool, so they don't understand why I'm such a complete dweeb.'

'How horrible,' I say. 'That's really cruel, Paskia.'

'I'm not a dweeb, am I, Mum?' she says. 'Am I?'

'No, you're not,' I say. I have to admit that I'm deeply flattered at what the cool girls have said about me, but I won't have them upsetting my daughter like this. 'They're a bunch of idiots,' I announce. 'Complete idiots.'

'They say they're going to come down to the ground on Sunday.'

'Good,' I say. 'If they do I'll be waiting for them. Now, how would you like to invite your nice chap round for tea on Friday night?'

'OK,' she says. 'For a Fourth of July tea?'

'Yes. Good idea!' I say. A special tea party. Marvellous. I'm not quite sure why the fourth of July should warrant a mention, but if Pask wants to celebrate the date, then I'm up for that. I'd celebrate the date every day given half a chance.

Friday 4 July

Technically, I'm not sure whether I've committed a crime by harbouring criminals on the run, but I certainly don't imagine that the country's law enforcement agencies would look kindly on me if they knew.

The three men headed off there once I'd told them where the key was kept, and today I went down there with food and shed-loads of drink. It's OK there, actually.

'This is just like camping,' I say, which seems to make them laugh. The place lacks a woman's touch, what with the guns, knuckledusters and other criminal paraphernalia scattered around, but, like they keep saying, it's a darn sight better than where they were planning to hide out. Let's just say I don't think they were expecting to be drinking Cristal for breakfast with LA City Raiders' premier Wag. Funny what life throws up.

4 p.m.

Dean makes it home early for tea, as he promised he would, and looks quite taken aback by my efforts. I managed to find out what was so special about the fourth of July and the house is now decked out in stars and stripes and I'm sporting a skin-tight boob-tube dress made from the star-spangled banner. I have big, chunky red, white and blue platform shoes and my newly spray-tanned skin is covered in red, white and blue glitter.

'Good Lord!' he says.

'Don't mention the Lord when the little religious boy gets here, will you?' I say.

Paskia and Joseph arrive half an hour later, and my daughter comes straight over and gives me a kiss. Not just a cursory 'Man, you're so embarrassing' but a proper kiss . . . in public! This is great.

'Food?' I say, inviting them through to where the table is laid with the most astonishing selection of foods. We could hold a Fourth of July party for everyone in the street and we'd never run out of food.

'Wow,' says Joseph, taking in the goodies before him. 'This is great. Thank you, Mrs Martin, and happy Fourth of July.'

We all raise our glasses and right there, in that minute, it's as if all my problems melt away. Here with Dean and Pask and a lovely new friend called Joseph, dressed up to the nines and with a drink in my hand. I want it to stay the Fourth of July for ever more.

'I've got fireworks for later,' I tell them. 'Just a couple of sparklers and things to mark the occasion.' Actually, I have enough fireworks to blow up the White House.

Sunday 6 July

So, this is where we are now. It's important to summarize your situation to yourself every so often just so you're clear in your own mind about what you're doing and where you're going.

The car that was stolen from me while I asked for directions from three criminals is now in a garage that I've hired at the end of the block, all smashed up. I don't know what to do with it because if I tell the insurance company it's been miraculously returned to me they'll ask all sorts of silly questions starting with words like 'How?' and 'Who?' and they'll tell the police, who'll want to fingerprint it, and my new little friends will be in even more trouble. I have no desire to defraud the insurance company, but how can I tell them without making things harder for the B brothers? I don't want to cause any more trouble for my hidden criminals than is strictly necessary.

OK, so what else? Oh, yes, in addition to the criminal fraternity that I have got hidden in the former office of Raiders soccer club, and the car that I have got hidden in a garage down the road, there's the other issue I've been wrestling with all morning – the fact that Jamie took a quarter of a million bucks off my dad and disappeared into thin air.

I don't think Jamie's stolen the money because the cheque wasn't made out to him, so he can't have cashed it, but I do think he's being a real pain by not getting in touch and helping me sort this out.

My dad phoned twice during the week asking whether he could have a quick word with Dean, and on both occasions I said that Dean was at the club, working really, really hard, and had actually been staying there overnight.

Raiders are playing today, thank God, so I have a valid excuse for not taking Dean with me, but what of this paperwork that I can't produce?

Perhaps I should go to the bank and take out a loan for $250,000. I'm sure they'd give me the money if I borrowed it against the house. Then I could pay Dad back without Dean knowing, and it would be I who had invested in Jamie's company, so I'll just have to find him and sort out the paperwork directly with him, cutting my father out of the picture and sparing him the financial loss if things go wrong.

'You OK?' asks Paskia-Rose.

I didn't even see her standing there in the doorway, looking at me.

'You look really worried,' she says.

'No, of course not,' I say. 'I'm fine. Are you OK?'

'Not really. Look at this.'

She shows me a text that has been sent.

'You r sad, fat, ugly cow. We're going 2 ruin yor soccer game.'

'OK,' I say. 'Leave this with me,' I say. 'You go and concentrate on getting ready for the game.'

11 a.m.

I get to the club early so I can have a quick chat with my hidden criminals. I explain to them that my daughter's in trouble, and jointly we make a plan. If the girls turn up and start being rude to Paskia, I'll lure them to the outhouse and leave the rest to them.

3 p.m.

It's the start of the match when the girls come down, more dressed up than ever – thick black eyeliner and earrings all the way up their ears. Gosh, how I admire their style. Why do they have to pick on my daughter?

I stand back from the crowd and watch as they begin to taunt her, shouting 'Hey fatty!' when she gets the ball.

OK, time to act. I walk out of the shadows and over to them, and the heckling ceases at once.

'Hi,' they all say. 'We just love your column in the paper.'

'Oh, thank you,' I say. 'Would you like some champagne and cigarettes?'

'Gosh, yes please,' they say.

Like lambs to the slaughter.

'Go over to that building over there, and I'll meet you there in five minutes,' I say, and off they troop.

They're gone for longer than I expected and I do have a momentary panic when I think I hear a shriek, but I don't move. I stay watching the match, pretending I have no idea where the schoolgirls have gone.

Then I hear the booming voices of the criminals, and the sight of three girls running for all they're worth back to the pitch side. They all look pale and terrified as they watch the football match unfold.

'Come on, Paskia,' they shout every time my daughter touches the ball. 'You're the best. Come on, you can do it.'

'If you ever insult my daughter again, those men will be appearing wherever you go,' I hiss. 'I mean it. Don't fuck with me.'

'No, we won't,' the girls say, and looking at their faces I'm inclined to believe them. 'We're going home now,' they say as they hear the final whistle, and they leave the ground with their heads bowed and their confidence sapped.

Paskia comes running over as soon as the coach tells them they can leave.

'Can I go for ice cream with Joseph afterwards?' she asks. 'His dad said he'd drop me off.'

'Of course,' I say. 'I've got a few things to do, anyway.'

The first of those is to head off to visit my father.

7 p.m.

I cut short my visit to my father's house because it was awful. Dad asked me time and again when Dean would drop the paperwork in.

'Next week,' I promised.

'There's no problem at all,' he was keen to emphasize. 'I just need to get the paperwork signed so that I can properly account for the money I've invested. My business accounts look a bit dodgy with "Gave cheque made out to Dean Martin" written in there!'

You see – that's an important point. Jamie can't have cashed the cheque because it wasn't made out to him.

'I don't think Dean's put the cheque in the bank yet, actually,' I say. 'I think he's planning to sort out the paperwork before paying it in. So if you want to cancel it, then you could reissue it when you've had time to talk to Dean about it all in more detail. Dean wouldn't mind at all. In fact I think he'd be relieved. He's so busy at the club right now that he has no time to even think about the business.'

'No, the cheque's been cashed,' says Dad. 'It was cashed straight away.'

8 p.m.

I couldn't go straight home. My mind was spinning too much. I ended up getting the taxi driver to go round in circles. Dean texted to say that the team had won again and he'd be back after Tai Chi. I don't want to be at home thinking of the madness of what's going on. How does Jamie manage to put a cheque made out to Dean into his account?

With every question I ask, and every turn I take, things get more complicated. Things get horrific, nasty, illegal and vile. I need to get my father out of this web before our relationship is irretrievably damaged.

I have to get a bank loan, but I fear that my husband's club is bankrupt – will that count against me? I've no idea, and I've no real idea how to find out, but there's someone who might be willing to tell me the full story about how short of cash the club is – Sian.

'Hello stranger!' she says, kissing me fulsomely. 'Come in. Poppy's inside.'

The sitting room is filled with candles burning and whale music gently wafting. It's a sea of calm and tranquillity with Poppy in the middle, sitting in the lotus position in a pale-pink loose-fitting tunic top.

'I haven't seen you for so long,' she says when I walk in and plonk myself down on the sofa. 'Macey was asking after you this morning. She said she hasn't seen you for ages. A party's always so much more fun when you're there, Tracie.'

Admittedly, since I started hanging out with my long-lost father and an assortment of violent criminals I haven't seen so much of them.

'Have you lost weight?' I ask Sian, who looks thinner than ever.

'Don't think so. Don't think I could. Besides chopping off a limb, I think this is about it for me, thin-wise.'

I laugh and take the drink she offers. I must have forgotten just how skinny she is.

I take a sip and I'm almost sick. 'What the fuck . . .?'

'Sun-dried tomato, grapefruit and lime. Nice, huh?'

'Nice with vodka,' I say, and she laughs . . . but doesn't move.

'No, I'm serious. Do you have any?'

With a shake of her head she disappears into the hallway. Eventually she comes back with a bottle, splashes some into my glass and turns to walk towards the window where Poppy is now standing, breathing deeply. I take the bottle and pour a great slug in. I have to take the twirl of lime out to fit the necessary quantity in, but that strikes me as a fair trade.

'Listen, can I ask you a question?' I say. I might as well get straight on with it.

'Sure,' says Sian.

Poppy offers to leave the room but I figure I trust her, and her contribution might be valuable.

'You know how the club's completely broke?'

'Broke? What do you mean?' says Sian.

'There's no money at the club.'

'There's loads of money at the club,' says Poppy.

'But Sian said the club had no money. When I first got here. That's what you told me.'

'No, I didn't,' Sian insists. 'I'd never have said that.'

'You did,' I say, trying to remember when she said it. 'It was when I was asking why you wouldn't continue to employ Jamie as a driver. You said the club couldn't.'

'That wasn't because the club couldn't afford it, it's because Jamie's a nasty piece of work. He fleeced one girl out of about $50,000 by telling her he was going to set up a company selling vintage football clothing, and then he told another girl that his mother was dying and he needed money for hospital treatment to save her life. He's evil, Tracie. *That's* why we didn't employ him at the club. He's a con artist.'

'He's the most vile person I know,' confirms Poppy. 'A really horrible man.'

Monday 7 July

Why does daylight have to come round so quickly? I don't want to get out of bed ever again.

'What are you up to today, my love?' asks Dean as he slips these awful pyjama-style yoga pants on and does a ridiculous dance around the room. 'Something fun?'

'Probably write some notes for the *LA Times* thing, then . . . I don't know really.'

And, the truth is I don't know. I don't know what to do. I guess I should go straight to the police because I know that's the right thing to do, but that means telling my father, and what if he never forgives me? That's too high a price to pay.

I spent my whole childhood believing that my father hated me, and that I was a bad person. I've finally met up with him, discovered he's lovely and he likes me very much, and now I've messed it all up. As usual.

As Dean jogs down the stairs, whistling football tunes to himself, I disappear under the covers. I cry like I've never cried before, not just for the lost money or the fact that someone I trusted has proved to be utterly selfish, money-grabbing and horrible, but because I've wrecked everything. My father will never want anything to do with me again. Jamie's stolen something that money can't buy, and it's all my fault.

Tuesday 8 July

'Tracie. Is letter,' says Alina, passing me a padded envelope that was left in the mailbox overnight. It must be from my stowaways at the club. I'm pleased to see that someone with much neater writing has been given the task this time. I tear it open, and a letter typed on a single sheet of paper falls out, along with a photograph. I stifle a giggle as I reach for the letter. They've clearly found some old type-writer left lying in the office, and have decided to have some fun.

Dear Tracie,

Do not show this letter to anyone. If you value your relationship with your husband and daughter, leave $5,000 in used notes in this brown envelope at the end of the block, near the disused garages. Do this by midnight tonight or I will pass this, and other photos like it, on to Dean.

PS. Remember – I have pictures of us two with your dad, and out at loads of different tourist spots, bars and restaurants in LA. Dean would love to see them.

He'll be intrigued to hear of all the lies you told in order to meet up with me.

The photo is of Jamie and me at Koi restaurant. He has my face cupped in his hands, and he is looking deep into my eyes. I remember it being taken. It was this picture, but it was not this picture. This is all wrong. The picture looks as if it's been shot from a distance by a paparazzi photographer. It looks as if I've been caught red-handed having an affair.

I look back at the letter and realize that I've been incredibly, incredibly stupid. Jamie's completely stitched me up. And he's right – I told loads of lies to everyone in order to spend time with him. With these pictures, it looks *exactly* like we've been having an affair.

11 p.m.

I've told everyone at home that I'm going to post a letter, which – kind of – I am. They have no idea that my letter contains $5,000 in used notes that I took out from the cashpoint. I had to use my platinum card to take it out because it's the only one that Dean doesn't see the statement for. Dean calls it my Tracie Treats card.

I'm terrified that I'm going to get attacked as I walk over to what Jamie called the 'disused garages' but which I know to be used because they're housing my beaten-up car. I lay the envelope on the ground, take a look around the place, then run as fast as my stiletto-shoe-clad feet will allow, running and running until I'm safely home. I shut the door, collapse on the sofa and think, Phew, I've dealt with the problem. I need a drink.

It's parents' evening at Paskia's school tonight, so Dean and I have dressed in our finest clothes and are sitting in the reception area, awaiting the arrival of Mrs Thompson. I felt like a teenager sneaking out on a date earlier this evening, as Pask and I were in complete disagreement about what was appropriate attire for a night at the school talking to her teachers.

'No other mums will wear hotpants,' she said, when I came downstairs with my chosen clothes for the evening.

'More fool them,' I responded.

'Mum, I love the fact that you're different from everyone else and have your own unique style, but just this once is there any chance you could wear something simple and elegant? Please? Could you blend in with the others for one evening?'

She wants me to look like a mother rather than the sort of woman who gets mistaken for a transvestite (no, I haven't forgotten that – just because I don't talk about it doesn't mean it doesn't still hurt).

'OK, dear,' I said, in the interests of continuing the happiness of the relationship that we have managed to strike up between us.

I headed upstairs and rummaged through my dressing area, realizing that I might have over-reached a little in my promise. Nothing in there spelt simplicity, and if you called any of it elegant you'd be done under the Trade Descriptions Act.

In the end I borrowed a white blouse and trousers from Alina and walked downstairs. The blouse was about eight times too big and the trousers could have fit the whole family in them.

'Oh!' said Paskia. 'Mum, you look so pretty.'

'You do look gorgeous, Tracie. Honestly, I've never seen you look like that before. You look, well, lovely.'

'Thanks,' I said, picking up my huge handbag.

'Do you need a bag that big?' asked Dean.

'I'd like to take it, love,' I replied.

'Let's make a move then,' he said, kissing Paskia goodbye.

We jumped into the car and I drove down the road in the direction of the school, waving to Paskia as we went. I signalled, turned right, then pulled swiftly over to the side of the road.

'What are you doing?' asked Dean.

'What the fuck do you think I'm doing?' I replied, pulling off the blouse to reveal a spangly pink brassière and kicking off Alina's navy blue trousers to unveil pink leather hotpants. I shoved the plain clothing into the handbag, pulled out long white plastic boots and a huge bag of makeup. Twenty minutes, much pink lipstick and vast quantities of sparkly blue eye shadow and foundation later, and I felt more like me.

'Right, we're off,' I said to Dean. He was sitting there open-mouthed.

'I thought you looked lovely before,' he said.

'Yeah, well, you've been out of Luton for far too long.'

So now we're here, and though people stop and stare at me as they pass, and though the French teacher walked straight into the wall because I bent over right in front of him, I don't care. This is me. That's what I am. If I didn't dress like this, part of me would be missing.

388

'Mr and Mrs Martin,' says a lady in a long brown skirt and fussy brown and red blouse with a pussycat bow at the top. She has ridiculous half-moon glasses on, which force her to look sternly down her nose at everyone, and her thick, greying hair is in a high bun. She's English, like many of the staff members at the school. I know this because of her accent, but you'd know it from four miles away. 'Follow me.'

We trot behind her as she strides off, talking about the weather and the air conditioning in the upper school library.

'Settling in OK?' she asks.

'Yes, thank you,' we both reply, because even though my world is completely falling apart and I see no way in which I'm going to get through the next few weeks, let alone the rest of my life, I'd never share that with Mrs Thompson. She's a teacher. Teachers are different. They're from outer space – from a planet where no one has first names and everyone does as they're told.

She tells us to sit down, and we do so.

'Not there,' she barks, so Dean, currently one of the most respected men in the multi-million dollar world of football, leaps up like a ten year old. 'Sit there,' she commands. 'That's Paskia's desk.'

'How's she getting on?' he asks.

'I'll come to that,' says Mrs Thompson, looking at him through her half-moons as she shuffles papers.

'Sorry,' he says, meekly.

'Right.' She pulls out a collection of papers. 'Well, the short answer is that Paskia-Rose is doing exceptionally well. Her grasp of complex arithmetic is astounding. Do you have any mathematicians in the family?'

'Er, no,' I reply, and I'm sure she looks me up and down in an 'I am *so* not surprised' sort of way.

'Well, the skill's come from somewhere,' says Mrs Thompson. 'She's really an exceptionally talented girl when it comes to numbers. In fact she's in the top three in her class in everything. We're terribly pleased with her.'

We sit there a little longer, being shown some of the work she's done, none of which makes any sense to me, then suddenly I have a blinding thought: Shit! It's Dad, isn't it? He's an accountant. That must be where Paskia-Rose gets her mathematical brain from. Gosh, isn't that amazing? It makes me more determined than ever to make sure I don't ruin the relationship with my father. For Paskia, if for no one else, I have to rescue this crucial relationship from the mess and conflict that Jamie has caused all around it.

'Thank you for your time, Mrs Thompson,' I say, rising to my feet and giving her a full-frontal, eye-line view of the crotch of my pink hotpants. Dean gets up too and we're out of there. I need to think. I need to put things right. Somehow I have to sort this problem out.

Thursday 10 July

I'm awake early. I have to give Dad his money back, and I have to do it quickly. He's been leaving messages all week, just to say when he's going to be in if I want to drop round, and how he'll happily come to pick me up if I want, it's no problem at all.

I want to go round there with the cheque and refund him. I want him, and our relationship, out of the sordid mess caused by Jamie's duplicity. My relationship with my father is too important to be dragged down by this horrible slimy man.

So, what are my options? First stop has to be the bank. I know it doesn't 'solve' the problems, but it's a short-term fix for the most important problem – that of Dad's trust in me. Once I've got Dad out of the problem, then it's just me and Jamie – and that's a fight I'm well and truly up for. He may have thought I was a push-over. He probably thought I was stupid. What a shock he's going to have. I've got nails that could slice through diamonds and stiletto heels that could pierce skin. He's going to regret ever crossing swords with me.

I found the bank's twenty-four-hour service on that Google thing on the computer, and they've made me an appointment for 10 a.m. I'm desperate to look the part. Unfortunately I don't have a sober black suit or anything like that. I've given Alina her blouse and trousers back, and she's gone off to the farmers' market. (Why do they sell farmers? It's always mystified me. Sounds like slavery.) I'll have to wear something of Dean's, so I pull out a simple, single-breasted black jacket. It's elegant and nicely cut. Perfect for this meeting. I put it on and look in the mirror. With the buttons at the top undone and a leopardskin push-up bra underneath it'll be fine.

It looks good with the bra, but it doesn't really show my waist off, which is a pity. I rush through to my dressing area and pull out a big, thick, pink patent-leather belt. I wrap it round the jacket and though the jacket does ride up considerably with the belt on, meaning I'll probably end up having to wear knickers, which is a shame, it does look much better.

I slip on some turquoise gladiator sandals that lace up to near my knees and by the time I've done my hair and makeup, putting vast quantities of gold sparkles on my chest and in my cleavage, I'm ready to go. My hair looks great – I've got large pink flowers in the front of it to minimize the masculine effect of the jacket.

The cab comes, and I jump into it without telling anyone where I'm going. This is the first time I've done anything like this on my own and I have to say it makes me feel very grown up. Being dressed in a professional and sophisticated way feels much nicer than I thought it would. Perhaps I should do this more often. Perhaps they'll be so impressed with me they'll offer me a job in the bank. That might be a fun thing to do. I've never been in a bank before.

'Hollywood Hills Bank, ma'am,' says the taxi driver. I slide across the back seat and clamber out.

Ooooh, it looks very posh from the outside – all black and gold and kind of rich-looking. I push open the door and am treated to a welcome blast of air conditioning. Lovely. But – oh – what a disappointment! It's not very sumptuous at all.

Judging by the décor and the general feel of the place, not many Wagalicious ladies work here. I think that even if they offer me a job I'll turn it down. Talk about dull and sombre. Browns and blacks everywhere. It's like a . . . well . . . I guess it's like an office, really.

'Mrs Martin,' says a boy. He looks about twelve years old and I just about manage not to ask him whether he's here on a 'bring your son to work day'.

All the ladies sitting behind the glass screens stop what they're doing and stare at me as I teeter past. Yeah, style, ladies. Watch and learn.

The boy leads me into a yet more dull room. It's small, dark and devoid of any of the little features that I always think make a room special, like throws, scatter cushions or life-size marble statues of Dean when he was at his football-playing best.

'How can I help you?' he asks. 'Tell me what brings you to Hollywood Hills Banking Corporation.'

'I'd like to take out a loan,' I say, bending over to pull my notes out of my handbag.

'Holy fuck,' says the boy, taking his seat.

'Sorry?'

'Nothing, nothing at all, Mrs Martin.'

'Oh, I know,' I say. 'I forgot to put my knickers on.'

Bank boy is the colour of the goji berry smoothies that everyone in this town seems to love so much.

'What's your name?' I ask him.

'Louis,' he says, straightening his tie and trying to concentrate on the papers I've put before him. 'This loan,' he comments, his eyes glued to the desk. Every time he looks up, he turns a deeper shade of red.

'Oh, sorry,' I say, realizing that my left breast has made a triumphant escape, both from the lace-top balcony bra and, indeed, from the jacket itself. I shove it back in and take the boy's hand. 'I've shown you my arse and my tits. What more do you want? Surely I can have a loan now?'

I'm joking, of course, and I'm being coarse because I'm desperately nervous. I need this loan more than I've needed anything before. However worried he may feel, with his dropping the paper, going bright red and stumbling over his words, at least he doesn't have known criminals in his care, a dodgy car in a lock-up garage, a father who's been fleeced and a husband who knows nothing about it all.

'So, I need a $250,000 loan, and I'll need it today. If possible, I'd like to take it away with me in a cheque made out in someone else's name.'

'I'm sorry, Mrs Martin,' says bank boy. 'I can't give you a loan without your husband's permission. If you can get him to sign the form and bring it back tomorrow, I'm confident that there will be absolutely no problem at all offering you such a loan.'

'What century is this?' I ask, though I have to confess that, as he's speaking, I remember Dean saying something about the account being in his name.

'I'm so sorry,' says bank boy. 'We at the Hollywood Hills Banking Corporation would be more than happy to make a loan to Mr Martin. Unfortunately, just because of the nature of the account you have, we can't make that payment to you without his prior and explicit authorization.'

'Please,' I say. 'You have to help me. I know I dress in a strange way, and you may think I look peculiar, but I'm a nice person and I've been really turned over by this guy and if I don't get the loan I think it'll all end up with my father hating me because he'll think I'm dishonest like my mum who lied to me and hated me. I couldn't bear it. I couldn't. Please. I'll do anything.'

'I just can't help,' he says.

'You have to.'

'There's nothing I can do,' he reiterates.

'There must be,' I shout, rising to my feet and running round to his side of the desk. 'I'm rich. My husband's rich. Just give me a loan. I'm begging you.' I'm on my knees beside him now, with my head in his lap and his hand in mine.

I see him move the other hand and I'm convinced he's going to comfort me and tell me it'll all be OK, but instead he hits an alarm button under his desk, and two security guards come dashing in. Oh, great.

'I just wanted your help,' I say as the guards attempt to lift me to my feet. 'Did you really have to do that?'

'I told you – I can't help,' says bank boy.

The two security men escort me out of the building while I'm still shouting at bank boy, 'Why? Why?'

'Sorry, madam,' he says. 'There's nothing I can do.'

Fuck.

Sunday 13 July

There's no way I can go and see Dad today as planned. How can I? I don't know what to say to him. If I tell him what I did, he'll think I'm a terrible liar just like Mum. Perhaps I am a terrible liar like Mum. Actually, there's no perhaps about it, is there? I am a terrible liar. I've caused absolute chaos by lying to the people I love most. Dad has left messages all day asking where I am. Shit. I'm going to bed and I'm staying there all day.

5 p.m.

'You OK?' asks Paskia-Rose.

She came bounding up the stairs as soon as she heard from Alina that I spent all day in bed. Bless her. She's a lovely kid. I really don't deserve her.

'I'm OK,' I tell her. 'Just a bit of a hangover.'

'Well, I've got some news that will cheer you up,' she says. 'Joseph's parents have invited you and Dad for dinner on Thursday night.'

'Great,' I say. 'That will be nice.'

Pask skips out of the room and I dive down under the covers. Bloody marvellous.

Monday 14 July

The phone rings bright and early and, of course, I don't answer it. Alina will answer it, then she will panic like mad about whether she's supposed to put the call through to me. I'm 'out' to so many people these days that the poor woman has to consult a long list every time she answers the phone, and I know she's terrified she's going to get it wrong.

Today it says Sian, because I don't want to talk to her in case I blurt out the whole thing and end up lumbering her with all my problems, which just wouldn't be fair. It says Keith, because it strikes me that it is increasingly likely that my father will call or turn up here in an effort to find out what's going on. I suspect that it's only the presence of Paskia that's keeping him from banging on the door. He's decent, you see, my father. If I've learnt anything about him, it's that. What a shame the same can't be said for me. I'm realizing these past few weeks that I must have inherited far more of my mother's genes than my father's.

'Is phone. I think is OK,' says Alina, looking terrified in case it's not.

'Hello.'

'Hi, Tracie, it's Sheila here, from Reunited. I just wanted to check that everything was OK.'

'Yes,' I say.

'Oh, good. Is everything going OK with your father?'

'Yes,' I say.

'Good. I'm really glad. He was a bit worried that something had happened. He said you haven't turned up a few times when you said you would, and he can't get hold of you when he calls.'

'That's because I'm ill,' I say. No point in stopping the lies now, is there? Might as well never tell the truth to anyone, ever again. 'I've got mumps and I've been told to stay in. Could you tell him I'll call as soon as I'm feeling better?'

'Of course I will, Tracie,' says Sheila. 'Wrap up warm and look after yourself.'

'I will,' I say, thinking that I might just have bought myself some time. Why didn't I think of mumps before?

Thursday 17 July
6 p.m.

It's such a pity that I can't tell everyone I've got mumps. It's such a ridiculous-sounding illness that no one would think I'd just made it up. We've got this dinner tonight with Joseph's family, and I would genuinely rather contract mumps than go to it. I know Paskia thinks they're wonderful, but they're odd. They've got a manic look in their eyes that makes me want to run for the hills. They don't look entirely trustworthy even though they're religious nuts, so presumably perfectly trustworthy in every way – they just look too pure and proper to be real.

'Remember we're having dinner with Mary, Joseph and their parents tonight,' says Paskia.

'Where is it? In a stable?' I joke, but you're not supposed to joke about Joseph – it's all very serious – so she shakes her head and makes me feel as if she's the adult and I'm a naughty child.

'Don't make jokes like that tonight, will you?' she says anxiously.

'What are his parents' names?' I ask. I can't call them Mary's mum and dad all evening.

'Don't laugh,' says Pask, which is when I know I'm going to howl with merriment.

'Go on,' I urge.

'Well, the dad's name is Noah.'

'Noah?'

'Yes.'

'Like the bloke that built the bloody ark?'

'Yes, but Mum, please, no ark jokes. Promise me.'

'I'll try my very hardest,' I promise. And I will. I like religion. I'm not religious myself, but it makes a lot of people very happy, so I think that's fine. I like the fact that they get all dressed up, I like the business with the wine in the church and I like that there are rules and stuff, so everyone knows exactly where they are. The Bible gives them advice for life, a bit like my *Wags' Handbook*, and they all walk out feeling happy. I'm all for that. I love crucifixes too. They always remind me of Madonna.

'What's the mum's name?'

'Genesis,' she says, 'so don't make any jokes about the first book of the Bible. OK?'

'I won't,' I say, thinking that if I were able to make jokes about the first book of the Bible I'd be on stage at the Hammersmith Apollo or something. I mean, how many people in the world could make jokes about the first book of the Bible? It's not a subject laden with comic potential, is it? No, it's the bursting into Phil Collins songs every few minutes that she'll have to worry about.

I've had no choice but to dress down for this austere occasion, so poor Alina has been forced to strip off and hand over her clothes again. The clothes are way, way too big for me, of course. It didn't matter when it came to the parents' evening because I knew I was taking them off, but if I'm going to stay in them all night I'm going to have to make a plan. First, a pink, sparkly boob tube under my shirt, with the shirt open. Second, a large, thick pink belt holding the trousers up and pulling in my waist. Sky-high pink sparkly shoes and really big hair, earrings, glasses and makeup, and I look . . . well, boring but with at least a nod to Waggishness.

Paskia-Rose has gone really over the top with a white sweatshirt, blue trousers and a small crucifix. She seems inordinately happy, though, hugging me and smiling at me in a way that almost throws me off balance.

'Thanks for coming,' she keeps saying. 'They're really nice people. I know you're going to love them.'

We arrive at their house and I hand over a large bottle of champagne and thank them for their hospitality.

'We don't drink,' they say, as soon as I present them with the bottle. This strikes me as the thing you least want to hear from your dinner-party host. 'And we'd really prefer it if you didn't drink either.'

No, I was wrong – *that's* the thing you least want to hear from a party host.

'Of course,' says Dean. 'We don't mind at all, do we, Tracie?'

It's OK for him – Mr 'I'm Teetotal so make mine a green tea'. I feel as if my life's falling apart.

'No, we don't mind at all,' I say through tightly gritted teeth, and against my better judgement. This may well turn out to be the longest night of my life.

Their house is furnished a little like a doll's house. I didn't get to see the sitting room on my last visit, but its defining feature is flowers. It has floral curtains that match a floral sofa and scatter cushions. There are pictures of flowers on the wall and vases of terrible dried flowers everywhere – dotted between the various items of religious paraphernalia on the mantelpiece and window ledge. Crosses, statues and prayers in photo frames. It's horrible.

'A floral feast!' I declare, stepping back onto something soft underfoot and hearing that high-pitched scream that is unique to a cat that's just been stepped on.

Happily, no one seems to have noticed, so as Noah hands me a glass of water I pretend I haven't just skewered his pet, and step away from the once sleeping fur-ball.

In the corner, Paskia is smiling up at J and hanging off his every word. They make a nice couple, to be fair. He's terribly nerdy but sweet enough. When he sees me looking, his little face blushes a soft pink colour and he pushes his glasses up his nose and does his best to avoid my eyes.

'Are you well, Tracie?' asks Genesis, walking into the room in a full-length apron. It's not one of those ones that's got boobs on the front and a bum on the back, like the boys at Luton used to wear whenever they had a barbecue in the clubhouse, but a proper floral, flouncy one. (Yes, there's a theme here. This woman *loves* floral like I love leopardskin.)

'I'm very well, thank you,' I say politely, while trying desperately hard not to step on the cat again. Why does the damn thing keep rubbing up against my leg like that? It should know better than to do anything to threaten the stability of a woman in stilettos. 'Are you well?'

'Yes, I am, Tracie. I had a few problems earlier in the year – just women's problems, you know – but they've passed now. I feel much better these days. Dinner will be served in five minutes.'

'Right, shall I come and give you a hand?' offers Noah,

but Genesis tells him to stay and talk to his guests. I can see by the look on Noah's face that he'd much rather be laying the table than exchanging pleasantries with Dean about the challenges of club football. To be fair, I think he'd rather be torched alive than discuss team tactics in Major League Soccer with a spiky-haired coach from Luton, but he's stuck, trapped in floral hell and made to talk about ball control and team dynamics.

'What I've found,' Dean continues, 'is that if you change the formation you might as well change the players. It's like – you can't impose a structure *on* the players, you have to create the structure *with* the players.'

'Yes,' says Noah. 'It must be terribly interesting.'

'Dinner is served,' comes a loud voice from the kitchen, and the three of us belt towards the dining-room table, thrilled to be relieved of our small-talk responsibilities. Paskia and J walk along behind us, never taking their eyes off each other.

'Tracie, would you like to say grace?' asks Genesis, and I look at her dumbfounded. I could no more do that than recite my eight times table in French, but they're all looking at me expectantly.

'Grace,' I say, hoping that they find me so amusing that they give the job to someone else, but they now have their heads bent over in prayer.

'Dear Lord,' I start, and I can feel Paskia's eyes boring into me, challenging me to say anything remotely offensive and she'll snap my neck between her fingers. Such is the power of first love that I bet she would.

'Thank you for family and for friends,' I begin, and I can feel Paskia and Dean relax. 'Thank you for the food we are about to eat and those we love. Thank you for the sun and the moon, the stars and the clouds.' (I'm struggling a bit now.) 'Thank you for . . . rainbows, trees and, um, sheep too. Um . . . thank you for the clothes we wear, especially the designer ones. Thanks for the new, modern hair extensions that can be fitted so quickly and look so great.' (Here we go. I'm on a roll.) 'Thanks for stilettos and jewels, for teeny-weeny knickers and little pink skirts. Thanks for makeup and perfume and *Heat* magazine and for the Beckhams and all they have done for mankind, and most of all for Wagkind. Thank you, Lord, for the coloured contact lenses and lash-lengthening mascaras that have transformed my eyes. Thanks for doctors and dentists who battle tirelessly to save faces from wrinkles, and for Botox, collagen and bust-enhancing implants. Thank you for –'

'Thank you for everything,' Noah butts in.

'Oh, right. Yes,' I say, looking up at ten eyes filled with a great deal of confusion and, if I'm not mistaken, a little disappointment.

'Right,' says Noah, rising from his seat. 'I'll bring the plates out, shall I?'

'Do you need help?' asks J, moving to assist him.

'No need, son,' says Noah. 'I'll bring them out two by two.'

And the funny thing is – no one else laughs. While I'm practically choking with hysterics, stuffing the tablecloth into my mouth to stop myself snorting and crying with laughter, the others are just looking at me in amazement.

'Two by two?'

No response.

'Noah . . . two by two?'

'Different senses of humour for different people,' says Noah, putting down two plates.

'Yes, sorry,' I say, containing my mirth, but I think he's wrong. Some things are just funny. OK, so not everyone laughs at the same thing, but there comes a point when something is just funny and if you don't laugh it's not because you have a different sense of humour, it's because there's something wrong with you. It's funny when Del Boy misses the bar in *Only Fools and Horses* and goes crashing to the ground. Basil Fawlty is funny when he's trying not to mention the Germans. It's just funny when someone called Noah says he'll bring the plates in two by two. No, in this house it isn't. I suspect that nothing that happens in this house raises so much as a smile.

'Are you religious at all, Tracie?' asks Genesis.

'No, not really,' I say. 'I mean, I care about people and I'd never hurt animals – well, not on purpose, the cat got behind me just then, I wouldn't have speared it intentionally. I don't go to church, though. It's a Sunday morning thing – not the best time for me. If they did it on, say, Monday afternoon, I might pop down for the bread and wine, but not on a Sunday morning.'

'If you'd like to come with us one time, we'd gladly introduce you to the Church of the Latterday Saints,' says Noah. Uh-oh, I'm being recruited. I wonder whether this is what Tom and Katie do when they get Vic and David round to dinner – try and drag them into the Church of Scientology.

'Let me think about it,' I say, moving a horrible pile of food around on my plate. It looks like school dinners

– watery mashed potato, soggy carrots and a small piece of what looks like rubber and smells like overcooked fish. It's got a horrible, globby parsley sauce on it.

'Food OK?' asks Genesis, and I look round to see that everyone has finished. I'm piling mine up to make it look less.

'We thought that instead of having pudding we'd spend some time thinking about people who have so much less than us,' says Genesis. 'Then we'll ask for contributions for the church and Noah will take it down on Sunday. Does that sound OK?'

It sounds fine because no pudding means we're outta here sooner.

'Yes,' I say. 'That's perfectly fine.'

'We thought we might do some sharing. How does that sound?'

'That sounds fine too,' I say, thinking that if we spend five minutes sharing our thoughts, then I can be homeward bound and heading for champagne heaven.

'Good, then let's go into the sitting room, shall we? Children, why don't you go upstairs? Dean and Tracie, perhaps you'd like to say prayers of thanks here and come into the sitting room when you're done.'

The four of them leave the room and Dean shakes his head.

'Bad decision,' he says.

'What? Coming here and eating crap fish with these nutters – oh yeah. Bad decision doesn't even cover it. We need a new word for bad – horrendous, awful . . .'

'No, bad decision to laugh at Noah when he said two by two.'

'Oh, sod off,' I say. 'That was funny. The old Dean

would have pissed himself at that. You've become too dull and sensible. I want the old Dean back.'

But he just shakes his head and suggests that we stop thanking the Lord and go and talk to Noah and Genesis.

'If we have to.'

I follow Dean into the sitting room, almost crashing into him when he stops in his tracks at the door and utters a strange, high-pitched noise, not unlike that emitted by the cat earlier this evening. I look past him and see that Noah and Genesis have cast off their slippers and comfy dress. The floral apron has been removed and they're both dressed in black leather underwear. Genesis cracks a whip and growls seductively from beneath her cat mask. Noah thrusts his leather-clad crotch towards us both and says in an astonishingly deep, gravelly voice, 'Let's share.'

'Let's not,' says Dean, screaming Paskia's name as we head for the door.

'Come on, Pask,' he says again. 'We're going. *Now.*'

She comes belting down the stairs and we push her out of the door, closing it behind her.

'What's the great rush?' she asks.

'Turns out we're no good at sharing,' says Dean.

Friday 18 July

I'm starting to feel much better about things now that I've bought myself a little time to think with the mumps ruse. I also feel much happier after last night. I thought I'd been such a fool to trust Jamie. I thought my instincts were all wrong and I'd been an idiot. I realize after last night that appearances can be extraordinarily deceptive and that you never know quite what's lurking under the skin or, indeed, beneath the floral apron.

'Can you do me a favour, Tracie?' asks Dean. 'Can you never mention last night again, not as long as we live?'

'OK,' I say.

'Good,' he says. 'I'm trying to get that image out of my head – it's doing me no good at all having that leather crotch floating round my brain. I need it to go, so let's, like, just not ever mention it again. OK?'

'OK,' I agree, but I don't know that I can go through the rest of my life without mentioning it to Mich and Suzzi.

Dean didn't rush off to the club this morning. He woke up looking startled after last night and hasn't quite summoned the energy to drag himself from beneath the covers. I have to say it's lovely to have him here with me. We're all snuggled up in bed. He's stroking my hair, trying hard not to snag his chewed-up fingernails on my hair extensions.

'You OK?' he asks.

'I'm fine. It's lovely having you here,' I say, but in my mind I'm thinking, Tell him, tell him, now's your chance, tell him for God's sake. You went through a bizarre, relationship-strengthening experience last night. Now's your big chance to tell him everything. But I don't, and then the moment passes as Alina knocks on the door and says there's a phone call. I'm thrown into a mad panic that it might be someone on today's banned list that I haven't managed to put together yet because Dean's still here.

'Is phone. Is OK?' she says, worry etched on her soft, round face.

'Of course it is, Alina,' I say, and the poor girl looks quite confused. She knows that she usually gets an inquisition from me before I'll take any phone calls.

'Is for Dean.'

Phew. Thank God for that.

'And is two letter for you,' she adds, handing me a brown padded envelope and a plain white envelope.

Oh, shit. I know what the brown one's all about.

While Dean says things like 'Really? Wow, that's amazing,' into the receiver, I throw the white envelope onto the bed and take the brown one into the en suite bathroom with its his'n'hers baths, toilet and bidet. I walk in, lock the door, slump onto the floor and open the thick brown envelope. Out fall three photographs. One is of Jamie and me playing tennis against Dad and Sylvia in which we look like a couple – there's no getting away from it. The second is of me holding his hand.

It's unmistakably my fingers, with their long, glossy nails. The third, possibly the worst, shows me lying back in Jamie's arms, smiling up at him. There is no way that any right-minded person could think that we weren't having an affair.

There's a note again, written in the same type, on the same paper.

Tracie,

Well done for leaving the money last time. If you continue to be a good girl I'll keep these photos to myself. If you don't, well then you'll leave me no choice but to have a long conversation with Dean. I'm sure he'd love to see these pictures. This time I need you to leave $10,000 in notes (used). I need you to put them in an envelope marked VARDIG, next to the showers on Muscle Beach. Make sure the money is put in there by 11 a.m. on Sunday. If it's not, I know where I'll be going for Sunday lunch.

'Tracie, Tracie. What are you doing in there? Come out. I'm dying to talk to you.' Dean's voice contains an optimism and excitement that I fear I'll never feel again. I'm the sort of girl who trusts people. I thought Jamie was for real. I thought he enjoyed my company and wanted to spend time with me while he wasn't working. I thought he welcomed my views on photography. Am I so deluded that I can't see when someone so close to me is just using me?

'Tracie, what are you doing in there? What's taking you so long? Are you doing a number two? If you are, remember the extractor fan.'

'Won't be a second,' I say, pushing the photographs and the letters into a tampon box which I then slide into a bag of sanitary towels. If Dean's looking in there, then I've got bigger problems than blackmail and extortion to worry about.

I flush the toilet, wash my hands and rub fake tan onto my face until it glows. Best to keep outward appearances as normal as possible, even in these most trying of times. As I walk out into the main room I see the white envelope lying on the bed, and it sends a shudder through me. What the hell is that one going to be? Jamie wanting more money?

'What is it?' I ask Dean.

'Oh, doll, I've got some fantastic news,' he says, and he's jumping up and down like a little girl as he speaks. 'The agent just put Roman Abramovich on the phone.'

'Oh, yeah. Who's he?'

'Doll, he's the owner of Chelsea. He's sending someone over to talk to me. They want to offer me a job, starting really soon.'

'Back in England?'

'Yes, of course back in England, sweetheart. I couldn't coach them from here, could I, silly?'

He looks over at me and takes in the look on my face as I mentally weigh up the significance of what's just been said, and think, Oh my God, Oh my God, Oh my God. This is the answer to all my prayers. He misinterprets this as disappointment.

'Sorry, I know you're just settling in here and everything, but it would be such a good move. We have to consider it.'

'Of course! Of course!' I exclaim, much to Dean's surprise. 'Let's do it! Yeah, let's do it. I'll pack now. Let's get on a flight straight away. There must be one going later today. I'll call Pask's school. She can meet us there. I'll get Gareth and the boys to pack the trunks and they can send all that on. Let's just get ourselves back to Luton as quickly as we can.'

I'm throwing things into a bag even as we speak.

'Whoa, sweetheart, slow down. No rush,' he says. 'We don't have to move that quickly.'

'No? What – get a flight tomorrow? Sure, let me call and book it. How do you do that?'

'Stop, Tracie. What's wrong? I thought you liked it here. I thought you were enjoying meeting new people. If I take the Chelsea job we will have to be back for the start of the season. I guess mid-August, something like that. It would be up for negotiation with the agents there. I certainly won't pull Pask out of school or anything, though. They'll have to wait until she breaks up.'

'She breaks up today, Dean. This is her last day at school. It's perfect timing. We'll get on a flight tomorrow at the latest.'

'Tracie, I'm not due to meet the agent until Monday. We won't know till then what they're offering, then the agents will have to haggle over contracts.'

'Monday? Monday? Can't we get a flight that leaves before 11 a.m. on Sunday?'

'Why would we do that?'

'I just think we should. 11 a.m. is a horrible time of day.'

'OK. Look, Tracie, I think you probably need to have a bit of a rest, you know, take things easy. You look tired.'

'I just want to go back to Luton.'

'Then we will.'

'Now.'

'Come on, Tracie, you know as well as I do that we can't just go. We need to do things properly, but we'll go home. I wish you'd told me before that you were unhappy.'

'Yeah,' I say, thinking, There are a lot of things I should have told you before. But I don't say this, I just shrug, tell him it's just my time of the month and I feel a bit low. I see him flinch and tell me he has to go.

'Don't mention the Chelsea thing to anyone, will you?' he says, then he sees the white envelope lying on the bed, unopened.

'What's this?' he asks. 'It's got the Raiders' badge on the back.'

'I don't know,' I reply, my heart pounding because I know it can't be good news. It has to be something to do with Jamie.

Dean tears open the envelope before I can stop him, and he sits down heavily on the bed.

'Oh, sweetheart,' he says, reading it through. 'Oh, I'm so sorry. Why didn't you tell me about this?'

Fuck. I'm buggered. Now he knows everything.

'I could have helped,' he says. 'You nutter. I didn't know anything about this.'

'No,' I say, not sure what to do. A lone tear escapes and runs down my face.

'Oh dear, oh dear,' he says. 'Come on, give me a big, brave smile. We'll talk about this later. I might even have a chat to some people at the club and see if there's anything that can be done. OK?'

'Yes,' I say, as he kisses the top of my head and leaves the room.

I pick up the letter and begin to read:

413

Dear Mrs Martin,

I am sorry to tell you that you have not been selected for the LA City Raiders Junior Cheerleading Academy. We appreciate that this will come as a great disappointment to you, but the judges felt that given your age (the academy is for under 16s) and the fact that you have no coordination, timing, stamina, strength, flexibility or rhythm, cheerleading might not be right for you just now. We would like to invite you and a friend down to watch the cheerleaders in action, though – so we enclose vouchers that will allow you to go to Raiders' next game for half price. Thank you for taking the time to come to the audition.

Yours in dance, Jazz Jones and all at the Cheerleading Academy.

Marvellous.

I hear the door close downstairs, and I rush into the bathroom to retrieve the brown envelope. I pull out the letter and plonk myself down onto the bed, reading and re-reading it. I can get $10k by Sunday. The trouble is – what then? Next week I'll get another letter, and the one after, and so on, until I've given him tens of thousands of pounds of our money, and still won't be any better off. He'll still hound me. And what if he comes to England? What if he turns up in Luton or something? If he finds out Dean is going to be the new coach of Chelsea, and really famous, he'll realize he has me completely over a barrel. What if he goes to the press in England?

I'm sitting in the car outside Sian's house for the simple reason that I can't work out where else to go or what else to do. I had half a plan to tell Sian all about it, but is that fair? I feel like I created all the problems, and I should clear them all up. It's not fair to burden her.

'Are you going in, or do you want to go back?' asks the taxi driver, bored.

'I'll go in,' I say nervously.

Sian's delighted to see me. She's got her ankles wrapped around her neck when I arrive, of course, and she's chanting some damn rubbish, but she soon unravels herself and offers me a glass of the most revolting drink in the history of raw food. Before long we're sitting on the sofa and I'm sipping a very strong vodka (I put the alcohol in myself because, with respect to the woman, when she does it I can't even taste it).

'Is there something you want to tell me?' she asks, and I feel a massive feeling of relief wash over me. It's like the door's been opened to my woes.

'Yes,' I say.

'It's Jamie, isn't it?' she asks, wisely.

'Yes,' I say again. The door's now wide open.

'I thought so. You've been having an affair with him, haven't you?'

Bang, the door slams shut in my face.

'No!' I cry. 'No, I haven't.'

'What's wrong then?' she asks, and I look at her sitting there, so exquisite and lovely in a simple soft white tunic top and matching flowing yoga pants, and I really wish I was like her. I wish I wasn't Tracie the Mad Wag who's always in trouble. I'm the woman whose life is always the root of much hilarity for so many people. It's fun being belle of the ball and butt of the jokes sometimes, but not all the time. I need help.

'I've been visiting my father,' I say.

'I didn't know your father was in LA,' says Sian. 'Is your mother here too?'

'No,' I say, realizing with a sinking feeling that in order to be able to explain the situation with Jamie I'm going to have to give her a potted family history.

I tell her that I'd been very unsure about going to meet Dad, but that when I did I was very glad I'd made the effort.

'Oh, great!' she says. 'Oh, that's brilliant news.'

'Yes.'

'So why do you look so upset about it? Isn't he very nice?'

'Oh, he's lovely. Really nice. I wish he weren't so nice, then this wouldn't all be so hard. I really like him and I'm worried about what's going to happen between us now.'

'What? You mean you want to sleep with him?'

'*No!*' I scream.

Is it me, or is she making this unnecessarily difficult for me?

'OK, listen – I've been going to see my dad and his wife and he's very nice and she's very nice, and I'm not sleeping with either of them. I've also been seeing Jamie – he's been very friendly, I've helped him with his photography and he's been good company. I'm not sleeping with him either.'

'Right,' says Sian. 'So what's the problem?'

'One day, in the early days, when I first started meeting my father, I was worried about going, so Jamie offered to come with me.'

'Yikes,' interrupts Sian. 'That was uncharacteristically thoughtful of him.'

'That's what I thought, but then when we got there Dad said, "Ah, you must be Dean", and he just said "Yes" because the whole thing felt too embarrassing. It suddenly felt odd that there was a man there who wasn't Dean, so I just went along with it, and agreed that he was.

'Things then got more complicated because Jamie ended up coming back with me a few more times because each time when we left my dad would invite us back again as a couple and say things like "We must play tennis" and stuff. So we just went, and even though I knew that I'd have to tell Dad the truth, and soon, it never seemed the right time.'

'So your dad still thinks that Jamie is your husband?'

'Yes.'

'Well, don't worry. Would you like me to come with you to your dad's house now, and we'll tell him the truth? I'm sure he'll understand that you were nervous and just panicked. I then think you should keep right away from Jamie. He's trouble, you know.'

'I wish I'd known that before,' I say. 'Things have got really complicated.'

'How?'

'It turned out that Jamie started going round to my dad's house on his own, "father and son-in-law bonding" and all that. He told my dad about his company and how he desperately needed money to get things started.'

'Oh, shit. How much did your dad give him?'

'He gave him $250,000.'

'Fuck! Quarter of a million bucks. Shit. What happened then?'

'Jamie left, promising to drop off all the paperwork that would make my dad, officially, a director of the business. No one's seen him since.

'I've ended up covering for him every week, promising my dad that Dean will drop the paperwork off really soon. All the time I believed that Jamie would. I never for a minute thought that he'd do anything like this.'

'Fuck! Have you told your dad all this?'

'No. It was only when you said that he'd swindled people out of money before that I realized what was going on. That's when I panicked, and I've been pretending that I'm ill so I don't have to go and see Dad, which is no doubt making him very suspicious. Dean doesn't know about any of this either.'

'Oh, Tracie, Tracie, you poor thing. I thought I'd warned you about Jamie. I wish I'd been more explicit. Shit, this is awful. It's hard to imagine anything worse.'

'Is it?' I say. 'There is worse.'

'I need a drink as well then. Keep talking.'

While I run through the blackmail photographs Sian fills both our glasses with vodka. No mixers, and no terrible green plants popping out of the top. It may be the only good thing to have come out of this mess.

I lay the photographs and the letter on the table, and Sian is speechless as she reads through.

'What the hell possessed you to let him take these pictures?' she asks. 'Did you not suspect anything?'

'Of course not. We were friends, having fun. I was enjoying his company. It was innocent. Dean was at the club all day, Pask was at school all day and even when Simon came over he spent the first two weeks at Raiders. I guess I was lonely.'

'Oh, Tracie, I'm sorry. This is all my fault. I should have made more effort to come round and check you were OK, but every time I called you were out. I assumed you were having fun with Simon. I had no idea. I'm sorry.'

'It's not your fault. It's all my doing. It's just that I kept bumping into Jamie. Everywhere I went I'd see him, and we ended up just spending more and more time together.'

'Bumping into him – ha! He manipulated all this from day one, didn't he? We need to go to the police.'

'No!' I say. 'Dean knows nothing about it. What if it all comes out and it ends up being in the papers or something?'

Imagine it? New Chelsea boss's wife has a sordid secret . . . see pages 3, 4, 5, 6, 7, 8 and 9 for full-colour photographs. Oh God. No.

'I just want Jamie to stop doing this. I want him to give my dad his money back, then I want him out of our lives. I'm telling you all this because I trust you. Please don't tell Chuck, don't call the police. Sian, I wouldn't have come to you if I had any idea what to do. I'm desperate. I felt so rotten this morning that I actually thought about eating something. You can't get fat from thinking about food, can you? Tell me you can't!'

Saturday 19 July

'I call this meeting to order,' says Sian, banging her hand on the desk. No one's talking; everyone's sitting quietly, waiting for her to start. There's no need for such high drama, but this is LA.

Today's the day when Sian and I put our plan into action. Our plan, sadly, involves nothing more than telling Gareth, Peter and Mark about the dilemma I'm in, in the hope that they can help in some way. It's not really a plan at all. If I'm honest, we don't have one of those – that's why we've called the meeting.

'Tracie has a problem and she'd desperately like your help,' says Sian. 'Everything said in this room must remain within this room. Please do not tell anyone. Tracie's had these problems for a while and has coped on her own because she didn't want to drag anyone else into them, but now she's asking for your assistance.'

'Anyone messes with her, he's messing with me,' says Gareth, cracking his knuckles and almost dislocating his fingers in the process. He jumps up and runs off for some ice, his top lip curled up as if he's about to burst into tears. The scene does not fill me with overwhelming confidence. While Gareth runs off, feeling sorry for himself, and returns with an ice-filled tea towel wrapped around his fingers, the others listen to the story of my downfall.

'OK,' says Mark, when Sian and I have finished explaining. 'It's quite simple really.'

'Is it?' asks Gareth.

'Yes.'

'We know Jamie's going to be on Muscle Beach at 11 a.m. on Sunday, so we'll be waiting for him.'

'Brilliant!' says Peter, and I do wonder what sort of intellect is required to be a live-in gardener.

'He'll see you,' I say.

'No, he won't,' says Gareth.

'He will,' I insist. 'He's bound to have considered this. He'll be looking out to make sure there's no one around.'

There's a brief silence.

'We'll be disguised,' says Mark.

'What as?'

'Details, Tracie. Details. Leave it to us.'

Sunday 20 July
9 a.m.

Today's the day. I start by phoning my father to tell him that I feel really ill. There's no way on earth that I can come round and see him today. He offers to drive over with Sylvia to see if I'm OK, to look after me, but I explain that I just need to get some rest and I'll be fine.

10.30 a.m.

OK, we're on our way, me and the boys. I'm in a new car – a hire car! I don't have a great track record with cars, on the whole. In England I managed to have my car impounded, then never got it back, and my American car is still in the lock-up garage. I've no idea what to do with it, or how to explain its reappearance to the insurance company and the LAPD who are, right now, investigating its disappearance.

Still, I was told I needed wheels for today's Operation Jamie so I've got some. I found just the car, and have hired it for a couple of weeks. It's a sugar-pink pickup truck and I love it. I've coordinated my lingerie, my clothing, shoes and even the rims of my sunglasses to match the truck, the hub caps, the steering wheel cover, the seat cushions and the head rests. Everything's in gorgeous bubblegum pink. I'm just a big pink blanc-mange on wheels driving out towards the beach. On the passenger seat next to me is a brown envelope with $10,000 in it. Behind me, three large employees with a range of domestic skills are crouched down, dressed as nuns. It was the only thing I could think of . . . there were nuns at the beach when I went last time.

The plan is for me to get out of the truck at the beach and walk over to the lockers. I'm to be as noticeable as possible, so that if Jamie sees me he'll concentrate on watching me go to the lockers, and not rather watch the large nuns climb out of the back.

I suggested that the fancy-dress nuns go down to the beach separately, in Gareth's car, and be wandering around the beach, totally away from me, but the guys won't do this. They want to be next to me when I arrive, and to be able to follow me – with binoculars, if not literally – all the time I'm on the beach. Also, it's generally consid-ered that it would be a good idea if the nuns spent as little time as possible open to public scrutiny because no matter how much makeup I put onto their skins the stubble pokes through, making them very unconvincing up close. So all I have to do is go to the locker, put in the envelope, return to my vehicle and drive off. The guys meanwhile will watch the locker, and when they see Jamie they'll jump on him and demand that he return the money immediately or they'll go to the police. Simple! We're all agreed that Jamie is, fundamentally, a wimp, and will do what is asked of him rather than risk a thumping from the boys, or an arrest from the Boys in Blue.

My job's quite simple, and I do it with aplomb – striding

across the beach, pausing with my arms outstretched and looking up at the sun. No one on the beach could miss me as I stumble along in my sky-high shoes and skin-tight clothes. If Jamie's watching, which presumably he is, then hopefully he's missing the sight of my religious accomplices.

I walk up to the lockers, making quite a performance of finding the right one, then I slide in the money and walk slowly back to the truck. I get in, drive off, and hope that the next thing I hear is that Jamie has been caught red-handed.

3 p.m.

'I still don't understand how,' says Sian. 'How did you let him get away?'

The three mournful-looking nuns sit before me, still wearing their wimples. Their misery and disappointment in themselves have given them a world-weary air that complements the outfits no end.

'He had a beach-buggy,' moans Mark. 'There was no way we could catch him while dressed in these ridiculous outfits.'

'Every time I tried to run I tripped over. How do nuns run?' asks Gareth.

'I don't think they do. I think they walk round the place slowly and serenely,' answers Peter wisely.

'What? They never run? Not ever?'

'Can we quit the fascinating discussion about the speed at which nuns move, and concentrate on the fact that Jamie has got away with a fortune. Did he see you?' asks Sian.

'No, he didn't see us.'

'Are you sure?

'Yes, I'm sure,' says Peter. 'We never got anywhere near him. I'm not even sure that it was him in the buggy. The person looked too small. I think he's got someone working with him. Maybe a woman, or a young boy.'

'It's looking like the police,' says Sian, turning to me. 'It's hard to see what other choice you have.'

'I could hope he doesn't come back and ask for more money.'

'What? And just allow your father to lose a fortune?'

'I can't go to the police, Sian. It'll be all over the papers.'

'OK. That's your choice, but you have to tell your father the truth – you owe him that. He might want to go to the police. He has that right.'

Monday 21 July

I'm lying in bed with the blinds still closed against the harsh Los Angeles sunshine when Dean marches into the room, full of purpose. 'I have something important to announce,' he says.

'Nothing important happens before midday,' I reply wisely, but apparently I'm wrong. Dean has been formally offered the job as coach of Chelsea before I've even left my bed.

'Congratulations,' I say, desperately trying to put on a display of happiness and joy, even sitting up in bed to mark the importance of the occasion. 'That's great. You must be chuffed, hon.'

'I am,' he says. 'And so should you be, Trace. We'll return to England and you can take on your rightful role as Queen Wag.' He bows before me in a playful fashion but I'm feeling about as playful as a hatstand so I just smile back. 'Doll, we're going to be famous.'

A few weeks ago the promise of fame would have been enticing. Now all I can think is, No, world, leave me alone. I need fame like I need another handwritten note in a plain brown envelope. I can't tell Dean any of this though, so I try unsuccessfully to be positive.

'Great,' I say, so half-heartedly that it just adds to his confusion.

'You said you wanted to go,' he says. 'I'm trying to do the right thing for you here – the right thing for all of us.'

'Yes, I do want to go,' I say. 'I'm just feeling a bit under the weather.'

'OK, sweetheart,' he says, backing off a little, presumably as he recalls that I said something about it being my time of the month.

'I'll get back as quickly as I can tonight, but I need to see my agent who's meeting their agent tomorrow to smooth everything over, and talk packages and dates and terms, etc.'

'OK,' I mutter.

'Just think,' says my husband, 'Tracie Martin – the new Nancy Dell'Olio! Won't it be wonderful? You'll probably be offered your own TV show. You could get Victoria Beckham on there! Just imagine it – Tracie's Transformations! You could take dull-looking people and transform them into Wags!'

'Cool.'

'Cool? Trace, surely you must think that's the coolest thing in the world – ever! What's wrong? I want my Tracie back. Will whoever's stolen her please bring her straight back to me?'

I smile half-heartedly at Dean, and eventually he gives up and heads off to the gym for a circuits class, promising to call me later.

'OK?' he says before going, and I do my best to be chirpy.

'Never better,' I say.

He shrugs and leaves and I'm left with nothing but dark thoughts pounding through my head.

I know I can't let my dad find out about our move to Chelsea through the papers. The poor guy deserves better than that. I can't face talking to him, though, so I take the wimpy way out and send a text. 'Dean's new coach of Chelsea. Still feel v.v.v. ill. Will call l8r and come round to see u as soon as poss. Luv Tracie x'

8 p.m.

'Paskia, hon. Can I come in?' I'm standing outside Paskia's bedroom door. I know she's in there. She rushed up there early this evening when I broke the news about Dean's job with Chelsea to her, but she won't respond when I call.

'Pask?'

Still no answer, so I push open the door to my little girl's bedroom and peer inside. The lights are off, the Luton Town curtains are drawn and there's romantic music playing on the stereo.

'Pask. Are you OK?' I ask, but there's no response. 'Can I put the light on?'

'OK,' she says.

I flick the light switch and a classic scene of adolescent pain is illuminated before me.

Paskia lies in the foetal position in the far corner of her bed sobbing quietly to herself, while some soppy tune by The Carpenters plays from the stereo. Her shoulders quiver gently with every breath she takes. I feel as if my heart might break.

She's surrounded by screwed-up tissues and half-eaten Hershey bars. In her arms she has a small blue teddy bear that I've never seen before. The Mormon Book of Prayer and a pile of photos lie by her side.

'Paskia, angel, please don't be sad,' I say, walking to the bed and sitting next to her. I stroke her head lightly and she whimpers like an injured puppy. 'I know you don't want to leave J behind but it doesn't have to be the end of your friendship. You can stay in touch and come back and visit in the summer holidays. How would J like a holiday in Luton? We could take him down the club and he could meet all the guys.'

'I don't know,' she says, sobbing as she speaks. 'He'll probably forget all about me the minute I'm gone and find new friends who are much prettier and much nicer than I am.'

'That's ridiculous,' I say. 'He thinks the world of you. You're a beautiful person, Paskia, inside and out. I think you and J will be friends for years to come.'

'Do you?' she says, turning to face me and reaching out for any reassurance or comfort being offered. 'Do you really think that?'

'Yes, I do, actually,' I say, feeling myself fill with joy at the happiness I'm managing to ease into my daughter's sadness. I'm not usually very good at this mother/daughter thing, but I seem to have cracked it this time.

I tell Pask that I know of lots of relationships that survive long separations (that's a lie, actually, but I think it's called for in the circumstances). I trot out all the clichés I can think of. I tell her that absence makes the heart grow fonder, and that the world's a very small place these days – with emailing, phoning and texting. I tell her that I'm sure everything will be OK.

She lies on her back as we talk, looking up at her

bedroom walls covered in posters of footballers. There's everyone, from Beckham and Rooney to Gerrard and Ronaldo, all of them standing proudly, smiling into the camera lens. It's always been like this in Paskia's room; ever since she was really young she's wanted pictures of footballers on the wall. I used to try and sneak up pictures of the Spice Girls and Sugababes but she'd always find them and tear them down.

I notice that two of the posters of footballers have been moved to make way for dozens of photos of her LA friends – stuck onto the wall with blu-tack above her bed. J is in every one of them.

'If you want the friendship to continue, there's no reason why it shouldn't,' I say to her. 'Now, why don't you come downstairs and have some hot milk?'

'OK,' she says, and to my great surprise she sits up, clutching her bear, and follows me out of the bedroom.

We wander onto the landing to see Alina, tears running down her face. Oh Lord, no. What now?

'Alina, are you OK?' I say, as Paskia sobs quietly into her teddy bear next to me.

'You go. I so sad. I love Martin family. So nice family. You so kind lady. I miss very much. Such fun in this job.'

Well, this is amazing. I always assumed that Alina tolerated us rather than enjoyed working for us.

'Come on, Alina,' I say, taking on the unusual role of carer. 'Let's get you some hot milk too.'

I lead the two of them down the stairs and put them on the sofa while I walk into the kitchen. I can hear Alina's loud sobs as I pour milk into the kettle and put it onto the stove. The smell of burning rubber wafts through the house. Shit. What's wrong now? I hear the familiar pat, pat, pat sound of Alina's footsteps as I have so many times over the past few months, as she's stepped in to sort things out. Now here she comes again, looking to sort out the mess I'm making of trying to sort her out.

I give her a big hug and tell her that she's the best housekeeper I've ever had and I'm going to really miss her.

'Thank you,' she says, then she looks at the stove. 'I do this.'

She lifts the kettle off and tells me to go back into the sitting room and see Paskia. By the time I get there Pask's got Fox Sports on and she's nose to nose with some footballer.

'Go on, stop him!' she yells, and the world is settled again.

Tuesday 22 July

We've got a leaving date. 10 August, the day after Raiders play Galaxy again. Now everyone knows we're going. Newspaper reporters have been calling up, and Mich and Suz say it's the lead story and on the back of every paper in the UK.

'You two are famous!' declares Mich. 'Are you still talking to me?'

'Of course I am, you fool,' I say, adding, 'Who is this again?' Just for fun. Mich doesn't quite get the joke and starts explaining that she's Michaela and don't I remember, we were really good friends at Luton.

There have been guys on the phone from Chelsea constantly, talking to Dean at all hours of the day and night, about players he could buy, film clips they're going to email over, and agents he needs to meet. Some influential agent is flying over to see him personally about some African player that Dean's already shown an interest in.

Suz says that the features pages have been doing profiles of me, and wondering how I'll get on in Chelsea. There was one today with the headline 'What will happen when the Wag meets the Sloanes?'

'Isn't that amazing?' says Suz. 'They've got some lovely pictures of you. We're all so proud. You should see the one of you taken at Luton last season – you're off your trolley and your tits are practically hanging out of your top. You look brilliant!'

'Cool,' I say dismissively. And it is cool – undeniably so. But I just can't get excited about anything at the moment.

'Then the *Daily Mail* did a page where they had cut-outs of your articles last year and it says "Return of the Wag" right across the top!'

'Major,' I say, but none of it feels at all exciting. It just feels threatening. It feels terrifying that I'm in the papers. I'm scared to death that people want to write about me, because I know there's a story here that would be well worth writing about. It's making me petrified. I don't want to raise my head so much as an inch in case anyone shoots at it.

Wednesday 23 July

Horror of horrors. I awake this morning to a message on my mobile.

'Hi darling, it's me,' trill my mother's dulcet tones. 'Hasn't Dean been a clever boy getting a job at Chelsea? Dying to talk to you, little girl. Call me on the mobile. Straight away.'

What does she want? Angie only ever calls me things like 'little girl' when she wants something. Shit. What's she after now? I'm not calling her. I've got enough on my plate, and what did that clairvoyant say: 'Don't encourage her, don't return her calls or communicate with her. Your future happiness depends on it.' Right. Not calling her then. That's simple enough.

Thursday 24 July

Another day, another message on the mobile.

'Tracie, call me. It's Angie. You've got my number. Call me straight away.'

What's she after? I'm too terrified to find out.

One of the best things about Dean joining a club like Chelsea, apart from the shed-loads of money and the chance for Dean to work with some of the world's best players, is the fact that everyone at the club is so incredibly organized. The lady I talk to there says they're used to helping people relocate from all over the world because so many of the players come from far-flung places. She phones and checks we have everything we need. Do we need her to sort out a temporary home for us in Chelsea?

'No!' I squeal. 'We'll be moving back into our little house in Luton.'

'Can I do anything to help you with that?' she asks. 'Just tell me if I can.'

I think she might regret making that offer because poor Lucy from 'Player Liaison' is now in charge of everything to do with our move. She's been brilliant, and has sorted out the lot, from getting our things packed and shipped back to England to booking flights, organizing change of address notes, informing gas, electricity and phone people and doing all those dull, boring things that come hand in hand with moving house.

Over in LA, I've been left with nothing to do except worry about Gareth, Mark and Peter.

'What will you three do without us?' I ask.

'It's not going to be quite the same,' they concede.

They'll be OK though because Dean, bless him, has arranged for them to be employed by the club to help the groundsman, who's about ninety years old, and to run the bar and act as drivers when needed. There was a rather unseemly fight at one stage for the role of head barman. I think the job eventually went to Peter after a particularly competitive game of rock, paper, scissors.

Sunday 27 July

'Tracie. I'm sick of leaving all these messages. Tell Dean to call me, for goodness' sake. I need to talk to him about him making me the fitness coach of Chelsea. It's important that he calls me straight away so I can work out when to announce the appointment to the press.'

Ah, so that's what she wants. I should have guessed. Nothing to do with me, that's for sure.

I'm standing on the same street next to a kind woman whose name begins with 'S' but in all other respects this meeting between myself and my father bears no similarity to the first time I met him. I was untouched by tragedy back then. My fears of meeting him were fears of the unknown. Now they're genuine fears of the known. I know that I lied and in doing so I put my father in a position that is very likely to lose him a quarter of a million dollars.

It's Sylvia who opens the door, and her face is a picture of delight when she sees me.

'Oh, Tracie, how are you?' she asks. 'We've been so worried. Come in. Are you feeling better?'

I tell her that I am, and I introduce Sian.

Dad walks through the house to greet us.

'Mumps?' he says. 'You're a bit old for mumps, aren't you? You had us quite worried.'

'Mumps?' says Sian.

'This is Sian, Dad,' I say. 'She's married to the chairman of LA City Raiders. I've asked her to come here today because I've got something to tell you and I know that if I came on my own I'd never find the words to express what I have to say.'

'What is it?' Dad asks.

'Do you mind if we all sit down first?'

Dad, Sian and I sit, while Sylvia remains standing.

'Do you mind taking a seat too, Sylvia?' I say.

'Well, I was just going to get some drinks,' she says.

'Sylvia, Tracie asked you to sit down, love. Why don't we just hear what she has to say?'

'Drinks? Oh, OK,' I say, urging Sylvia to stand back up again and get 'em in.

We have a glass of champagne each and it's difficult to think of any further ways in which I can delay this conversation, which I've been heading towards like Dean has been heading towards gardens, postmen and pedestrians since I started trying to teach him how to drive.

'Right. OK, well – I'll start at the beginning. You know when I first brought Dean round here to meet you?'

'Yes,' they both say, wide-eyed with anticipation.

'Well, that wasn't Dean. That was a man called Jamie, who I believed was a friend. He came along to give me moral support. You assumed he was Dean and I ended up not correcting you.'

'Which man are you talking about?' asks Sylvia.

'The man you think is Dean,' I say.

'The man who's been coming here?'

'Yes.'

'So there is no Dean?'

'Yes, there's a Dean – he's my husband. He's never been here. The man who's been here is called Jamie.'

'Right,' says Sylvia, but the look on her face indicates that she doesn't have a bloody clue what's going on. Frankly, who can blame her?

'It just seemed to get so complicated,' I say. 'That first time, you thought he was Dean before I'd had time to think straight. It was really difficult to correct you after that because we kept arranging to do things together, like play tennis and things. I just felt trapped in pretending that Jamie was Dean. I thought it was all harmless.'

'Well, it is, dear. No harm done,' says Sylvia. 'Now we know that the other man was just a friend, why don't you bring the real Dean along to meet us?'

'I can do that,' I say, 'but what is really worrying me is the money you gave to Jamie, believing him to be my husband.'

'Oh, no,' says Sylvia, her hand flying to her mouth.

'Oh, God,' says my dad, standing up and looking very angry. 'I thought the whole thing was odd. I didn't understand why he refused to bring over any of the company documentation. I should have known better. Shit!' He kicks the kitchen door aggressively and stands with his back to us.

I feel like I'm living out all my worst fears. Now my father does hate me. He's getting violent. He's going to start screaming and shouting at me, and there's nothing I can do. This is all my fault.

'Mr Skipworth, it's not your fault at all,' says Sian,

standing up and walking over to him. 'You didn't do due diligence, you didn't run any checks or sort out paper-work because you believed you were dealing with your son-in-law. I'm afraid what we've just established is that you were dealing with an out-and-out criminal, someone who set out to ease as much money as possible out of Tracie and in the process stumbled across you and real-ized that he could get much more money than he ever thought possible.'

Dad is silent.

'I don't think we should be blaming Tracie here. What Tracie did was wrong, and I know how mortified she is at her role in this gross deception, but it's Jamie who has stolen your money and I think it's he who we should be focusing on finding.'

'I don't blame Tracie,' says my dad. 'Not one bit. I blame myself. I've behaved foolishly because I was so desperate to give something to Tracie to make up for the terrible childhood she had, and the lies her mother told her about me. I wanted her to have some security for the future – a little nest egg – and it struck me that by investing in the company they were building up together I was doing just that.'

'You were,' I say. 'I've messed it all up because I was so eager not to rock the boat, and to make sure that everyone felt comfortable and happy. It felt like such bad manners to say, "Actually, this man isn't my husband." I kept thinking that once we got to know each other better it would be easier to say something. I thought that if you knew me and liked me, then me admitting that Jamie wasn't Dean would be something we'd just laugh about, rather than something that made me feel silly and like I was going to lose you all over again. I'm so sorry.'

There are plenty of reassurances and even a big hug to make me feel better about everything. Dad insists that nothing is going to come between us and that even if he never sees the $250,000 again it won't affect our relationship, but I'm still worried. How can't it?

Sian tells Dad about the subsequent blackmailing and our efforts to catch Jamie, and I watch as concern spreads across his features until his face is red with fury.

'You *have* to go to the police,' says my father. 'For your safety and for Paskia-Rose's safety. You don't know what this man will do next.'

'No, I don't,' I say. 'But please give me a week or so to try and catch him before we talk to the police.'

'I think that's a mistake,' says Dad. 'I think you've tried for too long to deal with this on your own. I think we need experts involved – people whose job it is to catch baddies.'

'*No*,' I say, suddenly realizing what I have to do. It's like a light-bulb has just gone on in my head. 'Dad, please, give me ten days. I know exactly how to sort this out. I know exactly who can help me. I can't say anything but I just know with all my heart that I can get him. I know people who are really good at catching baddies.'

'OK,' says Dad. 'Ten days, then we call the police.'

Wednesday 30 July

There's been so much post arriving in immaculate cream-coloured envelopes that I didn't think anything of the one that came this morning. I slit it open and pulled out a bill. Nothing unusual there. The trouble was, the bill was for $15,000. It was from Koi. I pulled out the accompanying information. The total was for meals and drinks at the restaurant nearly every day – twice a day sometimes. Shit!

The charges had been made to my credit card over the past few weeks without me noticing, but here was the end-of-month bill for all the charges incurred over four weeks. Bloody hell. Is there no end to what that bastard will do?

Saturday 2 August (my wedding anniversary)

'Tracie. I am furious,' squeals Angie. 'I'm livid and I'm sure my blood pressure's gone up. Make sure Dean calls me and sorts out this job offer.'

This isn't how I envisaged spending my wedding anniversary. I'm in the derelict outbuilding at the back of the LA City Raiders pitch with three criminals on the run for a selection of heinous crimes, three friendly employees and Sian. I told the criminals about my plight yesterday, then I told Sian about the criminals. The criminals think this is an easy problem to clear up, they just need to ring some bloke who's just got out of jail and he'll track down and kill Jamie. Call me old-fashioned but, despite everything he's done, I still don't think murder's the answer. Sian, bless her, just looked at me open-mouthed when I told her that I had three lawbreakers tucked away. She insisted that we call a meeting this morning to make sure things are done properly.

'Make sure you keep your dad briefed on everything,' she said.

I called Dad and mentioned the meeting, but couldn't bring myself to talk him through my three dodgy mates.

'There are just these three guys who could help us,' I said, which is the truth, if not the whole truth.

'OK,' says Sian, standing up at the front of the hut. 'Is everyone fully aware of the situation here?'

The door slowly opens, and three large men leap up and throw themselves, with extraordinary speed, behind the sight screen at the side.

'Dad!' I say.

Everyone spins round as my father walks in. The gang hurl themselves behind the table, with their guns cocked.

'Can I help?' he asks. 'I thought there maybe something I could do.'

'Hands up!' shout the shed's criminal fraternity.

'It's OK,' I shout. 'Put the guns away. You don't need guns. This is my father.'

'Ah, sorry man,' they say, dropping their weapons and going over to shake Dad's hand.

'Do I know you?' Dad asks them. 'I'm sure I've seen you somewhere before.'

'*America's Most Wanted*?' asks Bill, and if I'm not mistaken he looks like he really, really hopes that's where my father knows him from.

'Yes,' says Dad, and all three men look immensely proud.

'Thanks,' they say. 'You're welcome here, bro. Beer?'

He takes one and I introduce everyone.

'Now, where were we?' asks Sian, but before she can go on the door opens at the back and the bandits dive for cover.

'It's OK,' I say, seeing Poppy arrive. 'It's just a Wag friend.'

I say 'Wag' but Poppy is not dressed like any Wag I've

ever seen before and possibly like no Wag in the history of football. She's in a white linen trouser suit with a blue-and-white striped top underneath and has flat ballerina pumps on her feet. Her hair's in a chignon. The only thing that's right about the look is the sunglasses, which are large. I mean, come on, it's not exactly Girls Aloud on the pull, is it?

'Right, where were we?' asks Sian.

'We got some fuckwit who needs killing,' says Bob. 'We gotta track him down and rearrange his face so even his mother don't recognize him.'

'No!' says Sian. 'We've got to try and find him and take him to the police. That's all we've got to do.'

'Yeah,' says Bill, winking at me. 'Won't be our fault if he accidentally breaks his legs on the way there.'

The three wanted criminals on the run from the law across eight states chuckle to themselves, their heavily muscled shoulders rising and falling with each laugh.

'This is all wrong,' says Poppy, jumping up and looking down on the three men now doing high fives and saying things like 'Yo man', 'Easy target' and 'Dead meat'. 'We should just go to the police.'

'Whooooaaahhh,' say the men. 'No police. Don't say that word.'

'Sorry,' says Poppy.

'Apology accepted,' says Bill, rubbing his hands together and revealing his heavily calloused knuckles.

Poppy sits down and crosses her legs neatly at the ankle. It's bloody boiling in here. I'm in my hot bubblegum-pink PVC catsuit, but when I pull the white zip down my boobs keep bursting out, and hearing Sian shriek 'Tracie!' as if I've been caught with short hair or something is more than I can stand, so the zip's now completely done up and it's like a sweat suit. When I take it off, assuming I can get it off (it took two hours to put on and lots of talcum powder), the sweat will come gushing out.

On my feet I've just opted for very high-heeled, pointy-toed white shoes. I've got so many ankle chains on my right foot that it takes all three of my male members of staff to lift it when I want to cross my leg. Last time I did that I almost smashed my kneecap, so I'm just sitting still now, while the sweat runs in rivulets down my face, stinging the huge burn marks either side of my neck – my big gold earrings became too hot in the sun and when they swung against my neck they left their painful mark. No one said it was easy being a Wag.

'How about if we find him and bring him to you?' says Bill, suddenly.

'No broken legs,' instructs Sian.

'No,' says Bill with a grimace, and we can all see how hard that was for him to say. 'I won't break his legs.' He cracks his knuckles and shakes his head. It's like he's broken some unwritten code. I suppose him saying he won't break someone's legs is like me saying I won't wear makeup. I don't think I could do it. I admire him so much in that moment. So much.

'Good,' says Sian. 'What happens now then? What do you guys need?'

'We could do with a car that the police aren't searching for. You know – if we go driving round in that van they're gonna pull us over in no time.'

'Yes, you need the sort of car that no one will expect you to be in,' says Poppy. She is very wise, that girl. Pity

446

she doesn't put a little more of that brain power into her clothing selections.

'Like what?' asks Gareth. I realize it's the first time that one of the three guys has spoken. When I look over at them I realize how terrified they look next to my criminal friends. Not for the first time, I'm driven to wondering just how effective they will be as my accomplices in this mission.

'You can have my little pink pickup trick,' I say. 'No one would be expecting to find you in that.'

'I guess,' says Bill, dubiously.

'Yes, let's take it,' says Barry, and it seems like suddenly we've got the beginnings of a plan. Quite how the three criminals will catch Jamie is, they insist, their business.

'Yous just gonna have ta trust us on this one,' they insist. 'You just keep yourselves busy, and we'll call you when we've got news.'

'OK,' I say. 'So you don't need any more information from me?'

'Nothing,' they insist, 'unless you've heard anything from him since we last spoke.'

'No,' I confirm. 'I've discovered he's taken money off me too, but no – I haven't heard anything directly from him.'

'What money has he taken?' asks Barry.

'Oh, just this restaurant bill I received. I laid my card details down at the restaurant, and they charge it every time I go in there. I've only been a handful of times, but the bill came for a dozen nights out there. Jamie knew my password. He's obviously been going in there and charging it to me.'

'You got the bill there?' asks Barry, and I pull it out of my bag.

'It itemized?'

'Yes,' I say.

'So it shows when he was last in there.'

I look down the statement. 'Yes, just a few days ago.'

'You need to cut it off with Koi,' says Sian. 'Phone them later today, or he'll run up even more credit on there.'

'Koi?' says Barry.

'Yes,' I say.

He turns to the other two. 'Does Lightning still work the door there?'

'Yes,' the other two confirm. I immediately have a picture in my mind of the guy on the door with the lightning bolt tattooed across his knuckles.

'Good. Tracie, don't cancel the card. Leave it open. Don't do anything to arouse suspicion. Make him think that we're not on to him yet. We'll make a few calls, and the minute our good friend goes near Koi, he's ours. Let me have that statement, Tracie.'

I hand it over and he balks at the total. 'Motherfucker,' he mutters under his breath.

To: Mich and Suzzi

From: Tracie

Hi, thanks so much for all the help, girls. Mich – can you let the builder in? He's coming to make me a large suite of rooms called a dressing area. Once you've had one, you can't do without it. Make sure he uses exactly the right leopardskin velvet to line the shelves and cupboards, and the walls need to be pink, obviously.

Re: the welcome home party – yes, let yourselves in and get started. Dean and I will come straight from Heathrow and see you at the house. I won't mention our plans to Dean so it's a nice surprise for him when he gets home after an achingly long flight and finds his house full of pissed-up footballers. He'll be thrilled.

Love you loads. Can't wait to see you, T x

Wednesday 6 August

It's 1.30 p.m. when I get the call.

'We got 'im,' is all that Barry says.

Quite what we do now we have 'im is something that has not been discussed thus far.

'Take him to your place and I'll get everyone to come there,' I say.

'That's where we are now,' says Barry, adding, 'He came into the restaurant with someone, so we've got her too. What shall I do with her?'

'I don't know. Maybe let her go?'

I'm thinking that this is all between me, Jamie and my dad. We don't need some random tart that he's picked up, hanging around and getting in the way.

'I can't let her go, love. She'll tell people where we are.'

'OK, keep her there. I'll be there as soon as I can,' I say.

I call Sian and my dad, and I notify Gareth, Mark and Peter, then ten minutes later we're all standing outside the hut, knocking and waiting, all of us wondering what to do now.

Barry opens the door and I walk in. Jamie's standing there, and as soon as I see him my heart lurches all over again. He's so handsome, so strong and powerful. Perhaps this has all been a mistake.

'The woman's over there,' says Bill, and we all spin round.

'Macey?' I say. 'What are you doing here?'

'She was with Jamie,' says Bill.

'What?' says Sian.

But Macey just shrugs. Standing next to her is the man from Koi, the man I now know as Lightning. I have a sudden memory of the clairvoyant who couldn't locate Jamie's whereabouts because a flash of lightning kept going through her mind.

'Leave Macey alone,' says Jamie. 'This has nothing to do with her.'

'Yes, it does,' growls Barry, moving himself so he's nose to nose with Jamie, and snarling at him in a quite terrifying way. 'You've been in there a dozen or more times with her, haven't you? And you've paid on Tracie's credit card. Do you think that's fair? Or legal?'

'I don't understand,' I say. 'What's going on?'

'We just needed some money, that's all,' said Jamie. 'You obviously fancied me like mad, and you have loads of money, so I thought it might be easy enough to relieve you of some of it.'

'But I thought we were friends.'

'Yeah, whatever.'

'I thought you liked me.'

'Tracie, you're a joke,' says Jamie. 'Just look at yourself. Take a look at what you look like compared to Macey.'

Bob reaches in and grabs Jamie by the collar, threatening to punch him in the face.

'Don't!' says my dad, stepping forward and stopping Bob. 'I don't want you to do that, Bob,' he says.

'Why?' asks Bob.

'Because I want to do it.' With that, my father swings for the man he once gave quarter of a million bucks to in the belief that he was my husband, landing a punch right on the end of Jamie's perfect nose.

'No!' screams Macey.

'Oh yes,' say the criminals, high five-ing my father and muttering the word 'respect' a lot.

'How dare you talk about my daughter like that?' he says. 'How dare you? It's one thing that you come into my house and steal my money, quite another that you insult my daughter. Don't you dare talk about Tracie like that again.'

We get the money back, of course. Poor Jamie has no choice but to phone up his bank and transfer the money he stole from my father immediately. He pays for the Koi restaurant bill and he pays back Dad, and as far as we can make out he has no money left in his account.

'Where's the rest of your money?' asks Bill. 'Or was Tracie the only person you stole from?'

'I bought tickets,' he says. 'For me and Macey. We're flying to Australia to live. We're going tomorrow morning.'

'But what about Derek?' I say. 'You can't leave him here on his own. Isn't it bad enough that he's lost Nancy, without losing you, too?'

'Derek?' says Jamie. 'Who's Derek?'

'Your dad,' I say. 'You were telling me all about how much he relied on you after Nancy died.'

There's a silence, then Sian puts her arm round me.

'Jamie's parents are alive and well and living in Sydney,' she says. 'I think you've been completely conned.'

I look up at Jamie in utter horror. I think this is worse

452

than the money he stole and the lies he told to swindle me out of everything he could.

'So Nell and Nancy meeting in heaven – that was all a big joke to you, was it? Was it?'

I'm beside myself with rage as I approach him. My teeth are gritted and my hand has involuntarily formed itself into a fist.

'Tracie,' says Sian. 'What are you doing?'

'People die,' he says with a shrug, as I approach him. 'It's no biggie.'

And that's when I let him have it. With every fibre in my body and utilizing every twitch in every muscle, every moment of pain I've ever felt and the anguish of a childhood stolen from me, I swing my arm like I've never swung it before and I smash my huge, buckle-covered Marc Jacobs handbag into the handsome face of the man I'd thought was a friend.

Jamie goes stumbling back, and there are shrieks and cries of amazement from everyone around us. 'Noooooo!' howls Macey.

The three criminals step between Jamie and me, lest he's tempted to retaliate, and as Barry looks at me I see real respect in his eyes. They're among America's most wanted criminals and they respect me. How cool is that? I just hope my bag's OK.

'I'll be looking out for you for the rest of my days,' says Bob, with menace dripping from his tongue and teeth. 'Come back here, or go near anyone in this room, and I'll break every bone in your body.'

Jamie quivers like a baby. He's still holding his face.

'Get out,' says Barry, giving him a quick kick on the way for good measure. Lightning lets go of Macey and the two of them go, their footsteps disappearing as they rush off through the trees and hopefully out of our lives forever.

Once Jamie has been kicked out, we all sit round on upturned crates, drink champagne and put the whole story together. We realize how stage-managed the whole thing has been from day one. No wonder I never felt comfortable around Macey. What a shame that I didn't realize it was just her that was odd. If I'd realized that, I might have made more of an effort with the other girls.

I tell them about when Macey took me shopping that day – the same day that someone knocked on Dad's door, fitting the description of Jamie. Clearly since my dad wasn't in that day their plans were foiled, and they had to make me sit in a raw food restaurant the next day while Jamie went back there and, this time, was successful.

'I guess he put the cheque straight into the bank, into an account set up in Dean's name,' I say, trying to figure the whole thing out as I speak. 'He must have taken some letters or bills or something when he was round at mine. He then transferred the money to his own account after a couple of days.'

'But they got greedy, and probably thought they could get one more expensive meal out of you before you got the bill. By then, they'd have been on their way to Australia,' says Sian.

'What about the Beckhams?' I ask. 'Does he really know them? He said he used to work for them.'

'The Beckhams?' says Sian. 'No way. He came over from Sydney six months ago. He wasn't in LA before that.'

And that, my friends, is the worst deception of all.

Thursday 7 August

'Do you want me to come over?' asks Sian, but I tell her no. Really this something I have to do on my own. I'm not sure how Dean will react. He'll be pleased that I've managed to sort everything out, and he'll be pleased that I've been meeting up with my father, but I think he'll be disappointed at how reckless I've been and equally upset that I didn't tell him and solicit his advice sooner.

I've asked him if I can take him to lunch, so he knows something's wrong. I'm in the car on the way over to the club now. Gareth's driving, and of course Gareth knows everything.

'I'm dreading this,' I tell him.

'He'll be fine,' says Gareth.

'Do you want to tell him then?'

'No!' he squeals.

'Mmm, thought not.'

We get to the club and Dean jumps in. For the first time I notice just how amazingly healthy he looks. He's more muscular, and he's holding himself properly, instead of slouching all the time.

'What's this all about then?' he asks, and I glance up and see Gareth's face in the mirror, watching me closely.

'Let's talk about it over lunch,' I insist.

'But you don't eat, Tracie. I don't think I've ever seen you eat anything more than a glacé cherry from the Asti Spumante that Nell used to give you.'

'No, but only because I don't see the point of it,' I reply. 'I mean, if you eat, you get fat. I don't want to be fat so I don't eat. You can eat, though. I'll talk while you eat.'

'OK,' he says, and we head off to a lovely little restaurant up in the hills.

'Now, I think I know what this is all about,' says Dean, after ordering chick pea and lentil soup. The man at the table next to us orders the biggest cheeseburger in the world, and Dean tuts and shakes his head as it goes past. Funny how you can get huge meals in LA, and you can get desperately skinny, no fat, no wheat, no taste, vegetarian meals, but it's all the stuff in between that's so hard to come by.

'Do you really?' I ask.

He shoves his hand into the pocket of his tight-fitting trousers and pulls out a pile of pamphlets.

'I've spoken to some people at the club, and they say that if you practise really hard, and attend auditions in the UK, you might get into the Chelsea squad. Apparently standards aren't as high in England.'

'What?' I look through the leaflets in front of me. They're for cheerleading classes, dance classes and general fitness sessions. 'Thanks,' I say. 'Unfortunately, what I've got to tell you is a bit more serious than this.'

'OK,' he says. 'More serious than cheerleading, huh? Blimey. Better tell me.'

I explain about my father first, and try to make Dean understand why I went to visit him without talking to either Simon or him. 'I needed to do it in my own time, and without pressure,' I say. 'So I went to see Dad without telling anyone. Then, once I'd met him and realized he was nice, and that I liked him, I planned to tell you.'

'So why didn't you?' he asks.

'Well, once I'd met him and planned to see him again I felt the pressure all over again, because I realized that forming a relationship would mean taking a huge risk. I'd end up caring about him, like I cared about Mum, and what if he let me down? So I asked Jamie to come with me to the second meeting.'

'So Jamie knew you were seeing your father? You told Jamie, but not me?'

'Yes,' I say. 'It's hard to explain why. I think it's because I didn't know Jamie and so I felt he wasn't judging me. Taking him along didn't feel like a big thing at the time, but it ended up becoming this huge thing because Dad thought Jamie was you and I didn't correct him because I was so nervous and everything, and the whole thing kind of grew out of all control.'

Dean looks completely confused. It's hard to make him understand why I let things drift on.

'It was so silly not to correct Dad the first time that it felt absurd to do so further down the line. The other thing is that I'd got to really like Dad and trust him and I felt that the whole trust between us would be blown apart if I said anything, so I just let it drift on.'

'OK,' says Dean. 'I'm trying to understand this, Tracie, but I have to be honest – it's not easy.'

That's when I tell Dean about the stolen money and about the criminals hidden away in the outhouse. I tell him about the meeting and the capture of Jamie, and all the time he looks at me as if he doesn't quite know me.

'You should have told me all this. I'm your husband, for God's sake,' he says. 'Why would you feel you couldn't tell me?'

'I was ashamed,' I confess. 'You were always at the club, always absorbed in it. I didn't feel I could pile problems on your shoulders.'

'That's just plain silly, Tracie,' he says. 'I'm always here for you – always.'

'Thanks,' I say. 'So will you come with me to meet Dad? I know he would really like to meet you before we go back. Do you have any free time tomorrow?'

'Of course,' says Dean, and I give him a huge hug. On Saturday they play Galaxy. I know he's desperate for Raiders to win. I know that he'll have filled tomorrow up with meetings, plans, tests and discussions with the players.

'I'm so grateful, Dean,' I say. 'I know how busy you are.'

'Tracie, this is the most important thing in the world. Never think I'm too busy to do something like meet your father, for God's sake.'

Friday 8 August

'Hi, Dad,' I say, giving him a big hug. 'This is Dean. The real Dean.'

'Hi,' says Dean nervously. 'So nice to meet you at last.'

Dad smiles warmly and tells us to come in, and there's a slight awkwardness between them that really disappoints me. Perhaps Dad preferred the other Dean?

We walk out into the garden and take a seat, and I hear footsteps running quickly down the stairs, then Sylvia comes padding into the garden, her face alight with curiosity. Dean jumps up from his seat to say hello. Again, my husband looks terribly nervous. Still I suppose, given the circumstances, he well might.

'Did all the money come through OK?' asks Dean, and my dad says that it did. Dad then says that he did genuinely want us to have the money, and that he'd like to write a cheque to Dean for the amount.

'I've got a much better idea,' says my husband. 'I'm sure you know far more about investing than I ever will about investments. Perhaps it could be a trust fund for Paskia when she reaches twenty-one or, even better, it could be money spent for you both to come on a big long holiday to England once a year.'

'We'd certainly like to do that anyway,' says Sylvia. 'You know – to meet Paskia properly and to get to know you all much better.'

'We've got a big house in Luton. You'll be welcome any time. We'll designate a room for you. It'll be yours whenever you want to come, the more frequently the better.'

And so it goes on, and I realize that, while Jamie exuded charm, Dean's real, honest and decent, and he's charming on a far deeper, more meaningful level than Jamie.

He's asking Dad all about himself and the house, and about his children in England. Jamie never asked any questions other than about Dad's business. He tells Dad all about the club and then invites him and Sylvia down for the match on Saturday.

'David Beckham will be playing,' says Dean.

'And Victoria will be there!' I add, enthusiastically. Dean told me this morning.

'We'd love to come,' they say, and Dean says he'll get tickets sent over the next day.

Saturday 9 August. LA City Raiders against LA Galaxy!!

Raiders won!! Dean says that unless they behave like a complete bunch of tossers when he's gone they'll make it to the play-offs. No one in American soccer seems to be able to believe what Dean's done with this team. There were TV cameras and hundreds of journalists knocking around, trying to get a word with Dean, wanting him to say something about Chelsea, the Premiership, the England team or any of its players. He just stuck to his guns and spoke only about Raiders and how proud he was of the players.

Now we're in the bar, in the roped-off VIP area. We're waiting for the appearance of a woman who I've been dying to meet since . . . since, I don't know, probably since before I was born. Oh God, oh God, it's her. She's dressed in pink – just like in all my fantasies – and everything matches. Oh my God, oh my God. It's like the Queen's just walked in. All the players have lined up and are preparing to shake her hand. She's got this fabulous skin-tight dress on in the brightest pink imaginable – it's the exact point where fuchsia meets scarlet. She has on pink gloves which match exactly, and a tiny little hat. She's carrying a Kelly bag, of course, and she looks like a movie star. David's just ahead of her as they move down the line and he's saying, 'This is Victoria', in his sweet, sweet voice. It's just like when the captain of a side introduces the team to the Queen.

Now David's in front of me and Vic is standing there and I could reach out and touch her if I wanted to, which I do, I really do. But I'll try not to. I'm just standing there, open-mouthed. She's the most beautiful thing I've ever seen.

'Hello, you must be Tracie,' says David, and he takes my hand.

Let me say that again: DAVID BECKHAM TAKES MY HAND. I grip onto his hand so tightly that he yelps a little and pulls it away. He kind of looks nervous at this point, but his feelings hold little interest for me. Vic is standing there looking radiant, exquisite and perfect. The true Queen of all Wags. 'Meet Victoria,' says David, rubbing his hand where I squeezed it, and wiping away the blood where my fingernails have dug in too deeply.

'Hello,' says Victoria, putting out her hand. 'Nice to mee—'

'Tracie, Tracie, can you hear me?'

'Tracie?'

All the voices are muffled and all the people are blurred.

'Tracie, we need you to help us. Can you understand what I'm saying? Can you? Tracie, please answer me.'

'Her eyes are opening.'

'OK, blood pressure's normalizing and her temperature is dropping. I'm worried about her colour, though. She's quite orange. That could signify extreme liver malfunction. We need to keep her in for observations. Tracie, can you hear me?'

Slowly everyone comes back into focus. I'm not at the club and Victoria's not here.

'Where am I?'

Dean's lovely face comes into view.

'You're in hospital, Candyfloss,' he says.

'I'm whaaaat?' Has all of this been some sort of dream?

'You fainted, just before meeting Victoria,' he says.

Just before? Just before? Oh no.

I lift my hands up to my face and hold my head. I can't believe that the greatest moment of my life disappeared – like a bubble being popped before my eyes. Victoria, Victoria, Victoria . . . so near and yet so far.

A doctor with teeth so white that I'm temporarily blinded by them looks over me and feels my pulse. He's handsome in a rugged, outdoorsy way. He's the sort of man who looks like a doctor should. He's like a TV doctor. Too perfect for the real world, but then LA isn't really the real world, as I've learnt so well.

'How are you feeling?' he asks.

'Fine,' I say. I feel a little bit light-headed but nothing that a glass or two won't sort out.

'We're very worried about your colour,' he says.

'Sure,' I reply, with a knowing nod. 'Pass me my makeup. It's in the suitcase by Dean's feet. Careful when you pick it up, though. You'll injure yourself.'

'No, madam, it's not makeup, it's the colour of your skin.'

'How on earth can you see the colour of my skin?'

'We removed your makeup when you came in.'

'*You removed my what???*'

'Your makeup and nail varnish.'

'*How dare you!!!*' I shout. How dare he remove my nail varnish and makeup. My God. Who does he think he is?

'We were in the process of saving your life,' he replies.

'I don't care what excuse you have. You should never remove a woman's makeup.' I'm sobbing now. It's like those awful dreams you have – you know, the ones where you're running through the streets and you realize you're naked, and you think – oh well, never mind. Then you realize you have no makeup on and you think 'Holy fuck!!!' and you wake up soaking wet, crying and screaming. Oh no, I've just had the most awful thought. Too awful to contemplate.

'You didn't remove my makeup in front of Victoria, did you?'

'Victoria?' asks the doctor. 'Victoria who?'

Oh, for God's sake. Are there any other Victorias in the world?

'No dear, don't worry.' Dean's comforting voice comes to the rescue. 'Don't worry, love,' he says. 'Your skin was never on show to Victoria.'

Phew.

I ended up staying in that hospital all day for tests because they were convinced there was something wrong with my internal organs.

'I'm a Wag!' I kept shouting. 'Wags are this colour. Get over it!'

But, no. They washed my face just to check, and when the towels stained a vibrant shade of tangerine they realized that it was all artificial colouring and not some serious medical problem. Trouble is, no matter how much they washed me I was still a colour that concerned them.

'She's the colour of Homer Simpson now,' said the doctor. 'I do think there's something wrong here.'

'I'm fine,' I eventually yelled in frustration. 'I just want to go home.'

Gareth moved to the side of my bed.

'Home?' he asked, as he has on so many previous occasions. 'What? Home to Luton?'

'Home to Luton,' I said with a smile.

LAX Airport

It's not how I ever imagined my stay in LA coming to an end, but Paskia-Rose, Dean and I stand at the airport entrance waving goodbye to our friends. Poppy's here, dressed absurdly, but supporting me all the same. Perhaps it's true that you can't judge a book by its cover; more scarily, perhaps you can't judge a woman's intellect and moral fibre by the height of her shoes and the size of her sunglasses. Strange thought.

Sian and her family are here too, and I've come to realize that Sian is one of life's good guys – a genuinely nice person whom I regret not spending more time with. My views on Chuck remain the same – he's a complete throw-back to the 1980s. He's two red braces short of being a Yuppie, and that's not a good thing. I think he's a nice bloke deep down, but you have to dig through six foot of 'getting ducks in a row' and 'running things up the flagpole' to get there, so I stopped digging fairly quickly!

Paskia is sobbing into her hanky, poor love. Her eyes are red-raw from the tears she's cried over the past week. Her first love. I'm glad he was a nice boy, and I hope the two of them stay in touch. I'll definitely be coming back to LA to see Dad, so she and J will get the chance to see each other then. I know what it's like, though: a few weeks back in Luton and she'll barely remember his name.

Photographers have come to catch sight of us as we leave this bright, sunshine city to return to London, so we decided that it was better if Dad didn't come to the airport. He hasn't met Paskia-Rose yet, but he's coming to London later this summer to meet her, and to introduce us all to the other half of our family.

As we step back, away from the LA lifestyle of health and herbs that Dean has come to enjoy, and back to the life of champagne and shoes that I adore so much, there's a commotion as three big men tear across the pavement towards us.

'Hi,' I squeal. It's Bob, Bill and Barry – taking their lives in their hands to wish us bon voyage. 'I'm so glad you came. Thanks for all your help.'

'Thanks to you,' says Barry in that lovely voice of his. 'You're one cool lady.'

They hug me tightly, bash knuckles with Dean and kiss Paskia on the cheeks, then they race out of there as if their shoes are on fire.

The sound of police cars tearing through the car park with their sirens blazing drowns any further conversation. There are police helicopters overhead, officers running around clutching guns and a feeling of intense drama.

Dean smiles proudly, I wave girlishly and Paskia sobs quietly.

'Bye-bye, everyone. We'll miss you all,' I say, as we turn to go.

We stride past the officers who are handing out

'wanted' leaflets featuring the three faces of my criminal friends. The sound of helicopters overhead gets louder.

I'm really not sure what this next phase of my life will be like. I've got a letter from Angie in my Balenciaga handbag urging me to meet her when I get back to Luton and claiming that I promised she could be the fitness supremo at Chelsea. I need to sort out my relationship with my mother. I need to tell her what I really think of her. I need to confront her once and for all. Then there are the cuttings from British newspapers in my Mulberry overnight bag.

'Return of everyone's favourite Wag!' screams the headline. 'What will the Chelsea Sloanes make of her?'

I really don't know what they'll make of me. I guess they'll envy my fabulous taste in clothing and my ability to down champagne by the pint. I'm sure they'll want makeup lessons and a few hints in the decorum department. Let's face it – they're Wags and I'm the Queen Wag so they're going to be learning from me and admiring me. Oh yes, the Queen Wag is coming home. Get out the Cristal.

TRACIE MARTIN'S GUIDE TO LA – what to see, eat, and visit in the city of Angels . . .

Victoria Beckham. The greatest attraction that LA (or anywhere else in the world for that matter), has to offer.

Food – people in LA don't seem to eat much and instead exist on a wholly liquid diet (like me!) but instead of vodka and cokes they prefer to mush up fruit and veg! I ask you. Veg and fruit are gross, and pureeing them into something that resembles cat sick does not disguise that fact . . . the only veg I have ever eaten is the olive in a martini (is that a fruit?). They are happy to consume something that looks like it came from a village pond (wheatgrass) but you should have seen their faces when I offered them a Blue WKD. Where's the sense in that?

Nightlife – there's loads of clubs but sadly no Chinawhites. And they haven't even heard of S Club Seven or Blue . . . So don't ask for *Reach for the Stars*, no matter how much you want to hear it . . .

Style – it's all a bit underdressed for me. Even though the women are the right kind of skinny to pull off a pelmet skirt teamed with 7 inch stiletto heels, they seem peculiarly inclined to wearing the kind of flip flops that look like you are recovering from a painful in-growing nail operation. In their favour, they do have a penchant for the kind of boob job that looks like you have got a couple of grapefruit halves on your chest, which is always fab. I met some kindred spirits when I visited San Fernando Valley with Dean, and was admiring their PVC lace corsets and plastic leopardskin macs (which, oddly, they wore with nothing on underneath). And then one of them said that they were 'adult actresses' . . . but surely all actresses are adults?

Shopping – there's a fab store on Sunset Blvd called Hustler, which sells all kinds of cool clothes (and lots of DVDs with naked ladies, but I'm not sure why). I got a really brilliant PVC cheerleaders outfit which is perfect daywear; short enough to keep me cool, and wipe clean to boot. Don't know why Dean got in such a strop when I wore it to the match . . .

Tanning – California is known as the golden state and has 1,200 miles of beach, which makes it the perfect place to get that all-over golden tan. However, instead of covering themselves with chip fat and wrapping their limbs in Bacofoil before baking in the midday sun (all the better to cultivate a tan that looks like you have been doused in Bisto), these girls do things like playing volleyball? Which, if you don't know, is a kind of tennis that you play with your hands. Yes, it's as hideous as it sounds . . . and not to be recommended after a trip to Star Nails. How I was to know my 5 inch acrylic nails would pop the ball? Three times?

Travel – get a car, or a driver. End of.

FREE SESSION WITH A PERSONAL TRAINER

Visit our website, www.avon-books.co.uk and print out your own personal trainer session voucher and claim one free session with one of one of the participating personal trainers. Situated across the country, you're guaranteed a one-to-one service to help you get in shape!

- Visit HarperCollins website for a list of participating personal trainers.
- Telephone your chosen personal trainer in advance of your visit, stating that you are in possession of a "TLC free personal trainer voucher", to check availability, discuss the usage of the offer (restrictions may apply) and book your session.
- Hand in your voucher on arrival at your session.
- Proof of purchase is required, therefore a copy of the book "A WAG Abroad" and the book's till receipt must be presented along with the voucher. If this is not produced, you must pay the full price for the personal trainer session.
- Please read the terms & conditions on the voucher.
- Voucher valid until 30 November 2008.

TERMS & CONDITIONS

1. This offer is open to all UK residents aged 18 years or over for new bookings only. This offer is not available to employees of HarperCollins or its subsidiaries, TLC Marketing plc or agencies appointed by TLC and their immediate families.
2. The voucher entitles the bearer to one free personal training session, for one person at one of the participating venues, as listed on the AVON website: www.avon-books.co.uk
3. Proof of purchase is required, therefore a copy of the book "A WAG Abroad" and the book's till receipt must be presented along with the voucher. If this is not produced, you must pay the full price for the personal trainer session.
4. Only one voucher may be used per person. The voucher claimant may only claim one free personal training session voucher at a participating venue.
5. All additional customers will pay the full price and all future bookings will be charged at the full price.
6. Voucher valid until 30/11/2008.
7. Offer excludes Public Holidays and Bank Holidays.
8. The offer is based on advance bookings only and is subject to promotional availability at participating personal training venues.
9. The promoter cannot guarantee that your first choice will be available at a time or place convenient to you.
10. Voucher cannot be redeemed with a personal trainer you already have lessons with.
11. Customers must call the venue in advance of their visit, stating that they are in possession of a "TLC free personal training session voucher", to check availability, discuss the usage of the offer (restrictions may apply) and book their session.
12. The instructions listed form part of these terms and conditions.
13. If you fail to cancel your booking within 48 hours of the appointment, or do not show at the venue, a cancellation charge may be incurred.

14. The list of participating personal training session venues remains subject to change. Please contact your chosen venue to confirm continual availability of the offer.

15. Participating personal training session venues are all contracted to participate in the free personal training session offer.

16. Participating venues reserve the right to vary prices, times and offer availability (e.g. public holidays).

17. Prices (if any) and information presented are valid at the time of going to press and could be subject to change.

18. Neither the Promoter, nor its agents or distributors can accept liability for lost, stolen or damaged vouchers and reserves the right to withdraw or amend any details and/or offers.

19. The voucher may only be used once. Photocopied, scanned, damaged or illegible vouchers will not be accepted.

20. The free personal training session voucher has no monetary value, is non-transferable, cannot be resold and cannot be used in conjunction with any other promotional offer or redeemed in whole or part for cash.

21. In the event of large promotional uplift, venues reserve the right to book voucher holders up to 4 months from date of calling to make a promotional booking.

22. Neither TLC, its agents or distributors and the promoter will in any circumstances be responsible or liable to compensate the purchaser or other bearer, or accept any liability for (a) any non-acceptance by a venue of this voucher or (b) any inability by the bearer to use this voucher properly or at all or (c) the contents, accuracy or use of either this voucher or the venue listing, nor will any of them be liable for any personal loss or injury occurring at the venue, and (d) TLC, its agents and distributors and the promoter do not guarantee the quality and/or availability of the services offered by the venues and cannot be held liable for any resulting personal loss or damage. Your statutory rights are unaffected.

23. TLC and HarperCollins Publishers reserves the right to offer a substitute reward of equal or greater value.

224. The terms of this promotion are as stated here and no other representations (written or oral) shall apply.

25. Any persons taking advantage of this promotion do so on complete acceptance of these terms and conditions.

26. TLC and HarperCollins Publishers reserves the right to vary these terms without notice.

27. Promoter: HarperCollins, 77-85 Fulham Palace Road, Hammersmith, London, W6 8JB.

28. This is administered by TLC Marketing plc, PO Box 468, Swansea, SA1 3WY

29. This promotion is governed by English law and is subject to the exclusive jurisdiction of the English Courts.

30. HarperCollins Publishers excludes all liability as far as is permitted by law, which may arise in connection with this offer and reserves the right to cancel the offer at any stage.